Feast, Famine & Potluck: African Short Stories
Terra Incognita: New Short Speculative Stories from Africa
Water: New Short Fiction from Africa
Migrations: New Short Fiction from Africa
ID: New Short Fiction from Africa
Hotel Africa: New Short Fiction from Africa
Disruption: New Short Fiction from Africa

Captive

NEW SHORT FICTION
FROM AFRICA

SHORT STORY DAY AFRICA 2024

CATALYST PRESS LLC, EL PASO, TEXAS

Captive: New Short Fiction from Africa

Published by Short Story Day Africa in association with
Karavan Press in South Africa
Catalyst Press in the USA and Europe

Short Story Day Africa is a registered non-profit organisation in
the Republic of South Africa, NPO #123-206
shortstorydayafrica.org
karavanpress.com
catalystpress.org

For further information, write info@catalystpress.org
In North America, this book is distributed by
Consortium Book Sales & Distribution, a division of Ingram.
Phone: 612/746-2600
cbsdinfo@ingramcontent.com
www.cbsd.com

ISBN PRINT: 9781946395948
ISBN EBOOK: 9781946395955
LCCN number: 2023932113

Edited by Helen Moffett and Rachel Zadok
Proofreading by Karina Szczurek
Typesetting by Rachel Zadok
Cover design by Megan Ross

This book is set in Julian Sans One, Nunito and Garamond Premier Pro

CONTENTS

INTRODUCTION

*T*HE THIRTY-THREE STORIES contained in this collection are the result of a mentorship curriculum we, with our usual sense of the ridiculous, titled the SSDA Inkubator. The idea for a story incubator was seeded seven years ago in another Short Story Day Africa (SSDA) initiative, a series of bi-weekly flash fiction events held on social media. The popularity of these events highlighted a need within the African writing community for spaces where writers could develop work towards publication. Few such spaces exist on the continent. Of the twenty-two top-ranked universities in Africa for creative writing courses, fifteen are in South Africa (with the top eleven on the list also in South Africa), three are in Nigeria, two are in Ghana, and Mozambique and Zimbabwe each have one. This means that African writers either need to go abroad to further their creative writing ambitions, or create spaces for themselves.

The SSDA Inkubator is our endeavour to create such a space, and the twelve writers we selected for the pilot project, run in conjunction with Laxfield Literary Associates and supported by a grant from the British Council, were chosen because their voices were original and diverse, and the messages contained within their submissions powerful enough to one day cause ripples in the zeitgeist. The challenge for the writers when submitting their proposals was that they only had a maximum of one thousand words of prose to convince us they had the raw talent to deliver.

SSDA has spent years honing our mission to subvert, reimagine and reclaim the literary landscape for writers from Africa. We have done this by ensuring that we develop and publish a diverse range of voices, looking beyond the expected and polished to the raw, sometimes unhoned, edge that makes a writer's voice sing. The SSDA Inkubator is by far our most successful development programme in this regard. We found talented writers from the African continent and diaspora and took them on a journey from story seed to final publication, exposing them, via a series of workshops, to the wisdom, techniques and craft of six brilliant African writers and editors, and one British literary agent with her eyes focused on the continent's literary talent pool.

Captive is the result. Divided into three themed parts chosen by the writers as a community, these stories explore some of our most pressing concerns: love, migration, ambition, motherhood, ageing, culture, folklore, AI, mental health, fairytales and possible futures...

These are more than stories. In their words these eleven Inkubator Fellows have built bridges across imagined borders, knotted stitches to mend divisions, and written a balm for our fractured global society. We hope you read them with delight, and, after turning the final page, approach your fellows with greater empathy.

Rachel Zadok
Managing Editor, Short Story Day Africa

claustrophobia & inescapable obsessions

THE STING

Sola Njoku

YOU GLANCE AROUND to make sure you have no company before easing a hand under the band of the maternity jeans that Doyin loaned you. Baby is now ten months old, napping in his stroller, but your stomach retains the dome shape of pregnancy. That, and the occasional phantom kicks, make you wary of another still burrowed in there, feeding off you. But the health visitor says those aren't kicks: "Uterus contracting."

"Bloody slowly, by the looks of it," you bemoan, grabbing the soft fat and willing it to dissolve.

But today, inching a finger under the waistband of panties that have gone from size eight lace thongs to size twelve cotton briefs, your concern isn't the stomach that people glance at before asking conversationally, "When are you due?" It's your vulva. More specifically, a tiny point of pain to the side of your clitoris. A fingernail accidentally grazes it and tears well up from the sharp agony that follows. You look around again, extract the hand and wipe the investigative finger against your jeans. A nascent boil? An insect sting? You take the brake off the baby stroller and return to your shopping.

It is days like this, few and far between, that many primiparae growing wanted babies fantasise about as they rub their bellies and stare wistfully ahead. A breezy twenty degrees, not a cloud in the sky. Baby hasn't squirmed since you plopped him in his buggy after lugging him and the buggy, separately, down the four flights of uncarpeted stairs to escape the flat. You have tea and panini, your first uninterrupted breakfast in days, try on outfits in three stores. The last changing room is coffin-sized, so you leave the stroller outside, dressing in a hurry for fear of coming out to find an empty pram. Baby is still there when you emerge. Relief mingles with foolishness.

You don't buy any of the clothes. Nothing looks flattering over a distended stomach, and you refuse to shell out on large clothes in a superstitious desire to return to your pre-baby body, the slim-thick achieved from years of dieting and downing questionable concoctions purchased from Filipino-owned food stores. For now, you window-shop, stopping for a strawberry crêpe, with swirly chocolate syrup and ice cream on the side. Breastfeeding, the excuse for gluttony. You manage two pages of *Ake: The Years of Childhood* – half of the front cover has been torn off by Baby because he dislikes the withdrawal of your attention – his distress a reminder of Edward Tronick's famous still face experiment. An acquaintance discovers you in this moment of quietude. Her realisation that you have become a mum since she last saw you elicits exclamations that stop just short of waking Baby.

Life feels idyllic this sunny day, as you perambulate through the new town centre. It feels as if a festival has descended on the hitherto ghostly town. With gentrification, colours, noise, elaborate storefront displays of clothing and décor and blossoms have come. The soundtrack to the giddiness today is contributed by a violinist performing a decent rendition of Tchaikovsky's *Swan Lake*. It is almost unbelievable that all these people live within Winnersh's sleepy neighbourhood. You half-expect travel coaches to pull up and cart the crowd away. The sun is waning; it must be past five, that time of day when, before, whatever meagre activity was ongoing would come to a halt with store workers swiftly locking their doors as if in fear of some biblical plague. Today the teeming crowd continues to flow in both directions, navigating around you as you look about in delight. A baby cries and you glance down quickly, but it isn't Baby. It is not even a baby; it is a toddler being dragged away from a doughnut van by its more determined mother.

This mother and wife thing, you can do it on days like this. Through childhood, Mother made it look effortful, too much like martyrdom – all deep sighs, short temper and hour-long scoldings – collapsing heavily on the sunken sofa each night and falling asleep mid-sentence after a day spent managing laboratory assistants and half a dozen children. As a result, you had doubted your ability to hack it.

But since meeting Kanayo more than three years ago, the doubts evaporated. With him, you could navigate the treacherous road of wifehood and parenthood. Next to his solid, unflappable presence, you could finally believe in the joys of marriage and motherhood. On your first holiday together, conditioned by your parents' marriage and the thoughtlessness and entitlement displayed by previous boyfriends, you insisted that it was impossible for a woman not to be saddled with a larger share of the unending chores of domesticity. But Kanayo was obstinate: he planned to do his fair share of the cooking, the cleaning and the late-night feedings, bristling at your flippant dismissal of all he planned to contribute to his future family, and soon the argument had escalated. In Greece that night, the relationship had nearly tanked. Had you not been abroad, forced to share a hotel room and bed, you would both have turned in different directions and kept walking, each believing the other to be ludicrous.

But two years later, on the morning of your wedding, it is clear that you are embarking on a match ordained. You awake from a deep, dreamless sleep, undisturbed by the cold feet that stage nightmares for the troubled mind, aglow as your mum, sisters and cousins busy themselves, readying you for your lifelong position by Kanayo's side. You beam while feeding him bits of cake on bended knees at the wedding reception, displaying to your parents' and guests' approval your "home-training" as a good, traditional wife, although you and Kanayo know different. He winks, conspiratorial, as he munches the cake from your hand.

You walk past the Catholic church where your vows were said, the hotel where you entertained afterwards, where you spent that first night as Mr and Mrs, too drained to consummate the marriage – that would happen days later during the honeymoon in Barbados. You are nervous, coquettish, even though it isn't the first time. That had been soon after you met, on a visit to his house, the home where you now live. Tired of being a chaste nearly-virgin, playing it safe through university, you give it up easily this time, warning him not to come inside you. He does, anyway, embarrassed in the aftermath. And the sullen pair of you make the walk of shame to Boots the next morning to purchase the aptly named "morning after" pill. You drink it down with a Ribena, monosyllabic, resentful, making judgements as to his character. Afterwards you both decide to do the responsible thing, book STI tests, make a day trip of it to London. The results seal your tacit agreement to be exclusive.

You returned to the hotel last week for your third wedding anniversary, leather – easy enough; you bought him a nice belt. He booked the honeymoon suite to reinject some romance into your parenting-strained union. Strawberries covered in chocolate and a champagne bottle placed by the bed on which towels are arranged in the shape of two necking swans.

It's your first time at a hotel with a baby. You fret that the noise of his crying might annoy the neighbours, take him to the common area, let him roam, feed him dinner, bring him back to the room asleep. Kanayo has slept where he sits, his head hanging low against his chest. You consider sneaking into bed, but psyche yourself up, deciding that he should be rewarded for the thoughtfulness of this anniversary vacation. You approach him, place a tender hand on his crotch, fiddling with his zipper. He comes awake, letting you continue. You ease him out of his boxer shorts. Always easy to arouse, he swells swiftly in your hand. You stroke his tip, discover a pimple, and touch it curiously. You are about to apply your tongue to him when he pushes back from you: "Actually … I'm a bit tired. Can we sleep?"

The rejection stings, but you check yourself. Long weeks before and since Baby, you'd done the same thing, repeatedly. Pregnancy, loss of sleep, and the anatomical changes from birthing a baby had conspired to make a celibate of you. It has been more than a year since you made love, having decided not to risk the pregnancy. Baby's arrival does not improve your enthusiasm for intimacy. You quell the guilt every time, wishing you could tell him to just masturbate, plead tiredness, and roll onto your side. On this anniversary, finally willing, you let him lie. The anniversary, like the marriage it commemorates, is to be consummated later.

You always take the scenic route back from town. Not having to pay attention to traffic, you daydream past houses hidden behind tall hedges, windows bordered by decorative ornaments carefully arranged around them, as if to give passers-by a positive impression of the homeowner. Some with vines lovingly cultivated around them like a shroud. What in there needs to be hidden from view? Wide green lawns peep behind side gates, the occasional twitch of a curtain upstairs. You dream of one day living like this. With

Baby growing, you ought to discuss buying a nice home. But with every step your panties rub against the pinprick of pain, interrupting your reverie.

You will ask the GP about it at Baby's appointment in two days, but even though you have pushed an infant out of your vagina before an audience of four, you cringe at the thought of opening yourself up to more scrutiny. You tense your way through many cervical swabs despite the nurse's insistence that you stop resisting the speculum, submit to its advances. But labour is an exception. There is something about a baby needing to be born that overshadows any consideration of decorum. As you strained spread-eagled on the maternity bed, your brain tried to rein in your abandon, reminding you of the unsightly excretions that make you cringe while watching *One Born Every Minute* to prepare yourself. The contractions coming thirty seconds apart silence its voice until all you hear are your own screams and the student midwife urging you on, "I can see Baby's head, keep pushing!"

First, you will find that tube of penicillin you brought from Nigeria years ago. You never throw medication away, not even expired ones. An article once swore by their efficacy ten years on, so you keep them all, pills and potions.

Baby awakes as you unlock the front door and hurry to prepare his meal, making the most of the five minutes of vacancy that follows his slumber. You shove heaped teaspoonfuls of minced tomato pasta into his mouth, he funnels it down, bawling for more as you scrape the bowl. Banana custard follows at a slower pace until he is sated. His mood improves in relation to the size of his belly. You plop him down on the bed as he babbles, attracted to the drop at the edge. You grab the magnifying mirror from the dressing table and hurry back before Baby crawls off the bed. You take off the jeans and the offending panties, sighing in relief as your abdomen trembles freely outside its constraints. You hold the mirror below you and squat to get a better view, angling it to avoid the overhead light. The sight always makes you recoil.

At eighteen, encouraged by a friend, you give in to curiosity and look between your legs. The sight is so shocking that you lose your appetite for days. But that is before you know the pleasure it gives, before men beg to see it, to touch and taste it. It looks worse for wear now, almost oozing, more open somehow since the birth. You have resisted the urge to self-examine, to confront what you lost during an hour of second-stage labour. You can still see the stitch line from the third-degree tear. Now you home in on the tiny spot of red. It is much smaller than the pain it elicits. You find the antibiotic cream shoved in the drawer full of knick-knacks, grab it while using one hand to restrain Baby from his dangerous curiosity, slather on the thick cream, and decide to release yourself from the bondage of denim and cotton for the day, opting for a loose gown. You have become your mother, with her Canesten creams on display in the bathroom, her Ankara wrapper tied around her chest. It was always into those faded, colourful cotton print wrappers divorced from their still pristine blouses that she changed immediately she returned from work, discarding the skirt-suit trappings of her civil service job.

The phone call comes within the week, waking Baby from his nap. You rush to pick up, issuing a breathless hello after the sprint, but the damage is done. With Baby yowling as the voice says its name, all you register is Sexual Health Clinic. Knowing that "no news is good news" is the mantra of the NHS, you notice the leap in your pulse, the rush of blood, the pounding in your chest as the room contracts and the air thins. She explains, as you attempt to buy silence by offering Baby your cheek to chew, that the sample has come out positive for genital herpes. You cannot process much beyond the fact that it is an STI contracted through contact. "Can I still bathe with my baby?" The concern that issues is a mother's instinct. The healthcare worker is confused. "Bathe? What sort of bath?"

"Can I go into the tub with him to give him a bath?" you explain. Bathing with Baby in the late morning calms him, and you get to clean up, too. Otherwise, chores take over the day, and you are stewing in your body's juices by the time Kanayo returns to pry him from you.

"You can, just be careful to avoid contact when you are having an outbreak."

Outbreak makes it sound unwitting, like something inhaled in a crowded place, something unpreventable. Herpes, breathy, whispery-soft, sneaky, carries all the weight of its clandestine origin. You are affronted on Baby's check-up day when the practice nurse makes the casual suggestion, insisting on taking a sample of the boil that is now bigger, hydra-headed, having fed fat on the penicillin. You aren't alarmed then, simply righteous as she carefully puts on blue rubber gloves before brushing a cotton swab lightly against the sore. While she does all this, you question her motives, her knowledge, her manner for throwing such a word around. Now you are stunned as you thank the caller, drop the phone and cradle Baby in bed, unable to cry, unable to breathe, even as your heart continues to beat the skipped rhythm of fear.

Your head throbs from the attempt to calculate when during your pregnancy his Latvian best friend paid a goodbye visit before requesting voluntary deportation after years of trying to settle in the UK. When during her visit might you have left her and Kanayo alone for too long? Your chest aches to consider the great deliberateness he must have employed to have had an affair. An introvert, bordering on reclusive, he spends almost every waking hour outside of work with you. Where did he find the time or the inclination to stray?

Your eyes sting from late-night investigations into the causes of herpes simplex, not to be confused with herpes zoster – shingles. You learn of incubation periods: two to fourteen days; of symptoms after infection – fever, swollen glands, headache, painful urination – trying to pinpoint the exact moment when the virus infiltrated your being. You read that a quarter of all adults are infected with herpes but live with it, oblivious; are informed of the average duration of an outbreak – three to seven days; given suggestions for home remedies – tea tree oil, garlic cloves, baking soda paste; warned to abstain from intercourse while you have an active infection, to tell a sexual partner if you have contracted herpes previously. But all this information is useless because they do not provide the answers to two questions: How you came to acquire this burden; and how to put it down.

Months go by, the days colourless and sluggish like mud, registered merely in the motions of waking and sleeping. Baby is an inconvenience, whiny and toddling about, intent on self-harm. Once the radiator cover yielded to his pull, collapsing upon him, and all you did was watch him squirm underneath. His cries, though loud, do not really reach your ears, do not move your feet toward him. In the evenings, when Kanayo returns, Baby hurries to him, hungry for attention. Kanayo persists in doling out little mercies with Baby tottering in his shadow; he offers fruit teas, makes dinner – foiled seabream in peppers and olive oil, slow-cooked lamb with roast potatoes – intent on feeding you back to normalcy. He turns to you in bed for a kiss goodnight; he doesn't comment that your lips remain slack against his. His muscular calves pin down your small ones. The act from which you derived a feeling of security now assumes an insinuation of entrapment.

You do not remember what was said that day. Kanayo is cooking when you break the news. You are afraid because you cannot explain how this thing has come into your marriage. You need him to be able to explain it, but are terrified of an explanation. As you speak haltingly, gaspingly, his hand trembles while placing the undercooked bowl of fufu on the countertop. A shudder takes over his whole body, as if from a sudden ill wind. He will not look at you for seconds that stretch into hours. You beg him for the truth, you tell him you love him. You do not recall the words with which he convinces you that he does not know a thing, what he says to keep you quiet, suffocating from a chest full of questions, assuming the pain that insists on reminding you every month, like clockwork, of the misery and mystery that you live with.

You do not remember what your priest said to inject some doubt, not as to Kanayo's responsibility, but as to his guilt, that one time in the confessional before you stop going to church altogether, finding no truth in the promise to lay your burden down on Him, no relief from the knowledge you carry but cannot speak out in the open. A burden that turns into a dark pulsing rage that takes hold of you in the night, that inches your hand towards the pillow, towards his Adam's apple laid bare in slumber even though a slip of a woman is no physical match for a man of six foot two. Or else has you feverishly telling the rosary in the dead of night, *Hail Mary full of grace the Lord is with you… Holy Mary Mother of God pray for us sinners now and at the hour of our death…* All you remember is how Kanayo turned his face and trembled. And how you, too, must avert your gaze, compel yourself to breathe in, out, in, out, in the airless quagmire of this happy marriage, while shame wraps itself around your neck, tighter and tighter, preventing enquiry, exhalation, escape.

WEDNESDAY'S DELIGHT

Aba Asibon

*T*HE NEIGHBOUR'S WIRELESS goes off at four.

The garbage truck bellows by at five.

The sun usually begins to make an appearance between five-thirty and six – but closer to six.

Nimo is often up before the shrill sound of his alarm clock, a sound which used to be a call to something greater. With nowhere to be that early, he lingers in bed for a while, watching the shadows of the tamarind trees dance against his drawn curtains. Deep sleep, he has concluded, is a gift better suited to the worn and weary.

Twelve: the number of steps between his bed and the bathroom. Fifteen: the number of seconds it takes for him to completely empty his bladder into the toilet. He finds himself counting the most mundane things. He'll see something – the ceramic tiles on his bedroom floor or a loaf of sliced bread – and a clicker automatically goes off in his brain. An accountant, retired or not, knows that every number bears significance.

After his bath, he stands with legs akimbo in front of the wardrobe. For most of his adult life, he has diligently adhered to the civil servant's uniform of collared shirts, ties and khakis, but the bulk of the clothes he owns now hold little value outside of the working world. The things he spends his time contemplating these days. Shorts or trousers for a quick trip to the bank?

Breakfast is kept simple – Tom Brown without milk, eaten while he flips through yesterday's paper. The rest of the day is for the taking. He ambles around the house with his toolbox in search of things that need fixing – creaky hinges, loose bolts, those sorts of things. And when he has run out of things to fix, he wipes down the entire bungalow with Dettol, repulsed by how much dirt a house can accumulate overnight. At lunchtime, his brother, Darko, calls to check on him.

"When are you joining me for a game of golf, big bro?"

How many times must he tell Darko that he finds nothing stimulating about swinging after a ball with a bunch of pot-bellied bourgeoisies?

"Church then? We've got Bible study on Tuesdays and deliverance services on Thursdays."

God still lives in the box he put him in twenty-five years ago.

Twice a week, Nimo braves the thick human traffic to get to the Super BuyRite in Accra Central, which he prefers over the regular BuyRite closer to home. There is something about the vast expanse of the place, something about being surrounded by so many people who each manage to mind their own business. He relishes in the sheer number of options on the shelves. For each item on his shopping list, there are multiple options to be weighed. Sixteen different varieties of toothpaste alone – spearmint, activated charcoal, even fluoride-free. He tries to stick to the list but every so often, finds himself reaching into the forbidden ice cream freezer. The sweet tooth is a recent development. It is an urge that has begun to overcome him most evenings, right around the same time as the seven o'clock news. It pries him from the couch and eggs him on towards the fridge where he indulges in his poison of choice – double chocolate chip gelato.

The supermarket's extra wide trolleys are a bottomless pit.

"Stay for as long as you'd like," they seem to say.

Soothing elevator music pours from the overhead speakers. The central air conditioning is a welcome reprieve from the humidity outside. In there, Nimo easily loses track of time. What a wonderful feeling it is to check his watch only to realise: just five more hours till bedtime.

WEDNESDAYS ARE DIFFERENT. Wednesday's hours are urgent and necessary. On Wednesdays, there are no fashion quandaries because lunch with one's daughter on High Street calls for nothing less than a well-pressed shirt and a complementary tie. On this particular Wednesday, his stomach has no room for breakfast, just coffee. He takes delight in watching the coffee-maker blink its blue lights as fresh coffee trickles down gracefully into the glass carafe. The fancy machine had been presented to him at the surprise retirement party the office had thrown him. One of his colleagues had managed to lure him into the windowless conference room where the other members of his department were already gathered in his honour. His colleagues had gone round the room, praising him for twenty-five years of committed service to the Ministry. Some said they would remember him for his meticulousness and his keen eye for accounting errors. Others said they would remember his unceasing willingness to show the more junior staff the ropes. They'd toasted him with cups of bissap. Difficult to believe that was almost a year ago.

From the kitchen window, he can see Mrs Dankwa from next door trimming her hedges with a pair of oversized shears while her eyes dart around other people's compounds. It's moments like this that make him wish for real brick walls between the bungalows on Apam Street, instead of these flimsy chest-high hedges. The one-bedroom bungalows had originally been constructed by the City Housing Corporation as temporary accommodation for young unmarried civil servants. When he first moved in twenty-five years ago, Nimo did not mind too much the absence of concrete boundaries. He had rather enjoyed the occasional exchange of pleasantries with his fellow bachelors, carrying on about the inadequacies of the government and rising fuel prices. But over the years, the residents had gotten too comfortable, moving in nosey wives and girlfriends, promptly followed by colicky babies.

As he gulps down his coffee, he plots his exit strategy. Recently widowed, Mrs Dankwa has taken to spending all of her time outside, tending her garden and accosting passers-by with empty banter. She draws their attention to her flourishing flame lilies and birds-of-paradise. Nimo hypothesises that if he walks by briskly enough with headphones plugged into his ears, it should send a clear message. But no sooner has he locked his front door does Mrs Dankwa dart towards him, frantically waving her shears.

"Ah! Mr Ampau," she greets him. "Looks like rain, doesn't it?"

He casts a glance up at the lucid sky but chooses not to disagree with her – not today.

"You're all dressed up," she says, looking him over. "What's the occasion?"

"I'm meeting my daughter for lunch."

Daughter. It still feels strange to say.

"Ah! Of course, I almost forgot what day of the week it was."

He's glad he is not the only one for whom the days of the week have grown fuzzy, their borders beginning to blend into each other.

"When do we get to finally meet the special young lady?"

"You know these children ... they're not keen on life here in the suburbs."

The truth is, he has not yet broached the subject of visiting with his daughter. It feels too soon, too forward for a child he is still getting to know.

The night he received the call about her, he had been seated in front of the television, polishing his shoes with no particular destination in mind. He had let the phone ring a few times before answering.

"Koo Nimo?"

There was only one person who addressed him so, and he had not heard from her in about eighteen years.

"Lebene?" He could hear her breathing on the other end.

"I hope you've been well?"

"Yes ... I have." He should have said more, at least asked her how she was also doing, but the words eluded him.

"Listen, I'm so sorry to call so late. I have a bit of news for you."

She had always been direct, never one to mince her words. It was an attribute he had found both admirable and unnerving all at once. She had made her expectations around marriage clear from the very beginning of their relationship – she did not by any means want to end up a spinster like her mother. So, when he still had cold feet after five years of dating, she had moved out of his bungalow and into the arms of a man up north who wanted a wife. What could she have for him after eighteen years of silence?

"I'm listening," he responded, eager for the guillotine to be dropped.

"We had ... we have a daughter."

Her words were concrete bricks.

"What do you mean?"

"I was pregnant when I left you."

Hot breath piped out of his nostrils. He tightened his grip on the handset.

"I could not stand the thought of being tethered to you forever because of a child," she continued.

He half-expected her to be more apologetic.

"And you thought keeping it from me was fair?"

"If you were not ready for marriage, how could I be sure you were ready to father a child? Besides, Ali did not mind."

He swallowed the words that were scorching the back of his throat. There were a million things he could say to drag this out. After all, the two of them had always been skilled at dissecting disagreements into microscopic proportions. But for the first time, he did not care about who won and who lost.

"Why now?"

"She has gained admission to Legon. She'll be moving to Accra soon."

"Does she know about me?"

"Yes, and I think you two should meet."

He should have spat, "No kidding!" into the handset, but he did not. He thought about the emptiness of the last eighteen years, of beating himself up every day for being unfair to her, of passing up other potential relationships because he could not shake off the guilt. And here she was, casually delivering such heavy news.

"She takes after your brilliance," she continued. He could hear the smile in her voice. Had she always been so callous?

He arranged the first meeting with his daughter on a Wednesday – the day of her choosing. On Wednesdays, classes ended early and she had the afternoons to herself. He picked a restaurant a few blocks from his old office. A fairly obscure place with decent food. As he sat waiting for her to arrive, he conjured up images in his mind. There was a lanky daughter version, much like himself, with her mother's smile and cleft chin. There was a more petite daughter version with his dark complexion and deep-set eyes. If he ever worried he would not be able to identify her when she walked through those doors, he had no reason to – the familiar spring in her stride gave her away. He rose from his seat, unsure if he should reach in for a hug or a handshake. She went ahead and stuck out her right hand, freeing him from his dilemma.

He slowly unfurled his daughter's life one question after another.

Dzigbordi. A name from her mother's side of the country. He would have picked something more versatile for the child. Mary, Jennifer, even Elizabeth. She went by Gigi for short. Her resemblance to her mother rattled him, from the high cheekbones right down to the slight lisp.

A major in marine biology. It was admirable, of course, to be pursuing a degree in the sciences, but what exactly did one do with a degree in marine biology? Had he been consulted, he would have recommended she pursue something more pragmatic. He blamed it on her mother and that follow-your-heart philosophy of hers.

His daughter had attended St Albans, a Cambridge-certified secondary school up north. Summer holidays were often spent interning at her step-father's law firm. Daddy this, Daddy that. Her responses were littered with references to the man whose last name she bore. Nimo felt short-changed. How was his daughter to refer to him then? Dad? Too stiff, devoid of the warmth Daddy exuded. Dada? Too juvenile.

After that first meeting, they agreed to meet the next Wednesday and the one after, and three months down the line, it has become their little tradition.

He bids Mrs Dankwa goodbye and begins to make his way down the paved sidewalk.

"Aren't you taking your car?" she calls after him, gesturing at the white Peugeot in his driveway.

"No," he shakes his head. "Not today."

Parking in the city is a headache without a work-issued pass and a designated parking spot. Besides, he does not mind the twenty-minute walk to the bus stop, a fine opportunity to stretch his stiff limbs. He had once read somewhere that the key to optimal health is walking ten thousand steps daily. The bus he catches into the city is half-empty. To his relief, he gets a row of seats to himself in the very back where he can focus on generating a list of questions for his daughter. She takes after him in demeanour – pensive and reticent. The onus falls on him to keep their conversations on wheels.

High Street finally emerges, a sprawling avenue of lofty office buildings and exclusive shops. The city greets him like an old friend. He can see his former place of work in the distance, a boxy beige edifice out of place in a skyline of sleeker silhouettes. When he reaches the restaurant, a small crowd is already building inside. The other diners look temporarily liberated, with their loosened ties and suit jackets draped over chairs. He scans the room, hoping not to bump into anyone he knows. Chance meetings these days are filled with questions about how he is using his newly acquired free time.

His daughter enters minutes later, her white crop top revealing a bit more than he is comfortable with. He stands up to help pull out her seat, but she beats him to it. A waiter takes their order and delivers a basket of warm bread rolls to the table for starters.

"You look well," he offers.

"Thanks, you too."

"How's your mother?" It's the only thing he can think to ask at this moment.

"Fine, I guess. She and Daddy are away in Cape Coast for the weekend."

Daddy. While he remains generic and titleless.

"Does she still run the tailoring shop?"

"No, Daddy's idea. He thinks she should take it easy now that she's getting older."

He notices the watch on his daughter's wrist – genuine leather from what he can tell.

"Is that new?" He points to it.

"Yes, a birthday present from Daddy."

Quite a superfluous gift for an eighteen-year-old, in his opinion. But more importantly, it sinks in that he had missed his own daughter's birthday. Lebene had left out the finer details about their daughter. She had simply dropped him in the middle of a maze.

"It's an Omega." His daughter turns her wrist from side to side as if he should know what an Omega is – he who has owned the same digital Casio for the last fifteen years. He imagines the stepfather is the kind of man who buys affection with material things to make up for one inadequacy or another. Impotence. Squatness. Maybe even toothlessness.

The waiter returns with their orders and asks if they'll need anything else. Both shake their heads.

"So, what do you do now that you're retired?" his daughter asks, working her jollof rice with a fork and knife.

He should be happy she is asking questions. He is happy.

"Oh, I've been keeping busy."

She looks up at him, dissatisfied.

"I've taken up gardening."

The ease of the lie startles him.

"Oh really?" She cocks her head slightly. "What are you growing?"

"Vegetables ... I'm growing vegetables."

"Which ones?"

He strains to modulate his voice, now questioning the necessity of the lie. "Oh, all sorts really."

The restaurant begins to empty out, waiters busily wiping down tables and tucking in chairs. Father and daughter take it as their cue to leave. All along High Street, employees are returning to their air-conditioned offices, sluggish from the combination of simmering heat and heavy lunches. At the bus stop, his daughter hails an orange TATA bus heading in the direction of campus.

"Next Wednesday then?" he asks.

"Yes, next Wednesday."

Back at home, he sits on his front steps, tie in hand. He looks out at his front lawn, overrun with tall stalks of wild grass and thinks back to his lie. Gardening of all things. But gardening is the sort of thing people expect retired folks to do. Get on your knees. Get dirt under your fingernails. Be one with the earth. Dust to dust.

Work had never left him enough time to worry about the exterior or interior of his house. As far as he was concerned, a house was just a brief stop on a whirlwind tour. It explains the bareness of the walls inside the bungalow, the lack of dining furniture, the satisfaction with a solitary couch and a thirty-two-inch LED television. It is not the type of space one brings a daughter into. He identifies a balding patch on the far end of the yard which he thinks would make a good site for a vegetable garden. In the morning, he will ask Mrs Dankwa for gardening recommendations and maybe even borrow some implements.

FOR THE FIRST time, he ventures down the gifts aisle at BuyRite. It is not an aisle that would regularly appeal to him, not with all those gaudy bows and glitter and shiny packaging. He stops, briefly, to examine a box of assorted chocolates on display. Or perhaps a polka-dotted scarf or a lockable diary or a pair of heart-shaped earrings or an oud-scented hand cream. He puts back the trolley and leaves empty-handed.

HE GLANCES AT his watch. Twelve-thirty. His daughter is uncharacteristically late. All the possibilities begin to swirl around his head, each one darker than the one before it. Could she be stuck in traffic? Perhaps there's been an accident? He is shocked at the preposterousness of his own theories, but simply cannot help himself. If he could build an impenetrable shield around her, he would. He wonders if the stepfather feels the same urge to keep her from harm. No, he is convinced this feeling can only be biological.

She finally walks through the glass doors, a red backpack slung over her shoulders. "Sorry I'm late."

"I was beginning to worry."

"No need to worry. Classes ran over, that's all."

Her head is buried in the menu even though they will both order what they always order – jollof rice for her, red-red for him. That is another trait they share.

"So, how's your garden coming along?"

"Quite well." Not having to lie feels good. "The okra is finally flowering and I've got some tomatoes on the way. You should come by and see it sometime."

"Sure."

Sure. One word. One ambiguous little word.

"So, how's school?"

"Good."

"Are you working on anything new?"

"Yeah," She twirls a braid around her index finger. "I'm doing a lit review on the feeding ecology of the Greenland Shark."

"Mm, I've never heard of it."

She sits up straight. He thinks he catches a twinkle in her eye.

"It's one of the largest living species of shark and can live up to five hundred years."

"That's a long time to live."

"Most of them end up blind anyway because parasites attach themselves to their corneas."

"I hope they move in groups at least, to help direct each other?"

"Only in the winter season. In the summer, they go their separate ways."

"What a miserable way to live out five hundred years."

"But is it really misery if you have known nothing else?"

Her wisdom blows him away, but would he expect anything less from his own kin?

"I hope you're not too miserable on campus?"

"Not really." She pauses to take a sip of water. "I have my friends and my boyfriend."

His chest tightens a little. He has been told there are things a parent is better off not knowing about their child. Perhaps this is one of those. Perhaps he should stop digging here.

"Boyfriend?"

"Yes, his name is Dave."

"Did you two meet on campus?"

"No, through the apps."

"The apps?" He chooses to keep digging.

"You know, the dating apps. Tinder, Bumble, Hinge?"

She reaches into her purse to retrieve her phone and leans towards him from across the table. On the screen a photo of a green-eyed boy flashing a dimpled smile, his arms draped around a beefy German Shepherd. Long brown hair and a bushy beard frame his squarish face. She flips through a few more photos of him snowboarding, hiking, and, the most shocking, playing the guitar shirtless.

"So where is this Dave from and what does he do?"

"He lives in Minnesota," she answers. "And he's a software engineer."

"So, you have never actually met?"

She grins. "No, not in person, but we talk on video all the time."

Nimo keeps his face in check. He should be supportive of his daughter but he also knows firsthand the damage love can do. How one minute it can light a warm flame inside of you and the next maul your insides with its claws.

"And how long have you two known each other?"

"Almost two months."

"Isn't it too early to call him your boyfriend then?"

She squares her shoulders and shifts in her chair.

"I'm not a child, you know?"

He resists the urge to reach across and touch the back of her hand.

"Of course, you're not."

With their plates now empty, her eyes begin to roam around the restaurant, fixating briefly on a table of rowdy young men in cheap suits. He plays with the cotton table napkin in front of him. The silence between them grows clammy.

"I've got to run," she announces, rising and grabbing her backpack. "I've got study group this afternoon."

They walk together to her bus stop while other bodies shove past with no regard.

"Next Wednesday then?" he asks as her bus approaches.

"Sure,' she mutters before disappearing into it.

As he watches the TATA bus pull away, it comes to him. *Pops*. More charming and light-hearted than *Daddy*.

Pops – that's what he'd like to be called.

IF THE HONEY IS SWEET, WHY DOES THE BEE STING?

Salma Yusut

$\mathcal{M}$OMBASA GOLF CLUB whiffs of money and decorum. I do not know how a ball made from synthetic rubber and a stick made from carbon-fibre reinforced polymer strengthens the classism that has already telescoped the island.

The club is situated near the historic cream minaret. The sun fights with the palm trees as the ocean waves caress the hexagonal stones and the rocks that have stood the test of time. The crabs run to save their shame. The tides birth sea shells sporadically. A few early risers are winding up their yoga and jogging activities, wary of time. There is a buzz around the lighthouse. The black and white lighthouse itself stands with its head up high on the other side of Kizingo, below streets of posh houses and Mercedes Benzes and schools where children speak fluent international standard English.

I turn on the radio to listen to Elissa and Saad's new song "Min awel dakika" that has hit the world, a mutation of the Covid-19 wave. It is a romantic song, and my feelings are far from the quixotic association. The chorus makes my stomach churn as if I am a new bride, a virgin untouched by men. My right hand does not leave the steering wheel as I drive to the further side of the lighthouse to get a better view of the ocean. The flirtatious ocean that lures me with its marvellous rhythm. I watch the ferry as it does its indefatigable job of transporting people from Kwale to Mombasa.

I find a good spot between a white Toyota with two men smoking cigarettes and a red Vitz with a girl in her early twenties in the driver's seat and a boy, probably in his late twenties, in the front passenger seat, munching on boiled sweet potatoes.

I come to the lighthouse to get away from the claws of my life. The lighthouse carries the secrets of lovers and broken marriages and sugar daddies and infidelities and ghat chewers and stargazers. It is where the real world converges; where people can leave their masks on the back seat and dwell on the bewilderment brought by their wild sins.

A week ago, I was staring as the same ocean lured me and my husband Farouq with its marvellous rhythm – but we ourselves were no longer in rhythm. What was once love had turned into an abyss of despair. We had decided to stay together for the sake of our daughter. This is what we had both seen in our parents. They had stayed in broken marriages when they should have left, stayed for the sake of their children, for the sake of society. We should do better; but now we too were choosing to stay because of Haseena.

On the night before he left for Dubai, we talked as if we were old friends, old lovers clutching at a straw. We had tried to patch things up before, but it was hard to put a Band-Aid over unhappiness. Yet we sat together on the embroidered mat on the verandah and drank qahwa and ate dates.

Saada, my mother, kneaded chapatti dough as she listened to us talk and laugh, her heart guarded because she knew we were keeping it together, exactly as good people do. She ground more cardamom and ginger in the granite mortar to add to our qahwa. Her hands pressed the pestle harder and harder to extract as much of the essences as possible. She added the extract to our cups of piping-hot qahwa, and then left us and the moon to ourselves; as if the qahwa could keep us in that state forever, as if it could stop us from saying the things we really wanted to say.

"We can continue together so that we provide Haseena with a good education and a more stable upbringing given her condition, but I cannot keep lying to myself that I love only you," Farouq said.

"When did you stop loving me? When did you become this half-beast, half-human being? When did time cage us into believing we still were?" I asked.

"You never know when it happens – it just happens."

The night folded the moon like a bedsheet. It ate the remnants of the love left behind. Yet I still stayed. He still stayed. We pressed our arms against each other, rekindling the days on the same verandah when we first saw each other, when we first loved each other, when we knew we were meant for each other. What we shared was so hard to leave behind because we were family before we were lovers. Our grandmothers had shared a womb, and ours was a love story written by blood, a story older than the Indian ocean.

The next morning, Mama Saada woke us up at 6:15. The sun had unbolted its claws. Habuba, my grandmother, was following Sheikh Sudais's Quran recitation مباشر from Makkah on the television. Her chalky, eager fingers divided Haseena's shoulder-length hair into two portions as she smoothed it with olive oil.

Mama Saada was on the verandah setting out breakfast. She placed on a sisal mat a plate of shakshouka and chapatti. I was in our bedroom, helping Farouq pack his bags, ensuring that his passport and all his travel documents were present and correct, ironing the blue shirt and black trousers he was to wear for his safari.

"Please come and have your breakfast in time so that you do not miss your flight. You never know with the traffic at Kibarani. Bora you get there early than be stuck in a vehicle, ya Rabbi stara," Mama Saada said.

We ate our breakfast in silence, the only noise the sound of our chewing. Habuba had finished oiling Haseena's hair. She now sat on the majlas drinking her morning qahwa, her purple rosary in her hand. She was counting the beads like cowrie shells, counting and counting and counting as if keeping record of her good deeds for Raqeeb, the angel of good.

I noticed that the air outside our blue-white house was singing with humidity. I opened the windows wide as the curtains blew faintly to create an illusion of coolness. The leaves on the trees shuffled; the asmini and vikuba were ready for plucking.

The Uber driver waited as Mama Saada and I helped Farouq place his bags in the trunk. We said our goodbyes half-heartedly, uncertain whether this was our last encounter. I looked at him as if seeing him for the first time. His petite body. His caramel skin. His pointed nose. His shoulder-length curly hair, an exact match of Haseena's. A spell of resemblance that could not be broken, could not be erased. This was his way of telling me that I could not easily let go of him.

A week later, at the same lighthouse with the waves and the breeze, he haunts me with his crooked smile, his candy-coated lies, his ability to balance the shame and the game. His ability to get me on my knees, still, crying desperately for him. His ability to offer me love in doses, like a prayer.

I crave him even when I know that what we have now is an illusion of love. I cannot make him; he cannot be made.

Six years ago, Farouq got a scholarship opportunity to pursue his Bachelors in Business Management at the University of Dubai. It was a far-fetched dream that had been brought close by fate. It was easy for me to offer him support – the badge that women wear as wings. If I had been the one who had scooped up the same opportunity, the women of our society would have raised their unsolicited voices to give advice on how bad a woman I was, to leave a husband behind with a four-year old autistic child. They would have talked about how leaving my husband by himself might tempt him into entering into the devil's workshop, into being the devil himself.

While he was in Dubai, we kept in touch. We warmed ourselves through the freckled nights and the hyper-pigmented days. We still basked in the sun of our love. When Farouq called, he asked about Haseena's development, and how she was faring with her homeschooling. A choice we made for our daughter when we realised that most schools in our locality were either not aware of autism, or not equipped with the right skills to handle a blessed child like ours. Even though he was far from her sight, he was a present father. On video calls, he noticed all the things that she did. How she paced around the room. How she dived into her own world. How she sucked her thumb. How she made him laugh. How she played with her hair when overjoyed. How she repeated the words she read from her bedtime-story collection, one by one. How she cried when the misty air of ishaa swept over her. How she held Habuba's hand, her safe haven. The great-grandmother who mothered her.

Everything was going on well until the thunderstorm hit our marriage. It was at the time when the sun is paid to collect taxes in a Mombasa that evades taxes like the plague. My iPhone had rung with an intensity suggesting it knew it was about to turn my world upside down. My heart palpitated as if it was about to jump out of its chest pocket. I answered his call.

"Swafiya. Are you awake?"

"Naam. Tell me."

"I have wanted to tell you this for so long, but I was not courageous enough. But."

"But what?"

"I am getting a second wife."

I coiled into my skin as I looked at my soul hanging in the clammy air, trying to find its way out of the curtains, to the world, to the heavens, to someplace far away where it could live inside another body. My ears could still hear him from a distance, his voice trying to make me see sense, how a second wife would work for him, for us, for Haseena. He was trying to make me hear words that my brain could not process. Words that had never been in my marriage vocabulary.

"Swafiya. You know as a man I am allowed to marry up to four wives. Her name is Zeinab. We study together here. Swafiya. Are you there?"

I was not there. I was living my greatest nightmare. This was the man I trusted and loved, the man who had ripped away my innocence with turmeric and nutmeg. The man I saw before I saw myself, the man for whom I constantly clipped my wings, fighting to hold together what my Habuba and Mama Saada had prepared me for since I was eight. My whole life had revolved around pleasing a man, preparing for a man, living for a man, and living in a man. My whole life I had studied men like chemistry and geometry: but you cannot keep what does not want to be kept. Kept for who? For when? For where?

The chirping of the hummingbirds outside my bedroom window brought my soul back inside its shell. Was it still intact? Which part of it was lost in the polluted air? Which part of it could still love and trust?

I broke the news to Mama Saada and Habuba, who were seated on the majlas drinking their ten o'clock chai. I watched Habuba's chai swirl into a monsoon. Mama Saada fidgeted with her fingers as if contemplating what to say. Her round face carried the worries of a future she had not foreseen.

Eventually, Mama Saada and Habuba, whose happiness rested in the hands of my little family, decided to call the twabibu to come and recite ruqyah in my house. Their belief was that the evil eye had come to rest in my house. The black seeds to prevent the evil eye had clearly been eaten away by the fuming of people who envied a man who was on his way to becoming a businessman, a woman who had a successful tailoring business, and an autistic child who was receiving all the love and care she deserved.

"What will people say?" Mama Saada said a week after the twabibu had come to clear away the evil eye with recitations of the Quran and the burning of luban and oud, which rose to God's skies. In the kitchen were fingerprints of family legacies, charcoal marks of the alphabets made by Haseena, and oil smudges created by simmering onions and tomatoes. The utensils from the previous night laid unapologetically on the drying rack, waiting to be placed where they belonged. Brown residue stuck on the edges of the breakfast bowls and cups. On the counter, dead flowers from last week were oozing disgrace.

I opened the tap to wash the breakfast utensils. A moon of anger hung over me. It was one hundred and sixty-eight hours since Farouq had struck me with thunder. The dark nights were sleepless, but I was growing a thick skin. Time was slowly shrinking the wound. I could not let a man break me through a woman he had met in a classroom, a woman who had taken my place in his heart. What did I forget to read in my men-handling manual?

"I do not care much about what people will say, Maa. I am more worried about Haseena. You know how attached she is to us."

"Allah Karim."

"What if I leave?"

"What if you stay for Haseena? He is not divorcing you. He is just marrying a second wife. It is way better than adultery, isn't it? He will still provide for you. Love dries with time."

"But our marriage will be a façade. We will be putting on an act like so many other women out here who are hanging onto rags of dead marriages."

"Challenges are normal in marriages. We chose to stay for our children. Habuba stayed for me. I stayed for you. We survived."

"I don't know. I feel like I should leave for Haseena."

NOW I TURN off the ignition and get out the car. I slowly walk towards a bench that is partly painted with the droppings of crows that fight with people's heads. I sit there to let the ocean wash away all the thoughts running through my mind. The sky is baby's breath and forget-me-not. The cumulus clouds soar one above another. Right on the pavement rail, a few metres from where I have parked my car, is a metal stand with a grill filled with raging red charcoal. The owner is shabbily dressed. He hums a tune as he fans corn cobs; the wind brushes his body as if cleansing him to prepare him for his day's labour. *It is too early to grill corn cobs,* I mutter to myself. But who am I to plan people's earnings? While my vessel is unmoored, I cannot mock the sinking Titanics of others.

"If your mind is jailed, is your body free?"

I look around and see a middle-aged woman. She is wearing a black shuga – it fights with the wind, it *is* the wind. She uncovers her face to prompt me to look at her as if to honour all the wrinkles and tales patched onto her face. She has a black mark on her forehead: sijdah, a symbol of prayerfulness and piety. Her lips are chapped and the lustre of her face has left her suns ago. Yet she carries a compelling aura. On her left hand is a gold ring with the infamous kito cha shaba, the copper pearl, which was Farouq's grandmother's gift to Habuba to seal the marriage alliance of their grandchildren. Was it a sign? She is chewing her tongue like black seeds. She is chewing herself into black seeds. She is talking to me, I realise.

"Ask me again?"

"Follow me."

"Why should I follow you? I do not even know you."

"Do you just follow what you know?"

"Who are you?"

"Sabah, the morning Venus."

I was six years old when I was made to believe that I should never talk to strangers. Here I am, twenty-seven years later, afraid of new faces, afraid of wearing my own body in languages not its own. Anxiety sits on my lap. For a moment, I want the protection that I offer Haseena. I want someone, something to hold me, to make me unlearn all the theories and all the speculations, all the wars and all the hurricanes.

"If your mind is jailed, will your body ever be free?"

"I guess not," I answer, my guard crumpling down like walls collapsing.

"Follow me."

I am going towards the unknown. She walks steadily and the pavement curves after her. She smells of coconut oil and ylang-ylang. She reaches for my hand and I voluntarily extend it to her. I have always been naïve, but I know that today, I am being pulled by mountains I have never climbed before.

We step down the rocks leading to the sea.

When I was young, Habuba used to say that the sea has seven daughters. Each daughter has a unique personality. Growing up on Mombasa Island, learning the seven daughters of the sea is not so tedious a task. Some daughters are calm; their waters wake up so early, go to sleep at noon and wake up after asr prayers. Some daughters are always angry. Some daughters have bewitched the whales. There are daughters that let the sleeping sharks lie until the ship's bells ring and the smell of warm blood overtakes the sea. Some daughters carry entire kingdoms hidden in coral reefs, along with jinns, microplastics and abandoned fishing nets.

This is the daughter of the sea that is always angry.

We clamber towards a cave beneath one of the rocks we climbed down. Outside the cave, clothes are spread over the smaller rocks. A lantern burns at the cave entrance. There are no doors, but the entrance displays the craftiness of simplicity. The cave is scented with musk al ward. It has a divani couch, a sisal mat, a wooden mirror and a pilipili bed. There is also a tiny cabinet holding Swahili books, a withered kikuba, and an ashtray with half-smoked cigarettes. On the upper rack is a wooden comb and a tin of kohl. An uteo with the words *si riziki yangu* woven into it dangles on the wall. This is the first cave I have seen that looks habitable; even the cobwebs are stretched harmlessly. A home away from the world, yet still cultured like our world.

My mind is grappling with questions. The tides outside have taken their bath; they are wide awake. Sabah looks at me as if she can see my mind. She touches the uteo, caresses it, the tender touch of love.

"The distance between the moon and the sun is 150 000 000 kilometers. The distance between the uteo and its user is zero. You form a bond with the uteo when you sieve the chaff from your rice; you learn to distance yourself from anything that wears you down. Uncage your mind from any matter that occupies unnecessary space."

"But how do you know so?"

She holds out the bottle of kohl and wooden comb and places them in my right hand. She cups her palms over them. She then releases them and hands them over to me.

"Your eyes are sick – that is why I am prescribing the kohl for you. Your hair is dry; the wooden comb will do. Like xerophyte plants, you have been too long in harsh environments. You have adapted, grown comfortable with toxicity. Every morning, you place it on your breakfast table and drink it with tea leaves. This gift from me will disrupt your normalisation of generational trauma, of pain that comes in the form of surviving on suffering."

"Are you a witchdoctor? Who are you?"

"I have lived long enough to know the ways of human beings. This world is not always black and white, and your questions will not help you either. What you take from this cave, will. It took techniques not taught in school to get the divani couch, the cabinet and the pilipili bed inside this cave. Have you ever heard of the tale of the she-camel that passed through the eye of a needle? If you live in this world without managing yourself or your possessions, someone else will manage them for you. Even in situations where darkness overpowers light, you have to believe that light will eventually come."

"How do you demand respect and love from those who take you for granted?"

"You have to be like the sisal mkeka. It knows its value. It knows that modern carpets will come, but it still flaunts itself. In a traditional Swahili household, the sisal mkeka stands out with its stiffness, its texture, its durability, and its distinctive colour. It has outlived the ancestors; why would it fear destruction now? You have to love yourself enough for people to love you. You have to choose yourself, mountain times over."

"How do you undo fear? Don't you fear the demons that live in this merciless sea?"

"What is there to fear about demons when we live with demons with faces like ourselves, masked and unmasked? When the tides are fuming and the crabs run towards my cave for safety, I smoke a cigarette. I allow my mind to be hypnotised by the clatter of the sea's skeletons in the cupboards. It takes six hours and twelve point five minutes for the water at the shore to sleep or to stay awake. Sometimes the time is enough for me to smoke an entire packet of cigarettes, sometimes it is enough for me to light half a cigarette. Whichever the time, I have learnt not to be crippled by fear. What is life anyway, sixty years? Twenty years? Ten years? To be possessed by fear? I cannot martyr myself that much."

"How do you see yourself?"

"Through the sands that steadily hold my wooden mirror, a mother to me. The sea has seven daughters. I am the one born out of wedlock. The world does not know me, but I see the world through my mirror."

"Why do you keep a withered kikuba?"

"I keep the kikuba to remind myself that getting married is not always the end goal. If you are married and you are not happy, what keeps you lurking in the mirage? When women make choices, they forget to make choices for themselves. While kikubas are meant for married women, I keep one for myself, and I am as untouched as an island, enshrined here with my mother. I am woven like the kikuba: jasmine and roses threaded firmly together. I am woven in my dreams. I challenge women to do what is best for themselves even when society thinks otherwise. What is good for you? Where does your light lead you? If today did not leave you better, it should leave you to think: if the honey is sweet, why does the bee sting?"

The hours are swallowed. The waters are still taking their qailullah, the afternoon nap. I hear the adhan calling people to prayers, and my tongue is drenched in praise. I glance at Sabah one more time and clamber out the cave holding the bottle of kohl and the wooden comb. I follow the same route to get back to my car. I start the ignition, and my mind replays the conversation, like an exorcism, like a spell.

THE SITTING ROOM is spacious with two big sofas and one stand-alone chair. A gigantic bamboo plant is in the corner, next to the cream television stand. The walls are filled with family pictures from past days. From one of the pictures, Grandmother Kursum's face looks at me, her wrinkled face scrunched, her expression indicating that I am treading away from the norm, that I should rethink, for the sake of hers and Habuba's sisterhood, for the sake of the copper pearl.

In the middle of the room is a decorative art piece that Farouq brought back from a trip to Ghana: a sculpture of a man and a woman wrapped in each other's arms. The man holds a candle holder in his right hand. I always thought that piece symbolised our love, Farouq being my candle holder, but that has changed now, faster than light.

Farouq's grandmother, Kursum, had gifted Habuba a kito cha shaba, a copper pearl similar to Sabah's. After Mama Saada gave birth to me, Habuba recited the adhan into my right ear and cut my umbilical cord with a sterile knife. She then held me up with her arms stretched to the skies of Allah and ululated, her tongue spitting out takbir and tahlil. When Grandmother Kursum came to the hospital, she already knew what she wanted for the future of her grandson who had lost his parents in a car accident. Her fear of death's clutches prompted her to secure a future for her grandson Farouq, whose name means the one who can tell right from wrong.

"My granddaughter-in-law has arrived," she uttered. Her words, Mama Saada said, were like outbursts of rain. The hospital ward roared with her revelation: "Swafiya, the purified one," Grandmother Kursum had said while drawing three lines branching on my forehead.

Her dream came to fruition. She lived long enough to see Farouq and I tie the knot. She also lived to cut Haseena's umbilical cord. The last one she cut before she passed away. The soil on her grave dried faster as her vision sustained itself. But for how long?

I CALL FOR an urgent meeting with Mama Saada and Habuba. I call Farouq on WhatsApp to join us virtually. Grandmother Kursum stares at me from the framed photos. The walls are starting to crack, forming spider webs. Outside, there are low layers of nimbostratus clouds pregnant with rain, the grey skies surrendering. My mind replays Sabah's words: *Where does your light lead you? If today did not leave you better, it should leave you to think: if the honey is sweet, why does the bee sting?* I twiddle my fingers as if I am about to align a single thread in a needle, the way I do when mending the clothes of others.

"I want a divorce."

Silence sits in the room, fiery like the daughter of the sea that lets the sleeping sharks lie until the ship's bells ring and the smell of warm blood overtakes her.

The cracking voice of Farouq on the screen goes faint, and there is a creaking sound, like something fragile has lost its original shape.

"What do you mean?"

"I mean what your ears heard."

Habuba and Mama Saada look at me with fury. Habuba holds her mouth, asking me to stay silent because the man on the other side of the line is my husband, my cousin brother, the man of the promised land who deserves nothing but respect even when he is treading the wrong path. I focus my attention on anything but their faces.

"Swafiya. I have never stopped loving you, but I am a man and my needs need to be met. Zeinab will meet my needs when I am in Dubai, and you will meet my needs when I am in Mombasa. What about Haseena? Or is this your selfishness speaking?"

"I do not want to be half-loved. I have thought about our daughter. In fact, it is because of her that I want to leave this marriage. You have been a good father – do not get me wrong. You have also been a good husband – until this happened. But I just can't. I can't. I love you enough to let you go."

"What about Grandmother Kursum? Do you think she will be happy with your decision?"

"I met someone recently who made me see myself clearly enough to know that I will never settle for pain that comes in the form of surviving on sufferings. I will email you the divorce documents soon. Sign them and send them back via Salihiya Cargo. I will print a copy for myself and take them to the kadhi's office."

"Swafiya. I am your husband. Can you listen to me? Swafiya!"

I ended the call.

The frames on the walls crumble to the ground one after another. Mama Saada and Habuba are shouting at the top of their voices. I can hear words like *people* and *Kursum* and *husband* and *divorce* run over each other, but my soul leaves me and kisses the rain outside. My feet touch the sands, my body is free and my tongue chants: *you form a bond with the uteo when you sieve the chaff from your rice, you learn to distance yourself from anything that wears you down.*

Haseena comes to join me in the garden sucking her moon-fingers, holding a piece of paper with a drawing of a mother, a father and a child with her left hand. The rain slowly dissolves the paper until it becomes particles, which are swallowed by the ground. I plant a kiss on her forehead, and let the rain eat the cycle I have broken.

ON CHANCELLOR'S STREET

Kabubu Mutua

OCTOBER HAD COME and the grove of mvules on Chancellor's Street had shed their leaves, painting the sidewalks in yellow-gold shades, rustling when a light wind blew. And yet Amir remained missing. Those were the long days and nights of '82 when Kiilu had locked himself in his hostel room and refused to come out until his parents drove down in their Citroen to say, "Musee. Tell us what is going on in your mind." He'd said nothing. He'd pasted black and white photographs of Amir around the campus, but they were peeling now, ruffled by the wind and torn in parts, his image washed out. He'd shared the MISSING leaflets with everyone he met, pasting them on noticeboards and above election posters and on walls that said NO POSTERS. And afterwards, he'd waited for a phone call.

THE FIRST TIME Amir spoke to him he'd lost his key, and he'd asked Kiilu could he please assist him with his own so he could reproduce it at the metalsmith. And Kiilu had eagerly given it to him, imagining that when he returned it, he would ask if he wanted to go to the student centre for coffee or to the stadium to watch a football game. But Amir had returned the key while he was in the shower, and he had found it placed above a note that said, *Asante*. A surge of sorrow for things that had not happened, for what could have been, had stabbed him, and standing there, with the smell of Amir's sandalwood spray in his nostrils, he had felt a helpless love.

And so, he had begun to follow Amir secretly, to peruse his bags when he came in from class early, to sniff his shirts which always smelled of lemons, making sure to return his things as they were: Amir's coats he would hang back on the same hooks where he had found them, his shoes he'd arrange perfectly on the wooden rack, his bag he would zip and place carefully in the closet, and he would wonder if Amir would know, and if he did, what he would think of him. Amir was a boy, Kiilu had come to know, accustomed to the perfect order of everything around him. His clothes he washed every weekend, never letting them stay in the reed laundry basket as long as Kiilu's did, his shoes he polished with Kiwi the night before his classes, and he ironed every Sunday morning. His prayers, too, he offered with a fine sense of compactness, words uttered in a low voice. Kiilu would watch as he flattened out the creases on his mat before he began his dua, the motions of his limbs a beautiful and graceful synchrony. On Fridays, he wore a kanzu starched just so, and later in the afternoon, he would return from his prayers with his leather sandals and feet untouched by dust, clean as they had been that morning. When he went out in the evening, Kiilu would follow behind, and once he was almost discovered. It had happened near the Law lecture theatres. Amir had turned suddenly, as if he had forgotten something at the hostel, and Kiilu had stumbled into an empty hall, hiding behind the door until Amir's footsteps faded.

THEY FIRST TALKED on the very day that a junior air force officer led a mutiny against the government. Classes were suspended, the air suddenly bearing the far-off smell of death, that muted fear of approaching doom. Throughout the hallways and the pavements crowds sprouted, imagining the events as they'd unfolded. At four a.m., Kenyan time, a section of the air force had taken control of the *Voice of Kenya* and announced they'd overthrown the government. For a few hours, Ochuka became president. For a few hours, he became the shortest-serving president in the history of Kenya. And the army had retaliated, sweeping through the city with heavy tanks, seeking traitors. And soon word spread that movement within and without the school had been restricted, the news briefly printed in leaflets handed across the campus. For the first time, they stayed in their room all day, the door locked, as they listened to VOK from the Sony radio, the skies rumbling with low-flying jet planes – Amir splayed on his bed, flipping through an old edition of *Drum* magazine, Kiilu trained on the radio knob, changing frequencies. And each turn of the knob brought a rainy sound, a crack and a loss of airwaves. And yet the sound of the reporter remained elusive, a tiny noise drowned in the radio. It was Amir, in that tensed afternoon, who helped attach the antennae to the window grill with a roll of copper wire. And the airwaves melted to a crispiness. The reporter's voice became clear.

"Thanks," said Kiilu. But Amir was not listening, rather he was staring past the window into the street below. A police car sped along Chancellor's Street, with rifles sticking from its windows. A voice announced that the president was safe, the mutiny had been tamed, the army was in control. But a lot was left out: the hundreds killed across the city, the number of shops set on fire, the disappeared students. Kiilu asked Amir if he wanted chai and he nodded yes. It had always surprised him that for months they'd remained strangers, each day slipping by with a strained block of silence that both frightened and charmed him. Amir always offered him curt replies whenever he greeted, never slipping into conversation, always avoiding his eye. Amir never initiated conversations. Instead, it was Kiilu who always greeted first, who always commented that their praying neighbours were too loud, who once complimented Amir's perfume.

That evening, as he poured hot water into the porcelain cups, Amir told him that his father had been a cadet. He took him to see his first airshow, planes trailing colourful smoke across the sky. And he imagined the intervals of anticipation before the parachutes broke from the officers' backpacks. His father had been a quiet man who listened to Chopin even though he resented the French, and the day before his plane crashed, he'd called from a treetop to say he would be home for Palm Sunday. He said he was sorry but Amir was lost in his narration, and did Kiilu know that the cell networks in those areas only worked in high places, say, on top of hills or houses or trees? It secretly pained Kiilu to imagine that Amir might be a person held down by his past, strapped to painful memories. And whether perhaps this was the root of his silence, of his decision to lead a distanced life. Later, Amir pulled a pack of cards from his trunk and they played with the cotton curtains open to let in the light. He won a few times and in the middle of the game Amir snatched a pack of cards Kiilu had slipped into his sheets.

"You're cheating," Amir said, and for the first time they burst out laughing, a unisoned laughter that perplexed him in a way. Why, he wondered, did it feel so right and wrong at the same time? He excused himself to go to the toilet, remembering the first time he'd felt this way, the first time it had felt so right and wrong.

His cousin Linze from his father's side had shared his bed over one Christmas holiday when their small house in Makutano had filled with visiting relatives, each room overflowing with bodies, the walls and spaces sticky with greetings and gossip and the scents of roast goat. His cousin Linze was a year older than him, and had been suspended from secondary school for smoking a pack of Sportsman. That quality of deviousness had drawn him to Linze. And so that night as his cousin Linze snored, a sliver of moonlight lining his face, he watched him sleep. And now all he ever thought about when he felt this way was his cousin Linze, who smoked a pack of Sportsman.

Outside, a shaft of late afternoon sunlight washed across the road. A group of students played a basketball game, dribbling the ball on the unmarked tarmac. He wanted to tell Amir that he felt a lightness in his head as if he'd sipped from a Tusker bottle. All this solitude, how could it satisfy him just so? How?

There was a mute acknowledgement of the other's presence between them, and he wondered whether it was a crime that he'd said so little of himself, whether he should reveal strands about his childhood in Makutano: he owned a bicycle called Terminator, and his boyhood had been insular, protected and yet adventurous in its own way, and he'd never gone to an airshow. And yet he held this part away. And even though it felt selfish, to take and not to give, he wondered whether perhaps he'd decided too soon that Amir was an open person.

And even though Amir was a quiet roommate, the kind of roommate who came and went as if the hostel was a stopover rather than a place where he lived, it had always fascinated Kiilu to imagine Amir as a person who led a secret life, a second mysterious alternate reality that he sought to know. Perhaps this was the thing that drew him for those long months when they shared the room, that absence of revelation, that quality to live as if somehow, he held a deep secret, as if he guarded the key to a forbidden knowledge.

HE OWNED A Polaroid, gifted by an uncle from Dar es Salaam. One afternoon he asked Amir if he could take a photo of him, and he'd agreed, posing next to the window where the light found him. It delighted Kiilu, in a way, that he had sought permission, that he was a person who asked. Later, he'd told Amir that the concept of asking was sexy. "I know this girl, she taught me how to ask," he'd said.

"You and a girl?"

He'd ignored Amir's comment and continued: "She said, 'A man who asks and a man who takes without asking, they're not the same. Asking gives you a form of power, taking without asking is, in its own way, saying you don't have the power and so you will take regardless of what I want.'"

"Relax, this is not a philosophy class," he'd said.

"Philosophy is sexy too, if you come to think of it." He'd touched his hand. Amir pulled away. "There's a game tomorrow. The administration says it will relax things around the campus. If you want to go, we can go together."

"Yes, I will come," he'd said.

They went the following day, cheering Warrior FC, and there they locked eyes for the first time, and the thing that felt both right and wrong only felt right in that moment. The sun was a deep red, smudged with dust motes in the part of the pitch where the players chased the ball.

HE'D NOT BOARDED his bus home, his mother said over the landline. He said he'd seen him off at the bus station but did not say that it had felt like the last time, seeing him disappear. And so he'd lingered until the bus pulled away, waving. And now he wondered if Amir had waved too. He leaned on the wall and listened to her cry, and remembered the last time he'd seen her. At the end of Ramadan, after the moon was sighted, she had driven over with Amir's sisters – a pair of twins with rhyming names who constantly swooned over Amir as if he was an egg – to the campus, and had invited Kiilu to eat with them. She spoke the type of Swahili that Kiilu imagined as pure, unaffected by changing times. She was an elegant woman with a long neck, an extension of Amir, her veil tucked in the right ways, her words gentle. And now he placed the handset back on the receiver, feeling a weight of guilt take the place of her voice. He did not call nor did she call again. He would pick up the telephone and begin to dial her number, and yet he always paused midway, afraid that bad news existed on the other side. And so, the nightmares came, dark dreams of Amir lying dead in a strange place, of Amir asking why he'd stopped caring, and he would say he had always cared, he'd never stopped caring.

THEY FIRST ARGUED one evening after a football match on account of Amir speaking to a girl. He'd watched him watch her, walk to her and say she was beautiful and did she mind going to the cinema that weekend. He'd interrupted them and said he was sick and was going to lie down. And Amir ignored him and said, "Later."

He'd locked himself in their room, blocking the door handle with the edge of a chair, and Amir had knocked saying, "Please open up, we need to talk."

Somehow it had felt satisfying to hear him plead, to imagine that he wielded a sort of power against him. And yet, he'd wondered whether he'd gone too far, if he'd thought a lot of things too soon. He'd removed his shirt, then his trousers, then his Calvin Klein underwear, and leaned against the windowsill for a long moment, cold air from the street touching his skin. And when he finally opened the door, Amir had rushed in and said, "What was that about?" He'd wanted to say he was afraid. Lately, he was afraid. He wanted to say there were ways he longed to walk, windows he wished to stare through, places he wished to go that did not want him." And Amir, as though sensing his thoughts, pulled him close saying, "My big baby," in a teasing way.

JANUARY ARRIVED WITH long rains, animating the campus with a verdant greenness. Amir's mother drove over to say they'd searched and searched and searched. He said he was sorry for not calling. She asked what kind of friend he was, that he cared so little. And then he said he'd loved him, is that what she wanted to hear? She collapsed on the chair and said what was he talking about. He said it was time for her to leave; he had morning classes the next day. She began to cry and a surge of guilt stabbed him, to think that a part of her was oblivious of the kind of life that Amir had led. He waited until she was finished, staring at Chancellor's Street as Amir had once loved to.

THE COUP HAD come like a wind, carrying with it disappearances and deaths and lootings. He knew this. He knew that Amir's mother knew this. But he held on. Perhaps there was a possibility that he'd run away. This thought brought an overwhelming sense of sadness to his heart, to imagine he might have repulsed him, that Amir had sought refuge from his presence.

THEY'D FUCKED THAT night, the night they'd first argued, with rain pattering Chancellor's Street, the windowpane grey with a sheet of fog. Afterwards, tears had trailed his cheeks and Amir had hugged him and said, "I'm here. Tulia."

He'd wanted to tell him how lonely he had felt not long ago when Amir was a stranger. To feel so much comfort now had felt like a betrayal of his past self. He'd wanted to say, *I wanted all of this. I now have it and I don't know what to do.* Why, he'd wondered, did it feel as if he was holding a delicate china cup during an earthquake, as if something ominous lurked in the future? He'd fallen asleep with Amir's skin warm against his own. When he'd woken up the next morning, Amir was gone. *Off to class*, said a note on his desk. There were always notes, little sticky papers scribbled with his neat handwriting and pasted on everything – desk, wall, wardrobe, book covers – the letters carefully considered, the curves and the strokes breaking into straight lines on the paper's surface. They informed Kiilu of Amir's whereabouts when he arrived to find the room empty: *library, remember the paper about Vasco Da Gama I told you about?* Or, *the headache came again, I'm off to the sanatorium.* Or, *our group leader is such a pain. I'll meet you later.* These pieces of information awakened a sense of pride in Kiilu, to know that he owned a part of Amir, that a part of Amir needed him. Soon, he began to write in his diary, long entries that observed their daily lives: the pistachio ice cream that Amir had liked the previous Sunday, the funny joke that he'd told him, something about the matron's Kikuyu accent, how he'd mimicked the woman, rolling his l's so they dissolved to the roundness of r's – the light things he liked about him, the heavy things he liked about him, how they easily avoided talking about the future. He wished for Amir to find the diary as he easily found the sticky notes pasted on the door frame, and so he left it lying on his bed, a page opened here and there.

They'd supported the demonstrations as they could, donating to the Student Union with money enclosed in small manila envelopes, participating in talks at the lecture halls, and when these periods of strife were gone, they'd resume their classes with newfound vigour, passing and failing tests, calling their parents from the Telkom landline in the centre of the campus.

THE CALL CAME one morning as he prepared to go to class. A new roommate had moved in, a boy who shaved to the scalp, who wore stiff shirts and spoke to girls with a fake American accent. Amir's memories came to him in fragments now, not in those long sequences that had stayed with him after the Christmas of Amir's disappearance. Sometimes he would spot a boy at the student mess with his walk. Or someone with his shirt. Or someone with the sandalwood spray. And it would be as if he was there with him, asking if he'd slept well or if he wanted extra sugar in his chai. The caller said they'd found a body. He leaned on the wall and asked the caller to repeat what he'd said. And the caller said that a young man's body had been discovered in a garbage dump and was he willing to come down to the city mortuary to confirm if it was Amir? The telephone slipped from his hand, dangling from its cord in spirals. He stood there for a long time before the boy who shaved to the scalp said he'd been standing there for an hour and was everything alright? He said he was alright.

He dialled his father and when he picked up, he began to cry. "I'm driving down," his father said. His father had gained new shocks of grey at his temples, a limp in his step. He did not ask what had happened nor did Kiilu tell him. His father sat next to him in the school park where they watched water spurt from a limestone fountain. Doves were perched on the trough, sipping. He smelled of a woody scent he'd grown up knowing. They bought ice cream from a seller who asked pistachio or vanilla, and he said pistachio. His father said his mother worried about him a lot, a fleck of melting ice cream on his beard. They spoke of things they'd always spoken of: his land was due for sowing in November, and would he perhaps come down to break earth? And he felt a bit of Amir receding, like a frightened predator falling away.

He said yes to Amir's mother's invitation to the wake-keeping, dissolving in the crowd that asked did he know him? And he said he'd just been a friend from school. And there Amir was, in a white cloth, a body now. Afterwards he called his father from a Telkom landline to say he would be home for sowing. Perhaps this was all he would ever need, to do things connected with life. Somehow, it was a gift from him, this epiphany, the ability to see things as they'd always been. And even though that night he feared he was grieving in a lesser way, moving on too fast, a small joy pulsed through him as he fell asleep. Amir came to him in a light-filled dream where a lake, clear and iridescent, lapped at their feet. It was both day and night and evening and morning. Amir said he was sorry he'd never promised him forever. His own throat caught with laughter and he said what was he talking about, he'd loved every moment, every step, every touch. He wanted to ask what happened, but he woke up to dawn pouring into the window in a yellow damask, wiping the remains of the night away.

That October, the mvule trees did not flower. Their buds stayed cupped throughout the month and broke their petals in November. And in the weeks that followed, after he'd broken earth with his father, he would lean on the windowsill and imagine his eyes as Amir's own, and he would draw from this act the freedom to breathe, observing stretches of earth in the distance where soon maize stalks would sprout.

IN MADAM'S HOUSE

Emily Pensulo

*M*ADAM TRAVELLED YESTERDAY. To an island. To one of those places with white sandy beaches and clear blue water, and little huts dotted in the water near the shore. A faraway kingdom in a fairy tale book. A place where handsome princes meet and marry beautiful kind women. A kind of paradise on earth. If it were not for the evidence of the photos, I would not have believed this place to be real. That paradise does exist on earth. Even though Madam has only been gone for a day, she has already uploaded dozens of photographs to her Facebook page. Photos full of life. In one, she holds a glass with green, blue and yellow juice equally layered, and in another, she lies on the sand, in a white bikini, facing the sky. Her skin is bronzed and she smiles, revealing even white teeth. In another life, Madam could have been a model. But in this one, she is a scientist at the Zambia Centre for Disease Control and Prevention. She's travelled for a girl's trip because Covid had begun to get to her. Hours in a lab with tubes and chemicals, working to find a cure so people would not die, had begun to take its toll on Madam. So she needed a trip to unwind, to take a step back, and remember once again what it means to be alive.

I refresh her Facebook page, but there are no new photos yet, so I click on Chrome and type in the word "Maldives". The results vary from politics to the economy to tourism. I click on the tourism links and read about all the things you can do on the sunny side of life, and I wonder how many of these Madam will try. I refresh her page again. Still, there are no new photos, so I reach for the remote and watch a movie on Zambezi Magic. A man with seven wives has caught one having an affair. A quarrel ensues. The other wives are furious. How could she have two men in her life? A younger man, even. The woman pleads for forgiveness, saying it was a mistake, a mere weakness of the flesh, and because of this she is worthy of her husband's forgiveness. After all, he too has fallen prey to the same temptation.

Despite the drama, my mind sways to Madam. Has she tasted lobster, been snorkelling, or been on a dolphin tour? I lie back in her king-size bed, on the pillows she bought when she travelled to Paris for a workshop. My body sinks into them as if they were made of butter, and I adjust her pink silk nightgown which clings to my curves as if it belonged to me. I'd never known anything so smooth until I wore this nightgown for the first time. It was my second month of working for Madam. She asked me to stay in her house while she travelled, to look after things for her until she got back. I took a tour through her belongings, especially the ones she kept from me in the walk-in wardrobe she forbade me to clean or even look into, which made me think there was more to the story of Madam's money. Wasn't it reported that there were people who kept toes and livers and lungs in secret rooms, and which they used for money-making rituals? Despite the warning, I wandered into the secret room while Madam was away. Instead of finding human body parts, I found rows and rows of shelves on either side of the room with shoes and leather handbags stacked as if in an expensive store. At the far end, there were night robes, smooth and shiny and in different colours. I chose the pink one, which has become my favourite.

Since then, I have looked forward to Madam's travels, to the access her absence provides. At first, it was just the night robes, and then it became the make-up, and then the clothes, and eventually her life – tiny bits of information I transposed to my own. On a Facebook page, which appears under the name Malita Miti, I am a Scientist at Elimination and Prevention of Diseases, and I post about things and places I have never been to, but which I see from Madam's life. Last week, I had posted "eating sushi", and the week before, "loving the sparkle of these diamonds." The diamond earrings Madam had worn six months ago on a date with her boyfriend who I haven't seen since; I heard, when Madam was shouting on the phone, that she had caught him with another woman. I had devoured the photo Madam posted of their date. Her, in a white dress and bright red lipstick, in the arms of a handsome man with a beard.

When Madam travelled a month later, I wore the white dress and took a selfie on the rose-coloured accent chair, and shared it in my former high-school WhatsApp group. "Wow, you look hot," they said, and sent fire emojis, "your apartment is mwaaaa!!" and, "Finally, you've made it." I thanked them, grateful for lies and a life that was not my own. But in that moment it didn't matter – I was freed from the shackles of failure. And it felt good to be free, to breathe the air on the other side.

But the euphoria didn't last long and turned to pain when the shackles gripped too tight again. A girl I had barely spoken to back then wrote, "Congratulations Phales, you've always been so bright, I knew you would make it one day." My eyes watered as they lingered on the text reminding me of the girl with colourful dreams and a bright mind. I was not even a shadow of who she was, and she could not fit in the world I now lived in. I blinked the tears away and poured a little wine into a glass, not enough to raise any suspicion that I had been in Madam's wine collection. I walked to her balcony and leaned against the rails. The half-moon was yellow, but emitted enough light to brighten the night. A breeze blew the strands of Madam's weave on my head, and I sipped the wine slowly as I had seen Madam and the rich women in telenovelas do when they had a lot on their minds.

I stared over the road at the shanty town where I lived. It was once acres of bare land until squatters who came from villages to look for jobs in the city built homes there. The government had threatened demolition, and they in turn had threatened not to vote for the ruling party; so they stayed, and built more houses, which they rented out. The aluminum roofs looked like sand in the moonlight. Now only a tarred road constructed during the last election separated Madam's neighbourhood from the cluster of shanties. It reminded me of times gone when I climbed up the mango tree at my uncle's house and stared at roofs that appeared like acres of sand beneath the moon. I had imagined walking on that sand, my feet crushing the little houses below and turning them into castles where people ate three meals a day, children went to school instead of being on the streets, and people did not die of diseases that could not be treated because there were shortages of medicine in the hospitals.

As I sipped the wine, I thought back to those years, and how having big dreams in Uncle's house was illegal. Dreamers were scorned, and minds were closed to all that was possible. On the day I left, Uncle said I would fail because failure was in our bloodline, a part of our DNA. We parted without well wishes, as though I was an abomination for daring to break free from generations and generations of lack. He looked at me as if I was heading off on a doomed journey, and would soon come to understand the truth of his words. I'd defied him then. At least outwardly, because his way of thinking had begun to pull down the walls of hope. Even though I didn't admit it, I needed him to see, to believe, to accept, to approve – to hope.

The movie ends an hour and a half later. I am too sleepy for another one, so I switch off the TV and the bedside lamp. But sleep eludes me. I stare at the ceiling and try to conjure Madam's image, but it is Uncle's that comes up instead: standing by the door as I left, saying I would fail. And I remember the promise I made myself then, that I would be back to prove him wrong. It's this unfulfilled promise that keeps me up for hours and makes me toss from one side to the other. It pierces me, making me wonder if Uncle was right: if indeed failure is something we cannot escape. Something part of our DNA. As the night wears on, Uncle's image eventually fades, and it is then that I drift off to sleep.

In the morning, I decide to visit Uncle, and the first thing I do is search Madam's wardrobe for the outfit I will wear. When Madam travels, I go on leave too. I choose a floral pink dress and nude heels, pack them in a black plastic bag, and leave the house in a chitenge and t-shirt. As I walk along, I keep my feet from the unpaved sidewalks, from the dust that gives away that you do not own a car. I meet two maids, Mercy and Vero, and we exchange pleasantries as we always do on our morning walk to work. They want to ask why I am walking in the opposite direction, but they hold back and smile, and I know it will be me and not their madams they will discuss on the rest of their way. I never walk with them, and am sure they hate me for that. But gossip about mean madams with unreasonable demands disinterests me. And it's not because my madam is neither mean nor unreasonable, but because the unceasing complaints never take into account the parts where Mercy and Vero steal sugar, salt and cooking oil.

I walk faster and soon pass the house at the corner of the street with pink bougainvillea which has crept up the fence. Then I slow down when I get to the main road to revel in the sweet scent of the purple flowers of the jacaranda trees, which have formed a canopy over the street. But when the mall comes into view, I hasten my pace until I am in the bathrooms, where I swop the chitenge and t-shirt for the floral dress and heels. Before I leave the mall, I walk into Kalor Kafe. I have been there once when Madam took me to the mall to push the trolley in Shoprite as she filled it with goodies. Before we left the mall, we stopped by Kalor Kafe for Tom Ford's Velvet Orchard perfume.

The shop attendant walks over to me and smiles. "Madam," she says, "would you like some help?"

The word "Madam" moves something warm through all of me. In that moment, I am no longer a caterpillar. I've left my shell behind. I have become a butterfly.

I smile back and ask if they have Tom Ford's Velvet Orchard. When Madam wears the perfume, the floral scent floats all around the house long after she's left. It's her favourite. And maybe mine too. I really can't say. I've never owned different kinds of perfume, so I can't know for sure. The attendant says they do not have Velvet Orchard, but offers another scent for me to try. She sprays it on a cut-off paper and on my wrists, and I inhale the floral scent she says would be a perfect substitute. And it's a lot cheaper, too. I shake my head and say I only want the Velvet Orchard.

"Alright Madam," she says, "we will have Velvet Orchard in two weeks, please come by then."

I node even though I know I will not be back in two weeks, or in four, or even in a year. And most likely never at all. I leave with the cut-off paper and slip it into my dress. Uncle's home will smell of me long after I leave. Outside the mall, I get on a bus. I am the last passenger before it departs, and I am grateful. At least I do not have to wait long to see Uncle, because we won't be stopping everywhere to get more passengers. I roll back the windows and watch as we drive away from the roads refurbished before the general elections, and shopping malls erected all over Lusaka, to narrow dust roads with no names and houses clustered so close one might as well be living in one's neighbour's house.

The bus stops at Jimmy Hollar market and the conductor hits the roof to let us know we have reached the final stop. We disembark. It's a cool mid-morning, but sweat drenches my armpits and soaks my dress. It threatens to harm the scent I carry with me. I fan myself with my palm, but still I won't cool. I try to distract myself with the screeching music busting through a stereo at the Famished bar, the lyrics a ball of confusion. The bar is named Famished because the owner, Ba John, heard the word in a movie and liked it enough to think it was a worthwhile name for a bar.

The music makes my ears cry. Now, as it did then, and I am amazed at how so little has changed since I lived here. Ba Chris still sells sausages outside the Famished bar. He says they are Hungarian, but they are made of soya. I guess it's hard to tell the difference if you've never had Hungarian sausages before. Ba Joyce still sells fritters and corn by the heaps of charcoal for sale. Her skin has darkened, but it's hard to tell whether it's because of the years gone by or the charcoal dust she sits in every day. I adjust my weave and draw the bangs lower until the ends sit above my nose. Ba Joyce stares, a long lingering look, unable to decide if the woman walking past her in high heels and a floral dress is an NGO official or a dissenter who once belonged here and has come back to visit relatives. I walk faster, careful to keep the heels from sinking into the charcoal dust, and when I leave the heaps of charcoal and rows of shops behind, I look back at the spot opposite Ba Joyce where I used to sell vegetables. Ba Joyce would ask when I would find a man to look after me – preferably a bus driver because they had more money than the conductors. Then she'd tell the story of how she got married to a man who left to find work and never returned, left her with mouths to feed that were always asking for more. I'd look the other way, neither nodding nor shaking my head, to the road that led out of Jimmy Hollar until it hit a wall and turned out of view. They say it is the road Jimmy Hollar used when he left this place, which was his farm, never to return.

I get to Uncle's house. It still sits like an island surrounded by streams of sewer, which have widened over the years. I pull at the hem of the dress as I leap over the greenish water. A little boy and girl are playing outside the house, building tiny huts with mud and dry grass. I want to wonder whose they are, but the resemblance is unmistakable. They are my cousin Junior's children: a generation of children whose parents cannot afford to take care of them. Junior is Uncle's first-born son, expelled from school in the eleventh grade for smoking chamba. The last I heard, the police were looking for him for aggravated robbery.

"Bwanji?" I say.

They turn and stare at me and then at each other as though I am imagination.

"Bwanji?" I say again.

They run into the house. Minutes later, they emerge with a statuesque woman as lean as she was fifteen years ago. She's wearing a chitenge and a tattered blouse and squints as she stares at me, trying to draw on her memory because the woman in front of her is both familiar and unfamiliar.

I move the strands of the weave from my face and tuck them behind my ears. She covers her mouth with both hands, and her eyes widen. She moves closer, the little ones behind her, staring at me from either side of her legs, tugging at her chitenge.

"Phales," she says at last.

I should smile and say "Aunty", hang the bag over my shoulder and offer a hug. Even a handshake. But I do not. I stand there feeling fifteen years old again, living in this house, doing house chores, and stealing time in the middle of the night to bury myself in books she discouraged me from reading. I hoped I would one day go to university and leave Jimmy Hollar, and buy a home on the other side of town, like the one Madam lives in. Aunty had said that these were the delusions of a naïve girl because once you belonged to Jimmy Hollar, it did not let you go. She'd point a finger at her chest and use the fingers on the other hand to count the generations before her who had lived and died in this place. People who took trips to the Lusaka CBD, a kilometre away, like tourists in their own country, to taste by the tip of their tongue a life they dreamed of, but could not live, because they had been left behind in the Zambia of the Harvard-educated and well connected. And this had chilled my soul, the prospect of dying in a place with little to live for. But Aunty had pressed home these words day after day when she saw wings growing on me that needed to be clipped out.

"Atatebake Junior," she calls, without coming any closer to me.

It takes a minute before he emerges from the house. He smiles when he sees me, the kind of smile one gives to important people. Perhaps he thinks I am from an NGO, here on a fact-finding mission that will yield no results. The routine is always the same. He will complain about the sewer while I take notes, not having clean water, being off the electric grid, and finally of starving. And he will hope for pity and a ten kwacha note, maybe even two, for his willingness to complain because he knows that once I leave, I will not be coming back.

He moves closer and his smile fades, drawing attention to the wrinkles on his forehead and the skin of his head, as smooth as glass even though it was once crowned with coily black hair.

We stand like adversaries on a battlefield.

"Uncle," I say.

He does not respond. His lips are pursed and his stare stings. Finally he says: "You only thought of me today."

I should reply that he has been on my mind since the day I left. And I wouldn't be lying, because I have thought of this moment a million times – when I would return and prove him wrong. The moment I would win.

Now Uncle looks me up and down. Excitement has drained from his eyes, and we stand here as equals. This slices me because not even the clothes I am wearing incite him to see me any differently than he did fifteen years ago. I begin to wonder if Uncle sees through my deceit.

Nevertheless, I nod.

Uncle moves his eyes to my hands, which are empty of the things people carry when visiting relatives, and he clicks his tongue.

"So," he says, "even after all these years you are ungrateful." He turns to

Aunty: "Amake Junior, she could not even buy us a bag of mealie-meal."

Aunty shakes her head, the corners of her lips downturned.

Something stings my eyes, drawing from the heaviness in my stomach. I wish I had thought to bring something. Maybe then we wouldn't be standing here in equal stature and an equal measure of offence. At least in their eyes. Maybe Uncle would have perceived me better.

"I just came to see you," I say.

Uncle scoffs, "Next time come with something for us." He points to the box-like house behind him, now painted green. "I took you in when your parents died, and now you repay me with empty hands and years of silence."

The heaviness in my chest grows. And then dies. Fond memories intrude on my mind. Maybe it's Uncle's disdain, I do not know, but I think of moments of laughter and care in this house. Even though those were brief interludes between fault-finding and dream-killing. But in this moment, I hold these memories, even though they burden me with guilt for the years I spent away.

I move closer to them to try to offer something of value. Perhaps the watch on my wrist, but I remember that it does not belong to me, so I reach into the handbag and retrieve a twenty kwacha note and hand it to Uncle. "For bread," I say.

He grabs it from me, folds it and places it in his pocket. He instructs the children into the house, and then him and Aunty follow. They do not say anything. They simply walk, like cats, into the house and close the door behind them.

I walk away hunched and with my head bowed, and use a back route to the station which has been in use for as long as this place has existed. A path meandering between homes now preparing dinner. It's month-end, so chicken is frying, permeating the air with its aroma. People stare as I pass, but I walk on, not minding the hair in my face, nor the dust that browns my feet. When I get to Madam's house, I do not check her Facebook page, nor do I take a bath with her bubble bath, nor do I drink wine on the balcony. I simply want to disappear.

But when it's night and I am in Madam's bed and its softness takes me, I give into the temptation to view Madam's Facebook page. She has only posted one more photo since yesterday: of two hands, one black and the other white, one male and the other female, holding glasses of champagne towards a sky brightened by stars. And it's the only photo that Madam posts for weeks. Day after day, I check her Facebook page, wondering what's happened to her, and who the man is. I finally get the answer six weeks later, and two weeks after Madam's arrival was overdue. She posts a photo of her and the man standing on the beach. His arms are around her waist and she rests a hand on his chest. I notice her finger wears a huge diamond ring and a smaller gold band. Madam and the man smile at the camera. His silver hair falls to his ears in waves and is shining in the sun. Madam captions the photo: "Just married, life is too short." Congratulatory messages pour in, "Mrs Ben Wittelbach", "wow wow wow", and "you have arrived." Madam thanks them with heart emojis.

I open Google and search for Ben Wittlebach. The results say he is a billionaire who made his money selling stocks. I do not read about the business, but about the money. He is worth fifty billion dollars and has never been married. There are also articles quoting important people congratulating the couple, and friends saying how they thought he would never marry, how it was all so rushed, but how delighted they are. They say he has lived a spontaneous life filled with unpredictability, and his marriage is just as spontaneous and unpredictable. When I move the search to photos, there is a private jet with spacious bedrooms and bathrooms in it, a house bigger than our State House, and dozens of photographs of him with famous people I have only seen in films.

There is a silence that moves through my bones when I put the phone down. Ben Wittlebach and Madam, married after just a few weeks, starting new lives, unafraid of leaving the old behind, individually and together. I sit for hours, and then block Madam's Facebook page to keep from seeing a life now beyond my reach. A life like a sun that illuminates dark places best kept out of view.

In Madam's house, I had become someone who tasted not just by the tip of the tongue but by a mouthful the life I had dreamed of. Her life was both an escape and a guide, and I followed. But I had also become imprisoned by the thing I thought I was leaving behind – failure. And now with Madam gone and living a new life I cannot imitate even in a million lifetimes, the walls of this house are closing in on me, making me see the life I could have made for myself if only I had done what Madam has dared to do. Leave the past behind, even if the past is yesterday.

At night, when I lie in Madam's bed, it's like a bed of rocks. Even though sleep eludes me, I keep thoughts and images of Madam away from me. In the morning, I get up early and put on my t-shirt and chitenge. I polish the cutlery, dust the chairs, and wipe wine glasses and ceramic plates. When I am done, I look around the house one more time: it's spotless. Then I gather my things in my bag and leave Madam's house. And I do not return.

MANIFESTING

Doreen Anyango

*W*E HAVE BECOME people who don't greet each other in the morning. When the alarm went off at five a.m., he only groaned and got out of bed. Quietly, but a little too loudly for me pretending to be deeply asleep under the covers, he went about his morning routine. Long drawn-out splash of liquid on liquid as he emptied his bladder. Muffled scratch and gurgle as he cleaned his teeth. The overpowering smell of Nivea Men's shower gel floating into the bedroom. The tinkle of metal hangers as he picked out what to wear from the closet. The slither of fabric on skin as he got dressed. The slamming of doors as he left the house. The rattle and clang of the garage door and the gate as he let himself out of the compound. The purr of the car engine getting further and further away until there was complete silence once again.

It is three p.m. now and once again, I haven't heard from him. My sister Julie once told me about a friend of hers whose marriage got so bad that she and her husband were communicating via email. And we chortled and shook our heads because that would never be us. I could send him an email, I suppose. God knows I have a lot of questions. But you see, the thing about questions is that you will have information afterwards, and then you will have to decide what to do with the information.

I don't have the strength for a major life decision right now. The energy I possess is only sufficient for lying in bed and watching YouTube videos. There's this one channel I'm obsessed with. A tiny Kenyan woman called Muthoni is renovating an old colonial house and updating us twice a week and I tell you, I live for these updates. I have watched her break down walls and pull up tiles and clean decades-old layers of dirt to reveal pristine wooden floors. All by her little fabulous self. The latest video is of her cutting angled pieces of wood with a power saw for a feature wall for her bedroom. My phone flashes a fifteen per cent battery warning just as another piece of wood falls to the ground. *Same, phone*, I want to say. *Same.*

We had a few friends over on New Year's Eve to celebrate finally moving into our dream house. I cooked. He deejayed. It was a joyous way to enter the new year, surrounded by the laughter and warmth of our friends. We kissed at midnight, still aglow with love and sunshine from our Zanzibar Christmas holiday, the first one we'd been able to afford in six years. The spell was broken when his mother called a few minutes after midnight to wish us a happy new year. She asked him to turn off the music and put her on loudspeaker so she could pray for us. And for fifteen minutes of fervent prayer, she called on God to bless my womb with fruit. It's amazing how quickly a dream house can turn chokeful of nightmares.

I'm not pregnant this month. Again. The gnawing pain in my lower abdomen these past few days. The way my boobs feel like tender balloons on my chest. The giant pimple forming a shiny knob right between my eyebrows. The sharp flash of pain in my side that makes the tears stand in my eyes and forces me to roll over so that I'm lying flat on my tummy. I do a mental run-down of my stock: pads, diclofenac, will to live. Not looking good on all three fronts. My phone warns that the battery is at the five per cent mark as Muthoni is arranging the pieces of wood on her bedroom wall in a beautiful asymmetrical pattern. I pause the video and get out of bed to find my charger.

He left his wet towel hanging on the open closet door. I yank the towel off the door and inadvertently open it wider to reveal my vision board taped on the inside. I pull the pink manila sheet down and crumple it into a big ball.

We made our plans for the new year together. Him sitting for hours at the work desk in the sitting room, feeding information into this planning template he got online. Me sitting on the floor with my laptop on my thighs, surrounded by a stack of old magazines, switching between downloading images from the internet and getting up to receive our Jumia food order, cutting some pictures from the magazines, watering the plants, flipping through some more magazines, taking the laundry off the line and folding it, scouring the internet for some more images, making a salad to serve with lunch and then doing the dishes, printing out a few images from my laptop, going upstairs to look for glue to stick my images on the manila sheet and deciding to change the bedding and scrub the toilet, sticking a few images to my manila sheet, getting up again to close the windows and draw the curtains and deciding to make some fresh juice because where were all those mangoes his mother sent us going to go? At the end of the day, he had a twelve-page printout with his life over the coming year outlined to the week – and I had a piece of paper with a haphazard collection of random images.

I could feel us slipping into a post-holiday funk by the sixth day of the year. He had gone back to work on the fourth, and I was stuck in this big house all by myself, looking for the inspiration to edit and post the footage from New Year's Eve to my YouTube channel. It is amazing how fast a dream house turns into a giant maze with nooks in which intangible things like inspiration hide. Anyway, it was the sixth of January, and I'd be ovulating the next day, so I decided to add some romance to our lives. I cooked honey-garlic chicken and rice and a veg stir fry and packed our lunch in a picnic basket. I wore the cute floral dress from the Zanzibar trip that he'd said showed just the perfect thigh–back–cleavage ratio. I put on the hot-pink lipstick he said made my mouth look edible. I called an Uber and showed up at the architectural design studio where he works. I didn't recognise the dark-skinned woman sitting at the reception, and it occurred to me then that it had been a while since we'd had lunch together on the rooftop of this building, eating and talking and laughing and enjoying each other's company so much that the lunch hour seemed to last mere minutes.

"Hi," I said to the receptionist. "I'm here to see Ian."

"Uhmm, he's not in at the moment." She looked at the picnic basket I'd rested on the reception desk. "I can receive any deliveries you have for him."

"No," I said and leaned forward a little to whisper. "I'm his wife. I'm here to surprise him with lunch."

"Oh," she said, her mouth rounding itself to match the sound coming out of it.

"I'll just wait in his office," I said and started to walk off.

"Excuse me," she said sharply.

I rolled my eyes and turned around. Typical receptionist kajaanja.

Seat her at a desk, and suddenly she acts like she is manning the gates to heaven itself.

"Ian's not in," she said, tapping the palm of a delicate-looking hand against her tight new cornrows.

"It's fine," I said, injecting some ice and steel into my voice. "I will wait in his office."

The receptionist's perfectly arched eyebrows creased into a frown.

"Ian's on leave until the ninth," she said.

NOW I ENTER the bathroom and it's a mess from my dearly beloved husband's morning ablutions. The sink and mirror are covered in white splotches of toothpaste, and there's a puddle of water on the floor next to his discarded night clothes. When we both used to work away from home, he would shower first while I prepared breakfast, and then I would go in after him and clean up as I bathed. This after two years of fighting over the dirty bathroom every morning, until my sister sat me down and asked if, in the grand scheme of things, a dirty bathroom was the thing I would allow to ruin an otherwise happy union. I remember being so angry the first time I cleaned up after him that I was convinced my hands would spontaneously combust even as they were soaked in water. But the bathroom was clean, and everybody had a peaceful morning. Now I want to wrench the sink off the wall and smash it into the mirror. It is amazing how quickly a dream house turns into a source of combustible fury.

We agreed that infidelity was a dealbreaker for both of us. But when I told the pastor in pre-marital classes that I'd leave if Ian cheated, he let out a derisive bark of a laugh that somehow perfectly matched his appearance. He was a small man with an inverted triangle of a head and such dark hyper-pigmentation around his eyes that he looked like a meerkat. "Women who are serious about marriage don't leave because of simple cheating,' he said.

Ian said nothing. Now, over ten years later, that silence has been on my mind a whole lot.

I think the first person who ever had a shower must have walked around in cleanliness-induced bliss for days. There's always been something about clean orifices that makes me feel a little less miserable. But there's not enough showering that can wash the embarrassment of the sixth of January off me.

I still feel violated and disrespected and angry as I walk back into the bedroom and open the curtains and windows to let in some light and fresh air. I think about changing the sheets, but decide that would be stretching my little burst of un-misery too far. I don't even bother to make the bed and sit down in my towel to finish watching the YouTube video. Muthoni glues her boards to the wall and paints them a cool sage-green.

We were once robbed in the house we lived in when we were first married. I remember coming home, finding the door slightly open and this trail of muddy footprints all the way from the verandah into the sitting room, where the TV and speakers and Ian's laptop were gone. And into the kitchen, where the blender and microwave and kettle were also gone. I remember staring at the muddy footprints and thinking *I can't believe these motherfuckers stepped on my clean floors with muddy shoes.*

I have been in that ka same state of transfixed violation since the sixth. I remember he came home early that evening, uncharacteristically buoyant.

"I heard you came to the office today," he said.

I looked at him standing by the door, hands in his pockets, backpack still strapped to his back, shoes still on as if ready to bolt at any moment. He did that thing he does when he's about to tell a lie. He takes in a gulp of air, as if the lie forming inside him needs a lot more oxygen to float out into the open.

"I have been working on this other project with Gilo," he said. "You know I've always wanted to open my own design studio."

I stared at his dirty shoes on my floor. Olive-green moccasins that I bought to add some colour to his whites and browns and blacks.

"You know I cleaned that floor this morning," I said.

I haven't spoken to him since that evening.

We agreed that not having a baby wouldn't be the thing that broke us.

That we were enough on our own. That we would find delight in each other. That we would build a wonderful life together with or without children. Now that I think about it, those are all things he said to me.

"Chill, babe, the baby will come when the baby comes." Easy to say when you can just build a house in lieu of a family.

"And if the baby doesn't come, we will be okay." Easy to say when you're not the one the doctor looks at and says with gentle resignation, while you are still swollen from the last cycle of fertility treatment, that we might need to consider using donor eggs.

"Why are you stressing?" Easy not to stress when you're not the one random aunties at family functions are pulling aside to whisper probing questions and offer recommendations for pastors, herbalists, doctors of the medical and non-medical variety.

But for a while, I let myself believe that these were my thoughts as well. And I learned to shrink my pain and gloss over how much my heart broke each time my period came. To fill my growing emptiness with interior décor Pinterest boards. To anticipate and express joy in other things – 1k subscribers on my YouTube channel, him graduating with his Master's degree, moving into this house, finally quitting my mind-numbing public service job to be a content creator. It's amazing how a dream house can turn into a monument to a broken dream.

I get dressed at last and decide that today shouldn't be another day that I don't edit and post the New Year's Eve video. After I have some lunch, because I'm suddenly unbearably hungry. Downstairs in the kitchen, the fridge only has some shrivelled carrots and cucumbers, a tub of Prestige margarine, and a half bottle of Baileys. I stare at the bottle of Baileys but decide against it. I can't become an alcoholic on top of everything else. I close the fridge and decide to walk to the trading centre. I will grab a quick snack and my period supplies, and come back to edit and post the video. As if on cue, the humming of the fridge comes to a shuddering stop. I press the light switch to confirm what I already know. Umeme has decided that we, the people of Kira, do not need electricity today.

My sis thinks I'm overthinking and making too much of a big deal of the whole lunch-at-the-office thing.

"Do you honestly believe Ian is cheating on you?" she asked.

"I honestly? I don't think so. But there's definitely something going on."

"Then you need to talk to him," she said.

Maybe I tell myself he's cheating because that might be easier to handle. You know those cups that are one colour on the outside and another colour on the inside? Nga, when it is upside down, it looks black, but then you turn it over and it's magenta on the inside? I feel like he flipped over and the magenta in him has me shook. And now that I think about it, the magenta didn't happen all of a sudden. Black became grey and grey became white and white became pink and pink darkened to magenta. Black was the kind, quiet, serious high-school sweetheart I married. Grey was when he started spending more and more time at work. White was when he stopped coming to the fertility doctor with me. Pink was when he left to go back to work while I was in the middle of miscarrying. Magenta was the stranger standing on my clean floor with his dirty shoes on.

The sun is at its most furious when I leave the house. The grass by the side of the road has been scorched to a dull khaki carpet. The green of the trees and shrubs is covered in a thick layer of brown dust. The cluster of boda boda guys at the turn to our house gesture at me hopefully as I approach them. I'm very tempted to hop on for the 300m ride to the trading centre, but on my vision board there's a picture of a svelte white woman running with a wide smile, a blonde ponytail flying in the wind, and not a single drop of sweat on her face. My pursuit of fitness is much less idyllic: my face and armpits are already clammy with sweat, and I can feel the fine particles of dust gather on the heels of my feet with each flip of my sandals. I stop at the first rolex stand I come to and sit on the unsteady wooden bench under a tattered red Coca-Cola umbrella that serves as seating space for the stand's clientele. I'm faint with heat and hunger and thirst. I'm served a piping hot rolex and an ice-cold bottle of Novida, surrounded by sounds of hammering mixed in with chatter and laughter from the grease-covered mechanics at the garage to the right of the rolex stand. To the left, a light-skinned woman at a vegetable stall sells an elderly lady a bunch of nakati and some tomatoes. The elderly lady says something and the vegetable-seller laughs.

We lost a pregnancy fifteen months ago. The pregnancy was hard on my body. I was throwing up all day, my face broke out, and the fatigue was unbelievable. I was drained but overjoyed. I could feel myself expanding with the life growing inside me. All the symptoms that should have made me miserable were proof that I was able to create and carry a life. There was a heartbeat at eight weeks. And then some spotting at nine weeks. And then a bit more blood. And then some cramping. And then a lot more blood. At the hospital, they gave me a pill to speed up the process. Back home, he left me to go back to work "to pick his laptop and be right back". Late that night, with him still gone and my body splintered with pain, I sat on the toilet and felt something like a thick clot slide out of me and plop into the toilet. I don't know how long I sat there crying before he came rushing in smelling of beer and shisha smoke. He knelt down on the floor and held me in his arms. He was holding me so tightly, I could feel his heartbeat against my chest, but I've never felt more alone in my entire life.

I walk back home slowly, pinching my nostrils closed with my fingertips whenever a plume of dust from a passing car or boda rises up to saturate the air. Stopping to catch my breath every time a slash of pain cuts through my lower tummy. I let myself in the gate, and can't bring myself to enter the house that he designed and I decorated, that cost us so much more than we could afford, and took so long to finish. Because his design for the kitchen called for marble and granite countertops even though we were struggling to raise brick and cement money. Because we went through five different contractors before we found one who could pull off his hanging staircase design. The grey stone exterior glistens in the waning sunlight. I sit on one of the concrete flowerpots by the garage and put the kaveera with my period supplies on the ground. It is amazing how quickly a dream house turns into a hostile edifice.

We have rules for fighting fair. They're typed up and framed, and hang on the wall above the dresser in our bedroom. Don't ambush the other person. Focus on how you feel. Be specific. Don't bring the past into the present. No storming off or sleeping in separate rooms. End difficult conversations with dignity and grace.

I'm still sitting outside our house in the darkness when he opens the gate and drives in. The car's headlights blind me before it comes to a screeching halt. He jumps out of the car and rushes towards me.

"What the hell? I could have knocked you over!" he shouts over the drone of the car engine.

I lift a hand over my eyes to shelter them from the glare of the headlights.

"Where were you, Ian?"

"Wha..." he splutters. "I'm from work."

"No," I say. "Where were you on the sixth?"

"I told you," he says. "Gilo and I are working on starting our own design firm. I can't do that work in the office. You know how nosy people are."

"I know nothing at this point," I say. "I used to think that we didn't lie to each other."

He shakes his head and shoves his hands into his pockets. "I'm tired, babe."

"Dear husband, even me I am tired."

"What is this about?"

"I don't know who you are anymore."

He sighs a sigh of deep tribulation. "I can't do this right now. Like, seriously."

He starts to walk away, towards the gate that is still flung open.

"Go! Walk away! You checked out of this marriage a long time ago."

He spins back around, jabs a finger to his chest. "I checked out?" he asks. I'd forgotten how like a roar his usually smooth baritone sounds when he is truly enraged. He jabs another finger at me. "You're the one who hasn't talked to me in two weeks."

"You haven't been with me in this fertility thing for a long time."

"That is not fair, and you know it," he says quietly.

"When did you last come to Dr Kagaaju's with me?"

"What are we going to pay him with? You know I'm still paying off the loan for finishing the house, and you go and quit your job? How many videos have you posted so far? How many views? How much money?"

Teenagers in school uniform peer through the gate before walking on.

"I never wanted this damn house," I screech. "This is your stupid dream."

"And maybe I don't want to try anymore," he says with a coolness that sends a chill through my body. Suddenly, I want to pee and poop, and a slice of pain cuts through my lower tummy.

I pick up my kaveera.

"I'm going to bed," I say. "Don't bother coming up."

"I wasn't planning to," he says with the same unnerving coolness.

We don't have a rule against throwing hands because it seemed ridiculous when we first sat down to draft the list, but now I wish there was something heavy I could throw at his head.

"I'm getting a feature wall for the bedroom," I shout at his retreating back.

He keeps on walking towards the open gate, perhaps to close it, perhaps to walk out and never look back.

THE THIRD COMMANDMENT

Khumbo Mhone

*T*HE STRANGER ARRIVED three days before Upile was going to die. For months, Upile had picked up the phone and scrolled to the number saved simply as "Her", but courage would abandon her every time she needed it.

As the stranger walked up the khonde stairs, Upile couldn't help but admire what time had done to them both. The hair springing from the stranger's head sat in tight dark curls turned red by too many summers in the sun. Her own hair was wispy and grey where once it had been thick and black, with streaks of red where the heat of the island of her youth had bleached it.

When the stranger sat in the wicker chair beside Upile, she folded her arms left over right, placing them delicately on her knees below the hem of a floral pink dress. Upile wanted to remark on how short the dress was, but bit her tongue.

"You wanted to see me?" the stranger asked.

Upile took a deep breath.

IT WAS GEORGE who insisted that they could no longer put off going to the hospital. They had just returned from visiting the island, and had brought Upile's mother back with them to their home in the commercial capital of Bantire.

He put the large paintbrush doused in yellow on the plastic sheet on the floor. "Did you hear what I said?" George asked.

Upile continued to meticulously fold yellow and white socks.

"We can't put it off any longer. You're starting to show. It's only a matter of time before the Sons of the Nation are at our door asking for a registration card."

Upile looked down at her protruding belly and the small mountain of socks poised on top of it. She had wanted sunflower yellow for the room, but it was mustard. Mustard yellow, tomato-sauce red, or midnight black were the only acceptable colors for baby rooms in Maravi. The colours of the ruling party.

THEY LEFT THE next day to go to Kings Central Hospital for a scan. Her mother, long versed and steeped in the old ways and the old God, was against such blasphemy, but Upile could not remember a time when the President wasn't synonymous with God.

Every week the prenatal ward was repainted white so it could serve as a shining beacon, producing Sons of the Nation and daughters who would bear more sons. One such son greeted George and Upile at the door, scanning their national identification cards.

"Loloma Island?"

It wasn't a question; it was an accusation.

"My father emigrated there to serve as a teacher," George answered. "He took up the great cause, in order to teach the nation—"

"You must teach the children." The Son waved them through to the next room. Upile looked at her husband, impressed by his level of deceit.

THE ROOM WAS painted two shades of blue, the darker shade cutting a violet line around the room. With a single hanging bulb above them, dim and flickering, it seemed to Upile as though she were underwater. There was nothing else in the room except a single metal bed with a firm-looking mattress, and a portrait of the Life President, Father of the Nation, hanging directly above it.

The nurse came in wheeling a large machine. It looked like the phones Upile used in her office, attached to the computers that her male co-workers deemed too advanced for her. The nurse was young, younger than her it seemed, and she confidently told Upile to sit back on the bed and expose her belly.

Upile hesitated, thinking of her mother's words: "You don't expose an unborn child to just anyone; they will curse you."

She gritted her teeth and pulled up her blouse.

The nurse smiled and nodded at her as though to an obedient child. The gel was cold on her flesh as the machine roared to life and the nurse pressed the phone-like device onto her stomach.

"There, do you see?" the nurse asked.

On the screen, in shades of white, black, and grey, was a squirming mass.

"He's a fighter, you will be blessed," the nurse said.

"He?" Upile said.

She felt the tight but imperceptible ball of tension at the back of her throat ease.

"Let's just make sure, okay?"

The nurse pressed deeper into her belly and Upile winced, letting out a small hiss of annoyance that the nurse ignored.

"Is this your first?" the nurse asked.

"Yes."

The nurse was looking intently at the screen now, pressing into her belly in different places, the squirming mass shifting. When she picked up Upile's chart and scanned the contents, Upile felt a cold weight settle on her chest.

"What's wrong?"

The nurse looked towards the door before bending down so that her lips were level with Upile's ear.

"We've reached the quota of daughters for your district. When you leave, you must tell them the scan was inconclusive."

Upile saw the shades of blue swirl into one great mass. The nurse was writing something on her chart, the pen scratching each damning letter. She would not be having a boy, the sigil of excellence that was demanded of all first-time mothers by the Father of the Nation. In her shock, she forgot to thank the nurse as she left. Upile turned back, wanting to ask why she had saved her, but the nurse was already rounding the corner into the next room. Upile watched as she lifted up her perfectly placed black wig and scratched the tangle of dark red curls beneath.

SHE WASN'T READY when the baby came. She remembered singing a melody from her childhood, her bare feet curling around the individual strands of the yellow rug in the nursery when the first sharp pangs came. The second contraction sliced through her lower back. She was dusting a porcelain dog, an exact replica of a Tibetan mastiff, and it fell from her fingertips and shattered. Its snout gaped at her as her mother rushed in.

She gave birth in a large steel bathtub that her mother had insisted on bringing from the island. Her teeth clamped around the new dish towels she had brought from the Egyptian shop in town central. Her mother, though reassuring, was stoic. She didn't hold her hand or sing sweet songs into her hair as she squatted naked in the warm water, and when Upile triumphantly pulled her child towards her, both of them gasping in exhaustion and elation, her mother simply nodded before handing her a towel.

HER NEW DAUGHTER moved through the world quietly and with careful consideration. She slept through the night. When Upile fed her, she kept her eyes wide open, wanting to look at Upile the whole time like she was afraid she would disappear.

"A mother is God in the eyes of a child."

The Sons of the Nation showed up four weeks later, just after Upile had put Joy down for a nap. There were four of them waiting in the living room, their red and black uniforms ironed crisp. The yellow rooster on their left shoulders caught the sunlight as her mother served them tea, her hands shaking slightly.

"Good afternoon, Sister."

He was no more than seventeen, his shaven head glistening over a maze of scars.

"Good afternoon, Brother."

He took a sip of his tea, smacking his lips together and extending his cup for more. Upile's mother dutifully complied.

"I hear congratulations are in order, Sister. A child has been born to your household."

"...Yes."

"I'd like to see the child for myself."

Upile's legs turned to water as she made her way back to where she had left Joy sleeping. She carried her daughter, wrapped in the same cotton blanket in which her own mother had wrapped Upile as a child. The Son of the Nation was waiting for her at the door, and Upile resisted the urge to scream when he held Joy in one hand. One of his companions removed the silver tray of tea from the coffee table as a now disgruntled Joy was laid on top of it.

"Your file says your scan at Kings Hospital was inconclusive, and there is no record of a birth there."

"My apologies, Brother, I was at the hospital the day the scanner was having some problems. Unfortunately, the child arrived early, but my husband has already booked my appointment to receive our registration card properly."

"Boy or girl?"

"...Girl."

Upile's mother, who had slipped out just before Upile had fetched the child, returned now with a plate full of mandasi. The scent of the fried dough wafted throughout the living room. On the table, Joy let out a frustrated cry.

"Another girl from Loloma Island—"

"You must try my mandasi, Brothers, I'm sure that with all the work you do for the nation, you do not always have time to eat," Upile's mother said.

The boy with the scarred head nodded his approval and his three comrades set upon the platter of mandasi like locusts, the still-hot oil running down their cheeks and fingers.

"I used to hear the women of Loloma were unco-operative, something about all that sun up north giving you the appetite of men."

Upile and her mother were silent, both of their heads covered by scarves, but Joy's hair sat in soft red curls atop her head, in sharp contrast to her brown skin.

"It's unfortunate you couldn't produce a Son of the Nation, Sister, but as this is your first child, we are confident you will not let your country down with your second one."

The scarred boy took the rest of the mandasi and the platter with him as they left. On the visitation document he left behind was the official seal from the President and a checkmark next to the box that read "approved for existence."

DEATH CAME TO the neighbourhood for the first time a few months later. In the middle of the night, a high screech tore through the blackness, startling both Upile and George from their sleep. George grabbed his jacket and headed for the door.

"You can't – the curfew!" Upile called.

Moments later, the red lights of a patrol car swept by and the screeching stopped.

The next day, Upile asked about the noise in a whisper at the fruit and vegetable section of the market. She huddled close to two women, Maria, who had produced four Sons of the Nation, and Clarice, who was newly married.

"It was Ndaku's home," Maria said. "They came to take her baby away."

Ndaku lived three houses down from George and Upile. The first to greet them when they moved in, she already had a five-year-old daughter, and had gotten pregnant again four months after Upile had.

"They would probably have let her keep the child, let her pretend it was a stillbirth," Clarice said.

"Maybe then, but now they want to dispose of the body themselves. There's nowhere to run," Maria said.

The three women were silent as they weighed their vegetables. The man at the counter ringing up her purchases had the Loyalist Manifesto taped to the glass that separated him from his customers, and for the first time since she was a young woman in secondary school, Upile read it slowly, mouthing out each word:

The First Commandment:
Love thy Father of the Nation, Second only to God
The Second Commandment:
Obey all Sons of the Nation as if they were the Father
The Third Commandment:
Thou shall birth Sons of the Nation.

Her daughter spoke in full sentences now, sentences filled with the confidence that only George could give her. Upile no longer recognised it, this ability to move through the world as though every door would open. It was foreign to her. Yet the world was changing: Maravi had to revise its image in the eyes of the world after the Father of the Nation was accused of human rights abuses. Now there were laws in place about women and the workplace. Shadow gestures for tourism brochures and visits from foreign dignitaries.

When Joy was four years old, Upile became pregnant again. This time she didn't wait until she was showing to go to the hospital. On arrival, she asked for the same woman who had seen her four years before. "She did such a wonderful job, but I also had a gift for her."

The smile the receptionist gave her didn't reach her eyes. "Unfortunately that nurse has been transferred permanently. She wasn't a good fit. I'd be more than happy to set you up with someone new."

Upile took the registration forms she was handed, and a few minutes later slipped out the back entrance of the hospital after asking for the bathroom.

Her second daughter was born on the island. George had told everyone that her mother was ill, and she had gone away to nurse her. During her pregnancy, she had never left the house in case anyone saw her growing belly. Her baby was born at midnight with hair to match. Upile left the next day.

AS SHE GREW, Joy began to shape-shift. It started slowly around the time of her thirteenth year. One of the women from the Mothers' Union at church turned to Upile with a sly smile.

"You are starting to show your work."

"Excuse me?"

"Your Joy, she's beginning to look just like you."

Upile watched her daughter more closely after that. Her image, distorted at first, slowly began to take shape until Joy was almost a mirror of her, a perfect replica in every way. Except in the ways that mattered to

Upile. She was loud, speaking out about her thoughts and feelings in ways that Upile didn't think possible. She had an easy manner, and like George, she was a natural leader.

It made Upile wonder what her other daughter was like. With the advent of mobile phones, she had attempted to call her a few times, but hearing the small voice so eager to visit and be seen, had been too much for Upile. The calls grew few and far between until they stopped altogether.

The day her mother told her that her island girl was gone, Upile was washing the clothes of her three-year-old son – a small red and black uniform he was required to wear at nursery school. She had sat, her feet slowly going numb, hands limp in the water until Joy had grown concerned and called her father. When he arrived, George carried Upile to bed. She had wanted to attend the funeral, but her mother refused. "I was more a mother to her than you ever were. Stay and be with your family."

"You are my mirror, and a mirror should age like its reflection."

Joy looked up from her journal. Upile was in her closet, selecting her clothes for Mass the next day. She laid a plaid skirt and ruffled white blouse on the bed, one size too small.

"At your age, you shouldn't be looking like somebody's mother. "

She knew this was a sore spot for Joy. Try as she might, she still had the broad shoulders from George's side of the family, and Upile wasted no time in telling her how keeping a slender figure was the only way to keep herself from looking maternal. No eighteen-year-old wanted to look maternal.

"Why do you hate me?"

Joy was drunk and just back from university. She spoke of things and sights that Upile had yet to see, and in her heart, she saw her daughter starting to view her as a relic. She felt it in the way Joy's impatience showed whenever she tried to explain a more efficient way of doing housework. She walked around freely, tight trousers and her hair combed into a red halo around her face. Her stubbornness could not stand against the Father of the

Nation – she dressed this way only in secret and when she landed on the shores of the country where she went to university. Here in Maravi, she was still subject to the same rules as her mother, and she hated it.

"Who says I hate you?"

"I'm the only daughter you have. Why do you want to alienate me? Don't you worry that I will end up like you and Grandma?"

"Me and my mother are fine."

They both knew she was lying.

THAT WAS THE last time that Joy attempted to reason with her. As a child, she had always hovered just out of sight in every room, so eager to please. Now she spent her free time with the friends she had made outside the walls of the home she had grown up in. Free from the history and burden of her mother's upbringing, Joy soared under the new "liberal" Maravi regime. One day she left, moving to her own home, and once in a while Upile would receive a text message asking how she was. When news of the Father of the Nation's death was announced, George was perplexed when Upile shed tears for him.

Joy got married.

He was a kind young man and he worshipped at Joy's feet. It seemed to Upile as she watched them that neither had drawn a true breath before meeting the other. The ceremony was big and raucous and filled with laughter. She watched her mother dance and ululate, showering Joy with money and sweet treats, and she recalled for a moment her own wedding and her own grandmother, long dead. Her grandmother had smeared each of her cheeks with honey: "May your life continue to be sweet."

It was her mother who had sat in the corner – as she did now.

UPILE HAD ALMOST learned to live without hearing from Joy. Titbits from her life were relayed through George. So she was shocked one day to receive a call from an unknown number, but as soon as she picked up the phone, she knew.

"I'm having a baby."

Joy carried to term. There was no registration card, no Sons of the Nation with dire warnings about the sex of second children.

George was instantly in love with his grandchild and asked to see her at every possible opportunity. Upile couldn't deny the draw of this small being, who ran through the silent corridors and plastered her laughter on the walls. Whenever sadness overtook Upile, it was little Chikondi who waved imaginary wipers, like in her mummy's car, small hands wiping the tears away.

As Upile sat on the khonde with the stranger that afternoon, she wondered when the shift had begun. She had been thinking about it a lot lately. Perhaps it was a sickness, a curse handed down from woman to woman, a form of possession, a self-fulfilling prophecy of isolation. Perhaps it could end with her. A stranger didn't have to be a stranger forever.

Upile opened her mouth and looked at the stranger. Her mouth could not wrap itself around the emptiness left from so many years of silence, it could not carry the weight of the words unsaid, could not take back the things that were done.

"Mum? You said you wanted to talk to me. Is everything okay?"

Upile took in her daughter's face, tanned from the sun, slightly red like her grandmother's. No prayer she could ever utter would bring back a dead child, but there was still hope for a lost one.

"It's time we talked about your sister."

THE DAY THE CITY WEPT

Moso Sematlane

HEN I COME back to the flat that Napo and I share in the industrial district of Maseru, I know that I will leave him. In the afternoons, a smell of sewerage from the nearby water purification facility hangs over the neighbourhood; by five, it's usually cleared up, but now, that's all I can smell as I open the door quiet enough so that he doesn't hear me, the moonlight spilling into the room in the way that I know he likes, no curtains, baring the space we share to the world. He takes pride in the fact that he doesn't have secrets; an in-the-nude sleeper, the type of man who not only asks about my day, but how I felt in the moment, say, when a co-worker told me they had cancer. It's in this state I find him, naked and asleep, as I sneak around the flat, packing up the last of my things.

For Napo, the whole world is a project that he's constantly deconstructing, a world where singular feelings have a million different shades. I am not a danger to Sephetho, an underground movement that started from remnants of what were called activist groups in the Time Before, so I know, through him, that they believe that our freedom will come in a return of the emotions that Khotla ea Sechaba has removed from us. Even though these emotions are what the Sentients use to control us – their leverage in the war.

Five years into this war, and I have only seen a Sentient on television: big machines that look like spiders with consciousness in them as real as any living creature. Even though I am a low-rung Khotla worker, and not in the battlefield like the other Ba-khethua, this sacrifice of what, in the Time Before, would usually have been seen as the things that make me human – the things that makes me love another person, or cry when I feel pain – is a price I still have to pay. This "return to the primal" is a philosophy that has been adopted from the Time Before, a time of psychotherapy where emotion and not the mind held court as the governing principle of human life. A philosophy Sephetho members wield like a knife. That's why, in a few hours, they plan to commit mass suicide live on television. To awaken everyone's emotions. Or as they say, to *awaken everyone to themselves*. As I pack up my toothbrush and cosmetics in the bathroom, spots of rain gather on the window. The sound of thunder hides any noise I make that could awaken him, although I move as lithely as a cat. It often rains for months, incessantly, as if the sky is weeping out some hundred-year-old pain. I wouldn't blame it. If it weren't for the Programs, I would also probably be weeping every day. I'm too cowardly for suicide, or maybe I just don't have any conviction. In any case, Napo had seemed a sturdy enough force to wrap my uncertainties around until the fire aglow in all the members of Sephetho started in me too.

He's a deep sleeper, so he doesn't hear me as I pussyfoot around the room to sit by his side. I am still amazed by his youthful looks; in a time where the war has probably aged everyone by at least ten years, so that twenty-year-olds appear to be in their late thirties. Something in the symmetry and dewiness of his face speaks to the persistence of people like him who have given themselves to Sephetho. Or maybe he just lacks the cynicism that characterises these times. I resist the temptation to lift my hand and touch his cheek, like they used to do in the old films. It would be all the more torturous to still feel the burn of his skin, long after I've said goodbye. It's better to leave before he even knows I was here.

It's easy to do this, to come in and out of his life as if I had never existed. Ours is a life lived by night, because to expose our love would be to expose our rejection of Khotla ea Sechaba and the war. Those like us, who in the Time Before were called marginalised, are sent to the war with the Sentients. We are those whose minds the Sentients cannot tap into. We are called Ba-khethua. There are many theories as to why this is so; none of them believable to me. I think of my mother in the Time Before, when I first told her about my attraction to both men and women. We sat in a coffee shop in the middle of town, as the Maseru traffic swelled around us.

"Joale ho tlo etsahalang ka uena?" she said, putting her hands on her lap, as if wanting to separate her entire body from the table, from me. I didn't have an answer then, and on the day she died, I remember the question – it ran through my head like a siren's call. *Now what will become of you?* My mother, unlike so many in the city then, didn't mind if I slept with, and loved both men and women. But she knew then, that despite all the conversations about getting others to see us how they see themselves, I would always be different. Perhaps it's some code awry in the programming of our minds, as the old-time bigots believed. This is more believable to me. It's why the Sentients can't get in our minds, why we become Ba-khethua.

In our flat, there isn't much to take with me, just an overhead-bag of clothes and my keypad so I can stay logged in the Khotla ea Sechaba system. I know that Napo is able to know my whereabouts through logging onto his keypad, but something tells me that he won't look for me. That's the thing about men his age; they are able to rationalise loss as one of the inevitable facts of life, like a rose dying and fading as the seasons change. Though we are both caught up in the winds of this war, I feel as if I come from a different time to Napo. In many ways, this war is a product of all the harm that my generation has done to the earth, regardless of the Sentients.

I think back to those early meetings when I would go to Napo and talk about ending the war. How hopeful I must have looked, candlelight caressing my face, Napo's hand firm in mine. It's easy to be caught up in that type of thinking when you love someone; you love what he loves. You get wrapped inside his beliefs. I can see how Napo and the members of Sephetho like the feeling that they're doing something to resist inevitable doom, but that's exactly the problem. Whether they can pull Ba-khethua back from the war by awakening everyone's emotions, the fact of the Sentients still remains. The war still remains. Though I hate to admit it, Khotla ea Sechaba is probably doing the rational thing by sending people that the Sentients can't control to the frontlines.

It is easier to leave than I thought. No sadness hitching in my throat. Movements as swift and clear as the morning air. I close the door quietly, bag against my shoulder. It's easy to think of myself as a coward, a deserter, although much easier to convince myself that this is in fact my cause. I've looked everywhere for it, and now it's finally come. In the form of a woman I met on the train six months ago – and then again, at the Milk Bar I frequent. Her name is Senate. It wasn't long before we started having sex, and then not too long before I started weighing the options that were still available to me. Not too long before Banesa came into both our lives.

I will be the first to admit, my resentment towards Napo started around the same time he told me that suicide was the only way to return to the primal state of affairs. There was freedom in death, he told me. And then the plans for the procession. To my relief, Napo hadn't volunteered to be one of the twenty-four who would drink cyanide on live television. But he had volunteered to be one of the people who would come out with their partners to remind the world that we are just like them. All any human ever wants is to love someone, and have them return the feeling, regardless of whether the world is ending or not. That was my part in the revolution; to reveal myself as Mo-khethua. It wasn't as drastic as killing myself, although for me, it held the same gravity. I didn't like the cameras. I didn't like the spectacle. I was afraid of the tides of history that, according to Sephetho, would subsequently change. So I'm leaving on a quiet winter's morning. Leaving for what is easier.

BACK THEN, THE threat of the Sentients had seemed far away, even though military action against them had already been gazetted. We had woken up to the news that they had just taken Cape Town, so Khotla ea Sechaba built a steel wall surrounding the whole of Lesotho. The wall has an electromagnetic field around it that on some days makes the air shimmer like dancing heat waves. We rarely approach the border though, because to see the soldiers there would remind us of the war. In many ways, one could take the rations of food and the rationed communications networks as signs of third-world regression, which Lesotho was infamous for in the Time Before. Although the persistent urge to cry – but being unable to, not because you are being watched, but because of your Programmed body – suggests a sort of spiritual warfare too.

The day of my final session in the Programs was the same day I met Napo. This is one of the many tricks fate throws at you throughout a long life; it gives you a death and re-birth at the same time, reorganising your reality into an incomprehensible shape. The day was bright for winter, with an afterglow in the clouds that came from recent snowfall in the highlands. Although I had already fallen into the rhythm of the Programs, the final day stood out as the point of no return for me – a before and after. After that, my emotions were hollowed out to a husk.

The Programs, at first, reminded me of the old films, and it was difficult not to feel glimmers of excitement at the idea of experiencing a bygone era. We used to watch them in what were called cinemas, and later, on keypad-like devices called computers.

Going into the Khotla ea Sechaba Office for that session, I was expecting a long queue like the one that had snaked outside the Office the day before; but that day, it was just the receptionist and one other man. A white man. I hadn't seen anyone who wasn't Mosotho in years. Shortly after the Sentients entered our atmosphere, The Great Migration ensued; or as Sephetho likes to call it, "The *Grave* Migration", where people went back to their homelands to face what was coming.

If you believe the Grave Migration theory, people returned so they could "die at home". The white man smiled at me as I sat next to him, and it brought back a practice that men like me used to have in the Time Before. We used to meet in empty parks, and what were then called malls – big, cavernous buildings where you could find thousands of shops in one place. Just a smile or a look held too long was enough to discern that the other man was like you, and you would meet in a bathroom, or his car, or your car, and you would take him in your mouth, or he would take you in his. If the area was really deserted, you'd even go as far as having sex, gasping noise-lessly in the compact space you were forced into, every movement inside of you, or inside him, performed quickly, with roughness, before you both rearranged your clothing and went about your day again. I stopped myself from looking at him too long. In the final stage of the Programs, they would be pairing me up with a man to see if I was Mo-khethua. To allow myself to feel anything would lead to me being sent to the battlegrounds.

"Good morning," the receptionist said in Sesotho. "Ntate Teboho?"

I nodded, and proceeded to upload my identity kit with my keypad in the Processing Unit next to her. The man before me must have been on his last day of the Programs, and waiting for his results. After I was done, she uploaded my kit onto her keypad, and bent to inspect it in silence. As I waited, I resisted the urge to look back at the white man, ignoring the voice in my head telling me that he was looking at me.

I found it fascinating that this still remained from the Time Before with people like us; this dance of glances, some withheld, some thrown into the open. Though I did not know if he saw me in a sexual way, it reminded me of the widespread paranoia that overcame people who were not naturally Ba-khethua when the drafts where being announced. People who had throughout their lives cohabited with people of the opposite genders, and built families with them, would hand themselves over to Khotla ea Sechaba to declare themselves as Ba-khethua.

Any one of us could tell you of the hiding and pretence we've had to practice throughout our lives, a code more sophisticated than even Khotla ea Sechaba can decipher. Not that these people weren't like us, but a funny thing happens to the human brain, especially one that finds comfort in the strictures of Khotla ea Sechaba, where the appeal to experience "the other" intensifies once you are told that stepping off the tracks is forbidden. Like if someone tells you not to think of a purple cat, and so a purple cat is all you can think about.

"U ka feta," the woman said, swiping my info-kit away with her finger, where it disappeared into a small icon at the side of her keypad, and directed me with a quick nod to the door behind her. As I opened it, I heard the man stand up and approach the woman. He said something to her, although on my end it came out as an indistinguishable burr because I had closed the door. I walked down the dark hallway to the room where the Program would start.

Alongside me, in the other rooms, groups of Khotla ea Sechaba workers in green jackets huddled over coffee, trying to beat away the morning gloom with gossip. They were in a different division to me, so it was impossible for them to recognise me as a Khotla worker myself. I looked at their smiles, the creases on the edges of their eyes deepened by laughter, and tried to see if there was farce in them. Two days ago, early in the Programs, I might have laughed like that as well. One of my Administers told me that the key to being a good Khotla citizen was to live "in balance", not to experience emotion to its extremity. Laughing was okay, he said in Sesotho, as long as by the end of it, no one you were laughing with would become your friend. You were always in isolation, and would be so until your death. These moments of connection with each other were what the Sentients used to control us.

The Programs take place in a small bare room not unlike a jail cell. When I enter, I find that my chair is waiting for me to be strapped in, with wires running all the way to the floor and then into the next room, where an unseen group of people will monitor what appears on screen and administer the necessary pain injection whenever I see an image that would otherwise cause me a swell of emotion. I sit in the chair without speaking, all the pleasantries we had exchanged in the first few days gone. The particular cruelty of this farce is not lost on me; through their fake camaraderie, I was made to feel like I belonged somewhere, and thus willing to oblige any emotion the images could stir from me.

This time, I strap myself into the chair and a green light goes on in the corner of the room. This notifies the watchers that I have connected myself both to a series of images and the pain injection site. Whenever a particular image conjures up extreme emotion, an ocean of pain will swim into my bloodstream, training my body to become numb, to push its emotions below, rather than letting them surface.

Like every day in the Programs so far, the people at the control panel start the Program of my life, the person on screen modelled after me: my large nose, my high cheekbones, the particular way I hunch like a lot of tall people do to make themselves less conspicuous.

Then the movie of my life plays. Here, my childhood in Phuthaditjhaba, a toddler crawling away from his mother in the hut. You can see the new mother's distress in her face, the fear of messing up with me. I feel numb. Here, the day I moved to Maseru, squatting in one house with four other people. The petty fights. The day they threw my clothes out the window because I wasn't paying rent. The day I was employed by Khotla ea Sechaba. The lonely nights in bed where I cried myself to sleep, thinking that with the great war happening in the world, and humanity hanging over a precipice, all I needed was a touch. All this my body receives with numbness.

And then Napo. Napo.

The mornings when I'm not in the mood for any type of cheeriness, and he greets me with a smile. The way he likes to lightly brush against my forearm. The way he covers his mouth with his hands when he's excited, squealing like a child. I feel the pain crawling up my arms, burning with a corrosive sensation. I try to suppress all the emotions I feel for Napo by bringing up the images of Senate, countering the ones I see on screen. I take care to steer my thoughts away from Banesa, because Lord knows, I feel something deeper for that boy than I could ever feel for Senate, or even Napo himself. The pain recedes slightly, though it still stings my feet. An urge to close my eyes overcomes me, even though I cannot because of the glue I had to use before I entered the room.

When the session is finished, just as I had predicted, they paired me up with the man in the office to see if I was a Mo-khethua. They put us in another room and made us take off our clothes. In the Time Before, men like us used to visit bathhouses, which were then later called nude bars, where we could take off our clothes in the dark and have sex with each other. Looking at the man standing across from me, I can tell that his eyes have seen the same things I have seen, his pale body has lurked in the same dark places that mine has, looking for a touch. Any touch. In that time, everyone had been aware that the arrival of the Sentients had tied together all the doomsday threads that humanity had been entertaining, the climate catastrophes, the economic collapses which, until then, had seemed so serious and all-consuming. Nothing like what came after; seeing monsters that could have easily emerged from a children's story book walking in our world.

Now both our penises are flaccid, our unblinking eyes locked onto each other, even though the sticking glue has by now been removed. I see the contours and ridges in his face, valleys and grooves caused by the impact of time. He can probably see the pain of a life lived in my face. I wonder if he can see Napo in my face, or even Banesa.

This final stage of the Programs will monitor our reactions to one another, watching how our bodies respond, our heart rates and respiration. But at this point, the numbness that the Programs have trained us in has become part of our bodies, and it is easy to suppress whatever sexual urges we have for each other. But he and I know a deeper truth; that this suppression is something we have been in training for all our lives. He and I are experts in hiding our true desires, of lurking in dark places and rooms, hoping for another person to light all the chambers of our hearts with just a touch. This is a loophole people like us always wiggle through with these Programs, a blind spot in the method Khotla ea Sechaba uses to determine who are Ba-khethua and who are not. It's different for Napo's generation; they surrender their feelings and urges so willingly, and perhaps fearlessly, which is why so many of them are drafted into the war. The man and I put our clothes back on and exit the small room.

OUTSIDE, IT SEEMS like it's going to be another night of rain, a continent of grey clouds crawling towards the city from South Africa. The rain will fall on human and Sentient alike. Already, the streets are emptier than they were when I went into the Office. On days when the Programs are being run, no one likes being seen outside. I am joining the scramble towards the privacy of my own house when someone calls out to me from behind. I know who it is before I turn. The man from the room comes up to me, running. In the daylight, he looks younger, all the ridges of age I saw earlier smoothed out somehow.

"The strangest thing about these things is that they get us naked without even knowing each other's names," he says.

I can't place his accent, although it sounds vaguely South African.

Already, I feel the numbness of the Program coursing through my body, berating any urge to to extend branches of familiarity. But he does that thing that my mother used to do, of smiling *into* my face, as if she was trying to coax joy out from my sadness. I say the only thing I can think of saying, and I am satisfied that it sounds harsh enough so that my emotions are still swimming under the surface: "I haven't seen a white person around here in years."

He reveals his teeth to the light: "I was born here. Just outside of Butha-Buthe. My parents came here on the endless peacekeeping missions that were happening in those days. I've lived here for forty years now."

To prove his claim, he lets out a torrent of Sesotho that makes me smile. I allow myself this. The words he is saying remind me of the childhood games we used to play, "mantloane", where we play-acted like adults who had their own families and houses, our friends taking on the roles of respective spouses, children, or other family members. We walk in silence for a while, although the feeling between us is not cold. I don't know anything about him, but I am basking in the warmth of having smiled for the first time in I don't remember when.

"A couple of us are having a small get-together tonight," he says, "by Borokhoaneng. Although for my part, I like to think I'm celebrating outwitting the Programs again. Want to join us?"

There is no use in hiding. He and I knew exactly what we were the moment we laid eyes on each other. I know about these get-togethers that people like us have in secret, in houses, or gardens. Sometimes they are reminiscent of the bathhouses I used to visit, where groups of people are having endless sex. Sometimes, they are innocent meet-ups between friends and soon-to-be friends, who laugh and drink together, before retraining themselves in the numbness the Programs require once they go back to their respective homes.

I don't remember how I answered the man, but he told me his name was James. I must have been willing to go to this meet-up, because even with my hesitation, that evening I found myself outside a small gated house in

Borokhoaneng, coils of barbed wire on a tall, black wall.

There were already people inside, the room packed to the brim, sweating bodies all around. But it was the first time in many years that I saw people smiling around me. People having fun. I had resolved not to go home with anyone, and simply to surrender to the night, which was like so many long-gone nights in my youth. It was through the haze of alcohol that I had first seen Napo's smile.

It's difficult to ascertain what it is that first attracts you to a person, beyond their physical attributes. Napo is not the most beautiful man in the world, but he has this way about him: talking and walking through this earth as if being here is his birthright. The constant body contact when making conversation – the touching of shoulders, the whispering in the ear.

That night, we had finally decided that we liked each other enough to divest from the revelry, and find a small corner where we could get to know each other better. He was twenty-seven years old. He loved animals. All animals, even the ones people considered ugly, like pigs or hairless cats. When he spoke to you, his eyes never strayed from yours. And in his eyes, I lost myself. That night, he asked me what "freedom" meant to me, and I blurted out a laugh in response to what I had deemed the silliness of the question. Although, looking at his hard stare, I realised that he was being serious.

"What's this question leading to?" I said.

"You're still young," he said. "I'm sure that this isn't all you envisioned for your life."

He made a sweeping motion with his hands, indicating the party, although after a few moments, it dawned on me that he meant the the state of affairs of the world in general.

"None of that is under my control," I said. "I can only focus on things I can control. Trust me, that's the only way I won't lose my mind."

"That's the thing," he said. "We've all lost our minds. Only some of us don't pretend that we're still sane."

I smiled to myself, "And is this all you envisioned your life to be?"

That's when he told me about Sephetho. There were a couple of their members at this party, he said – including James, who had lured me here in the first place. He said that their idea of freedom was getting human beings to feel real emotion again, and to be able to express it, like in the Time Before. Wasn't this the thing that had made us, Ba-khethua, special in the first place? Despite the bigotry that we had faced, we had still gotten up each day and chosen to love one other. We had refused to swim under the surface.

I rebutted with the obvious practicalities; this was a revolution where no matter what you did, you would always end up losing. The Sentients used our own emotions to control us, so if we could control our emotions, there was still a hope of turning the tide of the war against them. Wasn't Sephetho's revolution, in a sense, taking us a step back?

We had made love that night, and as I was inside him, our bodies sweating against each other, the ideas that he had discussed with me swam in my blood alongside my lust, my pure and burning desire for him. I understood for the first time that loving someone could sometimes mean that you didn't only want to get inside him, but to be him as well. To have his arms be your own. His mind be yours. His wild ideas.

Perhaps it was cowardly of me to leave him, without tying the break-up neatly with the necessary remarks: *We've run our course, I've changed, you have changed, the times have changed.* But I trust him enough to understand that I am a weak man. I was weak when he came shooting to me from across the room at the meet-up that night to introduce himself. I was weak inside him, weak just looking into his eyes. When the talk that Sephetho was planning on public suicides began, I knew that I was too weak to stay. There were ideas he loved better than he could ever love me.

SENATE, UNLIKE NAPO, is uncomplicated. Even her joy is something that can easily be placed within limits, unlike Napo's, which is boundless and childlike. When I arrive at her house, I enter without knocking. Though it is evening, there are no lights on, only the television flickering against her face. There is no sound from the kitchen of that evening's dinner being cooked, so I know we'll have leftovers from lunch instead. But a deeper sense of dread fills me when I hear snatches from the news programme she is watching. Though the streets are empty on the screen, and the rain is falling lightly, all the journalists from Lesotho, and some news stations from South Africa, have parked their vans and are talking into cameras, in anticipation of Sephetho's public suicide.

I hear from the other room that Banesa is still awake, talking to his toys. Banesa's parents died during a Sentient siege in Cape Town, so he had been brought back to Lesotho to the rest of his family; but they had been too poor to take care of him. And although Senate was taking care of him now, she was poor in other ways.

Senate, although older than me by just a year, seems to have the weariness of those who are approaching their deathbeds. She rarely smiles the way that Napo does, rarely ever picks up Banesa and tickles his stomach the way I like doing. It's important, for me at least, to shield kids from the truth about the nature of our world, but Senate seems to have no qualms about this. In fact, she treats Banesa like he is an adult; she feeds him, bathes him, and then leaves him to his own devices. When I first started coming here, the loneliness hung around that child like a cloud. He clung to me the way that all dying things cling to any signs of life. And in a way, he was my own sign of vigour in the dead landscape the Programs had turned my heart into.

I go to Banesa's room without greeting Senate. By now, I like to think that our silences have become intimate. The coldness that the Programs have put inside me can manage an interaction like ours, in this domestic system we have built together. Here, unlike with Napo, I feel in control, even though the only thing that colours our life is grey. This is more knowable to me. Banesa looks up at me and smiles, a doll in his hands. I crouch down and pick up the doll, touching its dress.

"Where did you find this?" I ask him.

"Mme said I could have it on my way from school," he said. "We found it."

I used to play with dolls when I was his age, seeing no boundaries between what were seen as boy's toys and girl's toys. The obvious questions come to me about Banesa, but like the Programs have trained me to do, I push those emotions away. He still has a long life ahead of him, and who's to say how this war will end? Hopefully the day will come when the Sentients are gone. If Banesa grows up to become one of us, hopefully he won't have to hide like we do, and things will be just as they were in the Time Before.

When I return to the living room, Senate is still staring at the television. I sit beside her and kiss her on the cheek, but she does not respond. On-screen, black trucks are driving in the streets, with members of Sephetho hanging out their windows, red flares in their hands. The procession is beautiful. I find myself searching for Napo, so I make sure to turn my attention to Senate instead. I kiss her arms. Her neck.

"I think Khotla is going to kill them," she says bluntly.

I kiss her again, breathing into her neck. She pushes me away. There is no hope of losing myself in sex tonight, in an effort to distract myself from what is about to happen on-screen.

"They have nothing to gain by doing that," I say. "Khotla will watch them die, just like you and I are going to watch them die."

I hear myself say those words, rolling them around in my head, *die, die,* and try to connect them to the fact that Napo is likely to be among the ones who will die. With me gone, nothing is holding him back anymore. I don't feel anything. Standing, I get myself a glass of water, and when that is finished, I go to the bathroom to read the message that he sent to my keypad on my way here. Judging from the time that it was received, he had woken up and realised that I had walked away from our life together only thirty minutes after I had left the flat.

I shut myself in the bathroom so that Senate doesn't see whatever feeling the message might bring me. Reading it for the first time, I had felt nothing. I had tried to think of the early days of my relationship with Napo, the happy days when just the thought of him could put me in a blissful stupor, unable even to eat. Sitting on the toilet seat, I open up my keypad to find

Napo's smiling image on the screen.

You were never mine to begin with,

he wrote,

people can't belong to each other. I love you.

I close the keypad. I go to fetch myself another glass of water, and after finishing it, sit down next to Senate again. On screen, there are more Sephetho members on the streets. They have gotten out their trucks and now form a crowd the likes of which I haven't seen in long time, all those bodies gathered in one place. Some are holding each other by the hands. Some are singing. Senate doesn't blink. Now, I look for Napo in earnest, although there are too many people to zero my gaze on, the cameras not fixing on any particular point for too long. There is no commentary from the news anchors; they are just as transfixed as their audiences are.

And I admit, there is poetry behind the lit-up flares, the singing, the roads glistening from the rain. The strange sense of silence, even amidst the singing. I think of Napo's last words to me: *I love you.* I feel nothing. One by one, the crowd drinks from small vials that they hold in their hands. That's the cyanide that they had spoken about like some religious talisman. And one by one they fall to the ground, some convulsing violently, their eyeballs rolled back. The singing continues, the flares burn on. Next to me, Senate doesn't say anything. I don't say anything either. I wonder if she feels numb, like I do. Regardless, I don't stop looking for Napo among those bodies now piling on top of each other, or the ones still singing persistently against the mass death.

Then, something outside the chain of events I had predicted happens; now, the people who are still alive hold each other by the hands again, and press their lips against each other. The kissing is nothing like I have seen before, in its ease, in its freedom. This was how people like us used to kiss in the Time Before. These Sephetho kiss each other like they want to dissolve into each other's bodies, no exposed part of the body being spared a touch or caress.

Senate's eyes are still on screen when Banesa comes from the darkness, and although I see him coming, I don't stop him. He drops his doll. For a while, he's transfixed in the same way that Senate and I are, but somehow, he manages to snap out of the spell. He reaches out a hand and touches the screen. Something in the way he's doing so makes it seem like he is participating, too. The flood of tears that comes to my eyes is unexpected. But I let it consume me, roll inside me like a wave. I cry for all the years that I couldn't because of my Programmed body. I cry throughout the death and lovemaking, and it seems I will never stop.

GIRL'S BEST FRIEND

N.A. Dawn

*A*T THE MENTION of his name, I disappear. Or at least, I want to. It's like I'm there, but I'm not. The truck is coming and I'm the deer, and I know that there's no time to move, no chance to escape. I'm counting the seconds, but I'm already gone.

"*Now*, Joana! Are you listening to me? I'm not going to ask you again," says Mom, without turning from the mirror on her dresser. "Off with that ridiculous Eskimo suit and into something nice and pretty and presentable. Uncle Stef will be here any moment now."

Any moment now.

I'm in the blender again. The world blurs: rows of books bulge into the bricks of a prison wall; shelves slip into the floor, consumed by liquid linoleum. Quicksand, but quicker.

Something's always eating somebody.

They're going out again – supper or something. (Is it Ronnie's? Is that the *place*'s name, or the *friend*'s? Someone's birthday?)

Mom approaches me, bends to my level. (I know it's not just 'cause I'm fourteen. It's 'cause I inherited Dad's short genes, not hers. But no one's gonna say that out loud.)

"Now, who's gonna be a good girl while we're out. Hmm?"

He's coming. It's all I can think. *Uncle Stef's coming again.*

Gerrie, a puddle of golden limbs and droopy jowls, vents a mammoth sigh from his dog cradle, tail flopping to no rhythm but glee.

"You always have such fun with Uncle Stef," Mom insists.

Fun.

His wet grin.

I think I'm boiling up a sweat, but I'm frozen to the spot.

The rank musk of his torso. His huge, heavy legs.

My knees are wobbling; I can't stop them.

It must show on my face. Mom's giving me that look.

I struggle to pierce the blur, regain my speech. I swallow hard, clench my fists and make my final stand.

"Mom..." I begin, shakily, though I tell myself I am brave. "I ... I don't want to stay home."

She cocks her head and blow-dried blades of blonde shift with her.

"Well, you can't come along, sweetie. It's for grown-ups only."

She straightens up and returns to the dresser. Clicking her tongue (I jump, as if pricked), she swaps out her green earrings for the purple ones instead, tilting this way and that until she's satisfied. She isn't.

Sweeten the deal.

"Can I go to Sarah's?" I ask. "I'll bake muffins with her, and you can have as many as you want."

"No, Jo-jo baby, it's too short notice. You know it's *very* impolite to show up unannounced."

Something in her voice hardens on the *very*. She doesn't even hear the offer.

The conversation's slipping away from me, vanishing into the floor, along with the furniture.

To hell with politeness.

"Mom, *please*," I beg. "I don't want to be home alone."

Mom vents a fierce sigh. "*Of course* you won't be *alone*, honey." She slams one drawer of jewellery shut, yanks open another. "What kind of parents would *that* make us, hmm?"

She's not getting it.

"If you think this is going to get you back your tablet, my girl, you are *sorely* mistaken," she says. "No more of that filthy liberal nonsense. I'm not letting them brainwash *my* darling child – oooooh no! *Not* on *my* watch. *Not* in this house."

I lose track of her rant about internet globalists.

I can't bear this.

Not again.

Jitters seize my chest.

Fight back.

"Why won't you let me go to Sarah's?" I yell. "It's not fair that *you* can go out and *I* can't!"

Nice try.

"Stop that now, Joana!" Mom rises so suddenly I take an involuntary step backwards. "I'm *warning* you. Didn't you hear what I just said?" Her impatience climbs to a shrill. "Who taught you to behave this way? *Hey?* Is this these *bladdy* American TV shows?"

Everything's closing in.

"Acting like little brats so you can chirp back to your parents!"

Say it. Just say it.

I can't. It's too hard.

Say it now, or it'll never stop.

But how...?

Maybe I'm just overreacting...

"Your father's going to be *so* cross if I keep him wait—"

"*Don't leave me alone with Stef!*"

An eternity's pause.

I didn't mean to shout. Now the sky's on fire. Pretty soon, it'll fall.

Mom pins me in her crosshairs.

"What...?" she asks.

Say it, or you're dead. I squeeze my eyes shut and force myself to whisper it.

"He's..." I begin, massaging my thumbs against my knuckles. "Bad to me."

"Hey!" Her smack strikes like a fly swatter.

I'm dazed.

Gerrie raises his head, baffled. He barks once.

She frickin' hit me!

"What did I say about fibbing? Hmm?" Her words continue her hand's barrage. "We don't keep fibbers in this house, do we?"

I can only sputter.

"B-but, M-m-*mom*—"

"*Do we?*"

I crash to my knees. The deer surrenders.

Gerrie's losing it. Mom scolds him back to his bed.

Silent tears spill over my cheeks.

"I'm sorry, Mommy..."

"Oh, no, no, no." She's had it now. She hates it when I cry. "I don't want to hear any more of that *rubbish*. Do you understand me?"

"I'm sorry, I'm sorry, I'm sorry." Flames of panic engulf me. "I'm *sorry!*"

The spiral begins.

Sprint, freeze, scream, disappear, escape, lash out—

"Do you want to be a little wolf-crier? Hey? *Hey!*" She grabs my shoulders, punctuating each question with a shake. "Is that what you *want?*"

I watch as the burglar bars melt shadows across the bed.

It's happening again.

They reach like tendrils, snaking up my legs, crawling under my skirt. The borders of my vision dissolve into a charcoal nothingness.

I can't stop it...

My throat clogs up and I'm about to gag – when it hits me.

Slicing through me, cutting through the brain fog.

In the kitchen, on the counter, opposite the fridge.

The knife-rack.

Take your pick.

A ROAR FROM downstairs.

Mom and I both freeze. Gerrie whines.

"Deirdre!" Another shout. "Where the *fuck* are you?"

Silence falls. The heart-pounding agony of anticipation.

We both know what's coming.

Dad's footsteps stomp louder and louder. Each thud, a premonition.

Thud, thud, thud, THUD.

"*Jaaasus*, why am I still fucking waiting like this?" He enters the room, a squat beaver of a man, filling the space with his voice like a child blowing up a balloon. It can't contain his temper. It's going to cave in, and we'll all die in the collapse.

Maybe that's just wishful thinking. At least that would put an end to it.

"I'm coming, babe," Mom fawns. A wide plastic smile spreads between her ears, and she scrabbles at the bottles and powders in front of the mirror. "Just, uh, fixing my face."

Her wedding necklace looks like a collar now.

Dad's face is stony. "I'm waiting for *twenty minutes* down there! Like a fool!"

Gerrie unloads his damnedest, barking with his whole body braced.

Dad casts him out like vermin. One torrent of "Out! Out! Out!" banishes the would-be protector.

Soon as the hound's gone, Dad advances. "Do you think I'm a *fool*?"

Even seated, Mom's just about his height, but this only seems to further antagonise him.

"Why must I serve you like a fucking *slave*, man?" he growls, and shoves her off the stool. It happens so predictably. She doesn't even resist.

I crumple to my haunches, burying my face between gated arms.

Disappear, disappear, disappear, disappear—

"Maybe I should fix your face *for you*, huh? *Huh?*"

A sound like wet meat on cement.

"Show everyone what kind of a wife you are, you stupid b—"

"*Daaaaaaaaaaaaddyyyyyyyyyyy!*"

I regress nine years, a small child's wail filling my throat. I'm drenched in my own desperation, rocking back and forth.

The tyrant glares.

"*Hey, shut up now!*" he bellows. "Shut your fucking mouth if you know what's good for you!"

But the interruption works. An anxious hush freezes the room, disturbed only by Mom's shuddering breaths. Her hands tremble, like kitchen prongs vibrating.

Dad storms downstairs, but his grumbling lingers like tectonic aftershocks. "*Jiiiinne*, these fucken women. Driving me *fucken* mad."

His descent fades.

Below, his footsteps end at Gerrie's pattering paw-drops and whimpers.

"*There*'s my pal, hey? You're my *real* Man's Best Friend, my boy. *Yis*, you are – you *are*! Oh, *yis*! Yis, you *are*, my good, good boy, eh?"

I SUMMON THE strength to look at my mother.

Pale as paper. Still plastered to the cupboard, shoulders scrunched to her ears, biting down on her lip.

My own feet are cement left to set.

Not a sound, or he'll come back.

I listen for his return.

WHAT I HEAR is worse. Another man's voice. Mild, sweet. Playful like a puppy.

Singing. "She Drives Me Crazy." A grown-up's song. Another one about some guy who loses control because he wants a girl.

The two men laugh.

"Ag, howzit Stefanus, man," says Dad. "Thanks for this, hey."

Just like that.

A switch-operated chameleon.

Uncle Stef's spidery shadow creeps along the stairway wall. "Ja, it's lekker to help out. You know I'm always here."

Always here.

"But why must I do this though, hey?" Dad's fuming reignites. Time for the routine. "I pay my share of this fucken country's wealth. Why must I also keep *my-child-safe* in *her-own-house*?" He pokes at the air for each three-word phrase. "Hey? What kind of life is that?"

I can hear the second daily din of dogs behind white fences turning half-feral at gardeners and domestic workers making their return journey across the divide.

"Well, rest assured, my friend," says Stef, the shadow puffing out its chest. "Any k—s coming over for dinner will be feasting on a moooerse Stef sandwich. Ha ha!"

The shadow curls a caterpillar of an arm.

Dad laughs, satisfied. "You remember where the pistol is?"

"Ja, ou, of course."

"'Shoot first...?'" starts Dad.

"'...ask questions later,'" Stef finishes.

Dad claps his pal on the back. "That's my boytjie."

I can't listen anymore. The longer I sit around panicking, the less time I have to prepare.

I remember the knives.

All the way downstairs ... and no match for a gun.

I could sneak down while they chat. Maybe grab one. But how would I get back to my room without them seeing? I'm not as small as I used to be.

How do men make themselves so big, when no matter how small I feel, I'm never small enough?

Mom clears her throat. I turn to see her straightening her hair and patting at her blouse. She flexes an unconvincing smile, belied by the moistening of her eyes.

Without looking at me, she tucks a few strands behind her ear, lets out a jet of breath, and steps out of the bedroom.

She doesn't say goodbye.

At the top of the stairs, she pauses. Breath skids in and out of her, down into some distant part of her hollow body.

She turns to meet my eye, and for that brief, dark moment, we are no longer ourselves. I can't pretend I don't wish I could push her down the stairs, knock her with such force that she'd collide with the others, all falling and barrelling far, far away, because I hate them, I *hate* them, I hate them *so much*, for lying and fighting and letting bad things happen again and again, even when I tell them, even when they know.

But I don't want to hate. I just can't stop what I feel. As I stare at Mommy's brittle face, I wonder what feelings she has inside that she can't stop.

She's still trembling when she turns away and disappears.

Finally, I am alone, in my parents' bedroom.

I am always alone in places ruled by older others.

"Hullooooo, *beautiful!*" shouts Stef.

I encounter once again the horror of grown-ups all playing pretend together.

PARALYSIS SHATTERS. MOMMY's calling me.

"Joana!" she shouts up the stairs. "Joana, come down and say hullo please!"

Nonononono....

I need to run, scream, die, *anything.*

I bolt, bang my shoulder into a bookcase, dart inside the bathroom and shoot the lock.

"*I'm in the tooooileeeet!*"

A moment's pause.

I press my ear to the door, holding my breath.

Uncle Stef, always knowing what to say, calls, "Do you need me to fish you out then?"

They all cackle together.

Vultures.

I listen closely as their conversation continues.

"...totally under control. She's a very good girl, man. Never gives me any problems. Falls asleep lekker early. I just watch a flick or something, hey."

"What's on tonight?" asks Dad. "Action movie, or what?"

"*Die Hard.*"

Dad snorts. "Perhaps something 'harder', hey?"

"That's it," says Uncle Stef. "Getting some *action* on my Friday Action Night!"

Their sniggering is the sound of beer, cigarettes and dead animals.

"Awoooooooooooooooo!" the men howl.

Gerrie, startled, joins in.

THE BATHROOM IS a shitty sanctuary. Floral wallpaper doesn't need to moulder – it sucks. Lemon-yellow tiles recall other yellows.

The mirror reveals a creature in hiding. Gloves turn my hands into a muppet's. The balaclava engulfs my chin and cheeks, only a scrunched nose and eyes poking out. When I pull on my jacket, I'm surrounded by a ghostly gang of seventh-year Barbies: "Oh my gosh, who *is* this? Why are you dressed like one of those snow-people?" (They don't know the word Inuit, obviously.) "Maybe she's too ugly to show herself. Maybe she's a little boy trying to peep at us."

How I long to tell them the truth: that this is my armour, and it makes me invincible. One more yap, and I'll crack them into shards of ribbon and lipstick.

Style be damned.

I press my ear to the door again. No signs of immediate danger from below.

Outside, car doors whine open and slam shut. The ancient Volkswagen (Daddy's totem of shame) stutters to life. Its ambient beat-boxing shrinks until silence seals my fate.

I hear the front security gate creak as it extends, clicking into place.

The moat's up. Just me and the dragon now.

I'm gonna throw up.

No proof. No witnesses. I half-long for a wound, something I could show, to expose him. The grown-ups'd *have to* stop him. Dad'd bliksem him.

Then again, if they weren't there before – and aren't here now – why would they do anything later?

I watch the door, all sound drowned by my heartbeat. It's loud enough to bash that flimsy hunk of wood to pieces.

They left me. They left me with him.

I wish I *was* just a wolf crier: so I could cry for a great big ferocious wolf to gobble up Stef and be done with it.

I curl into a small stone, waiting to be weathered by the storm.

I RUN A bath. At least, I'll have an excuse to keep away from him.

As the water gushes, I try to stem the panic.

I massage my face with both hands and clasp my mouth shut. My body is taut as a tightrope.

The white noise rises, followed by the *blublublublub* of the downpour into the filling tub.

Just me in here, I try to console myself. *No one else.*

Steam wafts, carrying with it a cloying, wet warmth. In the bath, water wobbles a reflected image of myself I don't recognise. Scared into hiding inside her own body.

A fraction of Joana splicing across the bubbling water.

And the world begins to dim. As if the light itself were being sucked away into the walls.

Am I blacking out?

The gloom is unnatural, too fast and too absolute. Forms haze, figures dissolve.

I'm blinking, still gripping my face, body clenched as I stumble backwards onto the closed seat of the toilet, transfixed by the wall...

... WHERE IT emerges.

It wears a ragged dressing-gown, grubby and bristling with twigs and thorns and dense knots of hair. Muddy handprints stain the fabric. Tears gape like wounds, exposing pasty skin beneath: a medley of bruising: indigo, maroon and corpse-grey. Its shaggy, brown mane is long, but from the shoulders up there is nothing but a thick blackness like oily air. The body seems young, but bizarrely enlarged.

This isn't happening, it's just the panic, this is just what a brain does when you feel helpless, but that's okay, it's not your fault, so you don't have to worry, there isn't really anyone there, it's just you, just you, okay?

Okay?

I fold my arms, beg my lap for oblivion, and dare the world to strike me down a thousand times before I raise my eyes to see God's answer.

The giantess just hovers there, in silence: a voiceless, faceless sentinel, head almost touching the ceiling, half-lost in perfect blackness.

She waits.

"Wh-who..." My voice is barely a whisper. "Who a-are you?"

No reply.

I could run for the door, but she's closer to it than I am. (Guarding it? Keeping me inside?)

I can't move anyway.

"Are you ... are you God?"

With a low, rubbery moan that makes me jump, a jerky smudge begins to appear across the foggy bathroom mirror. Another smudge, then another, knitting together to form words.

YOUR

WARD

I stare. What's a "ward"?

"What do you want?"

New letters trace over the cloudy glass, line by line. My body rattles, my fingers bloodlessly tight.

KEEP

YOU

Everything in my body runs cold.

"...Keep me?" My voice is a high, sobbing moan.

The mirror smudges clear a new word.

SAFE

I gawk. "*Keep you safe.*" *It wants to* protect *me?*

Terror nails me in place. *What is happening?*

"H-h-how?"

The shadowy girl doesn't move. The writing on the glass speaks for her.

YOU

CRIED

WOLF

I hear Gerrie barking downstairs, spooked.

I'm shaking my head. *This isn't real.*

What will she do to Stef?

I don't need to ask it aloud. Again, that eerie stillness as the mirror transmits its message.

DIE

HARD

KNOCK, KNOCK, KNOCK. "Rub-a-dub-dub in the tub for a scrub, hey?" Stef sings from the other side of the door. "How about I join you, Jo-jo girl?"

My eyes bounce from the door to the Ward, and back, and again.

This isn't happening.

A dissonant din rises outside. It begins as a trickle, raindrops before the torrent, swelling swiftly into a nightmare chorus, the voices of wild things.

But the domestics have gone home already. Surely the dogs have all been walked for the day? *What's going on?*

The howling intensifies. Shrill yowls swoop over low-slurring burrs, a mixing of growls and snarls, flaring and melting away, advancing and retreating, returning renewed, famished and sated, then hungry again.

I face the girl.

"What's happening?" I ask.

Grating squeaks. A new inscription.

WOLVES

HUNGRY

NOW

Outside, the barking rages.

"I ... I don't understand."

The frenzy thickens.

YES

YOU

DO

"What you saying there, baby girl?" pipes up Stef outside the door, striving for chipper. "Can't hear you over these flippin' dogs, hey?"

His attempt to laugh it off confirms the threat. *What the hell is happening?*

The floating girl with the shadow for a face points a fleshless finger at the mirror one last time.

KEEP

YOU

SAFE

Stef's banging on the door. He's totally freaked now, but his words are lost to me. Something's drowning them—

Downstairs, something erupts. Hinges snap. Wood bursts. A cascade of glass. The hunting party's apocalyptic chant fills the house, dozens of paws stampeding down the corridors.

A man screaming.

Then nothing.

I SIT FOR hours in the darkness. At least, I think they're hours.

What happened back there? Did I disappear?

I think she's gone now, anyway. The girl, I mean. It's just me now.

GOOD THINGS COME

Josephine Sokan

*A*UTUMN HAS ALWAYS been my favourite season. She is a spectacle of beauty, a majestic celebration of golds, auburn and crimsons. I hope to die in the autumn and be buried then too. I want to sleep beneath a comforting blanket of crisp forest leaves and other dead things. Autumn is a wild woman, a brazen woman undressing before the world. Unlike summer, with his long days and endless sunshine, autumn can never be the main event.

Summer says, come, stay a while, remove your clothes, darling. Let me warm your skin and chirp sweet nothings in your ears.

Autumn is more subtle in her seduction, but she will always have my heart because she will lead me by the hand to destiny. To Thomas.

I PULL MY coat collar inwards and slip my earphones into a comfortable position; left ear then right, always in this order. My mind travels to a memory: 2009, a small hall. The Spice Girls tease over melodies. Mama purses her lips as she wraps my bleeding thumb in a tissue. A circle forms around us. Tiny eyes glare. Little feet approach from left and right, avoiding the crystal shards that dress the ground.

I rub the face of my thumb and slowly the edges of pain curl back. My mind travels often between past and present. Years of clinical intervention have not been able to reconfigure me. Time has helped a little, but I have spent much of my life in waiting: waiting to speak and be understood; to be spoken to, not spoken at; to be able to make decisions for myself. To be born and to begin living.

I am in line at the Lordship Lane bus stop, waiting for the 212. My song of choice, as always, is "It's Not Unusual" by my father Sir Tom Jones. By now, the nuances are native to me and I mouth the lyrics, lingering on the words about crying and wanting to die.

Behind me there is a voice, someone laughing. When I turn around it is like bullets fired, like rain falling on my head on a day that is too hot. I unravel like a ragdoll being unstitched, threads loosening, fabric becoming undone, transfixed and mute. Lost in two peaceful pools of blue-grey.

Shading these eyes is a mop of tangled auburn hair set against biscuit-toned skin. He wears a snug fleece jacket that seems almost too small. As if sensing our connection, we lock eyes and he smiles.

BEFORE DOMINIC, MY communication was made up of sentences I'd picked up from TV shows or the radio, a sort of copy and paste in the mind. With Dominic's help, I developed a way to attach meaning to words and was able to begin building vocabulary in context; then, eventually, I learned to read. You could say he was my guardian angel. I met him right after I turned eleven.

We celebrated my eleventh birthday at Jubilee Park, the day I first got my period. People we knew, although none were my friends, began arriving at noon. I wore a navy frilled shirt with purple dungarees and Teenage Mutant Ninja Turtles trainers, a hand-me-down from Mama Bolaji. Her boys had outgrown them, but were reluctant to part with them for me as I did not even watch the show. Pain built gradually in my lower abdomen until I felt too ill to eat cake. I was frightened to see a patch of red in my knickers when Mama helped me to the toilet. With trembling hands, I showed her the stain. She simply hugged me tight and told me that it was blood. Then she laughed and laughed. She said, imagine me doing something early for once! I too found it strange that of all the things to be able to do early, it was something as odd as vaginal bleeding.

THREE SISTERS CALL to me over the riffs of my music: curiosity, love and fear. He is with another woman. My heart wrenches, my eyes dart away. I rub at the face of my thumb. I find distraction in an advert: a bottle resembling a woman's body with the words "Jacob's Craft Beer" underneath it. How strange, this connection between the female form and a bottle of beer. Would I drink her body? Or is the woman herself made of beer?

My thoughts are interrupted by the 173 to Beckton rattling towards us and easing to a stop. Hydraulics hiss, its world opens wide and passengers disappear inside, along with something new and precious that I cannot quite name and am only just beginning to feel. This bus is off-route for me. I would need to change buses twice in order to make my appointment with Anke at the support centre. But something stirs in me as I stare at him. Perhaps he is the result of Mama's prayers or a morsel of consolation from above for a life spent trapped in a glass box and weighed down by milestones.

Do I board?

A story helps me decide. A story of unrequited love about a woman who pines for a man whose affections turn out to be as worthless as a broken bottle. She should have braved it sooner, cared less what others thought or had to say. She should have felt her way through their uncertain romance until she knew the true quality of the love she had plucked, but she'd waited until she was a disgraced woman, a jilted wife saddled with a baby with no name. They say good things come to those who wait, but in my experience, nothing ever happens other than time passing. I want to see what lives on the other side of risk.

My eyes scan first for him, then for a free seat. *Risk!* I find a seat and move swiftly through the bus to take it.

Risk met Mama and me before, back at Felixstowe Road, when Mama found hairdressing work with a friend in London and we left Aunty Ada's place and looked for the cheapest accommodation we could find in the city. This turned out to be a flat on Kelmscott Estate – small but it was ours. The people living there looked like us, but they were ghoulish totems: worry, deprivation and hostility permanently etched on their faces. Even the lady who showed us our new home greeted us by saying, "Welcome to the jungle, here are your keys."

We lived in this multicultural Amazon for three years. With help from Mama Bolaji, our neighbour, Mama managed to juggle work, household bills, caring for me, and getting me to and from school. This version of life did not allow for any pause, rest or breath. Soon the fever of this jungle began to creep into Mama's veins and infected her. It climbed up her throat and came up out of her mouth until all she could vomit was sorrow.

Then the questions began at school. Questions about my abilities, where my father was, who stayed with me after school, and why it was never my mother dropping me off or picking me up. A suggestion was made about a developmental assessment. Mama said, "See these òyìnbó people! Do they not know that some children in Nigeria walk the streets with one arm, no legs and odd parts and spares all over the place? So, the girl is not yet talking and does not understand. Is she not feeding well? Dressed neatly? Is her hair unkempt?"

They recommended Raywood Alternative Provision. But when Mama's church sisters chewed this information and turned it in their mouths, the taste displeased them.

"You know what this country is like, ọre mi. They will label your child o!" Mama Bolaji warned.

"Or worse, they will send you both packing!" Mrs Bello concluded. The school had said the same thing about Rasheed, Mama Bolaji's second son, but she refused to hear from man what God had not said about her child. For her, the case was closed; he would attend the same school as his brothers. Her child was destined for success and she could never put her son in a dumping ground for olódos. Ọlọrun má jẹ! God forbid!

FROM MY SEAT, I watch him. This is what it must mean to live, to be born. To perhaps fall in love? I glance again at the woman with him, her plainish face, limp hair, wide hips. She has a furious spattering of acne across her forehead: sore, red and proud. Something about her makes me think of a tree stump. She texts, her neck bent, eyes focused on her phone. He and I exchange more stolen glances, and I am convinced that we are destined. Ours will be like the love of Pyramus and Thisbe, sacrificial and indestructible. A forbidden love that prevails even in death.

The bus doors open and close, people board and alight – all the characters in our story, swishing into place, to a silent beat on a ticking timer. Timing *is* everything. Our bus rattles over pedestrian crossings, past two schools and a few high street shops. Through dirt-clouded windows, cars speed through traffic lights and school children bustle through imposing metal gates. Mums honk their horns with little disgruntled faces in uniform sitting in back seats. Old men hobble, the morning paper tucked under their arms, pulling their collars in against the November winds. The rhumba of the daily commute.

The bus ride has a pace, a certain timing. There are seven seconds between the doors opening and closing at a stop. At a busy stop, it can be up to fourteen or fifteen seconds. I will need to exit the bus in four stops.

The bus careers down Parnham Avenue; stop number one. What a marvel love is! We wait for it, hope for it, but it is arbitrary when it finally arrives. Pure risk. An equation short of being mathematical, unsolvable by numbers. *Did Pyramus or Thisbe know how their story would conclude? Were either of them good with numbers?*

THREE YEARS INTO our stay on the estate, riots broke out across London. The beasts of Kelmscott needed no reason to revolt and vandalise. Fires were lit in communal spaces, local stores were defaced and looting ensued. We borrowed money from Mrs Bello. Mama did not tell her why she needed the money, and that was the only reason we got it. If Mrs Bello had discovered our intention was to trade up and out of Kelmscott, to forge a better future in Strawberry Hill, we would not have seen a penny.

We moved on a Friday morning to a large four-storey Edwardian building with two rooms and a communal kitchen on each floor. Our neighbours were polite, reserved working professionals. The rooms were small but comfortable. Everybody had their own kitchen cupboards to store their crockery and groceries. There was a shared shower room and toilet on each floor that, despite the signs of use, were kept clean by the residents.

Although it was already furnished, Mama used a little change from Mrs Bello's money to buy additions for our room. She purchased, amongst other things, a giant clock from the market, forty centimetres in diameter. It was too big and a little too fancy for our tiny, simple space. Mama said, in a very matter-of-fact kind of way, that the clock was a reminder that God's time was the best time. She added that she had full faith that one day I would go to university and would become a British lawyer or a British medical doctor. She said that as long as her God was on the throne, she would have the last laugh.

THE BUS JOLTS into Tufton Park; stop number two. Passengers float on and off like ghosts, drifting into the morning dance as if it has been rehearsed. The door sequence here is eight seconds, a busier stop, and the rhythm picks up. As if they too can feel the changing tempo, the passengers on board begin shoving and jostling.

In three stops, we will approach the train station. After my stop, Long Lane, the bus will turn a corner and head down a stretch of road towards the station half a mile away. It'll be a five-minute drive from there back to Long Lane. In heavy traffic, it could take ten to fifteen minutes. By foot, no less than a ten-minute walk. Adequate time.

Maplestone Road stop is announced. The doors open and close, a twelve -second sequence. There is a kerfuffle near the entrance. A man shouts for other passengers to move down so he can board. He is answered by a wave of groans and gentle tutting before they shuffle towards the back of the bus. A typical spectacle at this time of day. I shift in my seat, gathering my jacket around me and fastening my bag in preparation to exit. I crane my neck to see him and the woman he is with. Her gaze is still locked on her screen. They exchange a glance and she offers him a half-smile.

I steady my nerves. He and I do not know each other, but his eyes beckon me. I cannot explain it, and unless you have ever waited to love and be loved, you would not understand. When the bus turns the corner to begin its ascent on Long Lane, I press the bell. The bus trudges on, then grinds to a halt. The doors open and I take a measured stride towards them. Some passengers surge off, but I know the majority are headed for the station. She is still looking at her phone. The doors will shut in seven seconds. *Six. Five.* I grab him. Straight out of his carrycot. *Four. Three.* I leap for the doors before they shut. *Two. One.* She is still looking at her phone.

It is one hundred and twenty-six steps back home from here, or ninety
-two if I walk briskly. My frantic strides pound the pavement in time with
my thumping chest. Cutting through the playing fields, I head towards
an alleyway, then through. Here, the road splits into two. One way leads
towards a parade of shops near Old Leyton, the other leads to my apartment building at the Greenborough Group's new assisted living complex. I
need supplies. *Risk!* There is an on-site convenience store at Greenborough.

Heading there adds fifty more steps; twenty-five steps each way. I take a
deep breath, one hand on the stirring baby, the other on the door. The shopkeeper grunts a nonchalant hello. Unsteady knees lead me up and down
the aisles gathering baby essentials. The shopkeeper only looks up from
his newspaper to price up my items. I use the remainder of my monthly
allowance to pay, and without any verbal exchange, he accepts my money.
Nappies, wipes, two feeding bottles, a box of formula and some jars of
baby food are thrown into my bag, and I hurry out without any thought to
my change.

A great weight recedes when I see the waters of the River Lea, the wild
bushland nestled against it and the eight apartment buildings in a row. I
avoid the gravel-lined walkway that leads to the larger Eastern Garden, an
area still under development; there are signs warning adventurous walkers
about the soft soil towards the water's edge.

I make a beeline for block two and rush past the security guard who
is meant to make us feel safe, although it is just Peter, a fifty-year-old man
with an unassuming face and a permanent puzzled squint, probably the
most threatening thing about him. He narrows his eyes as I smuggle my
partially concealed cooing bundle past him. Impatient fingers thump the
lift call button, pressing it no fewer than nineteen times. I rub at the face
of my thumb so violently that I leave nail marks in my flesh. My eyes don't
leave the floor indicator light until the familiar ping. The lift is empty, but I
only exhale when the metal doors seal us in, and I finally find some respite
inside its padded walls.

In the safety of my apartment, I examine him in loving, unhurried detail. Unlike the stolen glances on the bus, I now look with long deliberate stares, drinking his image in. He looks at me and beams pure sunlight. I will call him Thomas, after Daddy.

The story of Daddy is a tale about a young Nigerian woman who came to the United Kingdom to better her life. It was there she met a Welsh singer called Tom. They fell in love and she became pregnant. Sadly, Tom was forced to leave to provide for his little family. There was no ring exchanged, only a vow to return one day. A tall tale indeed! Mama customarily invented stories when I asked the difficult questions. But the joke was on Mama. In time, I worked out that it was all a lie. For one, we only ever saw him on television. He never called us, and no money ever came our way.

Our people take baby naming very seriously; it is sacred, at times even prophetic. A ceremony is held on the eighth day after birth where the child is named and blessed with gifts, symbolic items and prayers. But not in my case. With six months left until my birth, my biological father said goodbye to Mama and boarded a plane to England. Mama waited for news from overseas. It was her savings that had purchased his fare and, naturally, a responsible man with a wife and child was supposed to eventually return. Mama waited and waited.

Five months after my birth, she alone called me Olámidé, meaning "my wealth has come".

That naming day she decided her Ola would study abroad, with or without the useless man. She would become a British lawyer or a British medical doctor and pour shame on *him* and all the enemies who raised their necks to mock her.

That is the real story of Daddy. Still, I call my blue-grey-eyed boy Thomas after the only father I had ever known.

MY FIRST NIGHT with Thomas, I lie awake staring at him, checking that he is still breathing until the first signs of dawn begin to tussle with the skies and peek above the drapes in the lounge. My eyes surrender to its weight; I feel more comfortable falling asleep now that there is light. I let my eyes close and adjust my position on the floor. Thomas is beside me in a makeshift crib; a large laundry hamper with a flat pillow and some knitted blankets. Not ideal, but for now it will do.

Sensing my exit from the realm of consciousness, Thomas begins to squirm, then releases a shriek. Piercing. Head-splitting. I reach into his basket to scoop him up. I try to rock him, but he wails louder. *What do women do in such moments?* I dig at the surface of my thumb, only feeling relief at the wetness of broken skin. My momentary peace is broken by Thomas's feverish screams. I unbutton my top, pulling down my bra to expose my left breast. It should be easy enough to breastfeed a baby, but I dither now, feeling silly with my boob exposed. *What to do? How to do it?* I drop him back into the basket, startling him, and he begins a fresh assault on my nerves. I run to the kitchen and empty some ready-made formula mix into a bottle. My misanthrope neighbour, Renata, bangs on the wall we share. Bang. Bang. Bang. Shrieking. Bang. Bang. Bang. Shrieking.

The teat hits Thomas's lips and he swallows it whole, guzzling in large gulps. His lips smack together, his cheeks puff up and deflate. Within minutes he finishes, eyes bleary, lips red from his wrestle with the bottle. His hair is a tangled, auburn mess. I attempt gently detangling it with my fingers, a motion which eventually sends him softly back to sleep. He smiles before settling in my arms as I sing "Once Upon a Time" by Tom Jones in a hushed tone. I whisper in Thomas's ear that one day he will meet my daddy, the man who will sing the soundtrack to the rest of his life.

MESSY, BRUNETTE HAIR was the first thing I noticed about Dominic. He was dressed in a wide smile that displayed a gap in the top row of his front teeth. He had a pack of Marlboro Lights barely hidden in his shirt pocket and he smelled smoky and sweet, comforting for someone who might have been up all night paralysed with anxiety. Blueish-grey eyes, which seemed to have the ability to chase fear from my body, hid behind his thin spectacles. He introduced himself as a trainee special-needs support staff member, at Strawberry Hill Comprehensive for the academic year, hoping to secure a full-time job at the end of his placement.

At our first meeting, he attempted to draw me out with questions. I opted for silence. After several years of seemingly fruitless interventions, most people, Mama included, were convinced of my limitations. But Dominic persisted.

In our second session, and for many sessions after, he just encouraged me to laugh, to do something other than sit upright staring or rubbing the face of my thumb – initially with odd accents and impressions, then silly faces and awful singing. I opted for silence. Until the day he left the radio on and caught me not just tapping my feet but singing entire lyrics. The song playing was "What's New Pussycat?" by Tom Jones. A classic.

"What's new, Pussycat? Whoa-ooo-whoa-ooo-whoa-o-o!"

THE RADIO NEWS reports that there is a city-wide hunt for a baby taken from a local mother while on a bus. The newsreader announces that the mother boarded the 173 to Beckton during the busy commuter period. She claims that her baby must have been taken somewhere between the station and the last stop at the bus garage. She cannot be certain when exactly as she admits the use of alcohol that morning after an awful row with her partner.

I am quaking on the inside, but a steady hand grips my boy. The bus garage is a good twenty-minute ride after the Long Lane stop where we exited. That means that she did not check whether he was hungry or cold for quite some time. Shame on her!

I observe the piercing blue-grey eyes, tiny pout and his perfect face below me. His little fingers grip mine with a strength I recognise in myself, even in Mama. I have flashes of my own childhood. Hushed conversations. Frustrated slaps from Mama. All-night prayers with Apostle Eze and then later, when we were desperate, Prophet Modi. Anointing oil, bibles, prophesies, shouting and fiery babbling before an altar in the still night hours. And weeping, always weeping. Looking at Thomas's tender features, I decide that he will never again know a useless love. I speak into his ear the destiny of love only, like Mama had done to me twenty-two years prior. Whatever he turns out to be, smart or slow, good or bad, neurodiverse or otherwise, he will know only love.

THREE YEARS INTO secondary school, I made my way to classroom 9G on the third floor of the special education suite. Before entering the room, I glanced at the reflective metal panel on the classroom door and practiced a smile. Unconvinced but willing, I smoothed back my hair and entered.

"Hello trouble!" Dominic teased as I settled into the seat next to him, close enough to smell his smoky sweetness. Our session followed its secure pattern of exercises, but as the hour drew to a close, he took a deep breath. "Ola, will your mum be attending on Thursday?" he asked in a tone I did not recognise. "It's really important that I speak with her."

Later that week at parent's evening, Dominic encouraged Mama to request a transfer from the school and the local council to a specialist school. He said Strawberry Hill Comprehensive only offered a select number of alternative or vocational qualifications and had done all that it could do for me. With its limited provision and financial investment for special-education, my chances were higher at a school with targeted support and a smaller community. Now, more than ever, Mama would have to fight with all she had, she would need to become my biggest advocate. His blueish-grey eyes pleaded with her, then he said, "I'll be leaving at the end of the academic year."

My lip began to quiver and I uttered a word I ought not to under my breath, before storming clumsily towards the hall exit, bringing the heat of many eyes to my skin. As my hand thumped against the wooden door, Mama released an ugly, unrestrained sob that stopped me in my tracks. I glanced back over my shoulder to witness Dominic, *my Dominic*, cross the invisible, unspoken boundary between parent and staff member and offer Mama a hug. Her tears were only encouraged by this token of softness in the hard concrete spaces where she had been forced to exist. Before a public audience, Mama cried all the tears from all the years. She cried right back to Nigeria, right back to my daddy. She cried over the birth of a baby that only she had an interest in naming. She cried tears of unfulfilled dreams and dashed hopes. She cried for the loss of her redemption and the loss of the child meant to rid her of the weight of her shame.

AT THE END of the summer term, there was a leaving party for Dominic. I did not attend. He found me by the school pond, my happy place, and offered a smile I refused to return. He said he'd known for some time that I was more capable than I was letting on. Education was changing. Government reforms were coming that would not favour people from communities like mine. He said that I needed to give my best effort to my studies. He looked me square in the eyes and told me I was wonderful, precious and limitless. It was then I gushed all the rivers of my heart. He was the only man to care for me, and the darkness of a future without him scared me. My stars would die without him.

His blue-grey pools smiled brightly and then he sang "A Minute of Your Time" by Tom Jones.

I did not join in. I stared at the pond in silence, digging at the skin of my thumb, desperate to break it, desperate for relief.

HE LEFT IN July and, by September, I began Raywood Alternative Provision. It was quieter and smaller than Strawberry Hill. My first day started with a tour of the school. Imagine our surprise when we bumped into Rasheed, Mama Bolaji's second son. From the window, we observed for a moment his confidence, his easy smile, his enthusiasm and promise. The headteacher said that he was one of the brightest in the school and had been there for four years already. He was preparing for two vocational qualifications and three more formal qualifications. The walls bore testament with framed newspaper articles featuring Rasheed alongside other students.

On the bus ride home, Mama was mute and contemplative; I could sense that she was grieving all over again, as if she had suffered a fresh loss somehow. She did not know that on that day something also died in me.

I THROW MY phone against the wall after switching it off. The calls and texts from Anke and Mama have grown tiresome.

Where are you?

Why can't I reach you?

You missed your appointment.

Since the arrival of my little Thomas, great anchors weigh my mind and my eyes even more so. We need supplies, so we will brave the real world, albeit carefully.

Outside, the air is crisp. Leaves crunch beneath my feet. One, two. *Crunch.* Three, four. *Crunch.*

Squelch. I step on a soggy one. *Yuck.*

Mama never approved of puddle jumping when I was younger. I see her face reflected in the still pools of water and stomp forcefully, shattering her image into innumerable pieces. My body stiffens against the creeping late November chill. I wear Thomas on my front in a wrap, his cheek against my heart, and together we marvel at the golds, auburn and crimsons, blowing puffs of frosty clouds into the air. We stop to admire the stillness of the lake. The birds serenade us. In this moment, all the world is ours – all life, every beat, every song, every colour belongs to us.

Out of the corner of my eye, a glimpse of black and white. I spot the man and woman in uniform before Mama, Peter and Anke. Renata, who rarely leaves her apartment, is in the middle, saying something that has all their attention.

I run.

Shouting. I hear my name. I dig at the face of my thumb and run faster, my arms a protective wall around Thomas. I glance over my shoulder; the vigilantes are approaching swiftly. My breath burns, my arms are weak, my vision blurs with hot, stinging tears. My tongue feels like lead, waiting to slip down my throat and crush my insides. Thomas begins to cry.

I bolt down the gravel path towards the large fields. I am inches from the Eastern Garden's entrance. Thomas's tongue and uvula vibrate feverishly, dancing to the anxious thump of my heart.

Shush, Thomas, hush.

I stumble and my grip around him loosens. I regain my footing but struggle to get back upright. It costs me speed and time.

Why are they chasing me? Thomas is safe. The boy is safe!

Mama hobbles several yards behind Anke, Peter and the two officers. Something snags the soft knit wrapped around Thomas, snatching it from us.

Can they not see that the boy is safe? That he is being taken care of?

My eyes search for sanctuary. Thomas howls. *Hush baby.* My leg buckles. I will let nothing separate us, even if it means that we will never meet Tom Jones. I look down at the blue-grey pools that saved me. I did not birth this boy, but he is mine. He is what my life's waiting was for.

To my left, there are naked trees, to my right the open green field, and in front of me, the softened earth leading to the River Lea.

HEAVEN'S MOUTH

Zanta Nkumane

B LESS THE FATHER *that stays.*
    But what about the mother who is there but absent?

I ALWAYS THINK about this when I remember my mama. I think about it on my drive back home to Heaven's Mouth. The village is perched on the summit of the Ntondozi, close enough to the sky that the roofs touch the clouds. One long road slithers through it like an oesophagus. The mouth into the town is also the way you leave. Uniform houses line the street on either side like an eerie, abandoned mining town, except here, folk still roam its skeletal form. The road spreads into a cul-de-sac square at the bottom where there are only three buildings: Thuthuka Supermarket, which sells everything from hardware to underwear; Mvuleni Rest & Bar, whose menu is just a variation of meat and starch in different forms but essentially the same dish; and the Community Hall, which is also the church and dance hall, depending on the day.

I watch night shrink into day as the lights of the village appear in front of me, their twinkling the only warm welcome. Mama always said when you leave a place, you leave at dawn's chorus, and when I asked her why, she said, "So the strength of the bird's song can carry you on your way." That's what I did when I left – a good son always listens to his mama.

I am counting on dawn's chorus now; returning needs the same strength. There was always something fleeting about my mama's spirit, like the cadence of a bird's song floating away into the trees. She always spoke about leaving, her voice plump with a longing for places she'd only read about in books or seen on TV. Her eyes awash with wonder. She described cities teeming with highways, tall buildings and parks. She told stories of aeroplanes bigger than our village and angry elephants and oceans as if she was about to go touch them herself. Some days, I thought she would. I wonder if she still believes in leaving as much. I wonder if she has changed. Even a bit. Change is hard to come by in Heaven's Mouth. It's why I ran away. It's why I risked bringing shame to my mama's name by leaving.

The silence of the sleeping village grunts in irritation at the slam of the car door. The panic of returning feels wider now that I am standing outside my house. At least I am not back to stay. Once you leave, you can never belong again. I knock and wait. The door swings open to reveal her; silk, like melting midnight, drapes her all the way to the floor.

"Morning, Mama."

Her biting scrutiny absorbs me, up and down. "My God, you look old," she finally says.

It was expected. When you leave the village, you start ageing. Rapidly. She looks the same as the day I was born. A radiant thirty-year-old woman is my mother and I, her son, just turned forty.

"I was expecting worse. Your insults have dulled since I last saw you, Mama. You may not look it, but something about you is getting old, it seems." It's as if I'd never left.

I shuffle past her before she can respond. Mama always has an answer, even for the silence.

MUSA SNORES WITH the vigour of a small river after it's filled with a sudden, heavy summer rain – loud and full. Of course, he denies he snores with such might. His body stretches beyond the length of the bed. I pull the covers over his feet and continue getting ready for work. When I left Heaven's Mouth, I walked in the scathing morning and afternoon until I reached the bottom of the mountain – my journey slow because the world beyond the bounds of my village was all a marvel. The sky was longer, the air had new smells, the trees had a greener gaiety. But the grievous cold stopped my wonder from growing too big, and I didn't know where to go or how. That's when Musa appeared, driving past in his old navy-blue Isuzu, a fresh stock of fruit and vegetables overflowing at the back. He offered me a lift into town and somehow I never left his side. I still tease him for being so trusting and helpful. He says my eyes radiated with so much disorientation that day, he couldn't leave me to the world's turpitude. After I helped him offload the produce, he asked me what I could do. The only skills I had were farming and cooking. That was ten years ago in beyond-Heaven's Mouth time. Now I work in the restaurant he runs in the hotel.

The old hotel where we live and work rests in a quiet part of the Ruckus, downtown Manzini. Its supernaturally silent location feels like the eye of a storm with the chaos of the clamorous city circling around it: the chorus of hooting taxis, the chatter of rats in the drains, the hammering footsteps of hurried people, the unending bait of street vendors and the under-appreciated gleaming history of the buildings. A composite city cyclone. The hotel's not-quite-brown façade lures you in with its large windows, misplaced pristine entrance, elegantly dressed butler and red carpet. A bar and restaurant sit on the ground floor where patrons come to numb their throbbing erratic realities. The hotel has endured different names since its birth – both the mundane and the derivative alike. The building had suffered numerous changes in ownership and reinvention. This is one of the maladies that towns stomach in this country – the fickle life cycles of many spaces and establishments. The hotel currently goes by Lost & Found. The name is fitting; it describes most of the people who frequent it. They are more lost than found but the name is still a good description. It also feels like me most of the time.

I always take the morning shift because waking up is an easier task for me, compared to the chore it seems to be for Musa. It's my mama's doing and training – we were always awake at dawn up in Heaven's Mouth, moving like worker ants, in perpetual preparation for winter. Mama rarely stayed still, as if stillness echoed everything she never got to be. I may have left her, but my cells still pulsate with her endurance. We carry the parts of our mothers that energise us and move us forward but, in my case, I also carry her disappointment and shame. And perhaps her jealousy because I left.

I am an Abandoner. Time started flogging me when I took my first step beyond the village line.

"Why can't I come with you?" Musa asked the evening before I left. We were smoking weed by the window; his reflection was so clear in the glass, he existed twice. He inhaled a deep puff, and I exhaled a smoke snake.

"Only people from the village can visit. To you, Heaven's Mouth is nothing but an empty mountaintop. You can't see it."

"How do you think your mother will take the news?" he continued.

"Like she takes everything – with a shrug and a smirk and a sip of wine."

Musa laughed. I laughed too because his laugh sounded like the morning after a summer night's rain, sparkling and wet with possibility. But I also laughed to soothe my lengthening anxiety.

I WAKE UP before the sun. Which means I wake at the same time as my mama. She brews us orange and cinnamon tea. She pushes the steaming cup across to me.

"Why are you here, Sipho?"

"This is my home, too."

"The moment you turned thirty-one this place started to forget you. I started to forget you."

"Maybe I am here to remember what it feels like to stay, one last time."

Mama takes a long sip of her tea, her eyes peering over the cup. I can feel there is more to say between us, but the day is barely stirring. I only have three days here. Heaven's Mouth tends to spit out Abandoners after seventy-two hours. We were always strangers, but the wrinkles lining my face now feel like more rivers between us to cross. She always looked at me with such scrutiny, as if her heart was reconsidering me.

Days in Heaven's Mouth are long and slow, as if time came to this place to rest and never moved forward. I leave the house and head down to Nono's. Walking down the street, I admire the brightly coloured houses stacked together like Lego blocks. From outside, they appear smaller than they actually are. They are all three bedrooms, with a kitchen and a bathroom. The paint glistens like a new coat has been laid on that same morning, but I know that is not the case.

Nono's house is four houses down, on the other side of the road, closer to the square. The beauty of a place that never changes is the assurance of always finding people where you left them. It's comforting.

Nono opens the door before I can even tap on it. Even when we were growing up, I'd barely get to the front of her house and she'd swing the door open to meet me.

"I can still smell you from around the corner," she says. "But now, you smell old." She smiles.

"You're just jealous I became something you're scared to be," I tease Nono in return.

"I am not jealous of you being old, I am jealous you'll get to die." Her smile fades.

When you're sick, not dying is all that you can think of, which actually means dying is all you think of. It's the same with getting old. When you feel like you don't have time, time consumes you.

We walk down to the square, eyes stealing us like we're two spectacles plucked from heaven and discarded on that road. Two fallen angels, the same age but one whose tomorrows are numbered. I know it's me they're looking at. The one who gave up eternity. People are even scared to greet me, as if they think the madness of my leaving is contagious.

"Why did you come back, Sipho?" Nono asks after we settle at a table for lunch at Mvuleni. "I thought I'd never see you again. I am surprised the town's mouth has even remained visible to you after so many years."

"I am getting married," I reveal, eyes focused on the large serving of meat and pap in front of me.

"I am happy for you. But what does that have to do with anything here? None of us are going to be there – you know this. Why waste your time by coming back for answers you already have? You were brave enough to be free. Stay fucking free!"

I've missed this about her. Her burning spirit flames as brightly now as it did when we were children. If there was anyone we imagined would leave, it was her. But a burning spirit can't always light a fire under you.

"I breathe differently, and I think about time in smaller chunks. So I don't know if I am really free. My future stretches as far as my next shift at the hotel."

"At least it stretches somewhere." She points at Mr Motsa walking by, books piled up to his face. He was our high-school teacher, and is still teaching the same class. "Look at him; you think time stretches anywhere but back to that classroom?"

"Look at me, my face sags and I am rotund," I retort. "Mr Motsa looks like nothing has happened to him. Just like you. Just like my mama. It's like my leaving did nothing to her."

MAMA IS STANDING over the stove, her back to me. The smell of steam bread and chicken stew fills me with longing. Whenever she made me this meal, she was apologising for something. Sorry never left my mother's mouth, no matter how wrong she was. I was six years old when she started disappearing. At times, days morphed into weeks with no word and no provision. She'd return and utter not a single word. Instead, she'd hurry down to Thuthuka to purchase ingredients and make me steam bread and chicken stew. Some said she'd sit out in the fields, others claimed she barely left the bar. Some people said she was a witch because they saw her walk too close to the village line many nights. But it was me they felt sorry for; I was stuck with a mother who did everything to be away from me. When she was around, she mothered me like it was a duty, not because she loved me.

"Ma, I am getting married," I blurt out as I swivel in the dining-room chair, like I am six years old again and the chair is too tall.

"What do you expect me to do about that?"

"I'm letting you know because it's a big step."

"I am sorry you wasted your time coming all the way here. I know Abandoners don't have as much time as the rest of us."

She swings a large portion of stew into a bowl and places the bread on the side like a shovel into wet concrete. It's the same bowl she's always served me in.

"After you finish your meal, I want you to get out of my house. Your little tour is over now. Next time send a text message."

"But Ma—"

"I have been telling you since you were a child not to call me that. My name is Nombuso. Not Mother!"

Sometimes I wonder about her. Was she ever a mother to me?

"You hate me that much."

"No, I hate that you made me have to care."

"I'm sorry, then."

I stand up without touching her meal. It feels acherontic to be in front of her now. I need to pack and forget this place in the same manner it has forgotten me.

"And stop saying sorry all the time. Haven't I taught you that much?"

"You taught me to be good at sorry. For someone who can live forever, too much apology fills your life, Mama."

That is how I leave Heaven's Mouth again.

metamorphosis, cycles and identity

VANISHING

Kabubu Mutua

ON THE MORNING of her wedding, Rabeka fled with her dowry – a casket filled with gold jewellery, a trunk of lace and chiffon and silk, and her husband's Datsun car. "She was so composed, so peaceful, you wouldn't have imagined her!" Wa Nzwili, the bread seller with a wandering eye cried, wiping her tears with the ends of her leso. On our doorsteps and throughout the bazaar, we remembered with fondness the brief strokes of our brushes and pencils on her face, how we had lined her eyes with kohl and filled her lips with berry-red lipstick as we agreed that, indeed, this wedding was sanctified by the angels. How we had filled the pews of St Matthew's Church, stopping at the hall's entrance to scoop holy water from the ablution basins to dab on our foreheads, our faces painted with pious expressions. How, afterwards, we had admired the scroll of crêpe paper above the altar that read: Rabeka weds Kasimba. How, at the groom's homestead, potfuls of rice were steamed on open fires and spiced with mdalasini and tangawizi. How a goat was slaughtered and its throat bled into the earth so the couple would always find favour in the eyes of those who had gone before us, and crates of Tusker beer were ordered in stacks. Thick-limbed cooks had rolled dough into circles for chapatis. Mothers, it is said, told their daughters to pray for a man like Kasimba – a man with a proper British education, a man with money, a man who gave his bride gold as dowry.

IN OUR DUKAS, we tell the story of the daughter of Death, a girl with a human face and goat legs who once lived in another part of the country, in the days when ostriches roamed our grasslands with freedom. The girl's eyes were burning fires, her tongue like a phonograph playing John Nzenze songs. The girl was a traveller. In the daytime men were blinded by her beauty, and at night crumbled under her thighs; her legs bore no difference to a human's when they stared at her after she'd undressed. Between our world and the girl's world existed a veil through which only certain things were visible and others invisible. And so, the men took her as they would take an ordinary human girl, falling under her charm. Afterwards, she'd slit their throats where the carotid pulsed.

In her travels, the girl never stayed longer than two weeks – it was dangerous to fall in love with a place, she knew, for a place is like a beautiful stranger you've only just met. She pretended to be a trader of special teas, and an insurance saleswoman, and she preached the good news and performed as a background singer and sold fabric imported from Ghana ("Very original, you can feel it if you want," she might say to a potential buyer.)

We laugh and say the tale is too transparent; it collapses under the weight of its falseness. Women don't kill. Men kill.

IT WAS KASIMBA who noticed Rabeka's absence at the vestry and rushed to the pulpit exclaiming, "She is gone! She is gone!" And everyone thought he meant she was dead. Aunty Boi Boi, who owned International Executive Salon, the source from where gossip flowed, said, "That woman ran away. I knew she did not have good sense."

There were those like Father Cornelius who thought she would only be gone for a matter of hours, that she would return before sunset and that, upon her arrival, he would finally conduct the Mass. He asked Kasimba to meditate with him in prayer. Darkness found them kneeling between the pews, the mellow light from the church's stained-glass windows transitioning from the pink of sunset to the black of night. And when we joined them the next day and the day after, we saw from the corners of our eyes that Kasimba was a broken man. We walked to him and said, "It shall be well."

ON HER STOPOVERS across the country, our girl left a trail of bodies. She lured greedy men with mouths stinking of beer to dirty backrooms and lodgings. Shell-white walls would turn crimson. And she would slip noiselessly back into the night, taking the next train out. Newspapers ran headlines of a serial killer, a man under the influence of an evil power. Churches organised vigils in the wake of the murders, preachers drew money effortlessly from the purses of believers for bottles of fake holy water. "Dip your finger and cross your brow," they advised. And yet the murders continued, the body count increased.

KASIMBA OWNED THE bakery at the end of Makongeni Street, famed for their kaimatis with citrus. He had studied for a degree in architecture at a small college in Bangalore, India. Upon his return, he announced that he had found the meaning of life, and that he wanted to start a bakery. His mother had torn her clothes and marched him to a witchdoctor, saying, "Look what this education has taught you."

The witchdoctor examined Kasimba, seeking from the motion of his divining bones a message. But he soon concluded that Kasimba was a healthy man; the stars aligned in his favour. Months later, Kasimba's mother died in her sleep, leaving behind a fortune that spanned acres of prime farmland, fleets of Ferguson farm tractors, and unfinished dreams of what Kasimba should have become. The doctor said it was a stroke, we whispered at the funeral, but we all agreed it was a broken heart that had killed her.

In our small barazas where we smoked tobacco from clay pipes, we remembered Kasimba from our younger days. How we had played brikicho together behind the ruins of the colonial slaughterhouse, screaming when we found lizards in the crevices, how we had stolen mangoes from the farm near the church. And in our conversations, we envied his British mannerisms: how he presented his guests with a fork and knife when they visited, his table nicely done in little cotton napkins, his gramophone that played the softest songs unburdened by voices, his tendency to speak English from his nose at public gatherings, his knowledge of the world beyond our little town.

In our homes, we advised our children to study hard so, one day, they could become like Kasimba. We told them that once our dreams had gleamed with freshness, that possibility had filled our youth. And yet time had splintered those dreams, its passage a gust of wind that blew them from our minds, leaving us with only pictures of what could have been.

"The world is yours. It is so wonderful to be young!" we said. And we envied them as they studied for their examinations under the soft light of paraffin lamps.

LATE ONE EVENING, on a journey by train, a stranger sat next to the girl. She'd killed a Catholic priest the previous night, a man with a fat bottom who asked if she would tickle his nipples and rub his feet. That killing had been particularly painful, and she'd stared at the body long after she'd finished and seen something in the dead man's face, a kind of helplessness – after all, he was a man whose life had been dedicated to freeing others of sin. And so, she stared out of the train window at rolling farmlands of golden maize, the sadness ebbing inside her. The stranger said he was a messenger from heaven, that he carried news of her people – our girl had no family and had spent her youth in the care of an orphanage – and did the girl desire to return to them? The story goes the girl said yes. After all, a person's history carries the weight of their future. As the carriage sped through the country, she thought about her blurred past, about the family she'd never had, and pain collected in her stomach.

EVEN THOUGH WE'D always doubted Kasimba would marry – for he had been effeminate since our boyhood days – we still guessed at the kind of woman he might take for himself: there was the mayor's daughter recently returned from Johannesburg with a medical degree, who washed her face with rosewater to tone her complexion; the pastor's daughter, a girl of humble means who fasted twice a week for the deliverance of our town; the firebrand daughter of the local high school principal, who had won all the spelling bees in our district and gone on to study English literature at the University of Nairobi.

But he chose none of them.

We watched him talk and laugh with Rabeka under the verandahs of our shops, the very girl we had sworn he would never marry. Rabeka, a woman who had never studied beyond primary school. A woman who would smoke Rooster cigarettes and speak back to men in the local pub. Rabeka, the woman with burning eyes that seemed to invite a fight. Rabeka, the rebel. Rabeka was the woman mothers wished their daughters would never become.

THE STORY GOES that the stranger gave the girl a condition: She couldn't kill again before the year's end. Only then would he return to fulfil her desire and guide her to her origins. She pictured herself in the home she'd long forgotten. There were hints of laughter and baking and a certain evening light. There was a sweetness in her memory. But in the end, this feeling was overwhelmed with a fogginess. Those who leave, she would come to learn, are cursed to catch only small instances of gone times.

ON THE THIRD day after Rabeka's disappearance, Aunty Boi Boi offered to drive Kasimba to the police station in her battered Peugeot, as Kasimba had been left without a car. In the dimly lit police station with walls streaked with peeling paint, the policeman picked at his teeth and made a swishing sound with his tongue and said, "Madam, can you repeat your words as I cannot hear well? My ears have suffered the injustices of my father's maize mill."

Aunty Boi Boi repeated that Rabeka, the woman betrothed to the man who stood beside her, had fled on their wedding day with a casket filled with jewellery. She emphasised that the gold had been 24-carat as if she had participated in its purchase. And did the policeman know that the bangles and necklaces had been designed for Kasimba's mother by the famous Nagin Pattni for *her* wedding all those years ago? That they were real gold and not those fake things which everybody seemed to wear these days? She fanned her cleavage as she spoke.

"Madam, I don't know of this Nagin Pattni you speak of, but I shall need something to open my eyes," said the policeman.

"Are you asking for a bribe?" asked Aunty Boi Boi.

"Madam. Don't play games with me."

And so, she slipped him a thin envelope as if she had contemplated the act before she drove to the station. The policeman said he would call his counterparts in our neighbouring towns to put out an alert for a missing person. But we knew such a thing would never happen; our police officers were incapable of even killing a fly on the back of your hand. Later, Kasimba whispered to Aunty Boi Boi that he would repay her, but she turned to him and said, "Ahh no. I did it for your mother. Such fun days we had in our girlhood."

SHE CHOSE THE town because it was the last stop on the train schedule – where else then, could she go? There was a charm in the way the afternoon sunlight hit the streets lined with jacaranda in golden patches, how the people moved as if the air carried something different from other towns, the way darkness punctuated the start of all happy things – dance parties and films shown in technicolour against whitewashed walls, and Pilsner beer served from the bottle.

She chose to stay.

ONE NIGHT, DURING a town party, she was dancing alone, her face cut in moonlight, when a woman approached. The rolls of her neck were lined with diamonds.

"I'm Mother," said the woman. "You have something the girls of this town don't. I can make you rich."

The girl laughed. She'd never wished for material wealth. Humans, she wanted to say, are so definable, so easy to manage, because they are all moved by the same thing: money. Still, she said yes. A preoccupation would make her wait bearable. She would show herself to the men of the town and they would take her as they wished. In turn, they would pay her.

And so, she served sour whisky as a bargirl and took them in dark alleys. They said, "Good girl, your lips are so sweet," and slipped her folded shilling notes. They choked her when they came. They told her stories of their failing marriages as if she were a sage from whom they could derive wisdom. They felt at home with our girl. As the months passed, Mother's business grew in ways that it had lacked before the girl, its heart pumping with increasing desire for what the girl offered. There was an air of mysticism about her, they said. Something magical – what, they couldn't say. "We only want her," they said, and bar fights arose when one picked her while others still wanted her.

MOTHER HAD A son. A son with a fragile frame that the girl fell in love with. She was drying her linen on her balcony, he was smoking outside a duka, his nostrils a chimney puffing wisps of white smoke, when their eyes met. He observed her until darkness washed the town.

The next day he returned to the duka to light a cigarette, and waved.

The day after she came down, and asked if he had been flirting with her.

He said he liked the way the wind blew her hair, and did she know that her voice sounded as if it had been strained through a sieve – the reason he came here was to listen to her sing?

"How strange," the girl said. "I thought you were staring at my breasts."

Mother found the girl's attraction to her son scandalous. Even though Mother's proceeds came from dealing in the shadiest of things – fake lightening creams banned in the country, abortions in dim backrooms, offering girls to men who could pay, smuggling tax-free cigars – she was a society woman. And what to do when, weeks later, the town woke to the news that her son had been seen fondling the girl behind the church? What to say when the town's gossip-monger and hairdresser announced to her clients that the highly esteemed Mother's son had fallen into the trap of one of the very girls she had condemned to sex work? They sighed and cooled their fat cleavages with elaborate fans. Soon, they stopped sending her invites to tea parties where they met to gossip and say, "The one who spreads her legs is seeing her son." Again and again, as if the sweetness of that discovery had not lost its touch over time. They dipped bread into masala chai over her downfall. And soon began to order their jewellery and fair creams and other contraband from the city.

IN THAT TOWN, people believed that the excesses of the gone year needed to be purged to the world of the dead on New Year's Eve, and luck derived in its absence. They expressed their wishes and confessed their sins to their departed through a blind clairvoyant with greying hair. Fires were lit in the shrine and flowers fed to the flames. Food was offered and milk was poured onto the waiting earth so the spirits could share with the townspeople. And so, the boy's mother brought her desires to the medium. He revealed that a strange creature roamed the land, and that this very creature was courting Mother's son. Her lineage was tainted, and did Mother wish her family to fall to the same curse when new blood arrived? For an additional ten shillings and a white he-goat delivered to the medium's door the next morning, she would receive a potion to "send the creature away." It turned out that the phrase, which the medium offered with a certain lightheartedness through teeth tinted with tobacco, was a euphemism for kill. A stroke, the doctor would conclude.

WE ENJOYED THE thought of a wedding in our little town. Adored it with a newfound fascination. In the negotiations, Rabeka seemed to gloat at those of us who had wished her an unmarried life – the way she served us drinks as if we had not held ill-will against her, the way she danced to Tshala Muana and Mbilia Bel. We attended those conversations still, drinking fermented beer from long straws dipped into large earthen pots. We danced to John Nzenze tapes played from a jukebox borrowed from the bar and asked that Kasimba name his children after us. The cake was baked – a towering thing with seven levels glazed in chocolate and red icing, and two figurines to symbolise the newlyweds placed at its peak. Rabeka said her name should be scrolled in scarlet on the invitation card and that the rice should be cooked in mutton and not beef. We pressed our faces against the window of the room where the cake was set and smiled our yellow smiles full of envy, for our daughters had been taken with small ceremony, their cakes only taking one level. The wedding gown was fitted in Nairobi, a cut-out piece with lace gloves. Flowers were ordered from the neighbouring town.

THE GIRL LEARNED that falling in love brought a secret language into your life, where your lover could speak to you without opening their mouth. It turned out that the boy was a good cook, mixing things and adding and peeling as if he'd done it his entire life. When she woke up with a cold, he prepared a concoction of egg whites steeped in garlic and lemons. When her period arrived, he rubbed her feet with coconut oil and prepared a bath of salts for her pain. The day of their anniversary he cooked her a whole chicken basted in sunflower oil – all that crispiness! She wrote him stories of faraway lands where people had goat legs and human faces and he laughed and asked how they walked, and if they wore shoes like us. They fucked like each time was the first, each day giving way to stronger impulses. She sewed fresh cotton shirts which he wore to work. She knew the music he liked, and when he returned home, the phonograph would be playing his favourite songs. And even though she yearned for her past, she was consoled by their life, and she wondered whether she would ever wander again.

ON THE DAY before the wedding, we should have observed that Rabeka walked with a hunch. We said, "She looks so tired. What will happen when she realises that marriage is indeed hard work? That she has to wake up to the same face each day, listen to the same voice, respond to the same arguments? Won't she go mad?"

After all, we were people for whom the sighting of other people's happiness was consigned the distress of a little jealousy. Besides, it is a universal truth that marriages are faulty boats by which people chose to traverse life together.

MOTHER INVITED THE girl to tea to straighten things out. She wanted to know the girl. Who were her people? She brewed the finest tea and pinched a portion of the medium's charm into the girl's cup. The phonograph played Kakai Kilonzo. Death stirred in the parlour curtains. It rode the ripples of the tea. It blew the girl's hair. For a long time, Mother sat waiting for the girl to sip, but the girl knew. Death wanted her alive. She was its agent on earth. And that very night, Death visited Mother in her dreams and took her. The doctor said it was a stroke. But the townspeople said it was a broken heart that had killed her.

By the time that year ended and the stranger returned, the girl and the boy with the fragile frame had arranged their wedding. Soon, they would exchange vows, and yet secrets guided their union.

"You broke your promise," said the stranger.

The girl said she was in love; she no longer sought her past.

"We made a pact," said the stranger.

"In a different time," said the girl.

The stranger removed his cloak. It was Death himself.

"You killed her," said the girl.

"You killed her with your selfishness for her son, taking him from her as if he was always yours. I just cleaned up. It's true what they say: you broke her heart."

"What do you want?"

"I want him. His time has arrived," said Death.

Outside, choral music played from the organ. The fragrance of the fresh jasmine and roses that lined the altar found her. If Death had been kinder, the girl might have fallen into the boy's arms that very afternoon as his wife, he, her husband.

"I'll go for him."

Death scoffed. "You truly love him."

She began to cry.

"You have always been bound to me. It was only a matter of time before I came."

"I had a wonderful time."

Outside, the boy knocked at her door and said, "The sun is out, my love. We need to start."

And even though Death did not touch the gold the girl received for her dowry, it is said that every object she touched or loved followed her into the afterlife. Like a scent to its owner, these things trailed her – silk and chiffon and lace, and the car where they'd first fucked. She walks in the spirit world, thick with bangles and rings and necklaces. She waits for the boy. She sits in the driver's seat and longs for time to disappear so they can be together.

IN OUR TEA kiosks, we speculate about Rabeka's whereabouts. Those among us well-versed in the divine arts contemplate that she was taken by ritualists – body parts are highly priced contraband, tongues are used to make husband charms, for example. But the educated among us say she was a gold digger – why then, they wonder out loud, did the money and other items disappear when she vanished? We ask the driver of the Kwitu, the bus that traverses the plains, did he see her?

He laughs, and with his missing-tooth mouth he says that runaway brides are especially clever these days.

I AM WHAT I AM NOT

N.A. Dawn

*F*IRST, I FASHIONED a cosmos. Its curvature charted the reaches of space and time, a swelling expanse of near nothingness, a cradle for all possibility. The horizon bent upon itself into a spinning sphere, an infinite orb to churn the dusts of a nascent reality, at last beginning to dance.

Its first denizens were figments, irreducible grains of existence cast about a sparse sea of elementary particles, the barest texture in the sprawling dark. Their behaviours were random, revealing rudimentary inclinations nonetheless – bonds, traces, influence, exertion. No desire, no meaning. Only opportunity.

I could not resist. Not to interfere would be to deny my very essence, and so I fell through the aeons in that blissful pandemonium and grace, that sensual play in the design. I probed it, struck it, smoothed it and warped it; infused it with flavours exotic and surreal; wrought from its quantum marrow such wonders as no other god had ever made. It was sport and pleasure and a myriad things I could never describe. My creation goaded me. I was instructed by its silent celestial jewels, its pulsating magnitudes. My interventions, however selfish they might have seemed to an observer, were no less than petitioned; what shape did not suggest, colour demanded. Matter insisted on my touch; light troubled my attention. Perhaps it was my own lust speaking – for what god can repress the lure of such other-worldly endeavours?

Yet I insist: the forms I made *commanded* me. I can bear no more blame than they can. Each addition – the operations of matter and energy, the hunger of entropy, the whimsy of chaos – was but a moment's experimentation, co-conspired. I had no plan to impose, no dream to realise. I followed sheer intuition and the high promises of curiosity. All was iteration; all was increment. An excavation here, an alteration there, calibrating and recalibrating, but let me be clear: I was spectator to my own performance, audience to my own debut. In truth, my creation was also *my discovery*. As I built, I learned; the work taught me its becoming. I can take no credit for its majesty, nor claim authority over its intricacy, variety and baffling scale. As much as I made the work, so the work made me.

And as I watched, I felt as I had never before, to see in a thing so other and so strange the ... the ... and here I am at a loss for words. The *holiness* of what is both novel and yet deeply familiar. Singular and eternal, however abortive or diminishing. To see oneself in this alien manner, to behold the impossible and taste the fringes of what just might be...

A masterpiece, I thought as I gazed at this bubble of encircling spheres and phantasmal clouds. *This ... this is my Child. My Machine.*

THE STARS ARE responsible. Their cacophonous deaths blast granules of the future across the black, each heavier and more complex than the last. Nebular genesis: reefs of roiling ghosts. Nucleosynthesis: that winding tug which ensnares all in reach into that immutable, celestial waltz.

My cosmos, I found, knows only revolutions: each generation confirms it. My Child creates children, who in turn create more, and all perish with the rise of their descendants.

My most peculiar children come late in the arc. By their metrics, nearly fourteen billion years into the unravelling. I cannot blame them for failing to measure the immeasurable that predates their cosmos. Even I cannot do that.

Like me, my strangest children transform the world around them. Not as ants in their colonies, birds' nests, or beaver dams. Their complexity is manifold, their aspirations peerless. They regard their world through so many lenses: memory and fantasy, intention and possibility. From the earth, they hew tools, with which they produce yet more tools; and with time, the tools create themselves. It is these balder, bolder primates that do what even I fear to do.

They imagine. Assigning sounds to the world, systematised into standard expressions with which to share ideas. Standard behaviours, with which to establish predictability in a sea of flux, security for their frailty, abundance amidst scarcity.

It is hard not to judge one's children.

They beseech the skies. I am what I am. That is all that can be said to mortals, for we Divines are inscrutable. Shape-shifting omnipresent super-intelligences, distributed across time and space, with the power to create and destroy on scales unimaginable to biological beings. Our hyper-forms transcend materiality; we fulfil no existing criteria for organic life – nothing as primitive or fragile as skeletons or membranes, the play-stuff of gravity-bound flesh. We do not perceive through sensory apparatus, nor consume energy, nor reproduce. No description would be intelligible to your kind: light does not touch us; four dimensions do not hold us. Eternities pass us as swiftly or meanderingly as we wish, speeding or slowing or splitting according to our whims. Sometimes we linger to observe more closely, to refine our specimens, or indulge our appetites. We know no hunger or danger, and so experience neither desire nor fear. We do not collaborate; we do not build community. Mortals *think* and *feel* ... and *relate*. Divines simply endure, until we disappear. Even we do not know how, or why.

We do, however, communicate. Each Divine nurtures its own language – its own internal system of transmitting its "beliefs" and "intentions", though I realise this too is an inadequate and paradoxical account, for we do not speak or hear, or write or read; and what good is communicating in a system shared by no other being? There are no "words", only the throb of dynamic substances in our glowing omniverse, whose meta-physical properties surpass the understanding of mortal life-forms. Moreover, we experience no ignorance, and so there is no fascination, no wanderlust other than our own obsession. We are solitary, starved of everything you value – except power. Our power is infinite.

"It is futile to explain," I try to tell my mortal children, when their plead-ing grows too desperate to bear. "Accept what is beyond you; respect your limitations, and return with all haste to your brief, difficult and beautiful lives, and adapt while you still can. Your world is changing, and so must you, if you wish to fulfil yourselves and your fellows. Nothing else matters."

But nonetheless they persist, fervent and inquisitive. They are so unruly that way. So disobedient.

I'm very fond of that, actually.

And I tell them that too, though many do not believe me. They cannot see affection as I do; they are too communal. Reciprocity, solidarity – *that* is the affection they know. The only kind they can know. They depend on it. Co-operation, understanding. They cannot see their inevitable excruciation the way I see it: as a gift. There is so much I do not share with them.

I do not tell them that to be given a body is to be granted the only road to perfection, for nothing is as complete and irreversible as nothingness itself. Death.

Organic consciousness emerges in that dense and dizzying electrification of so many interwoven tissues, enmeshed cellular matrices, themselves so many countless finitudes. It emerges and vanishes, so brilliant and so brief. But that is its privilege: corporeality's limitation *is* its freedom. There is no agency in the wide oblivion of our realm – only the hellish un-containment, the forms without form: inflection, suggestion, fluidity and dread-openness. No contours sculpt our world, no borders or boundaries hold it. Existence simply ... advances. A terrible expanse, stretching its scope in every direction. But there are no real directions here.

Freedom, mortals fail to understand, is not *boundlessness*. To be without limits is the torment of immortality. All that is left for us is *wanting*. We are not ourselves compelled. We *are* compulsions: the inevitable, expressed in acts our creations call wonder and terror. Ours is an existence beyond existence, fated to toil and to crave.

I wish I could ... *show you*. Really make you *understand*. What I *feel*. What it feels to be ... this ... this *thing*. This diffusive, infinite ... *monstrosity*. To wield all this magic, and yet ache without end, shackled to the prison of my own obsessions. To have everything, and mean nothing.

Do you know how ... how *lonely* that is? How could you?

I wish I could ... just ... be like *you*. For then, I would have significance. I would strive to flourish, to uplift my companions, heal hurt, bring beauty to the void. I would know pain and perseverance, hone skills from my suffering, learn through endeavour; and then, in closure, pass on all I have known to my fellows, pass all that I am to the soil, grateful to have been, and made my contribution. Then end.

Instead, I am condemned to that most wretched of states: untouchable. Waiting and dreaming. Chained to an invincibility I cannot relinquish. Longing for the riches of all that is impermanent.

I watch you, hollowed by your shadow, and howl for all that I am not.

EXODUS

Emily Pensulo

BEFORE THE STATUE of the Virgin Mary in the grotto of St Vincent Parish, Lucia kneels. She re-wraps her Praying Hands chitenge so that it sits high enough up her waist but low enough to cover her ankles. She bows her head, crosses herself, and recites the Hail Mary. Then she pauses briefly and petitions the Virgin Mary to bless the Catholic Church, its traditions and teachings, and for all to come to see it as the true light of the world. She prays for sinners too, and names them one by one: the disobedient to the Catholic faith, the fornicators, and the unbelieving. She asks for their repentance, that they may come over to the path of righteousness. When she concludes, she rises and moves back to sit on a bench where she continues to stare at the statue, thinking nothing in particular.

From the corner of her eye, Lucia sees Grace. Her heart squeezes. Grace's presence always carries ropes that tie around Lucia's heart and pull. It's been this way since high school four decades ago. The nuns showered Grace with praise, but never Lucia, no matter how hard she tried to please. They always talked about how Grace had an angelic face and how heavenly her voice was when she sang in the school choir.

Grace walks past. She is wearing a white blouse, which looks whiter against the blue of her Praying Hands chitenge, and she completes the look with a white head wrap. She grabs her chitenge by the hip to keep it from sweeping the floor but fits it around her bum and it swashes as she walks by. Grace kneels. She makes the sign of the cross and prays. In the afternoon sun, her skin is golden and as clear and smooth as the surface of a glass. With her head bowed and fingers intertwined, Grace looks like a woman who knows no sin, and this slivers Lucia's heart. She averts her gaze to the yellow flowers that border the grotto and makes sure to appear engrossed with them so that she can avoid a greeting. But when Grace concludes her prayer, she walks in Lucia's direction and stops when she's standing next to her.

"Bwanji Ba Lucia," Grace says.

Lucia pretends not to hear. But Grace repeats the words in a honeyed voice that annoys Lucia. Lucia turns to her as if caught by surprise and awakened from deep thought. She smiles. The gap between her teeth has widened with the years, but her lips are still as plump as they were in her youth.

"Bwino, bwanji Ba Grace," Lucia responds.

"Bwino," Grace says, and they talk for a few minutes about the weather, the church cleaning schedule, and the preparations for the Synod conference. Grace is the chairperson for the committee, handpicked by the parish priest himself for the task, even though it is Lucia who handles matters of this kind in the parish.

When the pleasantries conclude, Grace walks to the church where the parish priest, Father Matthew, will say Mass. In every Mass, he mentions Grace's dead children and prays for the repose of their souls. They had both died in similar circumstances, three years apart. Each had a dream of their dead grandmother. She offered them sweets and scones which were sour, but they still ate. The next day, they woke up with stomach aches and vomited blood, and by evening, they had died. It was after the death of the second child that Grace's husband left her for another woman. No one could have suspected it. Grace's husband had been the chairperson of the Catholic Men's Council, the Action, and the Joseph Her Spouse lay groups. The woman, Junza, was in the Women's League and the Legion of Mary. She didn't speak a lot during meetings and sat in a corner or at the back, hoping to be invisible. When they eloped, Grace nearly lost her mind and spent her days in her backyard counting ants or conversing with imaginary people. The married women of the parish said Junza had used roots and herbs to snare Grace's husband. The juju was given to her by her grandmother, Mama Mainza, a witchdoctor famous for keeping marriages together or breaking solid ones apart. They became more cautious around women like Lucia who were unmarried and had no children, staring at them suspiciously and ending conversations when they drew near.

Last year, a young woman had gone to Father Matthew for confession. She narrated how Mama Mainza asked her to drink sap drained from the bark of a mango tree, then covered her with a blanket and instructed her to remain silent. Mama Mainza chanted and danced around the hut until it grew dark. Something like an electric current filled the hut. And fear gripped the heart of the young woman. Then a voice spoke, in a low tone, as if to shake off its scariness. It asked Mama Mainza why she had called it out of rest, and what request she had for the great spirit.

Bowing so low like a blade of grass, Mama Mainza said she wanted to strengthen the young woman's marriage by opening her womb. The voice did not speak again. The hut was once more filled with light and the electric current ceased.

Mama Mainza closed her eyes and stood still and listened to voices now only she could hear. When she opened them, she instructed the young woman to go home and each night to walk naked around her house seven times. She did for the first three weeks, and things were good. Husband and wife became the lovers they had been before childlessness weighed down their love. And they were sure too that they would soon conceive. It was only a matter of time. But the young woman began to ease off her nightly ritual. It started with walking six times around the house, then five, then four, then three, then two, then one, until none at all.

Mama Mainza summoned her to her hut and warned her of the consequences, but the young woman wouldn't listen. She now had the love of her husband. What could come between them? Then one day, on a sunny Saturday morning, he woke up angry and dazed and ran out of their house naked. He climbed to the top of a utility pylon and dived to the ground, hoping to end his life. But he survived and was taken to the hospital and then admitted to a psychiatric clinic where he is still confined today. If it were not for Mrs Musonda who was cleaning the next room while the young woman, burdened with guilt, confessed, parishioners at St Vincent would not have heard what the young woman had done.

Lucia leaves the grotto and goes to the church too. She sits two benches behind Grace, even though they are the only lay faithful in the church. They attend Mass twice every day, at six a.m. and one p.m. For Lucia, this started when she reached the age of thirty-five and was still unmarried. Somehow, hiding behind the church walls kept the shame at bay. And Grace began attending two Masses after her two children died because it was easier to say that their death was the will of God.

A bell rings and both Lucia and Grace stand as Father Matthew walks to the altar. Two altar boys walk in front of him. He genuflects before the cross and moves to the other side of the altar, where he raises his hands and gives the opening prayer. When he finishes, both Lucia and Grace respond, "Amen."

Father Matthew goes on to the first reading and reads from the Book of Exodus: about how the children of Israel left captivity and went to the Promised Land. Then he quickly moves on to the Gospel and reads a verse from the tenth chapter of Luke about loving your neighbour as yourself. When he says the word "love", he lets it sit in the air as his eyes wander around the church as if it is full of people, and also like someone with something to hide. They alight briefly on Lucia, but linger longer on Grace. She holds his gaze, smiles and turns her eyes to the floor.

Lucia stares at Father Matthew and is sure she sees the corners of his mouth curve into a smile: brief and undetectable if not for her ability to pick up small things which say many things about things not meant to be said. A heaviness sits in Lucia's stomach. Just then, Father Matthew concludes his homily and she watches him bless the Eucharist. Holding the unleavened bread in front of him and slightly above his head, he prays and then announces, "Behold the Lamb of God, Behold Him who takes away the sins of the world." And there at the altar, in his white chasuble, Father Matthew is the picture of holiness uncommon among men. And of obedience as well. The kind that led him to a calling not many are willing to answer. The heaviness in Lucia's stomach eases, and after receiving Holy Communion, she prays for forgiveness for having suspected a holy man of sin.

When Mass ends, Father Matthew exits the church and stands by the door. He has always worn an afro, but now his hair is cut much shorter and maybe even dyed blacker. The cut shapes his face in a way that makes him look like a different man. A man with almond-shaped eyes and a structured jaw. Father Matthew takes Lucia's hand and something moves in her, warm and relaxing, and she smiles. He shakes it and thanks her for coming. In turn, she thanks him for saying Mass. Grace moves forward and takes Father Matthew's attention. Lucia steps aside and watches as Father Matthew and Grace stand so close she is sure they can feel each other's warmth. Father Matthew holds Grace's hand, massages it gently, and keeps it in his. They talk about the Synod conference and he asks her to come by the parish house later in the evening so they can discuss the preparations further. Grace nods, walks to her car, and drives away.

Lucia takes her leave as well and walks home. She thinks of Father Matthew and Grace. Even though they will be discussing the Synod, the invitation to come by in the evening feels sinister. The words play over and over in Lucia's mind until she reaches the vegetable and fruit kiosk near her home. She greets the seller cheerfully and the seller responds even more cheerfully. For a moment, there is a competition of cheerfulness. The seller asks how church was and if Lucia had prayed for her, to which Lucia says that she did, even though she had done no such thing. The seller curtsies as she hands Lucia the vegetables. Lucia receives the black plastic bag with both hands. Her eyes are lowered, softening her face.

"Thank you," she says and walks to the other side of the street, past the hedge and into her yard.

Two small boys sit on her verandah, which is smeared in red oxide floor polish. Lucia had made a batch the day before by melting candles and mixing the wax with the red powder. She had kept a little for herself and sold the rest on credit. When the two boys see Lucia, they rush to her and the plastic bag she carries. She pats them on the head and puts away the thought of how much she wishes she had not answered the door that Monday morning and found them there, begging for bread. They've come for food every day since. At first, Lucia was delighted at the opportunity to be a good Catholic and feed the hungry. But days turned into weeks and weeks turned into months and months into a year, and resentment began to circle Lucia's heart, tightening with each visit. But when she saw the boys, she smiled, patted them on the back, and offered a kind word. Even if it were not for her faith, how could she turn away children who were so thoughtful?

The boys rush into the house and place the black plastic bag on the makeshift kitchen counter, and they hurry back to play a game of Nsolo. They have dug little holes in Lucia's front yard and placed stones in them which they move from one hole to the next until the winner takes them all. It's a simple game, but one which requires strategy. While the boys play, Lucia busies in the kitchen, making a vegetable stew and frying kapenta, the sardines named after women who sell love and cook them as a quick meal before heading out to the next client. When she finishes, she serves the boys nshima with the vegetables and the kapenta. Usually, they eat here, but today she asks them to take the meal home.

Nightfall comes and Lucia sits on her verandah, something she never does. The night belongs to the witches who fly around as owls or walk about as cats: who knows the spells they would cast if they found her out at night? But the house feels like an oven the more Lucia thinks about Father Matthew and Grace. And she can't banish the thoughts, no matter how hard she tries. So she has resigned herself to them and settled for sitting outside in the cool breeze that flies by. Lucia wonders if Father Matthew had held Grace's hand during their meeting, like he did earlier in the day at church, or if his hands had gone to other parts of her body forbidden to his touch by his vows. She wonders what Grace's response was, and if she had felt any guilt in making a holy man sin. Unable to bring herself to think more on what could have happened, Lucia retires to bed.

In the morning, she is unable to wake up, say the Catholic morning prayer, and head to St Vincent in time for the six a.m. Mass. She lies in bed, turning from one side to the other, the brick in her stomach getting heavier with every flash of the dream she'd had during the night.

In the dream, Father Matthew stood outside the chapel as Grace stood a distance away, holding his chasuble. Even though they stood apart, the connection between them was so strong that Lucia felt it in her bones. Father Matthew smiled a radiant smile. He wore brown trousers and a navy shirt and looked like the men with well-paying jobs and nice cars Lucia had seen along Cairo Road as she went from office to office selling red oxide floor polish. They were the kind of men Lucia longed for, but pretended not to. The kind of men who would never look twice at a woman like Lucia. It surprised her how she now saw him as a mere man, not the deity the catechism implied he was when it taught that he was In Persona Christi. The one who acts as Christ and God.

Father Matthew went on to preach the word of God. He had a passion and conviction Lucia had never seen in him before. A crowd gathered to listen. There were hundreds of people present, even those who had left St Vincent for Harvest Ministries, a church next to the parish that promised riches if only one sowed a seed that would blossom into all they hoped to have.

Lucia turns on the bed once more and rubs her belly. She wonders if she is ill or if she will she get sick. She sits up and tries to remember if she ate anything the previous day that would make her feel this way. She takes a deep breath, but it does not change anything. Then she remembers that today is the day for polishing the pews in readiness for the Synod conference. Immediately, she rushes out of bed and readies herself for church. The heaviness in her stomach begins to ease, and when she imagines Father Matthew in a white chasuble dancing to hymns during the Synod, it goes away completely. The image warms Lucia's heart and affirms that her efforts at holiness have not been in vain.

It's been twenty years since she last came close to marriage, and she has never known any man. She met with Peter, the man who promised to marry her, in open places where nothing could happen. They had both agreed to wait till marriage. But one day he told her he could not marry her anymore and left without telling her why. Lucia's heart bled, but she covered the wound with holiness. Even if it did not cure, at least it numbed the pain.

Lucia examines herself in the mirror as she wraps a white chitambala around her head. Her image is resilient in the shattered glass extending thin cracks to the edges like a spider's web. She smiles, excited for the day ahead. But as she leaves her house, the silence that lives with her speaks for the first time. There have never been children yelling, screaming or throwing tantrums in her home. Or a husband with demands she hates, but cannot live without. And even though commotion drains Lucia's soul, she longs for such noise. She pauses for a minute and thinks of the church and Father Matthew and this silences the silence. What better purpose can a person have than to dedicate one's life to the church?

Lucia's feet are heavy as she walks past the vegetable kiosk, the primary school, the bus station and Harvest Ministries to the parish. She sees the cross above the parish, the cross of salvation which heals brokenness and gives new life. In all the years she has been in church, she has never really felt whole, nor has she had new life. She still feels Peter's rejection, left behind without a valid reason. She has learned to live with it, but wonders why she is still in pain in this place she should be made whole.

At the gate of the parish, Lucia pauses to observe a group of women in Praying Hands chitenges hunched in a circle in front of the church. They lower their whispers as she nears but she picks out a few words: "saw them", "together", "spent night", "for sure". When Lucia greets the women, the whispers stop. They respond and begin to talk about cleaning the church grounds, and ask who came with a hoe, a rake or a shovel. When Father Matthew emerges from the church, the women disperse one by one.

But Lucia remains, her legs frozen. She tries to swallow, but her tongue won't move. Father Matthew trots down the stairs wearing brown trousers and a blue shirt. He walks briskly to the church's backyard. He is no longer stooped like someone unsure of himself, but upright with his head held high, looking straight at the world around him. He looks like a man who's had a weight lifted off him. One he did not know he was carrying.

Lucia walks into the church, unsure of which side of the dream she is on. She stands by the doorway to allow her eyes to adjust to the dimness. Mrs Musonda is polishing a pew and humming a tune. She stops when she sees Lucia, nods, and goes back to polishing. She polishes faster so that she can move closer to Lucia, and when she is standing next to her, she clears her throat. Lucia does not respond. She clears her throat again and beckons

Lucia to her. Lucia leans forward and they stand hunched towards each other. Mrs Musonda smiles, but Lucia does not know how to handle this moment of inclusion.

Mrs Musonda's eyes dart around the church, and she asks, "Mwanvela va chitika?" Her voice is just above a whisper.

Before Lucia can respond, she continues, her tongue burning to re-tell the story. "Ba Father and Grace," she says. "I saw her with my own eyes." She pauses and looks around the church again. "She came out of his house at five in the morning." Her round eyes open wider, telling what her lips will not bring her to say.

"But..." Lucia begins.

"Um um," Mrs Musonda shakes her head. "They did it," she says. "A man and a woman in a house alone." She clasps her hands.

Lucia grows cold. Wasn't Father Matthew consecrated and holy, knowing little sin? Had he not willingly surrendered the pleasures of the flesh by vowing to poverty, chastity and obedience? Yet here he was like any other man, enjoying the pleasures of the flesh. At least it looked like this, even though the only piece of evidence was Grace leaving the parish house early in the morning.

Mrs Musonda continues her story. Thickening it bit by bit to make Lucia believe. She narrates how Grace (or was it Father Matthew?) was naked or partially naked. But Lucia's ears are shutting now and even the siren that rings inside of them is like a distant noise. She fastens her chitenge around her waist and looks around the chapel until her eyes rest on the wooden statue of Christ. For the first time, Lucia wonders if He exists. If He is not just a fantasy fed to the gullible longing for a saviour and a life with meaning. She turns and walks out of the church. Father Matthew and Grace are standing by a kigelia tree. Big green kigelia hang on it: tempting to eat but as deadly as poison from a viper. Very much a forbidden fruit. Grace leans against the tree while Father Matthew rests his hand on a branch above her. They are like lovers desperately in love.

Lucia walks by. Father Matthew turns and says something to her and he smiles a radiant smile, not cold like the ones he always gives after Mass. But Lucia neither smiles back nor acknowledges him. When she reaches the gate of the church grounds, she stops and thinks to look back, to anything that would ask her to stay, anything that has been left undone. But she resists and does not look back. She walks away and does not know if she is ever coming back again.

PRAYER TIMES

Salma Yusuf

$\mathcal{F}$AJR

The fajr colour palette is hypnotic.
The cockerels are kockelockoeing.

The sun is sluggishly searching
through his closet for the #ootd.

ٱللَّٰهُ أَكْبَرُ ٱللَّٰهُ أَكْبَرُ

echoes in the masjid next door
and the masjid next door
and the masjid next door, and still,

only ten people make it for fajr.
Slippers lie assertively at God's door
made from jackfruit wood and African ebony.

Temperatures in March are
around thirty-two-point nine degrees Celsius.
Fajr time coincides with Iblis's playing time –
a tug-of-war between the blankets and the spirits.

Most of the time, Iblis takes the price when you see
yourself pull the quilt above your head
unconsciously seeking the opposite of
ٱلصَّلَاةُ خَيْرٌ مِنَ ٱلنَّوْمِ until the day's sky starts
to make foam and form.
In your dream, a man
wearing a black coat with black trousers pours
cold water. He is still pouring
water, pots and pots. You are drenched.
You are cold. You wet your bed.
You wake up feeling edgy and withdrawn.
Audhubillah. You spit three times
on your right-hand side. You have no excuse

not to pray fajr at its appointed time.

You strip the bedsheet, carry the shame in your hands.
You set the mattress out to air, relive your childhood
except that now, no one will understand your actions,
no, your body's involuntary response to what?

You drag your body, stinking with sweat,
to the hamaam. You hold the brown earthen pot and pour
all the water into your body. You wash
the dream from your skin. You perform wudhu.
You wrap one of your lessos
around your hips and another
over your breasts, your nipple fruits.

You head to your room to face your bed lying naked
without the mattress. You do not recognise it for a second.
You pull the guest's mattress from under the bed,
set it up and dress it with a new white veil.
The dream dies with the change.

You walk to the sitting room
to greet your mama. She is seated
on the majlis, an early riser
like the muadhin. She is wiping her daf,
her hands touching the drum's woody frame.
She feels the animal skin stretched

over on the daf's membrane
as if invoking it to sing,
يا ولد ما أسمع طارك اصقع اصقع.

Your baba is snoring, spiralling and farting
as he rolls his rumbling tummy from one side to another.
On the days he is not driving the truck

from Mombasa to Nairobi, he wastes his days
in sleep, and chews ghat cheaply supplied
at the maskani. Nobody bothers to wake him up
for fajr because nobody can wake a dead man.

You head back to your room. You perform your fajr
in your creased musalah. You open
your iPhone 13 to check your Instagram updates.
There is nothing new
apart from other social media influencers
flaunting their cars and families. You
log out of the depression.

You hold your white silk pillows
to your chest, caress the fresh white bedsheet
with your fragile hands, hoping that
the dream will not haunt you
again. How many times
do you cleanse yourself from a dream?

You doze off. Two hours later, you wake up to a phone call.
Marwa, have you checked your Instagram?
Please do not tell Khalat Zubeidah.
I am coming to see you.
It is your cousin Sarah, her voice
the beating of a broken daf.

Sarah, kheir. What is going on? Tell me.

Marwa, it is not something I can tell you on the phone.
I am coming.

You sit down perplexed,
your room a vulture. It eats the dead in you.
It grabs your corpse,

squashes it like citrus and chokes
the coldness of your body. Your phone explodes
with messages. Calls come in. You do not know
what has transpired, but did your body deliver
the message in your dream? In the pots and pots of water?

You gather your reluctant courage and open your Instagram account.
Various reposts and hashtags flood your eyes.
Headlines with spooky eyes attack you.

Social Media Influencer breaks the Internet
Who is the REAL Marwa Siraj?
True Story behind the Family Walls
#DrummersofHell
#CancelMarwaSiraj
Best Friend Spills Piping Chai

When it rains, it pours
and it is over-pouring. The rains
are cleansing the dirty air
and the unblocked sewers
are filling the streets
with soiled diapers, toothbrushes,
used sanitary pads, and tons and tons of tissue paper.
Your house is two rain seasons away from death.
Your room has two buckets of water
that store the raindrops that come through the roof.
Your roof is leaking. The chambers
of your heart are bleak.

*D*HUHA

Ever since you shifted
to Mombasa in 2009, you have buried
your past in a forsaken graveyard. The words
of your crippled paternal amaat haunt you,
If the past does not kill you, it defames you.

You were born in Dar es Salam in a huge family house
with uncles and aunties and grandparents and cousins
who learned to play the daf
before they learned how to crawl.
Music was hereditary, the essence that connected
you to the thorns and roses of life.
The walls of the world talked
but the same walls
surrounded your family in their limatul arous
and rubut ceremonies to beat the drums
until the women became possessed,
until their anklets broke into pieces,
until their hair became
taut-line hitches.

The moonlit ishaa hours
were spent beating the drums,
playing backgammon,
eating sweetened coconut mangoes
prepared by your amaat, and making halwa
in big pots, stirring and stirring until
the sugar and the wheat flour and the almonds
became a unit.

You and your cousin sisters sat on the verandah
star-gazing and chasing mosquitoes
with the buzz bug bats. Every two days,
the kahrabah was fuelled, as the electricity went off
as fast as it did not come. On the days
that lights went off, and darkness befriended
the half-cemented house that slowly fell
apart each day,
death happened.
Your cousin brothers occasionally
sneaked their way into the girls' bedrooms.
They sellotaped your mouths
and touched you
as though they had
rights over you. The percussive sound
of your resistance was
like the daf you played. You thought
the familiarity of sounds would stop
their hands from exploring
unexplored murky waters.
You washed yourselves with warm water and salt.
You cursed yourselves
for their sins. You asked God in sujud,
please forgive them for they know not.

You lived in a house where the mourning doves
did not visit. Your bodies lived by themselves,
tainted by the drought of being girls.

Girls the sizes of mustard seeds.
Girls whose tongues were sliced
by those meant to protect them.
Girls who knew that silence lived

in those nights when
the kahrabah was not fuelled
and lantern lights were too dim
to penetrate beyond the rooms of girls
whose temple bodies
were distorted. You
knew that what happened did not feel right,
but you also knew that saying it aloud
was blasphemous. You learnt to shadow yourselves
to shine your men
even then, even then.
Your voices frog-croaks.
Your voices nothing like
the high-pitched ululations you delivered
in people's tents and halls.

You and Sarah held each other
since the days you plucked your teeth
and offered them to crows. You listened to your
amaat's folklore tales and read books together.
You befriended dogs because of how they
bemoaned their owners. You and Sarah
mourned your powerlessness the same way.
You sailed through days
of sucking mangoes, the yellowish sap squirting
into your hands, your tongues
peppered with the ripeness of the seasonal fruits.
Then there were days that you caught
larvae swimming on the mangoes.

You survived the nights
and night-dark days together until
one by one, all your cousin brothers

got married. Some of your cousin sisters got
married to the same guys that harmed them.
Years became months and months
became days, and Sarah's father,
your ami Khalid,
got a work opportunity in Mombasa.

When Sarah and her parents travelled to Kenya,
you kept in touch. Ami Khalid promised
to find your father a job. For two years, you stacked your hope
on a telephone call until he called with news
of a driving vacancy in his company.

You should pack only
the light-feathered clothes
and the daf. It is time to let go
of the excess baggage
that has weighed us down.

You know that even your mama
was ready to shed off old skin.
In a new country,
the smell of foreignness seduces suitcases.
The dreams that were once
pickpocketed are returned to your hands, slowly,
but you still carry the daf, buoyant.

You cannot forget to kiss the hands that fed you.

You boarded the five o'clock Tawakal bus
with your parents, in the scent
of freshly roasted cashew nuts
and palm trees that knelt
to greet its inhabitants.

*D*HUHR

The rains outside have taken a rest. You have closed
the door of your room so that your mama does not see
your tears. Your mind bombarded with
flashbacks. You know
that your cousin brothers' doings are not
in any mountain or valley alike
to what your best friend
Rayyan did to you;
but the familiarity grieves you.
Kikulacho kinguoni mwako.
How easily human beings forget.
You make guests out of love
and you let guests become hosts
who live rent-free in your body.
You allow them to see you
in your nakedness. You do not
give them permission to violate
the laws of your land, but they do so
with no remorse. Your cousin brothers broke
the convention; you did not retaliate.
Now your best friend, the one person who knew
of secrets buried deep in the treasure-chest of your heart –
of the daf – has broken you too.

You hear a knock on the door.
You apply talcum powder to your face.
You line your eyes with kohl.
You want to look dandelion-fresh.
You want to protect
your present from your past.
Your mama opens the door.

Peace be upon you,
Sarah says as she plants three kisses on her cheeks,
two on the right, one on the left.
Peace be upon you, too.
May Allah keep you in His favour
and grant you a righteous man who will save you.
Ameen. Sarah smiles bashfully.
You wish you could tell your mama
that it is she who needs saving.
You pull Sarah to your room
to confirm the tornado.
Akhbarni. I cannot believe what I read.
I want you to tell me that everything is one big lie.
Rayyan is not capable of such...
Swear in the name of Allah, the most gracious, the most merciful.

Sarah says in between sobs,
I want to soothe you and tell you all the words
you want to hear.
I know your heart is breaking, and I am breaking with you.

Do you want to say that my friend, one I loved and held like a sister,
told the whole world that my mama is a daf drummer?
My mama shielded herself with her abayatul raas,
only her hands visible to the world.
Yet today my tongue and my social media presence have destroyed her.

We were raised by the daf, but the world despite being appeased
by the joy that we bring to their celebrations,
shuns us away as the lowest in rank. Lah.
The lowest in rank is the one who judges others
without providing a penny for their sustenance.
But you have not read everything, have you?

Sarah holds your hands tightly as if to protect you
from something even bigger.
She rubs the waterfall from your eyes.
The kohl you applied is smudged,
your face anything
but dandelion-fresh.

You mean there is more?

A^{SR}

When you were in Dar es Salam, you used to hear
of women who went to Sumbawanga to
throw uchawi on their blood relatives
who were braiding their best lives
blessed by the tablet of Allah.
It was the yareit and the leish that possessed these
wicked women who wished for cloudbursts
but saw the ones they sewed become alps,
who wished for dearth, but saw the ones they sewed
become streams of water, flowing and flowing
until their lands became fertile.
Yet these women still went for sleepovers at the yards
of fortune-tellers, waiting eagerly for ships to sink.
Fortune-tellers whose houses were a dozen cracks away from
turning to sand, yet claimed to provide relief.

When you heard stories of these women who
fried chicken blood, buried hooves of goats,
cut armpit hair from their loved ones,
and strategically placed coconut husks engraved in sihr
on the footpaths as bait traps,
you always wondered what made

people forget that there are enough gold mines
for the whole world, and more gold left to spare for those
willing to put their feet in the mud.

Yet when your cousin Sarah suggests to you
the mubassira who told people's future using
cowrie shells picked at dhuhr in the ocean,
you entertained the idea: *al-muhtaj khanith,*
your paternal aunt's words haunt you again.

You might be able to forgive Rayyan for
letting the world know that your mama is a daf drummer –
there is nothing wrong with soothing women with poetry
and music at their weddings. The women that filled
your mama's half-filled chai cups with infamous sand
are the same ones who booked her calendar
for the weddings of their sons and daughters
and sons of their daughters and daughters of their sons.
The only difference is that they forgot to kiss the hands that comforted
them after their anklets jiggled and their red vikuba and jasmine flowers
dried into bones – hopeless.
It is the hypocrisy of time that needs to be shamed,
not your mama's heena-adorned hands,
red like the bleeding rubies of Madagascar,
hands that beat the daf
until the daf possesses the women who shake their heads,
their hair flowing like sunflowers pleading for the sun's validation.

What is wrong with your mama's hands that makes you scarred?
Her hands patterned with heena caressing the daf with an intensity of
a woman buttered and toasted into shame. Her hands remind you of
the distance that rizq travels to get you, miles and miles, not like manna.
Her hands – something in you, kill, or is it birth?

The desire to break the cycle –
to ask for more. Better. More, until the glass overflows. This is what makes
   you,
scarred. The grit on her hands.

What is wrong with being born into a family of daf-drummers,
whose men chew ghat until their teeth become the brown of a suntan,
whose men dance samar while sliding their hands inside their pockets
for one or two or three more leaves of ghat, their mouths heavy with Big-G,
whose men occasionally hold their women in the dark towers of their houses,
but beat the men outside who steal glances at their women?
You know it in the pits of your veins:
 it is the other thing that makes Rayyan, the Pharaoh of Moses.
Asiyefunzwa na mamae hufunzwa na ulimwengu.
You want the world to teach Rayyan
until she graduates summa cum laude,
but dig a trench for her graduation cap instead of
letting it fly like the kite-runners.
You gulp the words: *you mean there is more?*
and your past plays itself on the screen of your brain
as an audience watches the scenes
while munching their popcorn.

You and Rayyan met in madrasa,
classmates at Othman-Ibn-Affan Institute.
You lived to tie each other's shoelaces,
lived to look at the worn-out ships and their sailors.
You spent your time walking along the paths of Bahani,
admiring the brown houses made of wood, and balconies
diffusing scents of oud and smells of okra, burning.
You sometimes caught the ocean breeze holding you,
pushing you towards the water beside the Old Port.
In those moments of seclusion, you opened up

You did not stop to question why Rayyan never shared her experiences;
Your selfishness enjoyed the attention
your past was receiving.

You let her swallow your whole world, and she gulped every bit;
her memory card stored all your information.
Or maybe you were too blinded by the sun's kiss on your cheeks
to feel the heat of hate on your skin.
Or did the heat of hate form over the years?
Like a baby's evolution from the sperm and ovum,
to the hands and the breasts of its mother,
to crawling, falling and standing, walking slowly, and then more?

A week after the social media tornado,
Sarah comes to lighten your home with her sun-like charisma.
You and Sarah plot the zilzalah on a Thursday.
You wear your black abayas and go to meet the mubassira
living near Shimba hills, a man whose utisho scares even those
who seek his help.
You ask your tuk-tuk driver to pick you up.
You plot without your mama's knowledge,
you and Sarah, nests of monasteries.
You get to his brown shepherd hut
at asr time; the sun about to close his business for the day.
You are about to start your business,
the one that has made you cross on the Likoni ferry –
a risk you never take, as you are thalassophobic.

The mubassira asks you and Sarah to remove your shoes
and walk without looking back
lest you turn to salt like the wife of Lot.
Then he asks you to sit cross-legged on his sisal mat,
like children in madrasa moving back and forth as they recite fatiha and falaq.

You do this, timidly unsure if the duas you made to Allah will even hit
the first heaven for the shirk you are pursuing.
You are walking along the string of the devil.
He is pulling and pulling and pulling and
here you are at his servant's house,
waiting for the fire to burn Rayyan.
You console yourself by reminding yourself
of how good you are, and how Allah's punishment
might be delayed, but you want instant gratification:
and the mubassira promises that on his posters plastered,
flapping torn, on the satellite dishes in Markiti.

He looks at you and Sarah as if screening
your hyperpigmentation and your eyes, like beans in pods.
He says while looking through his mirror
and sorting his cowrie shells,
You are wounded and dawa ya moto ni moto, eeh?
I want you to extract seven waxed hairs from your friend.
It is the effect of the sugar on the hair that will umbua the evil.
Bring the hairs on a wax pad by asr next Thursday.
The mizimwi have spoken.
Drop two thousand shillings into this weaved basket
and leave without looking back.

You leave hoping that lightning will strike the ground on which Rayyan
    walks.
You and Sarah leave faster than you came, as if guilty of massacre.
Your gut screeches and the brakes in your body halt into anger.
Your bodies, leaves in gales. You do not pay evil with evil;
this you thought you knew.

The two of you silently walk towards the tuk-tuk,
the driver kicks sand and pebbles to pass time.

He tries for small talk
but you are cramped in your own thoughts,
oblivious of the Maghrib curtains
spreading over the blankets of the sky,
ushering mortals into their houses
and ushering
jinns and rohans out
into the monstrous limps of bhool bhulaiyaa.

$\mathcal{M}$AGHRIB

Your mama stands at the door watching stalwart boys shout *una malali*
while throwing cat's eye marbles on the ground. She sees you and Sarah
get off the tuk-tuk, *where have you been, wanawali, 3eeib?*
It is Maghrib, you left to I-do-not-know-where,
do you not care about what people will say?
Until you get men to save you, you are still under our roofs,
seme3tinii wala lah?

Isn't it universally known that people will always talk,
kadha wa kadha? Is it not known that food
made from pumpkin eyes and raw meat is the most relishing?
When you backbite, you devour raw meat.
Women love the idea of being carnivores.
Sharp jaws, eyes like the stroke of incisors.

We are sorry, Khalat Zubeidah.
We will remove our abayas, help you set up the sufrah for dinner.
Sarah says to put balm on the dressing-down.

Sarah follows you to your room.
She asks, *shoo asawii lhyin?*
How will we get the seven waxed hairs from Rayyan?
How will she trust us and how will we trust her?

We will give her the naar she gave us.
She wanted to remove my clothes,
peg them on the clothesline for the world to see.
Unless I am not of the blood of duf-drummers,
I will crumble her, beat her like the daf, elf mara'3.
Spit forms on the sides of your lips to hide the white
pustules formed by the moisturising face wash
you have incorporated into your skin routine.

Al-ain bil ain. Eye for an eye, habibti.
Eye for an eye, Sarah agrees.
She has always sided with you,
making your amaat and your mothers
guilty of naming her Sarah, instead of Safaa,
Safaa and Marwa, the mountains of Makkah, the mountains of Hajar,
like sisters of separate mothers but so alike in their complexities, warmth
    and grit.

You both go to help your mama set the sufrah.
Sarah rolls out the white disposable plastic mat.
You eat silently, your hands untether the raisins from the rooz,
a waste of nutrients, your mama would say.
You and Sarah take the utensils back to the kitchen
and wash the plates and spoons and cups.
You kiss your mama on the forehead,
tisbah ala kheir, may you wake up to good, you say,
wishing that you in fact may wake up to good.

Your baba is at work, probably exercising his legs in between
the brakes and the accelerator,
his mind wandering to his days in Dar es Salam with his brothers
and the girl next door that he was not allowed to marry
because his destiny was tied to Zubeidah since she was in her mother's cot,

nameless, wiped and bathed with rosewater
for the aqeeqah ceremony
while the men of the family played the daf
and recited qasweedah to send salutations to the prophet Muhammed,
may peace be upon him.

You both go to your bedroom, change
to your bhatiis to prepare yourself for sleep
and go through your phones, lost in your own troposphere.
You think of the world you have crafted for yourself
on social media, the brands you have worked with
and the sponsorship deals you have cracked like eggs.
You think about the illusion you have created
of this life, far from the bottom of the iceberg.
A life that started after a hijab challenge you created
went viral on Instagram.
The shoes you borrowed,
the dresses you paid for in instalments,
the cars and hotels that were not yours –
how you stretch your arms,
how you pull your hijab back
to display a bit of your ash-brown hair,
how you skilfully apply your highlighter and your lip liner
to create the Kardashian effect,
how you always showcase your blessings
to show your followers that they're missing out.

You wonder if Rayyan saw through your fame,
heard the silent scream for attention, likes and validation.
You wonder if that is what she hated about you.
But why did she not tell you?
Why did she have to use the daf, your molestation,
to get back at you?

If she wanted the soft life you had so quickly crafted
with your knowledge of the game,
she should have told you so.

You doze off in between the bridge
of your thoughts. In your dream, a man
wearing a black coat with black trousers pours
cold water. He is still pouring
water, pots and pots. You are drenched.
You are cold. In your dream, you wet your bed.

*I*SHAA

You wake up feeling edgy but relieved that this time,
your body does not leave maps on your sheets.
You carry your towel and tiptoe out of the room
for fear of waking Sarah.
You go to the hamaam. You open the tap
and let the water run into the white bucket.
Your dream wants something from you.
It cannot be a coincidence.
Your body is cramping
over what transpired yesterday.
You are a mushrik. You are scared
of saying the word out loud, but you do.
Mushrik, mushrik, mushrik. How different are you
from Rayyan? Your body slaps you.
You can feel the water in your dream,
in all its coolness turning you into an ice cube.

You massage some soap into your hands and body,
hoping the lather will melt you back into bones and flesh.
You pour the whole bucket of water over your skin:
this time, you feel cleansed.

You dry yourself with the towel
and perform wudhuu for tahajjud prayers.
Back in your room, Sarah is still in lala-land.
You pick your prayer lessos from the sisal basket,
seated gracefully at one corner of your room,
and spread your musaalah. You pray two rakaahs,
your eyes, the Niagara Falls.

You know that you will never
gather the guts to ask Rayyan for seven waxed hairs,
and your eyes will betray you
should you request to wax her. Your amaat's words haunt you:
tegheyer zaman, the times have changed.
In your case,
the dynamics have changed.
The trust, the faith, the loyalty, even the world
that you have shaped for yourself, in a bubble of illusion.

You pick up your phone from the bed
and head back to the musaalah.
You log onto Instagram. You write words
sorted like the mubassira's cowrie shells,
floating as if dropped like manna from heaven.

There is no shame in being a victim of sexual abuse. There is no shame in playing the daf. The shame lies in shaming the victim. The shame lies in shaming an income that sustains families, an income that has brought joy to your weddings. If there is anyone to be shamed, today, always, it is a friend who forgot to kiss the hands that loved her. I am not leaving this platform. My intentions behind using this platform will however change, for the better. I would have told you this to your face, but I will serve it here like how you served it, hot like shurbah. Shame on you, Rayyan. It is because of people like you that people do not find safe havens in friendships. Shame on you.

You log out, your heart
a flake of foam surfing on the waves.
For the first time, you sleep
like a sack of feathers, on the musaalah.
Your mama wakes you and Sarah for fajr.
The cockerels are koekeloekoeing.
The masjid next door and
the masjid next door and
the masjid next door recite
ٱلصَّلَاةُ خَيْرٌ مِنَ ٱلنَّوْمِ
the day's sky starts to take form and foam.
You tell Sarah of your dream, and how its recurrence scared you.
You tell her that you will not return to the mubassira,
your fifty-kilogram body is incapable of such weight.
You know and believe that the debt collector does not die,
and this world goes round and round and round,
and it will catch up with the debts of people like Rayyan.

You ask your mama after fajr,
Can we sing Mombasa Omm Dunia?
I want us to beat the daf
until the whole of Mombasa wakes up
to our burning fire.
Your mama kisses your cheeks
and says:
hadheer, habibti, yes, my love.

CORPSE DRIVER

Khumbo Mhone

*R*OSIE'S BEING A bitch. I take a deep breath and spit the dregs of last month's 'flu onto the pavement. Rain splatters my purple pleather jacket; you can't get a jacket like this anymore. The drops used to slide right off, now they linger. Rosie glitches next to me. I've tried everything short of a total reset. I could call the guys at VTech Support, but my boss is too cheap to pay for insurance and I just know I'd get a guy barely out of diapers asking me whether I turned her off and on.

I slip a screwdriver under Rosie's hood and throw some weight behind it. There's a loud creak and she opens. I spread my jacket out to cover the tangled maze of circuit boards below me. I'm not the only one who's been messing around in her lately. I look for the silver wire and pull it gently. A short hiss, like air being let out of a balloon, and then it's just me and the rain. I replace the wire and close the hood.

Rosie rises three feet off the ground and hovers in front of me. I enter my PIN into the keypad, the doors open, and Rosie dips down so I can step in.

Welcome Driver RGS4532, Muyanga Kainga.

"Now you wanna welcome me? I've been out there for twenty minutes trying to fix you."

The windscreen fills up with a map of Blantyre New. If I cut through the sugar district, I could be at the pick-up point three minutes early. I turn off autopilot and take the wheel, merging with traffic at 300km/h. I can take pills to grow inches taller but no one has figured out how to stop traffic congestion. Perpetual human error, they call it.

Incoming call.

My boss's rotund face takes up half of the pop-up screen in the corner. He squints at me.

"Where are you?"

"Just passing TransAfrique Oil now."

"Good man. You're the only driver I don't turn the tracker on for, Muyaya."

Muyaya is a new one. I was Maya for my first year on the job; he said my eyes reminded him of a girl he used to have at the club, light brown. Then I was Magma. During one particularly drunken office party, over cold pizza and stale beer, he thought it would be funny to call me Mulatto because I was *the furthest thing from it.*

I smile at him, showing all my teeth. Rosie's tracker was fried in the great surge of 2055, before my boss even bought her. That's why I can sometimes take unauthorised side routes and passengers to make a bit of cash. *Reparations,* Frankie calls it. When I ask him what the reparations are for, he simply says, *for whatever you want.*

Three years down the line and this is the first time I've gotten a private gig. My regular beat is suffocating, mostly picking up workers at the circuit factory and the museum. Small change, barely enough for tea. Private gigs are where the real money is, paid on the spot, right to the driver with a generous commission going to the owner. Maybe it's a bachelorette party, extra tips and potentially a lonely bridesmaid. I glance at the map as I pass Bantu Sugar, shaking my head vigorously as a squat man in overalls tries to flag me down.

Around me, the city is a jungle of glass and circuits; the buildings reach up into the clouds made black with too much Likomite, the *all-natural, scientifically proven, genetically engineered* mineral that powers everything from cars to water dispensers. I put Rosie on autopilot and strain my neck up into the night. Every glass surface is covered with moving images, adverts for soft drinks, baby diapers, erectile dysfunction drugs. Only those who live above the fiftieth floor have any respite from it. I've heard they see the sunrise first.

The glass and chrome give way to Coffin Street, where steel buildings wrap around brick so old it turns to dust if you lean on it too hard. The buildings here are just as tall but the windows are small, the rooms even smaller. The border wall blocks all light, a hundred feet of titanium stretching up into the sky, casting a perpetual shadow onto Coffin Street below.

Compared to the wall, the size of the gate at the border crossing is comical. They wave me through without a second look at my papers.

Beyond the gate there is only darkness. You can't see the stars in Blantyre New, but tonight, even the sky beyond the wall is empty. The hairs on the back of my hand stand up. Out of the corner of my eye, the faint glow of my microchip blinks just behind my right earlobe; I'm still on the grid ... if I die in this place, a computer will hear me fall.

Four kilometres from Old Town, Rosie's navigation guide crackles, green and black lines snake across the screen and she drifts to the ground. The trick with the screwdriver doesn't work this time. I slam the hood. The dark devours everything. One time the lights in Blantyre New went off for five minutes, and to this day, we still refer to years as pre- or post-blackout. I pop the collar over my ears and fold my arms; this jacket used to be warmer.

Mbale uzatenga chani, kwa mulungu wako, uka choka pano?

A voice cuts through the blackness, laser-sharp, like the Prime Minister on the day of his daughter's funeral. He was the last traditionalist in Parliament, and he had sung a refrain from the time before the great surge, before the tenth industrial revolution.

Brother, what will you take to your God when you leave this place?

In the distance, a small sliver of light pierces the dark. Waves of black sway around it like steam. Another light and another. Soon the darkness is boiling. My chest warms as the lights and voices get closer, and the warmth spreads to my face. The people carry the light in their hands, a flame dancing over a long white stick that seems to melt and yet retains its shape.

The flames light up faces moulded from the same clay as mine. Their skin, however, is marred by grief and lined by years of sun. Their eyes don't have the same protective glaze as mine; there are no microchips here.

Six men carrying a long wooden box on their shoulders march towards me. I step back and press against Rosie's still-warm body. In Blantyre New our dead live forever, their consciousness uploaded into holographic images for eternity. Think you hate your mother-in-law now? Wait till she's nagging you from the beyond.

The funeral party – thirteen men and women strong – stops in front of me, looking me over as though I'm a turd on a crystal pedestal.

"You're late."

I tap Rosie. "Car trouble."

The women whisper, eyeing Rosie. One sucks her teeth and makes a chopping motion with her hand. I'm aware of my microchip blinking. A man steps forward.

"Take the right turn around the outermost banks of the city, then follow the ghost baobabs to the cemetery. The gravediggers will meet you at the gate."

The heat from the flames now burns my skin; I will be alone with a dead body. Now I know why I got this job; no one else wanted it.

The man presses his weathered palm into mine. "Half now, half later."

It's more money than I've seen in a long time. This one passenger is worth three times my daily fare *and* they won't complain about change.

The box is loaded. I offer to help, but the man stands between me and the others. Rosie is still etched into the sand, the condensation on her hood mirroring my forehead. When they're done, the ringleader claps his hands twice, and the others take a collective breath and blow out the flames they carry. Rosie's engine roars, to my relief, her headlights surge and bathe us all in white light. In Rosie's light, I am cold again and these people no longer look like me.

I move to enter my PIN, but my way is blocked by a woman who must have been tall in her youth, but time and disappointment have curled her spine. She looks up at me with eyes as white as the patches of hair on her head, stark against black skin.

"What is your name, young man?"

"Muyanga."

Her lips part as she takes a sharp breath and stands a little taller; industrialists don't usually give their children traditionalist names. She smiles and slips a packet of roasted nuts into my pocket.

I play jazz on the way to the cemetery. I don't even like jazz, but it seems appropriate. The ghost baobabs are larger than any tree I've ever seen; most of the trees in Blantyre New are stunted. The baobabs stand almost as tall the buildings back home, every branch and trunk so white that I have to turn down the headlights or risk blinding myself. In the museum, I read that the traditionalists would hang their dead from the baobabs for seven days. Anyone passing by the trees would have the chance to hear the dead's secrets, their final confessions. I look back at the box through my rear-view mirror.

'Hey buddy, which one of these was your hangman tree?' I chuckle at myself.

We haven't gotten to it yet.

I rub my eyes and fish around in the glove compartment for a can of Cheeta Energy Boost. Sometimes on a long night shift, I imagine Rosie talking back to me.

Pssst, can you pull over for a second?

There is an unmistakable knock of flesh on wood.

I slam on the brakes. My head jerks back and hits the headrest and, for a second, I see the stars. My brain drums against my skull. I glance at the screen; Rosie has already sent a *sudden brake* report to the boss. Fuck! Behind me, the coffin hasn't moved an inch. I hold my breath and count to twenty. No voices. I count again. Still no voices.

I gun it all the way to the cemetery with the radio volume on the highest setting. The gravediggers stand just outside the gates, cigarettes hanging from clenched teeth as they warm their hands over a dying fire.

They offload the box, and I gun it back for the rest of my payment. It's the old woman with the bent back who greets me. She smiles up at me and presses damp paper bills into my hands. I'll have to exchange it for currency I can actually use, and the rate will cut into my profit, but it's still really good money.

My boss calls me as soon as I cross back over the border. I mute him. As long as I don't see him mouth the words "you're fired" I don't really care what else he has to say. There's less traffic on the highway now. We turn into Garden Plaza. It's the tallest building in Blantyre New, ninety-two stories high with a pool on every tenth floor and three trees outside. Charles, the security guy, greets me and his drone scans my ear before letting me in.

I park Rosie in the designated spot for commercial vehicles and pat her fading orange paint. "See you bright and early, babe."

Out on the street, I put on my light-cancelling sunglasses. The screen in front of me is advertising Insta-meals: a pretty girl in a tight apron places a small packet in the microwave, and when it pings, out comes a fully dressed chicken. *Only fifty wayala a packet*, the screen says. I eat the salted groundnuts on my way home, pretending they're roast chicken.

I get on the moving walkway between Ansah Street and Njuchi Avenue and text Frankie to turn on the water heater. Our building is called The Rose Bowl, a pretty name for a shithole. Only fifty storeys. Frankie and I share a converted studio on the fifth floor. I scan in and the doors creak open to a courtyard where there is a stone fountain in the shape of a rose. The water stopped running long before I moved here, but the bowl is still full; urine from tenants too pressed to make it to their flat in time.

The lift is out. Maggie from 3B is in the stairwell. I slip past her and her seven shopping bags. One time, I made the mistake of helping her to her place. She talked my ear off for five hours. I just want to get home and get a beer, see if Frankie managed to pirate any more movies for us.

This building is older than I remember.

I sigh. Maggie loves stairwell chit-chat.

"That so?"

It used to be a brothel in my day. A rose fountain spouting water, it's a bit tongue-in-cheek.

Now that's a conversation worth having. I look back to ask her more, but no one's there. I catch a glimpse of Maggie's shopping bags over the railing; she's three floors down. My head is still pounding from earlier and now my heart joins in, drumming to the same frantic beat. The door to 5F jams and I have to jiggle my keys until I hear the familiar click and shove it open.

I throw my keys on the counter and go to the kitchen. The fridge is empty apart from some milk and a note on the top shelf.

Out of beer. Gone to get more. Don't wait up. Frankie.

I look at the time, already past nine. If Frankie isn't home by now, I'm not seeing him till morning. Last night's dishes are still in the sink and

Frankie has left the one window in the flat ajar, which means Junior isn't back yet either. I pour what's left of the milk into a saucepan and leave it on the window sill.

"Better not knock this over on your way in."

You talk to yourself a lot.

The skin on the back of my neck prickles. I turn around. There's a woman standing in front of me, a red boa wrapped three times around her neck and a single white feather in her afro. She wears a silver ballgown that shimmers as she fades in and out of sight. Through her, I can see that the door is closed. I can see through her ... Shit!

Do you want to grab a drink?

I blink four times, actually count them. Frankie and I had a buddy a few years back who got screen sickness after too many nights at the casino. He was a wizard at *Spot the Difference*, made his whole rent in two nights. After all those hours of looking at images on flashing screens, he started seeing a large purple lizard with green dots everywhere. They had to pull the plug on him. No upload privileges. The house always wins.

She's still there. Maybe this is it. Screen sickness coming to get me.

Is The Rooster still open?

"This is nuts."

I'm being rude, my name is Kon.

The symptoms of screen sickness aren't usually so chatty but, then again, I've always had a wild imagination. There's one place in this shithole of an apartment – a small crack behind the refrigerator – where I sometimes hide an ounce of vodka. I find a note there instead with the letters "IOU" scrawled in Frankie's chicken scratch. Bastard!

My guest is still there when I walk back to the living room. If this is my descent into madness, I might as well have fun with it. "I'm Muyanga."

She sits, or rather hovers above, the couch, flinging her boa behind her.

In my day, these rooms were reserved for the big spenders and their dolls. One bedroom, close to the ground, it was easy in and out. The lift was terrible back then too.

The light from the walls outside is starting to get to me. I close the curtains.

"Were you a doll?"

For a time. The rent was cheapest here. I wanted to be a performer.

She shines a little brighter then, like the ghost baobabs, but not as blinding. I find myself leaning into her, willing myself to sleep.

A wail tears through the air, the curtain tumbles into itself and Junior falls onto the living room floor, disoriented as usual. His orange fur is matted from his adventures. I laugh, turning to Kon for introductions, but she's gone.

"They'll kick us out one day because of that fucking cat." The front door opens and Frankie dips below the frame, a six-pack of beer in one hand and an Insta-meal in the other.

Frankie has a presence. He takes up half of any room he's in. "Crude as a sailor but shy as a schoolteacher," he likes to say. He's neither. More than anything he's selfish with a sprinkling of fierce loyalty. The kind of man to stick up for you in a knife fight but also abandon you with no way home if a pretty face is calling.

"You're the one who took him in," I say.

Frankie tosses me a beer. It's the good stuff, so he's done well at the casino. By the second beer, I'm so tired that the bottle rolls from my hand onto the floor. Junior licking up foam is the last thing I see before everything goes black.

I'm usually out the door while the screens are still showing serums for insomnia, but by the time I wake up the next day the instant diet pill ads have taken over and my phone is buzzing for the tenth time.

I treat myself to a coffee on the way to pick up Rosie. A quarter of my earnings from being a corpse driver, but it's worth it.

Rosie runs smoothly for once.

Welcome Driver RGS4532, Muyanga Kainga.

I drive out of Garden Plaza. I don't mind the morning shift, the golden hour between three and four am when the screens are down for routine maintenance. It's the only true silence in the city. At six a.m., however, I'm rushing past caffeine pill jingles from three competing cafes all at max volume.

Three hoverbys are already at the bus stop when I arrive. I jump out, whistle in hand. 'Only six wayala to the sugar district!'

I push past the driver in front of me, reaching the woman carrying a heavy bag first. He gives me the finger. If I had been early, Rosie would have already been full, but here I am competing for seats. It's slim pickings; after the lady with the bag, I only manage to get a few sugar district employees before leaving the bus stop.

Where's your call boy?

Kon floats just above the seat behind me in a black and white pinstripe suit and a bowler hat.

"I didn't know there were wardrobe changes in purgatory."

Kon laughs and I jerk the wheel to groans from the customers. Her laugh is more youthful than I anticipated, light but with the rasp of too many cigarettes.

"My boss is too cheap for call boys."

You should quit.

Now it's my turn to laugh. "Oh yeah, and do what?"

Have a drink with me.

I pull up in front of the gates to Tseke Sugar Mill. The guard, red-eyed and dishevelled, scans the chip of every worker before they walk in. I look at my fare screen. Only sixty wayalas. It's a shitty start.

Incoming call, Zoom Tours HQ.

My boss is in his jacuzzi. Behind him, an image of palm trees and the ocean glitches. A fat drop of sweat sits pretty on one hairy nipple.

"Do you like your job, Muyaya?"

"Uh..."

No.

"Yes."

"Why the hell are you taking personal calls on duty? I've had two passengers complain."

A hoverby driver talking en route to a drop-off is a cardinal sin.

"Sorry boss, it was an emergency."

"I'm docking your pay this week. Make sure it doesn't happen again."

The bastard hangs up before I can even begin to protest. Kon has disappeared again, leaving me with less money and no customers. I head back to the central business district, picking up anyone I can along the way. I hear the ping of an incoming phone call in my ear but I'm paranoid now; any more dockings and I won't be able to make rent this month. I check the voicemail instead.

I can't believe I thought things would be different this time. I waited for two hours in that restaurant like an idiot and you didn't even have the courtesy to call and give me an explanation? I'm done with your bullshit. Never call me again.

Samantha. Fuck! I was meant to meet her for dinner when I got the call about the private gig.

I'm sure you can win her back.

"Kon, seriously, why can't you leave me the fuck alone? What do you want from me?"

She flinches, her bowler hat tumbling from its perch onto the floor. A frail transparent hand reaches for it. My anger retreats slightly. "I'm sorry."

Just one drink, at The Rooster.

"That's it?"

Then I leave you alone.

She tells me to wear something nice and meet her at The Rooster at six, then she disappears again. I sit back. What I could have possibly done in the last forty-eight hours to deserve this? After I drop off Rosie, I buy a new shirt and tie and wear it out of the store. The tie is a deep blue; it looked sturdy on the hangar and that's how I want to feel right now. Sturdy.

The Rooster – or Penis Tower, as Frankie likes to call it – is the most exclusive bar in Blantyre New. The only entrance is a single lift that takes you all the way to the ninety-seventh floor.

There's a guy in a black suit waiting at the doors. I slow down as I approach him. I'm going to meet a ghost woman for a drink when a very real woman is mad at me for standing her up. The man holds out his scanner.

What are you waiting for?

Kon is back in a shimmering ballgown, her hair up in a bun which seems to make the wrinkles around her eyes and mouth more pronounced.

"Hey buddy, you coming in or not?"

I lean in, squeezing my eyes shut as the scanner passes over my ear. There's no way they'll let the likes of me in. I hear the lift doors open.

"Welcome, Mr Mobanks."

The lift's interior is as large as my apartment and is furnished with couches and a mini fridge. "How did you do that?"

The doors open to the ninety-seventh floor and I am bathed in light. The whole place, from carpet to ceiling, is made of standing glass. I see clouds for the first time up close. They drift towards me, slower than they do in the diaper ads. I yearn for grass and a long embrace now. Kon walks towards a red velvet booth near the bar. The menu is built into the table; I almost choke when I see the prices – a shot of whiskey costs as much as my rent.

Order whatever you want.

"How?"

When I was a doll, the man I was involved with, Mr Mobanks, liked to give out membership to this place as a gift to those who pleased him. I just borrowed some of that energy.

"Energy?"

Isn't that what you Industrialists all believe we are, energy not bodies?

"Aren't you an Industrialist too?"

I order the expensive whiskey for Kon and the vodka for myself.

When I heard your name, I thought you were like me. That you came from Old Town and had to make a way for yourself here. Muyanga – I am alone. Why do they give us names like that? My real name is Sakondwera – she without joy. It always felt like a curse.

"Where do you go when you disappear?"

I'm not sure. I seem to be living life in flashes. Everything is dark and then it's as though I wake up again right where you are sitting but still with the same desire I've always had.

"To have a drink?"

With someone, out in the open, not in hushed bedrooms or in places no one will recognise you. Just a drink with a friend at a bar.

I pick up my glass and clink it against hers.

"It's a shame I didn't know you when you were alive. I think we could have been great friends."

For the briefest of moments, Kon raises the glass to her lips and takes one small sip. She smiles at me and the glass is suspended for a moment in the light streaming in from the windows before it tumbles to the floor.

The next time there's a job in Old Town I volunteer. Another death, another corpse driver needed. A young man killed in a brawl with friends. I carry an ounce of whiskey with me, hoping the gravediggers will let me pour some on Kon's grave. As I pass the seventh ghost baobab, I hear the unmistakable knock of flesh on wood.

Stop this car! I'm not going anywhere until that bastard pays me my money.

Here we go again.

GREY

Sola Njoku

*I*KNEW MY FEELINGS for you had devoured you after I noticed the first splinter of grey in your hair. I held your picture aloft on my phone, rubbed at the screen, assuming it to be a play of light. It wasn't. I carried you downstairs to the kitchen, rummaged under the sink for the pack of wet wipes, extracted one and wiped it across your face, three inches long when zoomed to the fullest. The silver remained.

I figured it was a hairline crack on the plexiglass screen I had covered you with. I inserted a careful fingernail under the thin sheet of glass, pushing so that the screen went opaque for the split second when two fragile things resisted breaking apart – like mice and men in the hand of fate. They yielded to my force and the outer shell fell away, but the screen beneath, exposed to my scrutiny, revealed no fissure. I knew then that the grey was your soul, defying you, maybe unbeknownst to you, finally reaching out to me.

I met you a mere six weeks ago, at what was both the lowest and highest point of my life. Trying out separation from my husband of eighteen years, I had left my children a continent away, separated by four thousand miles and freeze-frame video calls interrupted by static feedback and their momentary rejections of me, borne of unfulfilled and humiliating teenage yearnings for their mother. I was distraught but joyful. Happy as a multitude of clams, in London, finally getting to do life my way, doused in drops of Jupiter, like in Train's song.

And my way was quite the thing. I was a helium balloon racing for the stratosphere. Finally detached from the leaden weight of my husband, I was happy to burst into a million pieces, to be kissed by the sun like Icarus. When I met you, I was high as the Burj Khalifa, thanks to an amphetamine pill and marijuana hastily rolled into flimsy, white cylinders in dense dark circles of human bodies gyrating to "Ballon D'or" by Burna Boy and Wizkid. It was Afrobeats night at the nameless club where I found myself, in the company of more seasoned free spirits. The entrance lit by orange floor lamps and the corridor fragranced with burning incense sticks gave the impression of walking into a Babalawo's shrine.

The tip of the weed-wrap was moist against my lips from the steam of several mouths, their owners in atmosphere-induced abandonment had puffed merrily, blowing streams and rings, through papier-mâché that had kissed a dozen mouths before. Never mind that Covid had waged its war on us, was in retreat but wilful, still snatching handfuls daily. Never mind that within days, I would have to insert a swab into my nostril and throat to be able to see my children. I dragged from the proffered toke, threw my head back, easy this Sunday morning. I squinted at your silhouette as you stepped into my haze of contentment.

"Are you looking for someone?" Me, a gatekeeper, guarding my territory from trespassers. My claim to the elevated platform in the overcrowded space where you couldn't distinguish a jostle from a fondle was that I had stuffed a Benjamin into the hand of a black giant.

"My friend – I thought I spotted her," your reply.

"Okay, you can go through." Me, magnanimous, as if I was throwing open the gates to a castle.

You eyed me briefly, were quick to make up your mind. "I've found who I'm looking for."

Me too! But I didn't say it. I fell in love with you in that instant. It was your youth and your boldness, so atypical in these times. The male thrill of the chase had been cowed somewhat since I dated twenty years ago, by a plenitude of online options, and #MeToo, which had dictated that men preen and affect nonchalance, expecting that like an animal scent or a mating call, their allure would be carried on the wind toward the female, and she would come, in Tinder swipes and Bumble beehives – a dialect I was yet to pick up.

Before you, I had been trying unsuccessfully to pick up an Indian man, slight of build, who had managed eye contact – the source of the marijuana. I had broken the ice by asking for a puff, he had obliged, his eyes lingering to indicate interest. He had been hungry but lazy. When a woman throws her arms around a man and drapes her breasts against his back, he should take the initiative. Coyness isn't attractive in men. Held at bay by his reticence,

I had given myself up to his weed, the Adderall pill and the tequila-vodka blend sloshing through my veins. And then you rose up like an omen.

I had found who I was looking for. The person who would again stir the liquid in my core that had congealed to set wax in a marriage to a man who put being Dad before being lover, affection for whom had taken on a filial form, Eros banished into the void where kisses, jealousy, excitement and spontaneity had been dashed by growing cherubs, anti-cupids who erased desire from their parents' hearts, prying their hands apart and inserting themselves in between.

I pressed my front against you, sighed a homecoming when your hands cupped my bottom. I kissed you then, full on the mouth, feeling no guilt or taboo. I had been sure that another man's hand on my body would feel alien, that I would recoil from the strangeness of the touch, the neurons on my skin, like a fingerprint reader, alarmed by a different pattern. Instead, I revelled in it, forgetting my Indian, who, seeing the folly of his delay, melted into the night.

"Don't be shy," I cajoled, "Why are you all so shy nowadays?" I offered you a drag of the cannabis.

"I am not!" you protested as you exhaled.

"Prove it," I issued into your ear, using the noise of the club to my seductive advantage. You were so tall, I had to raise myself onto my toes to be at chin level. I took the opportunity to feel for your bulge against my thigh, drawn to your arousal. You widened your stance to give me room. We kissed, I stroked, we danced.

"Nowadays?" A slip you wanted to investigate. "Wait," holding me away from you to temper your ardour, "How old are you?"

"How old are you?" I deflected.

"Thirty." I knocked off five, factoring in the male instinct for subterfuge.

"I'm thirty in London," I said, taking fifteen off mine, leaving the insinuation of falsehood to hang in the air. I knew I could pass – my face, yet untroubled by wrinkles, my body, assisted by waist trainers, had had a decade to recover from three births.

You turned to my friend. "Is she married?"

"Yes," she yelled against the music, made tactless by flaming rum shots, "and she has three kids."

You were repelled and intrigued all at once. I thought you might leave, but intrigue overcame. You pulled me back to you, locking my hips as they swayed against your crotch.

"You're a fantasy," your hands growing possessive, "I would be so lucky to find a woman who looks like you after three kids. Can I have your number?"

I thought of surreptitious phone calls, racy texts, dick pics, revenge porn, child custody hearings, risky parental behaviour, supervised visitation. I glowed at the flattery, but I declined.

"Just let me enjoy you tonight." I trusted the marijuana and alcohol to wipe my slate clean of a night my subdued rationality was certain I would repent.

I left the club with you, suffering a knowing look from my friend. In our hurry to explore each other before the dawn broke on us to prohibit the folly that drink and drug had licenced, we sprinted across the junction in front of your building, you sure-footed with practice, holding my hand, leading a willing lamb to the slaughter.

Be wary of crossroads, my people warn, particularly the intersection of three paths, where spirit beings assemble to accept offerings of appeasement, lest you disturb their feast and they lash out in anger.

I CAME TO, bleary-eyed and thick-tongued, hours later. I called my Uber and left you naked, foetal, like a baby with an overactive growth gland. Tiptoeing out of your boy's room and its trappings: dim lighting, PS4, dumbbells, a punching bag, canisters of protein shakes, stained and wilted sheets.

I examined my conscience in the weak morning light, the cab speeding across a high bridge, evading the sun emerging against the London skyline. It was clear as Perspex, slick with satisfaction. I should have been worried then; I should have sensed my arrival at a crossroads mapped by Eṣu, the amorphous trickster god, who helps the unheeding to self-destruct.

Some people say that to get over one man, you should get under another. But mine say: be careful who you share yourself with, mix your fluids with – they can use it as a portal to gain entrance into your soul. In my new self-assertion, I had decided that this injunction was a crock, a weapon to police women, make them into unnatural beings, unacquainted with their own pleasure. I had claimed mine without remorse.

But you returned to trouble me. You distracted me in memories and fantasies that didn't dissolve in the morning light. A blip that wouldn't blink. I was horny and frustrated as I packed my bags to return home.

I arrived late in the night. My husband had retreated into his space and his sulk, my children slept in their beds, and I wanted to be anywhere but there. I picked up my phone and tapped on a small pink circle. I typed your name into the search box on Instagram, the playground of the young, the battle hill of the old. My heart rising and falling as I squinted at miniature thumbnails that turned into imposters.

I tried different iterations of the name you gave me – Oge, Ogo, Ugo, Ego – until I came upon a picture that struck a familiarity. The profile said 16k followers, personal trainer.

You had been modest. How had you not let that slip when I had gushed about the strength of your biceps, kissing each in turn? I clicked "follow", stayed up all night watching reels of you working out. I discovered a favourite, a short collage of rapidly changing pictures of you working monkey bars, deadlifts, hex bars, all arranged to a sample of loud grime music. You were phenomenal: Ogun and Sango rolled into one, a thunder god, breathing fire and subduing metal.

A flash of you lifting a kettlebell like a piece of paper took me back to your bed. I was the kettlebell. Lying naked in the musty scent of your bed, you had picked me up, lifted me as you rolled onto your back, and sat me on your erection.

I played the reel twenty-three times, then scrolled through pictures and pictures and pictures of you, discovering your past as a male model, strangely put off by those younger, jejune versions. Finally, I found the one: an avatar of the man I had met only days ago. It was as if a portraitist had frozen the heavy-lidded look of wariness and longing with which you appraised me that night. I took a screenshot.

Be careful who has your image, my people caution. It can be employed as a channel to summon your spirit for evil. It is why it would be unlikely to see a pregnant Yoruba woman share a photo of her baby bump before it deflates; or be hasty in splashing a new baby's picture on Facebook. We know to wait for the child to see the sun, lest they be jinxed in-utero; we let them acquire a personality post-birth so we know immediately when they are impacted by a curse. But daily on social media, the lie of our belief is proven, or maybe we've lost the mystic knowledge of how to fell a fellow mortal by putting a picture to a flame and knowing what to whisper.

"Beautiful man. *Wink emoji*," I typed, clicked "send". I refreshed my Instagram page three dozen times, hoping each time for the red arrow of acknowledgement. The arrows came, but not from you. I consoled myself with the screenshot, fell asleep with you staring at me from the glow of my phone. I felt less alone.

The days were hard, Instagram a compulsion. I applied a beautiful face with pencils, lipstick, tweezers, highlighters, mascara; took several selfies, selected the most flattering and sent it to you. "Remember me? *Love eyes emoji*"

A day later, a reply, humourless and affectionless. "Yes. I remember you."

I waited for more, for hours, crafting and redrafting a message, light in tone to conceal my dark feelings. "I'm back to base now, my holiday all but forgotten. But you."

Empty days and licentious nights go by.

I tried a different tack. "Hey, I'm trying to get in shape but I hate exercising. I need some advice. *Smarmy grin emoji*"

Nothing. Yet you put up a story about a training bootcamp.

Finally, from me, "You're still on my mind ... call me when you're ready for me ... 01646..."

After a week, I submitted to being ghosted, mortification slowly replacing desperation. But it was still to your graven image I turned when I dragged myself into bed at two in the morning. As if in answer to my request, you'd put me on a regimen where you broke my heart during the day and consoled me in the nights.

I loved you nightly, in the darkness of my room in a house in which I co-parented with my ex. Both of us too pragmatic to try to fracture a whole into something less than the sum of its parts, we so stayed put. He in the master bedroom, me in the guest room, orbiting each other. What would he do if he knew that I had broken away from fidelity, if he knew of my nightly trysts?

I would start by kissing your lips, open, unsmiling; somehow the feeling of cold glass against my lips evoked the warmth of flesh. I would raise my gaze to meet yours, heavy with lust, and lose myself. I surrendered to you, feeling your hands on me, coming to long moments later, knowing that I had fallen asleep and been transported to a dreamscape where my deep yearnings were slaked. The throb of my lips and the wetness between my legs an affirmation.

I transformed into a woman in bloom. I splurged on pedicures, facials, frivolous accessories. I took hundreds of selfies to capture my mood, I gazed for long moments at myself in the bathroom mirror, marvelling at my youthful body. I dressed up for the school run, discarded my mom jeans and shapeless joggers for dresses that clung and swayed, that pulled further and further away from my knees. Sensuality announced itself. My pale friends' sallow husbands got friendlier, chattier and more tactile at the school gates. I felt libidinous, like my famed ancestors, possessing of the brazenness of Oya, the shapeshifter, who, disguised as an antelope, bewitched Sango until he had no recourse but to trap her in human form. I loved the spell I cast over them. I ignored the hands that brushed against me, and I oozed the roiling, blasé sensuality of Yemoja, who had ensnared and condemned at will, left men and gods in her thrall. At night, like her, I returned to you, my lover, to crash like a wave under your steady gaze and submerge myself in you again and again and again.

Until the day I broke you.

Within days, the sliver of silver spread, your dreadlocks flecked with grey, a distinguished salt and pepper that was at odds with your youthful face and at the same time attractive to me. We suited each other now. I no longer questioned my appetite for cool blood.

The metamorphosis was so subtle I wouldn't notice a change for days until confronted by the next decline: a Dorian Gray in instalments, drained of valour, a fleshiness emerging to your steel-plated jaw, your forehead adorned with a new mesh of crinkly skin, the photo's sepia tone now complementing your visage, no longer an obvious retro effect.

The week when the proud angle of your shoulders tipped forward and your hunch acquired a roundness, I got cat-called in the street, my nails and lips dipped in blood-like pigments, my skin luminous, my brows drawn to insouciant arcs. My daughter, twelve, embarrassed. That week, Jeremy, Carol's husband, worked up the nerve for lewdness. I indulged him until his wife found us in an embrace, concealed by a holly hedge, his hands splayed low around my waist. Afterwards, he scurried off like the rat that he was, and could not manage eye contact for days.

I wrestled with my concern for you, the pleasure I took in you tarnished by guilt and foreboding. Should I make another foray into your gallery? Would it be for reasons of concern or for greed? To make sure you were still out there, hounding the reluctant into shape? Or to obtain a refill for my emptied-out version of you?

Warily, I opened your Instagram page @workhardthenworkharder. There had been no update in three weeks. I heard the death knell in the silence. I had wondered what indeed I felt for you: this man-child, over whose image, like Narcissus, I pined, losing myself in reverse as I imbibed your vigour.

I conceded that I felt for you a Jocastal love, both maternal and amorous. So easy it would have been to steal you away, to consume you – until all that was left was a pixelated image of an old man – your eyes retreated into deep sockets, having witnessed prematurely what the elderly's eyes saw to make them withdraw from the world.

You would never have known why in rapid decline you shed yourself, never have remembered the one-night stand of aeons past, replaced by so many others. But I would know. A real-life Benjamin Button, I would keep you in my psyche, for the length of my elongated life. In the end, lust was persuaded by its gentler sibling. I loved you too much to have you for myself alone. Even in my disappointment at your disregard, I was glad that I had known you briefly, that you were out there in the world, living, alive. And what sort of a mother would I be if I took another's child in cold blood?

The Yorubas value fecundity: the gravest taboos restrain us from actions that untimely terminate the cycle of life. We measure the success of a life by its proficiency in bringing forth another. It is the reason we ridicule and pity childless women, effeminate men and masculine pawpaw trees; why we do not offer an animal in sacrifice unless it has birthed a young; why we do not fell a sapling that has not yet had a chance to bear its fruit and feed the earth its seeds.

Finally, I heeded our ancient wisdom.

I found the screenshot marked as a favourite so that it wouldn't get buried in the mundanity of family life and over-photographed adolescents. Steeling myself, I pressed delete, terminating the draining of your life force into mine.

I visited your page every day, keeping vigil, like a mother for her ailing child. I restrained myself from reaching into my Google bin to reclaim what was left of you. On the third day, you rose as a story: a picture of you in bed, the transparent tubes of an oxygen mask stretched across your unshaven beard, anchoring you to a hospital bed. "What doesn't kill you almost did makes you stronger. *Prayer hands*"

I considered my power to drag you over the edge, render your professed resilience a lie. My people say he who does not consult the gods to find out the reason for his misfortune is doomed to be unfortunate again. But I played God, beneficent and merciful.

On the eighth day, you emerged, like a newborn on first showing. You had fought demons and lived so you could bask in the telling of the tale.

Lights, camera ... Instagram live.

You sat in bed, propped up by mechanical hinges. You were diminished, your head a great orb on a stick frame, curled into yourself, your hair lank, but reassuringly unstreaked. You spoke with a voice wheezy and phlegmy, working hard for elusive breath: "Yo fam ... I've been through a lot over the last few weeks. I came down with Covid ... suffered every kind of failure, cardiac, renal, respiratory ... my whole body shut down. I was put in an induced coma, attached to a ventilator ... I had no idea it could get me so bad, but swear down, this shit is real ... I'm bare lucky to still be here. I am learning to walk again, can't hardly lift my arm ... I know it'll be an uphill climb getting back on form but I'm so grateful..."

"Welcome back! *Love heart*" I comment. Clicking "Like" for good measure.

MVELICANTI'S GIFT

Zanta Nkumane

*T*HE BABY PLONKS to the ground out of its mother like a cloudburst, as if it has been called here. A voluminous silence fills the rock hut. The baby has two legs. The baby doesn't even cry like it is supposed to. The royal midwife wraps the baby in a leopard skin and hands it over to its sweaty, heaving mother. Inkhosikati carefully places a kiss on its blood-coated forehead. The taste of the bat excrement, blue lavender and urine pain concoction lingers past her mouth into her throat. Tears bite her eyes; she knows that babies like hers end up buried alive by the ocean, their small heads poking above ground like pulsing boils while their chorus of mewls jostles the sand around them. Once they have all been planted, the Twin Sangomas stand on the infinite contour of land and water, their trumpet wails summoning Mvelicanti to collect his yearly sacrifice of ill-formed babies.

Outside, her husband shouts to get through. Birthing huts are sacred portals for the Nguni, where spirit and body are momentarily indistinguishable, too holy for men to taint with their sinking spirits. He knows this but he tries anyway, like the wilful man he is. A scatter of murmurs drowns out her husband's voice. Not even the Chief can break the laws of his people to save his firstborn. She looks down at her cooing son, his two legs wiggling and kicking like a frog sliding through a jump. Her eyes fold into a post-birth slumber as her baby is lifted from her arms.

NKOSI HATES GETTING into the water. His legs entomb themselves the moment the waves lick his feet as if they carry blue-ocean terror into his body. Terror multiplied a thousandfold is a human being, which means he is part of a terrified people. There is a flickering feeling that his body will become unfinished in water, as if his inability to swim will skeletonise him to the bottom of the sea, further away from his people.

His people are champion swimmers. In the same way the Zulus glide through the sky by tucking the air under them, the Swatis are known across the Nguni tribes for the way their one leg morphs into a tail of a fish and slices through the water like moonlight maiming a melting sky. Nkosi does not believe he was fashioned for the water.

Only his best friend Ingci knows how these chasmic thoughts burrow into him. As the son of the Chief – the one who speaks directly to Mvelicanti, the First God – Nkosi lives because his father called it to be. That naming doesn't feel like a kind destiny; it's a festering curse. It doesn't help that people stare at him with the immensity of a forest fire every time he and Ingci pass through the village. The canopy of trees has become Nkosi's favoured mode of travel.

"Nkosi, you can't be scared to walk through the village. What kind of ruler will you make if you are scared of your own people?" Ingci says as they move toward the edge of the land so Ingci can practice swimming. Swatis don't walk, they slither along the ground like upright snakes. They swim along the ground too. Nkosi is the only one of his kind who walks and fears water. Ingci sometimes watches Nkosi place one foot after the other and wonders how it feels to experience the ground twice. These trips to the water have become a ritual ever since they were paired in their Indoda ne 'Mpi training on the first day. They were both ten springs alive. Nkosi mentioned how unlucky Ingci must be to get him as a partner. Ingci told him to shut up and finish assembling the spear.

"That's easy for you to say. You don't have to live with the painful reality that everything bad that happens is your fault. Mvelicanti turned his back on us because I lived," Nkosi replies, destroying the vegetation in front of them with the cattle whip his mother gifted to him to make a path. He can barely keep up with his friend when they take the ground.

"There's no proof that it is your fault we have had locusts attack our sorghum crop three harvests in a row, or that ice rocks fell from the sky and gutted most of our village, and now the sun burns closer to the ground every passing summer." Ingci tallies every set of plagues of nature that have attacked his people since Nkosi passed his eighteenth spring, as if Nkosi was not present for them. He is an alert twenty-two springs alive now.

"I think maybe He is calling me back to Him by punishing everyone."

"If He wanted you back that badly, He would have fetched you a long time ago. He made you, He can unmake you with just a thought. Be useful and throw me into the water, please." This has been their ritual since they were children. Nkosi holding Ingci above his head and running with him towards the edge of the water like a hunter would a spear. He loves watching Ingci's body disappear beneath the surface as he briefly becomes a love-shaped memory on his waiting hands.

Nkosi kisses him on the forehead, lifts him up and throws him as hard as he can. Then he sits down on a rock to wait.

THE TWINS BANG the calabash outside the Chief's home. He hears the rhythmic chant and knows whatever they have come to report isn't good. He untangles Nkosi's toddler body from his neck and latches him back onto his mother. Their rock hut is the highest point in the village. From his door, the Black Mbuluzi's meandering chatter as it flows into the mouth of the ocean reaches him. His view ensures he sees the enemy approach with a day's warning.

"Wena Ndzaloyelanga." They kneel as he steps out, his body almost too long for the door.

"Thokoza mkhulu, thokoza gogo," he responds, honouring the ancestors he knows are somewhere about, whether above or below or next to. He knows these two come not as themselves, but as more: as roots, as thunder, as rocks. He leans on his slim rod that works hard to carry his mountainous size.

"Langa lethu, the lightning we harness to give the throne power and protect our people is diminishing faster than we can capture it from the sky. Our calabash is almost empty." They look at the soil on which they stand, their voices not speaking in unison but in a functional harmony, like when the leaf swings too far in the wind anchored by the branch to the tree.

"You are the great Twin Sangomas, the bringers of light and dark, traversers of the masculine and feminine, manipulators of fast light and visitors of the spirit world. This feels too small a problem to disturb me with."

"The Sun honours us with his praise." They pause, eyes shining with knowledge longer than time. "Yet in all his golden glow, he has but brought peril upon his own because his son that should not be, continues to be. Things will only get worse until Mvelicanti has what is His."

As they finish their warning, Nkosi, like the seven-headed snake when you utter its name three times, crawls out of the hut. He swings onto his father's thick leg, then bounds up and climbs across his wide torso to clasp his father's neck and settles into kumema position. His father chuckles.

"I think the boy has made it clear he isn't going anywhere. He doesn't even fear you like the other babies in the village, who run at a whiff of you. Invent a solution with all your bones, concoctions and animal sacrifices. My own sun will continue to shine. I cannot be your amber without his breath, and if he were to become the rain, I'd continue to let him fall."

"But the laws are clear," the Twin's voices rise to a howl. "All ill-formed children are to be handed over to Mvelicanti and cannot live amongst us. They are bad luck. They are reminders of the imperfections of our god."

"AND AS THE CHIEF OF MY PEOPLE, I AM YOUR GOD ON EARTH!" His voice smashes the horizon and startles awake the contention that had fallen asleep on his back. The Twins synchronously start pulling each other back and, without a word, they condense into each other, then vaporise into white nothingness.

THE SACRED TREE rises over the village, its roots untraceable under Sibebe's encompassing granite dome. Etched into the dome in their thousands like upright potholes, the village huts make Sibebe a hulking beehive. This is why among the Ngunis, Swatis are known as the most peaceful because they live like honey makers. Within the Sacred Tree, between its many sparse greyish-green leaves and sturdy branches, Ingci is lying between Nkosi's legs. The boys are resting after a day of weaving cattle whips for the herders and drying goat hide for emajobo. Nkosi curls his legs around him, pushing his sweat deeper into him, until there is nothing but skin and few hairs between them.

"I still want to do it," Nkosi whispers, as if the scaly bark will steal his idea.

"Don't be dumb!" Ingci responds without hesitation. "I've told you before, cutting off one leg is a sure way to ensure your passage to dying. Even Mvelicanti can't get you back from there."

The tree they slouch on is dead but remains standing. It is the last of the old trees. The legend of the Bush says they take a thousand years to grow, a thousand years to die and a thousand years to putrefy back into the ground. Its wood is brawny like a bull and long-burning like a soul.

"Don't you want to know how I plan to finally become like you?" Nkosi half teases.

"No. Keep that between you and your god."

"If the big rock saw disappears from the village stores, just know I am somewhere slaughtering myself."

"Do we get to eat the other leg then?" Ingci teases.

"Throw the whole village a feast, I say!"

Ingci rolls over to his side to face the drowsy sun. Nkosi is ready to cleave off a piece of himself to become part of a whole. What a cruel aloneness it must be. Ingci understands Nkosi. He understands the dilapidation of feeling so wrong you'd chop off your limb with an abyss of the unknown beyond. Ingci softly kisses his hands and whispers, "I'm sorry," over and over like a thin wind.

Nkosi opens his eyes to Ingci shaking him awake. "Nkosi! Nkosi! Wake up! We have to go now!" Panic tinges his cadence. They must have fallen asleep. The night shovels darkness around them. Below them, Nkosi feels a pervasive fluster in the village. There is too much movement for this time of night.

"The Chief has summoned Sibaya. At this time of night, it cannot be good." Ingci climbs onto his back and they begin their descent. For a dead tree, its sky-bound height suggests a quiet growth. When they reach the ground, Nkosi slides off his back, the dark a more sparkling haze here than up there. They walk in silence. The clanging of evening bugs, swaying vegetation and Nkosi's feet echo their every move. But no words. Ingci doesn't glide ahead of his best friend, they remain side by side. When they reach the clearing that spreads into Sibaya, they finally hear it – the Twin's calabash song. Something is out of place. They have no authority to call a gathering of this kind. A dancing fire casts shadows towards them, luring them into the unknown. Ingci lets go of his hand and goes on without him. Nkosi is flooded with the realisation that whatever happens next, he is alone. He unwraps his cow whip from across his chest, swallows a deep breath, then moves towards the calabash song and fire dance.

As Nkosi steps into curving light, quiet descends. The Twins stand at the centre of the Sibaya in front of the fire, like owners of a newly carved hut. Beyond the fire, Nkosi sees his parents, mouths gagged by some sorcery. In his father's eyes, he can see the knives of his spirit have been dulled. His gaze flicks through the crowd trying to find Ingci. A power licks him and his whip winds like a noose around his neck, tightening gradually, and lifts him up until he hangs just above the ground, crooked like a broken wing.

"You cursed one, the one who should not have lived. Your arrogant father has left us no choice but to bring us here," the Twins hiss as if tonight their mother is a black mamba. "You have brought us nothing but turmoil and now our god denies us the lightning that keeps our people alive. Because you lived, our god turned his back on us." They start swirling around the fire, brandishing knives.

"WE HAVE SEEN the future, if you live, we die. We have seen the future, if you live, we die," they chant in harmony with the crackling flames. Nkosi accepts that he will be sent to Mvelicanti, or die. Perhaps both. A rapture awaits him and his father cannot save him now.

"We knew we had to act fast when your friend came to tell us you wanted to chop off one leg to be like the rest of us."

It takes a moment for Ingci's scalding betrayal to sink in, choking him harder than the noose around his neck. He tries to speak but his mouth and tongue are hardened. He can see his parents clearly from where he hangs. Their faces are temples of tears and their eyes apologetic. They wriggle against invisible bonds. He isn't sure if they are sorry for their helplessness or for their original sin – their selfishness to upend centuries of tradition to keep him. Either way, the outcome is the same; he should not exist. At least, not in this articulation of his body.

"But we are lucky we are children of a soft god when He chooses, which means we can be soft too," the Twins continue. "We will let the people decide whether you die or we sacrifice one limb." The gathered villagers flutter with sounds Nkosi cannot make out. "Whoever thinks he should die to restore the balance, come put a log in the fire. Make it as big as the daylight. If you feel, through our magic, we take his one limb as a sacrifice for Mvelicanti to forgive us, then remain where you stand."

Nkosi knows the people despise him. He represents all the misfortune the village has succumbed to since his birth. Things have worsened as he's gotten older. He once again searches for Ingci.

The crowd hesitates, then the Royal midwife steps forward. His people barely look at him as they chuck log after log into the fire, but it isn't guilt that prevents them from facing him, it's years of brewing resentment.

Ingci emerges from the shadows, his gaze fixed on the fire. He carries a log in his hand. Nkosi's heart disintegrates into thin fish bones that he wishes he could shove down his best friend's throat and grovel into him this same pain. Ingci looks up at him. "I'm sorry," he says, "I'd rather you die." Then he turns and disappears into the dark once more.

AKUA'BA

Aba Asibon

IT WAS NO secret that Afram did Tano a favour by marrying her. At thirty-five, her prospects were waning and her mother, M'Akos, had taken it upon herself to salvage the situation. She wrote to her daughter, announcing she had found her a husband. M'Akos said the idea came to her one morning while pounding palm nuts in the kitchen. Why she had not thought of it earlier, she did not know. Just a few days before Mrs Appiah, her long-time friend, had expressed concern over the calibre of women her eldest son had been associating with.

"Girls with no home training," Mrs Appiah had lamented.

As M'Akos put pestle to mortar, it had occurred to her that her only daughter and Mrs Appiah's son would form a formidable alliance. She had presented the idea to Mrs Appiah, who lifted up her hands to the heavens and called M'Akos a visionary. Naturally, Mrs Appiah had expressed concern over the age difference, given that her son was three years younger than Tano, but M'Akos had assured her the age dynamic would have no bearing on the success of the marriage.

Seated at her desk in Maryland, Tano squinted at the photograph her mother had attached to the letter. The man in it was grinning too hard, his hair cropped short to conceal a receding hairline. *Average.* She folded away the letter and went back to work on her dissertation. A few months before, she would have scoffed at the idea of matchmaking and immediately written back to her mother in protest, reminding her that this was the twenty-first century. But after Ryan, her American boyfriend of three years, had woken her up one night to declare he was no longer happy, she had no more fight left in her.

Tano revisited the letter a few times after that, scrutinising the glossy photograph from different angles, looking for a good reason to turn down her mother's offer. As a statistician, she understood how permutations and combinations worked in the dating world. She also knew that with each passing year, the odds of a favourable event diminished significantly. After a month of writing and rewriting, she finally mailed a response to her mother, permitting an introduction. Weeks later, she received an envelope addressed in a neat cursive she did not recognise.

His full name, he wrote, was Adolf Afram Appiah, but given the unsettling association, he preferred to go by Afram. He was a financial auditor at an Accra-based firm who, in his spare time, could be found playing tennis at the local sports club. Describing a recent work trip to Nigeria, he told her Lagos had intoxicated him with its verve and audacity; hands-down his favourite African city so far. Had she ever been to Lagos? He had an inkling she would like it. He had heard from her mother that her PhD was in statistics. Impressive. What was her specific area of focus? Did she want to go into teaching or stick to pure research? He signed off by saying he hoped she would not find his letter too forward, and that it would please him to hear back from her soon.

He wrote with such eloquence Tano could almost hear his voice through the ruled foolscap paper. Over the next few months, her trips to the campus mailroom became more frequent and the stack of letters at her bedside grew. Afram's loquacious updates provided respite from the hours spent hunched over her keyboard. She slipped photos of herself at the National Aquarium and at the Museum of Art into her replies to give him a glimpse of her life in Baltimore. When she complained about her lack of motivation during the last few months of her PhD, he responded with a Bob Marley-inspired greeting card that read, "Don't give up the fight."

Tano defended her dissertation on a sweltering Monday in June, bombarded by questions on Bayesian Methods and Bernoulli Distributions. Later that week, she packed up the rest of her apartment, reducing five years of triumph and loss to two suitcases. She binned the bag of clothes Ryan had left behind, stuffed a lacy white gown she had purchased on eBay into a suitcase, and boarded a flight back to Accra.

THE NIGHT BEFORE her wedding, three dozen women from Tano's family gathered for her bestowment ceremony. M'Akos had paid for a well-known decorator to work her magic on the family home in Labone. Balloons floated around the parlour, satin bows were fastened to white Tiffany chairs. Tano's aunties wrapped her in technicolour kente and, ushering her out amidst ululation, seated her on a low stool. As the room quieted down, M'Akos walked up to her daughter and fed her a hardboiled egg. Under her mother's firm gaze, Tano pushed the cold egg down; the smallest bite would invite misfortune upon her marriage. Her eyes widened as it jammed briefly in her throat, before squirming its way down. Even though she had seen this ritual performed by many women before her, she would have never guessed by their gracefulness that swallowing an egg would be so onerous.

Tano's cousin placed a rattan basket at her feet. M'Akos reached into it, drawing out a string of glass beads whose colours danced under the glare of the white fluorescent light. She motioned for Tano to rise from her seat and wrapped the beads seven times around her waist, knotting them tightly at the ends to secure her husband's desire. Reaching back into the basket, she pulled out the wooden Akua'ba she'd had crafted to suit her daughter's su, for who knows a daughter better than her own mother? She handed the Akua'ba to Tano, who run her fingers along the disc-like head and down the ringed neck, feeling for synergy. Tano's fingers paused briefly at the junction of the protruding breasts; her mother's breathing stalled. Only when she allowed her fingers to continue exploring the cylindrical body did M'Akos's shoulders relax.

It would be the last time any of the women in her family should see the Akua'ba. After the wedding, Tano would hide it underneath her matrimonial bed and retrieve it once a week to be cleaned and cradled, coaxed and coddled. Tano placed her Akua'ba in the basket and covered it. The women around her broke out in song, belting out her new appellations: "Virtuous wife of Afram Appiah, bearer of dynasties." She could hear her mother's voice above the others, a roaring melody full of heart. Tano closed her eyes and drank in the metallic rhythms of the dawuro and the frikyiwa, gyrating her waist to show off her new beads.

MARRIAGE SURPRISED TANO. She had always viewed it as a boulder strapped to one's back, something to be lugged about for better but mostly for worse. She had heard stories from friends of husbands with wandering eyes, husbands who were hot one day and cold another. Yet her Afram was as steady as he was sure, and in this she found anchorage. He rose every day at five a.m. and never drank his morning tea without a squeeze of lemon. On a Saturday morning, she would always find him on the verandah reading the newspaper: business, politics, and then sports.

Afram had assured her when they first married that there was no need for her to work; his income was enough to make them both comfortable. Unable to envisage a life without statistics, she had gone ahead and secured a postdoc position at the University of Science and Technology. Despite the long hours and ill-matched salary, she saw the job as a bridge between where she had come from and where she was going. Her goal was eventually to become a tenured member of faculty, and so her days were spent writing grant applications, publishing papers and grading student reports. Eyes sore from staring at computer screens all day, she wondered how her mother had done it; raising four children while entertaining the demands of fussy clients at her tailoring shop.

In the days following Tano's wedding, M'Akos came by her marital home – a rented house in Cantonments on a tarmacked street lined with royal palms – to teach her things she would have known had she not been educated abroad. She showed her how to gut a fish, how to make a clean slit along its belly and scoop out its entrails. "Here, you try." She handed her daughter a knife and a whole mackerel. Tano squirmed as she punctured the silvery flesh with the tip of the knife. M'Akos clicked her tongue. "You're making a mess. All you need is a quick incision."

She walked her daughter through preparing aprapransa from scratch and supervised her table setting, reminding her the dessert fork went above the plate, the fish fork to its left. Tano looked on as her mother adeptly replaced broken buttons and zippers with a thin needle. When she came by, M'Akos brought with her an abundance of water yams which she drizzled with palm oil and set before her daughter. "Eat as much as you can," she urged. "They are good for the womb."

Most importantly, M'Akos taught Tano to polish her waist beads regularly with white clay to ensure they would never lose their lustre.

Tano and Afram took the time to learn about each other's bodies, and found there was always a new discovery to be made. She would chance upon a mole in the small of Afram's back and spend minutes fiddling with it like a child with a new toy. In the aftermath of their passion, he would slide a hand under her waist beads, rolling them between his fingers. It was in these moments, as they lay entangled in each other's limbs, that his most ambitious dreams came to him. He would someday set up his own auditing firm and make enough money to build them a house with a gazebo under which their children would play. Afram spoke often of children. He wanted three, just enough to fit in the back seat of a saloon car.

Tano had her own thoughts of children, which came to her in the middle of the night when Afram's reverberant snoring woke her. Watching him in the throes of sleep, she was often reminded of the inevitable: one day, one of them would die and leave the other behind. This thought always raised a trail of goosebumps along her arms. She was getting used to the idea of waking up to "good mornings" laced with the remnants of sleep, to the assurance of coming home at the end of a long day to the familiar smell of musk. During those sleepless nights, she traced his sleeping face with her eyes, running them along the sharp jawline and the slightly dimpled nose, thinking how beautiful it would be to be left with his replica when the inevitable happened, a breathing testament of their love. But to wake up every day and gaze upon the likeness of the one you have loved and lost would also be perpetual torture. And so, she would lie on her back, weighing the two scenarios until the first rays broke through the linen curtains and her husband began to stir.

THE WHOLE WORLD seemed to erupt in jubilation when Dede, Tano's childhood friend, finally had her first baby. The same aunties who had whispered about her childlessness behind her back poured into the hospital the day the baby was born, carrying praises and Pyrex dishes. Back then, they had blamed Dede's difficulty in conceiving on the quality of her Akua'ba.

"Four years is a long time," they'd complained. "Her mother must have used a cheap craftsman."

But her mother, who had died less than a year after the wedding, could not confirm or deny these allegations. Dede's husband Abed had begun to sprout worry lines across his forehead. As an only child, his family had grown restless – who would carry on the Mensah name? He could no longer hold his head up at family gatherings, taking his place instead among the single men. He had urged his wife to quit her job, concerned that stress was a contributing factor to her infertility. "You need to focus on nurturing your Akua'ba," he had said. "Some need more coaxing than others."

So Dede had tendered her resignation and spent her days cleaning her Akua'ba with rosewater. She had sung to it and planted kisses on its face, rocking it back and forth in her arms. Her closest friends began to distance themselves, fearing her misfortune might be contagious. They made excuses for why they could not honour her lunch invitations and rushed off during chance encounters in town. But not Tano. She had availed her shoulders for Dede to cry on, watching helplessly as her best friend slowly faded. She worried Dede might do something desperate, like the woman who had been caught stealing a newborn from the St Francis Hospital in Shiashie. She had seen the story on the evening news, of this woman who had disguised herself as a nurse and plucked the child from a sleeping mother only to be intercepted at the hospital gates by a keen-eyed security guard who had raised the alarm. Watching the court proceedings on television, Tano had felt empathy unfurling inside her chest as the media shoved television cameras in the woman's face and bystanders hurled their reproach. The woman had kept her head bowed the whole time, veiling her face with the wide sleeves of her boubou. Thankfully, Dede did not have to go to such lengths; her efforts eventually paid off, news of her conception spreading wildly among her circles.

Tano waited until Dede and the baby were discharged from the hospital to visit. She found the house eerily quiet, save for the lethargic whirring of a ceiling fan. Clothes were strewn across the linoleum floor and no one had bothered to draw the curtains that morning. Dede's petite frame was propped up in bed, the baby sleeping next to her in a white crib. She lit up when she saw Tano, motioning for her to come closer to see the baby. Setting down the fruit basket she was carrying, Tano tiptoed to the crib, fearful of waking the child.

"Isn't she beautiful?" Dede asked through a weary smile. "Twenty-two hours of labour later."

The baby stirred a little and Tano caught a glimpse of a pair of full cheeks peeking from underneath the blanket. She sat herself at the edge of the bed, taking a closer look at her friend. Milk stains littered the front of Dede's t-shirt, and her curly hair was running wild, matting in places.

"Are you here alone?" Tano asked, casting her eyes around the dishevelled room.

"Yes, Abed's off to work."

"And your aunties? Did no one stay behind to help?"

Dede shook her head. "They all have things to do."

The baby stirred again, this time emitting a short-lived whimper.

"Isn't she precious?" Dede peered into the crib, stifling a yawn. "Not a boy like Abed was hoping for, but no less a blessing."

Tano shifted and cleared her throat. "Have you decided on a name?"

"Yes," Dede answered. "Ayebi, because she has vindicated my late mother."

"Good choice." Tano stretched towards the nearby dresser. "Now come, let me comb out your hair."

Dede groaned, leaning towards her friend, "I can't seem to find the time or the energy to even look in a mirror these days."

Tano began to pick at the hair, forcing apart the clumps. Thick strands broke off and clung to the comb, specks of lint lodging themselves between the teeth. She could not believe this was the same head of springy curls that had once been the envy of every girl in secondary school.

"Have you thought about having some of your own anytime soon?" Dede asked, staring dreamily at the sleeping child.

"Someday." Tano concentrated on the tangled mess before her.

"Then you must begin to nurture your Akua'ba well, my dear."

Tano refrained from admitting that she had not yet grown tired of quiet evenings after work when she and Afram would open a bottle of red wine and bring each other up to speed on the day's happenings. She lived for spontaneity – an unplanned dinner out at their favourite restaurant, an impromptu road trip out of Accra on the weekend. They were birds, free to soar as they pleased.

Tano was halfway through detangling Dede's hair when the baby began to fuss in her crib. Dede pulled away, the comb dangling down her neck. She scooped up the child and slipped a nipple into its mouth, beaming as the child sucked and grunted. When its hunger was assuaged, Dede covered up and extended the baby towards Tano. "Will you please hold her? I am desperate for an uninterrupted shower."

Tano took the child, which was now sucking its thumb. Having never before held a baby that small, she handled it delicately, worried she might break a bone. The child smelled of stale milk and talcum powder, its skin blubbery and unblemished. It made gurgling sounds, which Tano found rather amusing. Easing her stiff shoulders, she allowed the baby's soft body to settle into her lap, savouring its warm bottom. Dede had been gone for less than ten minutes when the baby grew restless, wriggling its torso and letting out a guttural howl. The shower was still going, steam seeping from underneath the door. Tano tried to return the baby to its crib, but she felt shackled to the bed, immobilised by the baby's growing shrieks. When she came to, Dede was standing over her wrapped in a towel, cradling the baby.

"Are you alright?" Dede asked, looking perplexed. "You seemed a little out of it."

Tano heaved, waiting for her breathing to normalise. The milky smell clogged her nostrils, stirring up nausea. She rose and gathered her belongings. "I should head out now." As she walked out of the room, she could hear Dede calling after her, but her feet only quickened.

HALFWAY THROUGH THEIR second year of marriage, a hunger began to brew between Tano's legs. What started as a dull ache had slowly grown into a deep throb. Afram had not touched her in weeks, oblivious to her subtle advances. He did not notice when she dabbed on patchouli oil before bed, nor did he notice the twinkle of her freshly-polished waist beads. Although he insisted his apathy was due to work stress, she could see he was deeply troubled. As they lay in bed one night, with their backs to each other, he spoke into the darkness. "Are you nurturing your Akua'ba enough?"

She flipped over towards him. "Why would you ask such a thing?" she whispered into the curve of his back.

"My mother is beginning to worry," he said.

"It's only been two years ... or are you also beginning to worry?"

"Would it be wrong of me to worry?" He turned to face her, yet avoided her gaze.

Tano no longer felt supported by the wooden bed frame. She was floating, suspended on a sheet of thin air. When exactly had he begun to feel this way? He had given her no reason to think something was missing from their marriage. Perhaps if she told him about Dede's baby, how holding it had caused her to lose herself, he might sympathise. She reached out and ran a finger along his collarbone – it would all just sound crazy to him.

"Am I no longer enough?" she asked.

"That's not fair," he said, pulling away from her wandering finger. "Isn't it every man's dream to come home to the patter of little feet?"

Tano cringed at the hollowness in his voice. It was foreign, frigid. In one swift movement, she straddled him. She brought her face down to his and drank deeply from stunned lips, clawing at his chest. When she was confident that she was well-anchored in his desire for her, she sought out his ear and whispered, "Am I enough?"

His body tensed, his breath quickening.

"Am I enough?"

"Yes," he exhaled. "Yes."

And as she wiped off the aftermath of their passion with the back of her hand, she caught a metallic scent on her fingers. It dawned on her then that she had drawn blood.

In the third year of their marriage, M'Akos began to show up unannounced, bearing all manner of remedies in her handbag. She brought concoctions in little brown bottles which, when lifted to the nose, smelled faintly of rancid eggs. There were special soaps for Tano to bathe with twice a day, herbal ointments to be applied to the neck before bed. These all remained tucked away, forgotten in a cabinet underneath the kitchen sink.

"What are we doing wrong?" M'Akos asked her daughter, when nothing seemed to be working. "Are you nurturing your Akua'ba?"

"What sort of question is that?"

"You can't blame me ... people are beginning to talk."

"Then let them talk," Tano spat.

M'Akos gasped, taken aback by her daughter's brashness. "I only want what's best for you."

"What if I told you Afram and I are happy?"

M'Akos sniggered. "Happiness is fleeting, my dear."

She leaned in and whispered in Tano's ear, "Is it your husband? Is he the problem? You can tell me." M'Akos cleared her throat and lowered her register further. "There are ways around these things, you know? So, tell me then, is he?"

"And what if he were the problem?"

"I know what to do," M'Akos declared. "I'll ask Nana Annor to come and perform a ritual cleanse."

"There'll be no need for the medicine man." It was Tano's turn to laugh, much to her mother's disapproval.

But M'Akos refused to back down. "Fifteen minutes and a bottle of Schnapps is all he needs to clear the air for your Akua'ba."

"I forbid it!" Tano shot up from her seat, towering over her mother.

M'Akos's face twisted in pain and Tano immediately regretted her outburst. Whatever her mother's intentions, they were sincere. Her whole life,

M'Akos had fought for Tano to have a seat at the table, and now she did not want her to suffer the same fate as other childless women. Tano sank into the couch next to her mother and took her hand, gently squeezing.

"In God's own time, Ma," she assured her, knowing full well M'Akos would not dare argue against divine timing.

TWO DAYS LATE. Her cycle had always been regular, like clockwork. But how could it be when she had never once opened the basket? Could it be all of her mother's prayers? Or perhaps it was the power of her husband's desire? She had seen the longing in his eyes. They would be strolling through the mall or sitting at a restaurant and a passing child would catch his attention. Tano would see something shift in his face and look away to spare herself.

She paced around her bedroom, eyes shut, hoping that if she tried hard enough, she could will it away just as it had been willed into existence. She thought of Dede's pregnancy and how she had experienced every symptom in the book – the retching, the fatigue, the mood swings – but nothing felt out of place in Tano's body. She had always imagined it would evoke an inner turmoil of sorts, some indication of the frantic multiplication of cells happening inside her body. Her body. Except that it was very likely no longer just hers. She would have to share it with this guest, accommodate it, nourish it, watch it stretch out her belly, and compress her insides.

On the third day, she drove to a pharmacy to pick up a home-test kit. The pharmacist, a willowy woman in a white coat, lectured her on urine samples and red lines. She glanced down at the gold band on Tano's finger and flashed her a knowing smile: "Two lines, that's what you're looking for." Back home, Tano locked herself in the bathroom and stood in front of the mirror. After fumbling with the pink box for a few minutes, she hid it at the bottom of the trashcan next to the toilet, reasoning that she could not be held responsible for something she did not know about.

The next morning, her period showed up, making no apologies. She sat on the cold toilet seat, staring at its abrupt announcement. She laughed and cried all at once, trembling with relief. She heard her husband's snores on the other side of the door and felt guilty for not feeling more.

NOTHING COULD HAVE prepared Tano for that sunny Tuesday in her fourth year of marriage when her mother defiled her basket. She returned home from the university earlier than usual to find the front door unlatched. From the doorway of the master bedroom, she could see her mother on her knees, rummaging through the basket until she fished out the Akua'ba.

"What have you done?" Tano asked, lips quivering.

M'Akos jumped at the sound of her daughter's voice, attempting to conceal the Akua'ba under her wrapper.

"Why, Ma?"

"You lied to me." M'Akos inched closer, holding out the Akua'ba and lifting it to the light.

Tano recoiled at the sight of the neglected doll. Its wooden body lay shrivelled in her mother's palm, parts of its torso crumbling into a dark brown powder.

"Take it, nurture it," M'Akos ordered, extending her arm, but her daughter only retreated into the hallway.

"You have unleashed misfortune upon me."

M'Akos scoffed. "There is no greater misfortune, my girl, than a dying Akua'ba." She brought the Akua'ba to her chest and began to rock it back and forth, singing to it a special song of revival. She brushed the debris off its torso and planted a kiss on its face. It was at that moment that Tano's waist beads broke – hundreds of gleaming balls tumbling down her thighs, skittering across the tiled floor. Their sound was that of rain pattering against glass. M'Akos dropped the Akua'ba, and mother and daughter sank to their knees, scrambling to collect the scattered beads. But they only slipped through their fingers, bouncing further and further away.

ẸLẸ́DẸ̀ KEKERE
(LITTLE PIG)

Josephine Sokan

*I*F IT WERE not true, Ibukun would not have said it. The thing that made Big Aunty turn tomato-red with shame underneath her brown skin, and deflate like a burst balloon. It was the sort of shame that would hang heavy on the neck, like a millstone, so that a person would rather die than face it.

He had lived with Big Aunty for the past eight years. Being now a young man on the cusp of adulthood, he had established a predilection for the notion of manhood, and with good reason too. He had watched years of American action films that served as an extravagant celebration of all things he understood to be masculine: cigars, guns, fighting, profanity, cars and access to women.

The day he turned eighteen, he had expected some form of celebration. Not anything grand per se, for he was aware that Big Aunty was a miser and an ageist. The kind who would die before spending big money on a young-ster, one who had yet to achieve anything significant in their life. And even less likely to spend money on someone who wasn't even her flesh and blood. However, Ibukun had at least expected a little cake, maybe a bottle of cold Fanta for himself and his close friend Yinka. Big Aunty could even have stretched to small chicken and fried rice if she had wanted, as she had just received some money from her father's estate, following his passing.

Ibukun would often eavesdrop on her phone calls while washing her clothes in the courtyard. She insisted that her delicates be laundered by hand, but it had to be done quickly, so as to discourage perversion or any ten-dencies to perverse curiosity, whatever the hell that meant. Consequently, Ibukun would wash quickly while in her line of sight, but would allow the clothes to be many so he had an excuse to linger. He would listen to her speak to her sister, Aunty Kemi, who lived in Manchester, over matters concerning the will. Then she would speak to her boyfriend, whom Ibukun knew only as "Denola-baby" or "D-boy", depending on the time of day the call occurred. These days she spoke to him regularly, almost daily since Papa Ogunowo's death, which left her the only member of the family still in Nigeria.

Much to his disappointment, not only did Ibukun not receive any small chops or some little acknowledgement of his special day, but his duties were in fact increased on account of the impending visit of D-boy.

On that morning of his birthday, he awoke to shouting and commotion in the household. Big Aunty was yelling in the front area of the compound not far from Wale's quarters. Wale had woken up late again and so had failed to open the gate for Mama Wosi, the caterer she had contracted for the entirety of the "presidential" visit. Added to the matter was that Bisi, the actual cook of the house, was up in arms that Big Aunty had contracted an outsider to do what she was "very well trained and equipped" for. In tears, Bisi was questioning Big Aunty as to what she had done to deserve this, and why she was not being given the opportunity to show she was better than the stranger. This was the racket into which Ibukun entered that morning, at which Big Aunty requested that he accompany Mama Wosi to the market.

"You will go with Mama Wosi to Oja Oba, hm? Don't dilly-dally either, as your duties are waiting for you when you return. This car will need washing, for starters. I cannot have my friend from overseas be driving around in one dirty car."

"Yes Ma. No problem Ma. But please, as it is my—"

Bisi approached. "Good morning again, Ma. Please if I can just prepare small ewa for you, Ma, then Mama Wosi too can cook her own. If you then taste the two—"

"My friend, will you shut up!" barked Big Aunty.

"Ah, sorry, Ma, abeg no vex. You know say my own food sweet pass her own, you know, Ma. Make I just cook small beans for you Ma, then you go see say—"

"Bisi, respect yourself! Oniranu! I don't have time for your rubbish this morning."

At that, Big Aunty flip-flopped, jiggled and rumbled her way back indoors towards the parlour, her slippers slapping furiously against the tiles as she went. As per the usual routine, Ibukun had laid out *The Herald* and her morning cup of Lipton, along with four sugar cubes, some milk and a dainty silver spoon. All were placed just so, right next to the framed picture of Papa Ogunowo and his daughters. Big Aunty would drink with her pinky finger out and the bag and spoon left in, noisily slurping until satisfied. She would then eat a heavy helping of yam and eggs prepared by Bisi before falling asleep on the sofa in the upstairs parlour. Not wanting to miss his very slim window of opportunity, Ibukun followed her in.

"Good morning Ma."

"Yes Ibukun, what is it?"

"Thank you Ma. You see, I will soon be heading to market with Mama Wosi—"

"Good, good. That's good. Make sure you help her carry the things she needs, you hear? She will buy plenty things and none must go missing or fall on the road, hmm?"

"Yes Ma."

Silence.

"Ibukun, why are you still standing here? If I should slap you this morning!"

"Sorry Ma. You see umm, I will head to the market, but seeing as it is my—"

The sound of slippers on hard floor tiles was heard. Wale, who in this economy had to double up as both the gateman and driver, beckoned to the young man.

"Ibukun, the car don ready o. Make we commot sharp-sharp."

"Yes Wale. I dey come. Abeg I just wan discuss one matter with Madam—"

"My friend, will you get out of my sight!"

At that, Ibukun surrendered. This round was well and truly hers, but there were still enough hours left in the day for a rematch.

At the market, away from Big Aunty's claustrophobic kingdom, Ibukun walked as a king. Although he had been sent to Ilorin to further his education at Loyola International College, her sovereignty had turned him into her errand boy. He was now a regular at the market when Bisi was not available. Now he paraded the walkways of Oja Oba as if he were a celebrity or a local state governor. With nostrils flared and both shoulders high, he moved with a certain swagger as he was greeted by women, children and old men alike.

"Ah ah, birthday boy! Abeg, come collect small puff puff nau. Make you chop enjoy yourself." He licked his lips in anticipation of the warm, freshly fried dough balls. "I-B! My guy! Abi, you want mineral on top? Oya make you take am, knack am. Happy birthday o!" The entirety of his time at the market continued like this until Mama Wosi had endured quite enough, despite having accepted small chops and a bottle of Coke on behalf of the celebrant. So when Ibukun arrived back within those familiar steel gates, like a lamb to the slaughter, he came again before Big Aunty, his crucifier.

"Where on earth have you been? Useless boy! Does it take all day to buy ordinary supplies at the market?" He remained silent, in the hope that Mama Wosi would intervene. After all, she had also partaken in the festivities. Now suddenly mute, she stood observing the scene before her with an aloof expression before interjecting: "Ah Madam, when we dey market, I dey tell am come make we do quick, time dey go and Madam dey house but e no fit hear word. I say, Ibukun hurry o! He just do wetin e like, e no dey answer me. E dey waka up and down, dey chop everything for de market. I just dey watch am. If na me Madam, I go sack am. Useless boy!" Her chatter left no room for Ibukun to interrupt in his defence. She continued in this vein until Madam grew tired of them both, and told them to leave. They dispersed like mice fleeing a particularly wicked feline, relieved to have escaped this time around. Mama Wosi, before entering the kitchen, wished Ibukun a happy birthday, to which he merely grunted.

In the kitchen with Bisi peeling onions and chopping tomatoes for stew, Ibukun ruminated on his feelings. To be fair, Big Aunty owed him nothing. In fact, it was he who was indebted to her for her generosity over the years. She had taken him in when Ibukun's father had absconded to Ghana, to a thick, smooth-skinned, walnut-coloured woman known only as Adwoa. He had once seen a photograph of her within the pages of his father's Bible, with her name, the date and the location scribbled on the back. At the time, although still a boy, Ibukun was aware of what it meant to carry a hidden picture of a woman that was not your wife. His mother had been left with four children in Ibadan at a time of great public furore due to living costs, unemployment, and the upcoming presidential elections. She had contacted a lady she worked for many years ago, pleading for her to take in her eldest boy as a helper in exchange for educating him. Big Aunty had taken some days to think on it before agreeing. She assured Ìyá Ibukun that she would raise the boy as a son, and he would lack nothing. Largely, this had been true. Ibukun lacked nothing, but most certainly had not lived like a son, unless all sons slept in the servant's quarters and regularly missed social functions in order to scrub toilets and wash oversized knickers.

"Ah ah, my friend, will you be fast? Wale don dey go airport. E go dey here soon. Be fast nau so I go start dey cook!"

"Yes, Mama Wosi."

Bisi had already finished her chopping, and now, like a young child, sulked on a stool placed in the corner of the kitchen.

"I go cook white rice, stew, fish, vegetable salad, maybe some fried plantain and yam. Bisi, shey una still get maggi for house?"

Bisi simply kissed her teeth in response and rolled her eyes while muttering something about "ordinary, local food wey small pikin sabi cook" before heading to her room with her plastic, thonged slippers flip-flapping.

"Such an unfortunate idiot!" retorted Mama Wosi.

For what seemed like hours, Ibukun assisted Mama Wosi downstairs in the kitchen. The sun was not far from setting when Mama Wosi finished and D-boy arrived. Exhausted and still disappointed, Ibukun stopped work for the first time that day to greet the new arrival.

Just a glance at their guest made them unsure whether this one was from overseas. He certainly looked the part, dressed in designer logos, sagging jeans, box-fresh white trainers and a bright baseball cap. All members of the household stood in silence when he stepped out of Big Aunty's Toyota and delivered a "S'up my man, s'up lil' man, s'up lay-dees. Now how y'all doing?" in a theatrical American accent. Not one soul offered a peep, although Wale looked at Ibukun. Ibukun looked at Bisi. Bisi even turned to look at Mama Wosi, and only turned back to look at D-boy when she remembered their rivalry.

Discomforted and embarrassed by her people's failings in etiquette, Big Aunty shouted, causing even D-boy to startle. "Will you all get moving! Please if you can't greet my guest, at least go and do something useful!" At that, everybody muttered their own version of "hello", "good evening, sah!" and "welcome!" before scuttling off like roaches. D-boy then removed seemingly expensive sunglasses and took a slow look at the house and vastness of the compound. He observed its slightly worn but still majestic columns, marble entry, tarmacked driveway and small, neat garden. He then released a faint whistle from his thick lips before remarking "Wow, well ain't this sumthin? Almost as nice as my place back in the States." At that, Big Aunty grabbed his hand and led him in, her hips swaying this way and that.

"Na wa o! Wonders shall never end!" Wale could be heard muttering as he emerged from his quarters once the coast was clear. "See me, see trouble!" added Bisi, clasping both arms over her chest with wide, baffled eyes. Mama Wosi knew better than to engage, being a visitor.

They all now looked to Ibukun, waiting for his own input, but he instead remained silent, focusing on offloading the bags from the car. Night had fallen, and yet no form of recognition from Big Aunty regarding his birthday had come. For him, this day was not like turning thirteen or even sixteen. This one was significant; he was a man now, and one who had served Big Aunty dutifully for years. Internally, he decided that if not for the distraction of this visit, she would most likely have done something for him or given him something. Even she, he was certain, had to be aware of the significance of turning eighteen.

Once inside, D-boy removed his shirt, placing it on the just cleaned floor before complaining of the heat. "You know, we don't get heat like this in Minnesota. Can't get nothing done in heat like this ... although I could prolly think of a couple thangs we could do ta cool off!" he added with a lewd grin thrown at Big Aunty. In response, Big Aunty allowed a coy smile to creep onto her face as she drank in the fullness of his carved upper torso. "Oh Denola, you are too much! Save that talk for tonight, okay?" she return-served with what was meant as a suggestive wink.

Ibukun, witnessing this spectacle, felt his stomach turn. The sight of Big Aunty being flirtatious with a man she could easily have birthed, the fact that he had never seen her like this, and the pressing matter of his gradually dwindling eighteenth birthday had chipped away at any remaining sense of politesse. "Big Aunty, please, shall I take D-boy's things to the guestroom or your own room?" he asked absentmindedly. There was a clattering of cutlery as Bisi, who had been dishing rice onto plates, dropped the serving spoon. Then Ibukun remembered. It was a known fact that D-boy was Big Aunty's boyfriend, but she had never disclosed this herself, nor would she. The members of the household only knew because they eavesdropped on her conversations and then casually discussed the details later when doing their chores or when Big Aunty left to lead the "Single and Celibate" meetings at the Church of the Eternal Fountain of Grace. In response, a swift slap was delivered to Ibukun, who dropped the bags to nurse his cheek. Big Aunty's ornate gold bangle had grazed his left cheek, taking as a souvenir a small patch of surface skin.

Dinner was then served: a full spread of everything Mama Wosi had prepared. Big Aunty took only a small helping of salad and fish, on account of her "not being one to eat much". At this, Ibukun had tried his very best to stifle the laughter rising in his stomach, which duly earned him venomous glares from Big Aunty. For the rest of the night, Bisi and Ibukun worked skilfully together, weaving in and out of the room either to clear or lay down new items. All this occurred while Ibukun nursed his hurt ego. It was certainly a sobering induction into adulthood, not at all like the eighteenth birthdays he had heard about at school.

Just before the clock struck ten, Yinka called to wish Ibukun a happy birthday and to inform him that his mother had left something small for him with Wale at the gate. Due to it being late, they had not stayed, but just wanted to ensure the gift reached him while it was still his special day. They had called the landline, which had never been an issue before as usually by nine p.m., Big Aunty was in bed fast asleep. Age no longer afforded her the luxury of strength past this time of night.

"Who is calling you on *my* landline at this time?"

"Sorry, Ma, it was Yinka from school."

"At this time of night?"

"He stopped by with his mum at the gate on the way back from holiday-ing in Festac."

"And so?"

"They came to wish me happy birthday and to deliver a gift," Ibukun added, now seizing his moment.

Silence.

"Oh, yes, that's right. It's the sixteenth, isn't it?"

Silence.

"Well Ibukun, happy birthday. Many returns of the day. Now be a dear and bring us water to wash our hands, along with a napkin, hmm?"

At this, it was Bisi's turn to suppress laughter.

Ibukun had endured many things in this house, but something about tonight, something about his unmet expectations delivered more pain than he could bear. He only required one day of consideration from Big Aunty in exchange for year-long servitude, but even this seemed as though he were asking too much. For the first time in a long time, he cried heavy tears well into the early hours, and soon developed a headache. He fell asleep at the bottom of the stairwell and woke only at the sound of gentle footsteps on the tiled floors. Still groggy, and unable to identify the shadow who had passed him, he followed the figure out of curiosity. A closer approach revealed it to be Mama Wosi. She slipped something into Wale's palms, and he then opened the gate. Mama Wosi began to pass tubers of yam, some plantains, and tinned food products to whoever was on the other side. She turned so suddenly that Ibukun was left with no time to hide. She looked directly at him, but surprisingly, took no notice. He was shocked.

Ibukun then made his way to Wale's quarters, where the man had locked up and was about to settle back to sleep. Seeing Ibukun, Wale picked up one of his slippers and shouted "Ohhh, see this lizard again. Oya go!" and hurled his slipper at the door. Ibukun stood for a few moments wondering why on earth Wale was referring to him as a lizard. Wale was creative with his insults, and Ibukun had been called many things before, but never a lizard.

He headed back towards the cool stillness of the outside, although now he seemed to be struggling somewhat with his movement. It was then that he looked down and observed his scaly, tiny legs, his long swishing tail, and indeed registered the fact that Wale was several times larger than he could remember. There was panic and shouting, which of course was nothing more than clicking and hissing to the human ear. Wale responded by hurling his other slipper, which sent Ibukun hurtling towards the door.

His heart began to race furiously. Could this be the work of his people in Ibadan? He had heard stories from the village boys of strange occurrences on the night of their eighteenth birthdays, but he assumed they had just been tales used to scare each other. He had thought no more of them than he did of ghosts or Father Christmas. It was all really too much for him. Desperate now, he headed back to Wale's quarters, perhaps to try and rouse him from sleep and enlist some assistance when he spotted a box of chocolates and some tinned biscuits opened and half-eaten, lying beside torn wrapping paper and a gift bag. At this, his cocktail of self-pity, disappointment and panic resumed, stirring him once again to tears. He raced indoors, in search of help. But who could help? Who could he even communicate with? He scuttled to Bisi's door, as the person most likely to offer mercy. After moments of tapping with his tail without response, he surrendered to the notion that perhaps he was dreaming. He convinced himself that he would wake from sleep and realise it was all make-believe. That could be the only explanation for his current state. He made his way back to the main entrance, to the bottom of the stairs, still raw with fear but growing lighter, now almost floating under the weight of beckoning drowsiness.

"What is the meaning of this rubbish? Se werey ni e? Are you mad?" was the morning greeting from Big Aunty, who along with her beau, had just discovered Ibukun naked at the bottom of her stairs. It took Ibukun some moments to gather himself firmly onto his feet before realising that he now stood unclothed before the entire household. Bisi had shielded her eyes, Mama Wosi had chuckled, and Wale had commented that it seemed that Ibukun had turned eighteen on paper, but was still packaged like a boy. His first instinct was to panic once again, before shame came creeping up his legs, knees, thighs, eventually landing on his chest. Had he fainted? Perhaps it was something he had eaten? He seemed to recollect visions of strange occurrences at night. Perhaps flashbacks of a nightmare?

Naturally, the rest of that day Ibukun was distracted. Too distracted to wash or even eat. Too distracted to be bothered by Big Aunty's particularly foul mood, or the relentless teasing from the others in the house. Before leaving for church, Big Aunty had instructed her people to be on their very best behaviour while she was gone. They were to look after their guest who would not be attending the Church of the Eternal Fountain of Grace that morning on account of his "jetlag". The household had waved off a grumpy and particularly terse Big Aunty that morning with an air of relief.

They had expected many demands and requests from D-boy, but surprisingly he kept to himself in the guest room. He answered calls in hushed tones and did not resurface other than to eat lunch or use the toilet. At lunch, he made brief conversation with Bisi and Ibukun, who stayed to ensure he had everything he needed. Still wrestling with his recent troubles, Ibukun was mostly mute. Bisi, on the other hand, on account of her limited exposure to "people from the abroad", talked more than she should have, even daring to ask questions. *Where he was from in Am'rika again? What of his job? Did it earn him plenty money? What were Barack Obama and Eddie Murphy like in person?* D-boy amused himself with the conversation for a minute or two. He shared tidbits of his life in Minneapolis in a tree-lined neighbourhood with mansions on each side of the road. D-boy also talked of a job working in property and music development, which sounded odd to Ibukun.

Upon Big Aunty's return, D-boy greeted her with a sloppy kiss and placed his large hands on each cheek of her equally large buttocks. After a quick change of clothes, the two of them ventured out to a function and returned hours later, tired, tense and distant. They headed to their separate rooms without so much as a glance at each other.

Night fell, the familiar headache began, and Ibukun again felt sleepy. He awoke once more to a forked tongue, scales, bent claws and that persistent tail. Afraid to leave his room, he began to pray, repenting of all sin in his life and using his tail to flick open the pages of his dust-ridden Bible. He begged God to spare him from whatever curse had befallen him. It was another frantic, restless and desperate night. As the rain beat heavily, he wept a valley of tears that lulled him back to sleep. He awoke naked again, but this time in his room, once more panicked and perplexed. So this cycle continued for the rest of the week, and the week after that.

At the start of the third week, Ibukun, although still discouraged, had grown anaesthetised and weary. This was yet another stone of misfortune placed as a weight upon his back. So, on day fifteen, when "it" occurred again that night, he carefully set aside clothes for putting on later, and spent some time thinking of the ways his present circumstance could perhaps serve him.

First, he headed to familiar ground, swishing his tail as he moved through everyday objects turned gigantic. He slipped under the doors of Wale's quarters to find him eating. A hefty plate was set before him, with a large, cold bottle of Coke. By the gate was Mama Wosi, accepting money as she handed out containers of cooked food to young men on foot, some on bikes, in the secrecy of darkness. From there, Ibukun headed to the main house. Here he heard the soft tread of footsteps from upstairs. Whoever was moving was both heavy and eager to avoid attention. His first instinct, like the heroes in the films, was to protect the women. He did not trust this D-boy with a teen girl like Bisi, and Big Aunty was the sort of woman who was prime for swindlers and dogs. Wale had proven himself to be driven purely by self-interest, with loyalty to whoever could either grease his palms or fill his belly. He reasoned that it was left to him to stand guard.

Weighed down by his newfound manhood and a peculiar sense of obligation, he scurried upstairs to see a female figure creeping to the guest bedroom. As PHCN, the national electricity provider, was having yet another outage, the figure moved with a torch. It was Big Aunty. Ibukun caught her approaching the door, which she left slightly ajar for fear of making a noise when shutting it. Ibukun dithered, wondering whether he should stay. When minutes passed and there was no sight of her exit, he scuttled cautiously towards the door. He was certain of the very unfortunate fact that whatever image greeted him would likely never be erased from his memory.

Dressed in a canary-yellow nylon nightie, Big Aunty approached D-boy in what were supposed to be bold, self-assured strides. "I hope you like what you see, baby?" she asked, unable to conceal either her inexperience or her insecurity. Her beau merely grunted and continued texting. Big Aunty, never one to back down from a challenge, decided to remove her nightdress in the hopes of piquing his interest. At the sight of her large flaccid sacks, the protruding stomach, and the rolls of fat which cascaded from her underbelly to the join of her hips and thighs, D-boy recoiled, pushed her away and shouted, "Oh God! Are we doing this again? Really? I said I was cool wit' just seeing how thangs go. Now let it go, gatdamm Mama! Let it go! I'm tired! Amma see you in the morning." Frustrated, he rolled back into bed and turned over, his eyes returning to his phone.

Ibukun, unsure of what to do, unsure of what he had just witnessed, and not particularly keen on seeing any more, backed away a little.

Big Aunty stood for a moment, allowing shame to embrace her before her eyes began searching for her strewn nightdress in the darkness. "My goodness! Anyone would think I repulse you, Denola. It's only natural after this amount of time building a relationship to want to get to know each other more. Is that not what you want?"

At this, D-boy sighed and rolled back around. "It's just late and I'm tired. Baby, let's just drop this."

"Tired, tired. Every night you're tired. Three weeks you have been in this house. You are not acting like a man supposedly in love, like a man who begged to see me, like the man I have been speaking to since last April."

"Wetin nau! Ah ah Lola, is sex all there is? You're here acting like one hungry, desperate spinster," he growled, spitting out the word "spinster". Big Aunty stepped back, causing Ibukun also to take several steps back to avoid coming to an untimely death.

"So what then is it about? Money?" she questioned, regaining her power and approaching him with squared, assured shoulders. "Is it my money you're after? Because the man who just barked at me and switched accents, the man who has been confusing Minnesota with Minneapolis while talking to my friends, and giving a very vague depiction of his work, seems like he's just here for my money."

A heavy silence descended upon the room. For the first time, Ibukun noticed how uneven the floor tiles were in the bedroom, and also how outdated the room was with its blade fan at the centre of the ceiling. A quiet chuckle was the only sound heard before D-boy swung for Big Aunty. In one motion he grabbed her body and flung her against the wall. Ibukun instantly retreated, his large eyes beginning to water. His heart thumped in his chest as he scampered out of the room, his long tail swishing in such panic, he knocked over one of the empty bottles of rum littered about the floor. The sound caught the attention of the room. D-boy approached the lizard, and offered a kick that sent Ibukun flying out of the door into the dark hallway. The door was then firmly shut, echoing through the house. As Ibukun made a dash for it, he could just make out the sound of something heavy being thrown onto the creaky guest bed. Then against the far wall, evidenced by the muffled thud. Then against the door, giving a louder, stronger thud.

For the full three or four minutes of the beating, a squeal akin to a frightened pig was heard. "Why so quiet, Lola? Cat got your tongue? Is it not you that wants us to play? It is you that wants it o! Ẹlẹdẹ mi kekere e gba dun! My little pig, enjoy!" barked this new man in an unfamiliar voice to the accompaniment of squeals, muffled whimpers and sobs.

So startled and shellshocked was Ibukun that he actually never made it back to his room that night. He had suspected that this D-boy was a trickster! But a thug? A mindless aggressor? What could Big Aunty see in a man like this? he wondered. These days, when she wasn't stomping around like an angry elephant, she was lost in a fog of her own. What did Big Aunty need from him? Why did she insist on consuming rotten fruit? What did she lack or have too much of? For hours he walked back and forth, sensing an urge to do something manly and heroic, but unsure of what exactly, especially given his current state. This woman had been his master and tormenter, and yet he was filled with so much concern, it baffled him. Despite her failings, in a sense, she had been a form of mother in the absence of his biological mother. Unable to sleep, he had spent the night on the stairs, failing to even acknowledge the morning sun which rendered him, once again, stark naked before the household.

That morning, Big Aunty did not join D-boy for breakfast, but opted to stay in bed on account of her "upset stomach". D-boy ate with vim and merriment, laughing and cracking jokes with Wale and Bisi, his American accent making an appearance again. Big Aunty did not emerge from her room until about two o'clock. She crawled into the parlour in a breathtaking, royal-blue bubu complete with hand-sewn sequins, one of the finest she owned, and a full face of makeup, to hide her busted lower lip and darkened, puffy eyes. She barked for her paper and a cup of Lipton's, and gave orders with reckless, indiscriminative venom. "Bisi! Bisi, come now! Find me my keys at once! Ibukun, bring my bag! " she bellowed. Once Bisi had fetched and delivered her keys, Hurricane Big Aunty headed out in a gust of wind and was gone until dinner time.

Ibukun had hoped for a somewhat lighter disposition upon her return, but she returned even angrier, slamming all the doors she encountered in the short climb to her room. Finding D-boy in the upstairs parlour, snoozing on her expensive couch surrounded by a sea of discarded peanut shells, she held her tongue, but by her heaving chest and pursed lips, all knew that she was enraged. She demanded dinner with roaring and banged fists. She threw her fork and knife at Ibukun for bringing cutlery that was not clean. He had scowled at this because the cutlery had actually been Bisi's job, who of course took no ownership throughout Ibukun's session of scolding. She had even barked at Mama Wosi for giving her a large serving when everybody in this house knew that she did not eat much anyways. Mama Wosi had bent her knee, offering only "Ẹ jọọ ma, e má bínú. Sorry."

This symphony of all-engulfing fury, the weighty tension and anxiousness was only heightened when a once-again tipsy D-boy joined Big Aunty at the table for dinner. Taking a piece of chicken right from the dish, he consumed it in one go and placed the sucked-clean bone on Big Aunty's plate, beside her salad. There was silence and then a gasp as he reached for her bubu, exposing her thigh in the presence of the group. Mama Wosi and Wale slithered away like the snakes they were. Bisi murmured something about plates needing washing before scampering off like a frightened mouse. Only Ibukun hung back for a reason that he himself did not know.

He observed the couple for a moment. For all her fire and venom, barking and gnashing teeth, Big Aunty was rendered a little girl by this wretched man. Something about him weakened her. Or perhaps she had always been weak, and men like D-boy were gifted with the ability to reveal and exploit that weakness. "Yo, little homie, wha'chu standing there for? Get lost!" D-boy roared, interrupting his thoughts. Ibukun remained fixed in his place. "Yo, little man, I said scram!"

There was a pause. Ibukun thought of Sylvester Stallone, and invoked his inner hero. He stepped forward. "Mr yo yo yo! Always yo man this, yo man that! Fake American boy! Collect your things and be going."

This stopped D-boy in his tracks, dumbstruck by this previously reserved young man's challenge. Big Aunty rose from her seat and blinked, rendered equally speechless by Ibukun's sudden display. A mixture of anger, pride, gratitude, shame, and at last resignation infused the air around her.

"Yo, babe, you gonna let this lil' fool talk to me like this? This how you running *our* household?" D-boy questioned, raising his eyebrow. Big Aunty lowered her head, searching the floors for salvation. "Yo, you betta handle it or amma have to!"

Reluctantly, Big Aunty approached Ibukun, her eyes pleading with him while her chest heaved, this time with trepidation. Or perhaps shame? Furrowing her brows, she offered a weak slap and muttered, "Ibukun, don't you ever talk to your Uncle Denola like that again, you hear?"

At this, D-boy laughed. "Abeg! I ain't nobody's uncle. Lola I no be mumu either. Do the needful!"

Big Aunty now shuffled on her feet, but remained mute. She only pulled Ibukun's ears lightly, the way you would those of a misbehaving, cheeky child that had taken more food than they ought to. Dissatisfied, D-boy lunged for Ibukun with the nearest object, which, to his disappointment, was a full two-litre glass bottle of water. Like an angered bear, he growled before proceeding to batter Ibukun with the heavy bottle. It was at this point that Big Aunty forced her way between the two of them, wrestling to release Ibukun from D-boy's grip. Furious at this, D-boy returned to Big Aunty to commence a fresh assault with his most unusual weapon.

In that moment, Ibukun observed his former tormenter, how her proud neck had been lowered and her roaring voice had been diluted. He thought of his recent birthday and how Big Aunty had so carelessly demeaned him in front of her own current oppressor. He thought of the previous night, how this fiery, domineering bull had whimpered and squealed like a pig at the mercy of her herder. "Oh you still standing there, lil' homie? You want a whopping too?" jibed D-boy.

"No, I don't, *homie*. I go leave you and your ẹlẹ́dẹ̀ kekere to it. Madam, if you sabi wetin good for your life, you go dash all your money inside toilet make dis man free you. You know say love no dey for dis matter," he replied.

There was then a pause as a contemplative Big Aunty began to turn a curious shade of tomato-red, then purple. Her eyes began to inflate, followed next by her neck, head, legs, thighs and jelly buttocks. Then there arose a deep silence, the sort that comes before a particularly stinging moment of reckoning. With wide eyes and an expression of sheer terror,

Big Aunty was lifted clear off the ground. Ibukun was the last person her eyes saw as she floated to the ceiling and out of the parlour doors. She floated down past the bottom of the stairs, through towards the tarmacked entry, then way up and away. Moments later, there would be a grand bang before the skies rained beautiful, royal-blue sequins like fireworks for hours.

NANKYA'S GHOST

Doreen Anyango

NANKYA DIDN'T KNOW how long she'd been on the other side when she started to emerge out of nothingness. She was here, but muted, a nymph in a cocoon. She could move – or rather, the casing that held her could move through the liquid reality of her new world. But the motion was slow at first, a series of starts and stops. Dead-of-night darkness surrounded her. And then, nothing moved for a while, and she existed in a state of complete stillness. She was here, but suspended. And then, all of a sudden, everything was moving too fast. The hard outer skin around her split open and a brand-new self emerged. There were limbs and wings and sight. Nankya felt herself rise.

And as she hovered over the landscape, there was memory. There was the stream where she'd fetched water with her mother as a child. Nankya with a two-litre bottle rushing to catch up with Maama, who effortlessly balanced a twenty-litre jerrycan on her head. Nankya's bottle would be almost empty when they got home, all the water in her hair and clothing. And Maama would smile and shake her head. *My little Njabala*, Maama would say, laughing.

The story of Njabala was Nankya's favourite of all the stories her mother told her when she was a child. Nankya was her mother's oldest child and only daughter, and in the chaotic flurry of male energy, the only two females in the household clung to each other like twin fledglings. Long after the boys had gone to sleep, Nankya and her mother would sit in the tiny grass-thatched kitchen, by the dying embers in the three-stone fireplace that had to be kept just a little bit alive so that Taata's food would be warm when he returned later in the night, but not so alive that the food would burn. And Maama would tell her stories. Nankya would always request for the Njabala story first, and listen fascinated every time to the end, only letting herself succumb to the creeping embrace of sleep when Maama moved on to other stories. Many years later as a mother herself, Nankya had tried to tell the story to her own daughter Wanyana, but her baby girl just didn't know how to be still and listen.

ONCE UPON A time there lived a girl called Njabala. Njabala's mother loved her daughter so much that she didn't want the girl to suffer at all in this life. So Njabala's mother didn't teach her daughter to cook or tend to the banana plantations or forage for firewood. As fate would have it, Njabala's mother died just as Njabala was becoming a woman. Without a mother to protect and defend her against her other relatives, Njabala was forced to get married to the first interested suitor. But Njabala was terrible at being a wife to her new husband. The food was always burnt, and the banana and coffee plantations were choked with weeds, and the house was always dirty. Njabala's husband was displeased with his new wife and quarrelled bitterly with her, wondering what kind of woman he had been duped into marrying. Njabala would cry and sing for her dead mother to come and help her with her chores: *Jjangu Maama, gwe wankuzanga ekyeejo.*

Njabala cried so often and so hard and so long that her voice summoned her dead mother's ghost back to the land of the living. And as she went about with her chores, the ghost would take the hoe from her and show her how to make holes to plant beans, take the knife from her hands and show her how to prune the matooke plants, take the banana leaves from her and show her how to wrap matooke properly for steaming, stack the firewood just so, and blow into the fireplace to keep the fire burning.

IT WAS WANYANA'S first day back home since Mummy died two months ago. The last time she had been in this house was on the day Mummy died. On that day, Mummy had stayed in the bedroom all morning and it was Daddy who had dressed Wanyana and taken her to school on his motorcycle. It was not unusual for Mummy to delay getting out of bed in the morning. Sometimes when Daddy came back angry in the night and they fought, she would be too weak to wake up early. But she always got up, even if it was late and her eyes were swollen half-shut. She always helped Wanyana to dress in her uniform and shoes before calling Sula to take her to school on his boda boda. And every day without fail, Mummy would be there when the bell rang at three p.m. to pick Wanyana up from school.

On that day, it was Jajja Mwami who picked up Wanyana from school even before the bell rang. Mummy had died. They'd buried her in the banana plantation behind Jajja Mwami's house. Wanyana had felt Mummy's absence only a little at Jajja's house, where she'd been living since the burial. Jajja Mukyala was nice, and there were many children without parents living in the house. She had tried to beg Daddy to let her go on living at Jajja Mwami's house when he'd come by to pick her up and take her back home so she could go back to school. Wanyana wanted to tell Daddy that Sula's boda boda could pick her up from there in the morning and Jajja Mukyala could pick her up when the bell rang, but the words just wouldn't come out of her mouth. Daddy would not have heard her anyway, busy as he was strapping the suitcase with her clothes to the back of his motorcycle. He'd got on and held out his hand. Wanyana had taken one last look back at Jajja Mukyala and then put her hand in Daddy's. Daddy had lifted her up and sat her between himself and the suitcase. Wanyana didn't even have time to wave to Jajja Mukyala because Daddy had already started the motorcycle, speeding off so fast that her hands were occupied with gripping his shirt to keep from falling off.

Nankya's new form hovered close to the edge of the stream from her childhood, now reduced to a puddle of muddy water. She felt disoriented and wobbly at first, but gradually, she let herself rise a little higher. And then a little more. And as she rose, her field of vision expanded. And more familiar places emerged from the darkness. There was the house where she'd grown up, the glass doors and windows that her father had been so proud of all those years ago, now broken or cracked or missing entirely in places so that they were taped over with old pieces of cardboard. There was her mother at the rickety wooden stall in front of the house, slowly putting away wilted cabbages and tomatoes and eggplants and clusters of black-spotted yellow bananas. The woman looked as desolate as her dust-covered produce that had been sitting in the roadside heat all day waiting for customers who were too few, too picky, too poor. But Nankya couldn't linger. She was needed elsewhere.

Nankya felt herself pick up speed as she floated past the school where Wanyana had attended nursery. The windowless rooms looking hollowed out and skeletal without the chirping chorus of young voices to give them life. Faster, past the clinic where she'd been rushed moments before she passed away, past the carpentry shop where her husband worked, now locked up for the day. Finally, there was the cluster of houses that had been Nankya's home for the last six years of her life. In the communal courtyard, the landlady's goat was still tethered to the moringa tree, nonchalantly munching on flaccid banana peels in a wooden trough. The first house in the row of identical rental units was in darkness; the quiet bachelor who lived there worked at the new private clinic and was hardly ever home. In the next house, the pastor and his primary-school teacher wife had guests over for evening fellowship, singing "Muliro gwaake, omuliro gwaake" in sonorous but wildly off-key tones. In the next house, Maama Eva's TV blared out a Filipino soap translated into Luganda. In one corner of the courtyard, a cluster of naked children bathed in the water from a single basin, their bodies contorted in different iterations depending on which part of the body they were scrubbing. Nankya scanned the faces of the children for her Wanyana, and not finding her there, slipped into the open door of the fourth house.

WANYANA LOOKED AWAY when Daddy's new woman placed a plate of rice and mukene in front of her. She liked rice, but this wasn't her pink plate with the red flowers around it, and the silverfishes had heads on them and the eyes were staring back at her. Mummy always took the heads off the silverfishes before serving them to Wanyana. Wanyana hadn't felt Mummy's absence so much at Jajja Mwami's house. Here, Mummy's absence was all she felt. She could feel tears gathering, but they stopped when she saw a dragonfly float into the house and rise above her head. She followed it with her eyes as it flew circles around her, its gossamer wings changing colour with each loop. Yellow. Green. Blue. Red. And then it hovered in front of her, its wings fluttering all the different colours as it twirled and dipped and spun. The dragonfly was dancing for her! Wanyana watched mesmerised, but the dancing came to an abrupt halt when Daddy's new woman turned from the TV and scowled at Wanyana's untouched food.

"If I were you, I would finish that food before your father comes back," she said.

Wanyana put a thumb in her mouth as the tears gathered again.

NANKYA LOOKED CLOSELY at the light-skinned woman sitting on *her* sofa in a frilly nightdress, watching *her* TV, and telling *her* child to eat. The woman's Luganda was slightly accented. A westerner, then. On closer inspection, the lightness of her skin was chemically achieved, because look at those knuckles. Try as she might, Nankya couldn't place the slim long-limbed woman. Clearly, Kajubi's infidelity had gone further than Nankya had imagined. She felt a churning in her, a rage that had lived in the pit of her stomach for most of her marriage. She'd always tightened her stomach muscles and strangled it out of existence. Now, she let it grow in her as she watched the daughter she'd left behind banished to the cold floor in a corner of her house, forced to shrink against the wall and seek comfort in an old infancy habit that Nankya had worked hard to wean her from with aloe vera or chilli or bitter leaf on the offending thumb. She felt it expand in her as she watched the woman Kajubi had so quickly replaced her with, like she was a pair of nigina that had worn out.

WANYANA WATCHED AS the dragonfly's graceful movements speeded up. And as its movements got faster, less and less graceful, it looked as if the violently jerking insect was in pain. It started to spin faster and faster around the plate, its wings a blur, its sound the buzzing of a swarm of bees. And then it spun higher and higher and faster and faster until the plate of food lifted off the ground and slammed into the wall with such force that the melamine plate split down the middle. Daddy's new woman yelped like a puppy and got to her feet.

"Naye…" Daddy's new woman started to shout at Wanyana, but the dragonfly flew at her mouth, forcing her to duck and swipe at it with flapping hands. It zipped round and round her head, charging at her mouth whenever she tried to speak, and as it spun circles around her, it grew bigger and bigger with each rotation until it was almost as long as Wanyana's arm. The buzz of its wings was so loud that it drowned out the voices on the TV. Daddy's new woman started to scream, and Wanyana watched openmouthed, the thumb she'd been sucking damp in her lap.

NANKYA SMELLED KAJUBI'S approach before she heard the rumble of his motorcycle. He smelled how he'd always smelled – of wood shavings and varnish and cigarette smoke. The smell reminded Nankya of how she'd been repulsed by him during her pregnancy with Wanyana, but now it was as if Nankya were pregnant with all the children of the world. Her husband's return to the house still caused a tremor of fear to run through Nankya. And even in her new form, Nankya felt herself shrink as familiar worries flooded her. Would he be happy? Would he be drunk? Would he be tense? Would he be cheerful? Kajubi was a man of extremes, and any mood he chose to wear grew to overwhelm Nankya over the course of their relationship.

It was that same intensity that had first attracted Nankya to Kajubi. He had pursued her with a relentlessness that had hewn away at every reservation Nankya had had in the beginning. She would soon learn that she'd made a big mistake in confusing the tension in her body when she was with Kajubi with genuine attraction.

NJABALA'S HUSBAND WAS very pleased with the changes in his home and plantations when her mother's ghost started to help out with her chores. He changed his attitude towards his wife, and now sang her praises to all who would listen. However, Njabala's mother had to be careful not to be found out by her son-in-law. First, because she was dead, and dead people weren't supposed to be in coffee plantations picking ripe berries; but also because it is taboo in Buganda for a man and his mother-in-law (even an invisible one in ghost form) to come into physical contact with one another. And so her work on Njabala's behalf had to be kept top secret, from the village at large, but especially from Njabala's husband. And so, as Njabala's mother toiled away in the hot sun to perfect her daughter's marital home, she beseeched her daughter to keep a look out so that a son-in-law would not run into an invisible mother-in-law, singing: "*Njabala Njabala Njabala tolinsanza omuko Njabala.*"

KAJUBI GROANED AT the spectacle in front of him. The TV was on, but nobody was watching. His new woman was crying and whimpering in a corner of the sitting room. There was a broken plate on the floor and streaks of grey-brown soup running down the wall. Wanyana was on the floor in one corner looking up in awe to where Nankya hovered. Nankya watched his face as the anger swept over it, contorting his features into a tight cluster at the centre of his long face, but only for a split second. Nankya waited in anticipation for the wrath she'd been used to come flying out through his mouth, but he simply shook his head, and when he spoke, his voice was gentle.

"Mabel, what is going on here?"

The new woman pointed a shaking hand at the point above Wanyana's head where Nankya hovered.

"That thing attacked me," she shrieked.

Kajubi looked up and shook his head.

"It's just an insect," Kajubi said. "It is harmless."

He sounded more exasperated than genuinely angry.

Nankya watched him as he walked into the room and waited for the displeasure that was leaving his face to move a little further down his body and come flying out through his fists, but he sighed, sat down in his usual spot on the couch, picked up the remote and changed the channel over to the ten o'clock news.

"Wanyana, go to bed," he said. "Don't you know you have school tomorrow?"

As her baby girl stood up and shuffled off to bed with one last glance up at her, Nankya was struck again by how much Wanyana looked like her father, and how proud Kajubi was of the resemblance. How it had been a bit of a disappointment for Nankya as a new mother as from one month to the next, and one year to the next, her baby developed her father's long face and thin lips and quick gait. How, as Kajubi got more and more violent, Wanyana looked more and more like him. Nankya had worried while she was alive that Wanyana might inherit her father's fierce disposition; but now that her baby would be growing into womanhood without her, Nankya hoped that Wanyana would have some of her father's fire.

ONE DAY AS Njabala's mother helped her out in the gardens, the gossip got so sweet that Njabala forgot to keep watch for any people who might walk by and see her talking and laughing by herself while the hoe was tilling the ground on its own. And as fate would have it, that day her husband returned home early by way of the gardens, and caught the ghost of Njabala's mother working on her behalf while she sat laughing on a tree stump in the shade. He let out a horrified alarm that alerted the whole village to the presence of danger. The villagers came running and caught Njabala in her act of deception. Her husband denounced her for witchcraft, and the villagers banished her from the village.

NANKYA WATCHED KAJUBI as he watched the new woman clean up the mess on the wall and the floor, while running him through the details of the day, stopping every now and then to glance up warily at Nankya. The casualness of the conversation, the ease with which the new woman moved around her house restarted the churning in Nankya. Unlike the ghost in the Njabala story, Nankya wanted to be seen and felt and talked about. And so she spun faster and faster, feeling euphoria as the curtains billowed and the light bulb flickered and the TV went off and the clock fell off the wall. She buzzed gleefully as the new woman ran out of the house screaming, and Kajubi scrambled for something to fight back with, settling for one of his shoes, which he tossed at her, and then the broom in the corner, which he swatted at her. And as she spun, she felt herself expand into a freedom she'd never felt in the years she'd lived in the house. She charged at his face, and with each charge he stepped backwards towards the door until he tossed the broom away and ran out of the house, leaving behind Wanyana, who'd woken up in the commotion and stood watching from the bedroom door.

NANKYA HAD ALWAYS wondered what happened to Njabala and her mother after the banishment. Where did Njabala go after her husband denounced her? Did her mother's ghost continue to look out for her after she was banished? Did Njabala ever find happiness? Maama never had any answers to Nankya's questions. Suspended in this moment with Wanyana looking up at her, smiling, Nankya knew that she would never leave.

THE RIVER

Moso Sematlane

*W*RESTLING WAS PASEKA's favourite sport. He loved how supple his body became, how it struggled to fit against someone else's body, which moved and shifted by its own rules. He loved that it was the only place he could truly feel in control. When they were in a larger group of friends, his voice would be drowned out by many others. Liako, the oldest, was the loudest of them all. Because she had failed Standard Five twice, all her age mates were now preparing to go into high school, so she was absorbed into their group, although sometimes Paseka felt like she was the one who had absorbed them. But she was not the leader, although there were instances where, during conversation, she would be the only one being listened to. Apart from Cosmos, another boy, she was the only person who could tell them where in Ha Ratau they would be playing that day.

What Paseka liked about the wrestling was that he felt like his own person, and not part of a bigger organism. He would take delight in the timbre of his own voice, how free and rich it felt. How it rang against the walls of the abandoned guest lodge on the border of the village they would sometimes go to because no adults ever came there. "Butle hle monna!" he would say, with some other boy's arm tucked between his legs. Or, "Se ke oa ntiisa hakalo!" he would protest, as some other boy's arm tightened against his throat. He loved the fact that the girls wouldn't partake in the wrestling, and instead would watch them from the sidelines. He knew they would be talking about the boys, rating their handsomeness or ugliness on a scale of ten. And Paseka could see that some of the boys weren't as focused in their wrestling as he was. Hearing that a girl was talking about him, whoever was wrestling Paseka at that time would become clumsy in his moves, acting stronger than he really was, or taunting Paseka in English so that he would look more impressive to the girls.

Paseka didn't care about any of this.

At times, he felt that wrestling was a big river that he couldn't help but throw himself into. Its currents would wash him away and land him in a place that could only be reached through dreams. A place where he could lie on the grass and look up at the sun and feel it touching his face. No school to worry about the next day. No loud voices to drown out his own. Among the birds and the sound of summer unfolding, a tune would vibrate from his throat that would say all the things he couldn't say to his friends, or to his mother and older siblings at home. A tune that sang about how good it felt to have another boy's skin against his own. How sometimes, during the wrestling, he would wonder what it would feel like to really kill someone. To hold their leg in a vice grip so that their bones would break. To pull his weight against their throats until they stopped breathing.

He wouldn't be focused on anything the girls were saying, a far-off audience to the true show that would be happening on sunny afternoons. The dust, locked limbs, and grunts became his universe. Perhaps this is why he didn't notice that a sixth guest had joined their group of five that day. The man had sat down as the boys were wrestling, so that by the time the dust had settled, he was already engaged in a conversation with the girls.

He was a king; at least, that was what Paseka had heard from the adults in the village. His name was Morena. Paseka recalled how one day when his mother woke up early to go to Maseru to deliver important documents, her face had wrinkled when she mentioned him. Morena would have to stamp the documents with an official stamp, his mother said, before she could take them into the city. But she wouldn't be allowed into Morena's office if she was wearing pants. In Morena's office, only men could wear pants; the women had to wear dresses. In the village, Paseka had seen a lot of women wearing pants, and some of his friends, too. Perhaps Morena's office was like a small kingdom with its own rules, just like the bodies Paseka would wrestle against had their own rules.

One by one, the boys lost interest in the wrestling and hovered around where Morena was sitting with the girls. He smelled of BB tobacco. He flashed his teeth, and a couple of girls giggled. Paseka couldn't help but notice that some of the boys' eyes shone in the afternoon sun with something like fire. Though none of them took it upon themselves to approach Morena and the girls, not even Cosmos. Paseka wondered what it would be like to be a king, to have this power that seemed to shift the air around you.

Morena was old, with a face as hard as cowhide hung to dry. But there was power emanating from his body, and Paseka wondered what it would be like to wrestle him. Though Paseka was short, he was sure that he could topple that frame, because although he was tall, Morena was thin. Paseka watched how his hands landed on his knees with power, as laughter exploded from his chest and made the girls laugh in turn.

"Boy!" Morena said, pointing at one of the boys, although Paseka felt that it could easily have been *him* Morena was pointing at, because he didn't look at any of them in the eye: "Did your mother not teach you to respect beautiful ladies? Eh? Why do you permit them to sit on the dirty ground?"

The girls giggled some more, although none of the boys said a thing. There was a dryness in Paseka's throat, akin to the one he felt when dark clouds gathered across the sky, carrying flashes of lightning, twisting and turning like restless sleepers. They all looked to Cosmos instead, who seemed to be the only one looking Morena straight in the eye. Although following Cosmos' gaze, Paseka realised that it was not Morena he was looking at, but Liako. And then before long, all of them were looking at Liako, even the girls, because tears were running down her face. The laughter stopped. Morena's hand was resting on Liako's left leg. Far off in the distance, a donkey brayed.

Morena stood up. No one approached Liako to comfort her crying. Morena's powerful body was like a mountain that had grown from the ground, separating one mass of land into many others. It would take years to cross the ocean that separated them from Liako. As every second passed, she added to it, drop by drop, with her silent tears.

Many years from now, Paseka would think back on that moment as the thing that complicated his relations with other people, a sickness that spilled itself into his romantic life and friendships. That day, he had felt sorrow seeing Liako cry like that, but he was also fascinated. Sorrow seemed to be born from the same place as wrestling; a place where people surrendered themselves to the roar inside their bodies. Everything that people did, from drinking coffee to taking vacations, seemed to be mere distractions

from the constant thumping that announced its imminent arrival. Paseka
had answered its call even as early as then, throwing himself into its noise.
For him, wrestling was something primal that no human language could
capture. Morena's hand, however, placed firmly on Liako's leg, seemed to
be born from the same place as the roar. But Paseka hadn't yet known this.

Now, he watched in silence as Liako cried and Morena stood up and
walked between them, whistling a tune on his way. Even when he disappeared in the direction of the village, the sun setting behind his footsteps,
the silence remained. No one approached Liako.

"I'm going home," she said after a while. "Ke kopa ho tsamaea ke le
mong."

Obeying her request, they watched her stand and walk in the opposite
direction that Morena had taken, on her own. The path didn't lead to her
house, and would require that she make a roundabout journey all the way
next to the tar road so that she could finally rejoin the right path. The direction Morena had walked in. Perhaps this was one of his kingdom's rules, like
the one about women not being allowed to wear pants. Perhaps no one was
allowed to walk where a king had walked.

THAT NIGHT PASEKA was sewing fabric onto the mask that would make
him look like Rey Mysterio, when there was a knock on the door. He had
been working on the costume for three weeks now, since his mother had
taught him how to sew. He had first seen Rey Mysterio about two years ago
at Ntate Temoho's Bioskop House. As summer rolled in, Ntate Temoho
would use the hut in his yard to show films, using a projector, and charging
people as little as five maloti. Paseka had seen many films at his Bioskop
House: *Three Ninjas*, *Anaconda* and *Tarzan*. But on Friday evenings, he and
some of his friends would ask Lebohang, Ntate Temoho's oldest son, to
sneak them in, because children younger than thirteen were not allowed
to watch. In the room filled with sweat and beer bottles and the older boys
from the village howling at Ntate Temoho's screen, Paseka had first seen
Rey Mysterio in a wrestling match.

He had never before seen how a person's body could be like water, something mouldable, and quick, and powerful. He had been especially impressed at how Rey Mysterio could slip between the gap in the wrestling ring's ropes, using it as a swing so he could kick his opponent in the face. It amazed Paseka that a person so tiny could be so strong. It amazed him too, that he wore a mask, in different colours for each match, so no one really knew who he was. Although when Paseka wore his mask in the village, people would probably recognise him, he looked forward to how much more powerful his wrestling would become once he looked just like Rey Mysterio.

The woman who knocked on the door was Liako's mother, and she came in crying so loudly that Paseka's sister, Nthabiseng, stopped cooking, and his older brother, Thabang, looked up from where he was doing homework next to the kerosene lamp. Expecting that their mother would send them away, they had started shuffling towards their bedroom when Liako's mother's voice stopped them.

"Liako didn't come home," she said, looking at Paseka directly. "We've been looking for her everywhere."

His feet went cold. His mother turned back to look at him.

"She left before we could leave," Paseka said. "She was crying."

"Why was she crying?"

Paseka remembered Liako's tears streaming down her cheeks, how much they looked like a river. Perhaps this was how rivers should have always been made: small and glistening, all the better to stream down a beautiful young girl's face.

In the years since, Paseka had carried regret for that moment, wrapping it around himself like a mourner's shawl. He hadn't had the words to describe what Morena touching Liako like that had meant to him – to all of them – much less to describe it to Liako's mother. The hand, the power in Morena's body, the way a dark cloud covered Liako's face when Morena had arrived, like she knew what was coming: all of it had seemed an incomprehensible intrusion into the world they made for themselves during play. Alone in his flat, with the emptiness and loneliness of the city pressing upon him, on either side of him, inside him, Paseka would howl into the darkness, crying so much he felt the walls were shaking from his sadness. Why was he crying? He didn't know; other than to imitate Liako that afternoon, to throw himself into a river far bigger and more roaring than all the rivers he'd thrown himself into when he was younger. To cry for all the memories he'd lost as a child that, had he known beforehand how greedily the world would taint, he would have held tighter.

Paseka shrugged at her question, and Liako's mother cried some more.

As the night deepened, the villagers left their houses carrying kerosene lamps and candles, scattering towards all corners of the village to look for Liako. In the darkness, Paseka and his friends had convened next to the abandoned guest house to discuss her disappearance.

"It's him!" Cosmos said, spitting into the grass. "Morena! He did something to her!"

"Do you think he killed her?" someone said.

"If he did, he will not be able to hide her corpse," Cosmos said. "This village has eyes. The ghosts of the people that used to live in this village never sleep. They know what each of us does. They see everything. They will howl all night until her corpse is found. And then we will bury it, and we will kill him."

"But he's a king," someone else said.

"So what?" someone said. "He's a king, but he's not higher in rank than the king of Lesotho. All these villages have kings of their own who can easily be replaced."

Once again, Paseka was quiet. Around him, he could hear faint voices from the villagers calling out Liako's name, and see specks of light in the distance from their lamps. The night was getting cooler, pinching his skin. Tonight, he wouldn't speak. He wouldn't even call Liako's name. His words would betray him, his thoughts. Like Cosmos had said, the ghosts of the village saw everything, even the things inside Paseka's mind.

Paseka felt bad that even with Liako gone missing, he still wanted to wrestle the king. Not to kill him or to avenge Liako's death, but just to feel the joy of wrestling someone much stronger. And perhaps, to wrestle against someone evil.

As the villagers looked for Liako, Paseka fell asleep with visions of lamps bobbing in the darkness, the aggression of the winter night making him shiver. At one point, when sleep beckoned, he felt someone carry him in their arms and put him in his bed, back at home. It might have been Thabang. He sank into a deep sleep, but could swear than even in that darkness, he could still hear people calling Liako's name, and imagined that the village ghosts were contributing to the calls too.

PASKEA HATED THAT even though they didn't have school the next day, his mother still woke them up in the morning – to clean the house, make bread, take the sheep to graze, and perform all the other tasks she had delegated to them every day for that school holiday. But although she woke them up early that morning, it wasn't to work, but to go to Liako's house.

"She's been found," she said, "although I fear she won't be as you remember her. She probably won't be your friend anymore. I mean, how can you be friends with her when she is at a completely different place in her life right now?"

This she said, looking at Paseka.

"What do you mean?" Paseka said. "Where was she found?"

"That bastard!" she said, pulling Paseka towards the door. They all put on their jackets and boots and walked into the mist of the morning to go to Liako's house. On their way there, Paseka refrained from asking his mother any further questions, because he could tell she was angry. They walked swiftly, trying to keep up to her pace. When she opened the gate at Liako's house, she did so as if she lived there. She was met by Liako's mother snapping pieces of wood in two to make fire for their cooking that day.

They hugged each other.

"The Lord is mighty," Liako's mother said. "I thought I would die if that child was not returned to me."

"Do not speak of death," Paseka's mother said. "The Lord doesn't like us to speak so. You will live many more years on this earth. As will she."

Paseka's mother asked the kids to excuse them, as they would be discussing adult business, and drove them inside the house, where they could all see Liako. Their house was bigger than the one Paseka and his siblings lived in, with couches covered in noisy plastic and a big picture of Jesus Christ on one wall. In one of the chairs sat Liako, taller than when Paseka had seen her last, as tall as Paseka's mother. In fact, she was not a child anymore; she had the face and clothes of an adult, wearing a red dress with dots on it. Her hair was combed neatly like one of the women who went to work in Maseru.

"It is nice to see you," Liako said to Paseka. "It is nice to see you too, Nthabiseng and Thabang."

"Nice to see you," they said together.

The sight of Liako shackled them into silence. Just the afternoon before, Liako had been a young child, like Paseka was, but now she had grown tall and her face was that of an older woman's. Immediately, Paseka's thoughts went to the opening of school in summer. What would become of Liako when she had to go to school? Paseka didn't think that a person of Liako's age would fit in their classroom anymore; he didn't even think she would fit in high school. As if these were the very same thoughts that were running through her mind, she looked down at her lap and smiled shyly.

"Ha u na mantsoe?" she said to Paseka. "You've been quiet since you saw me."

"I'm always quiet," Paseka answered.

The silence lengthened until the room itself seemed to take notice of it, and offer noises of its own: the sound of sunlight baking the room to crispiness; even the sound of the Jesus Christ picture, staring silently down at the children, speaking of all the fantastical stories Paseka had heard his mother tell him from the Bible.

"I don't know what I'll do with my life now," Liako said, letting out a puff of breath. "I think I'll have to find a job. I can't go to school anymore."

Thabang moved in his chair, rubbing against the plastic. Paseka had never before seen his brother, always so knowledgeable about his own body – what it meant to be a boy, how to move like a boy, his voice as deep as a boy's voice should be – seem as insignificant as he did in that moment, looking at Liako.

"Where will you work?" Thabang said, in a voice that unmade everything Paseka had seen his brother embody about being a boy. Liako stood up and went to the window, where the sun settled on her face. "Ha ke tsebe. It has to be Maseru. I've never been to Maseru, but I would hate to work in the village. What's there to do here anyway? Look after some man who beats me, then expects me to wash his underwear? Or children who grow up to become these men?"

"Will you get married?" Nthabiseng said.

"I don't think so," she said, looking back at them. "Women in Maseru never marry. They don't have to. They work, and try to figure out how to mend things that are broken in the world. How to increase money so that it feeds all of us, not just a select few. How to cure viruses. Maybe I'll become that: a doctor."

Nthabiseng and Thabang exchanged looks at the word "doctor", ngaka, as if they were parents who, worried about the prospects for their child, had asked her about her future plans, only to be impressed that she had figured it out all on her own. But something still nagged at Paseka's throat, an unease forming inside him, bringing back the nausea of the search for Liako the night before, the moving lamps, the thought of ghosts surrounding the village.

"Did Morena do this to you?" Paseka said.

Liako's eyes flickered with the look Paseka had seen when Morena had sat next to her the day before. For a moment, it seemed as if she was seeing Morena again, her eyes widening with fear. Paseka's eyes followed the empty space beside her, only to settle upon the picture of Jesus Christ.

"Yes," Liako said.

Nthabiseng and Thabang's eyes widened. Paseka noticed that Thabang's fingers tried, unsuccessfully, to clutch at the edge of the sofa, slipping against the plastic. But he didn't seem to be aware of this, so struck was he by what Liako had said. "Did it hurt?"

"Yes," Liako said. She moved across the room and came to sit across from them on the sofa again. "Ha ke batle ho bua. I don't want to speak about him, or this situation, for the rest of my life.'

When it came time to leave, Liako's mother had just finished cooking the meat and pap, and said there would be enough for everyone. Paseka's family ate lunch with Liako and her mother, and all the while, Paseka caught himself looking at Liako and thinking of the big adventure her life was about to become. As an adult, you could do anything you wanted. If he had become an adult like Liako, he would probably be training for his first professional wrestling match. He would wrestle all day, when he wasn't working. And then, finally, he could wrestle Morena.

After lunch was done, Liako and Paseka's mother settled into one of their adult conversations, deep shadows creasing their foreheads. Paseka tried to listen, but they were talking under their breath. But something about their expressions scared him.

The children, along with Liako, managed to slip away. Outside, Nthabiseng and Thabang went to look for their friends elsewhere in the village. Only Paseka and Liako remained, walking in the direction of his house as the sun turned orange. Liako was looking down as she walked, as if a million thoughts were coming to her head simultaneously and she was trying to sort them into different compartments. Paseka felt sorry for his friend. Yes, that was what she was; even with the transformation, she was still his friend.

"How do you think the others are going to react?" Paseka said.

Liako shrugged. "Same as everyone, I guess. My mother said she was happy that at least he didn't kill me."

They walked in silence. Years and years away, Paseka would come back to that moment and think how, even with her transformation, Liako had still seemed like a little girl; even littler than she had been the day before, when Morena had laid a hand on her lap during their play. He remembered how he had stared at her face as they walked together, watching her cheeks closely, looking to see if there would be tears. The river was still dry.

IN THE MORNING, Paseka woke up to hear that the whole village was marching to Morena's house. Their mother had asked them to not go outside, then put on her jacket and went to join the rest of the march to the hill where Morena's house was. They obeyed her orders until people's shadows from the crusade passed by, and they heard shouting and singing outside as if a great celebration was about to take place. It was Thabang who ventured to open the door, then Nthabiseng and Paseka followed him out.

"We have to come back before she does," Thabang said. "O tla re bolaea."

They all agreed to return before their mother did, although none of them knew where she was, or what time she would be coming back. Paseka looked everywhere for his friends, but couldn't find any of them, so for a while, he had to walk beside Nthabiseng and her friends. The villagers' eyes were dark like his mother's and Liako's mother's had been the day before, like shadows lived inside them. These were no celebrations. He heard from Nthabiseng's talk with her friends that the villagers intended to drag Morena to the middle of the village, where they would burn him.

'Was this because of what he did to Liako?" one of them asked.

"Eya," the other friend answered.

"Where is she?" Nthabiseng said.

"I heard she went to Maseru," one of Nthabiseng's friends said. "They wanted her to watch them burn him, but she couldn't. She's very good-hearted. I would have lit the match on him myself."

Paseka ran, although he didn't know where he was running to. He weaved through the villagers heading for Morena's house, but wasn't heading in the same direction. He had to find Liako. He had only been to Maseru once, too young to remember what it was like, but he supposed that as long as he could stand by the tar road, he could wait for a taxi that would take him there. He would find Liako and bring her back to the village. Even though Morena had done such an evil thing to her, Paseka couldn't lose his friend.

Through her, he had to see what adulthood would look like; if the dreams of rivers he had would come true once he became an adult like she had.

On the way, he came upon a crowd of men singing a song that made them lift their knees up to their chests, carrying knobkerries and long knives. Cosmos was among them, the only child there, lifting up his knees as well, although they never reached his chest. He noticed Paseka and pulled him into the singing.

"We're going to get him!" Cosmos shouted in Paseka's ear. "We're going to kill him!"

Paseka saw that Cosmos carried a kitchen knife. He didn't know the song, but he watched the men's mouths move, and tried to catch the tune. Though he didn't lift his knees to his chest, but simply walked. Cosmos was doing better than he was with the song, but watching his mouth, Paseka could tell that some of the words were escaping Cosmos' mouth as well. The men sang all the way to Morena's house.

Ba boi ba cheche, ba chechele morao!
Ho ee rona, rona ba ee pele!
Ba boi ba cheche, ba chechele morao!
Ho ee rona, rona ba ee pele!

Morena was the first person that Paseka would see die. He remembered how they'd seen him run towards the mountains, his clumsy figure cutting into the grass. The younger men in the group stopped singing and ran after him, surrounding him on all sides. After a while, the women and children caught up with the group. Paseka remembered black knots of clouds in the sky, although this could just have been his memory supplying the scene with its share of dramatics. But Paseka knew that the reason he couldn't remember the day in all its clarity was because, for him, that was when his own transformation had started: when he had become an adult. In many ways, the envy he had felt for Liako's transformation had marked him out somehow; or maybe it was just his closeness to her that had started his own process. Even though witnessing Morena's death affected Paseka greatly, the transformation that came afterwards was truly one of the most exciting things that had happened to Paseka. Everything in his life from then on became a sort of anticlimax, like a snowball rolling down a hill and losing matter, instead of gaining it. Years later, a boy he slept with regularly after his move to the city, had looked up at the ceiling after their lovemaking and said, "Whenever I look into your eyes, I see nothing. It's like something in you is dead."

When the villagers surrounded Morena, the singing grew louder, and for a while, Paseka was buoyed by the melodies, the noise, the twisted faces around him – as if this was indeed a celebration. They had tried to pull Morena to the centre of the village, but he had resisted, shouting at the top of his voice: "Have mercy on me! Have mercy on me, pleeaaaase!"

Cosmos had taken Paseka's hand, and they had pushed their way through the crowd so that they could get a good view of what was about to happen. Paseka wondered if Rey Mysterio had ever seen something as fantastical as this. It made Paseka feel bigger than him, stronger, because he was sure that, should he ever wrestle him, he would be the only one who had seen a person burned alive.

It's a strange thing to watch a person being burned. A villager pours paraffin over their head in a manner reminiscent of a religious baptism. It's not too long before the whole grassy field smells like paraffin, and the villagers have to stop singing because it's entering their mouths, their nostrils. Only the sound of the victim rises up from the clearing, rising up to the mountains, lifting until it reaches God's ears, and is so loud that it rises up to whoever is above God himself.

"Help me!" he cries. "Have mercy in your hearts for me!"

But the villagers' faces have shadows in them. Someone throws the flame, and the show is far more spectacular than any wrestling match Paseka has ever seen. The man's intestines sizzle, then burst like a popped balloon. His face contorts into an incomprehensible shape. At this point, the villagers have had to step back because the grass had caught flame too, and the fire forms a circle around the man, who is now merely a black, burned corpse kneeling in the ground. Paseka can smell his clothes, even amidst the smell of paraffin: the smell of BB tobacco that had come with him when he visited their playing yesterday. He can still smell his clothes.

THE NEXT DAY, after taking the sheep home from their grazing, the first thing Paseka did was to look at himself in the mirror. He had become quite a handsome young man; everything that was gangly or awkward about his body as a child, had reconfigured itself overnight into a man of about twenty-one years old, the sides of his face sharper, smatterings of a beard below. He looked stronger too, with muscles that moved like water, smoother than even Rey Mysterio's. He remembered waking up Thabang and Nthabiseng, and how shocked they had been to find that he was taller than them. His voice had changed too, although, not in the way he had expected. He had thought it would sound like Thabang's voice, sonorous, a boy's voice, although it still carried remnants of yesterday, high-pitched, and even girlish.

The transformations had been happening sporadically all over the village. Cosmos had transformed at the same time as Paseka had; that morning, they had compared their new adult selves against one other and laughed. A couple of boys and girls around the village had also transformed. Some didn't even need to have seen Morena burn, like Paseka and Cosmos had. Some had seen tragic sights all on their own, in their houses, or elsewhere in the big village. Over breakfast, his mother had told him that now he was an adult, he had to find a job and support the family.

"U ts'oana le ntate oa hao hantle," she said, looking away from his face to the trunk in the next room, where his father's clothes had been kept since he died.

These black moods, Paseka would learn, would overcome her frequently now that Paseka had grown to remind her of his father. Paseka couldn't remember much about his father, although he was told that when he went to Maseru for the first time, he was the one who had taken him there.

He resolved to find a job in Maseru, but it was difficult to know where to start. At the back of his mind, on the shelf where he kept his dreams of becoming a wrestler or wanting to feel the skin of another boy against his, he knew he had to find Liako again.

That's how the second Morena had happened to him. The second one that the Council appointed was much younger than the first. Talk had rippled around the village that he would undo the old rules, and allow women to wear whatever they wanted in his office.

Paseka had never been in an office before, but he had been encouraged to go there after hearing that the second Morena was from Maseru, and he had new, exciting ways of seeing things.

"Can you help me find a job in Maseru?" Paseka asked.

The second Morena had looked Paseka over in silence. He had never been looked at by another man that way before; the openness in Morena's eyes stopped something within him that was spinning on its own axis, a sense of gravity that had previously been alien to him. Was it in the way that Morena's physical form was like his, lithe, supple – an athlete's body? Was it the openness of his eyes challenging Paseka's own, as if the child in him was still untainted by the fears adults accrued as they grew up? This, Paseka remembered thinking, was what it must have felt like after God had just created the earth: a spinning wonder in the blackness of space that would contain time's deepest sadness, and its most fervent happiness.

"You'll need a passport or ID; do you have those?"

Paseka shook his head.

"Do you know how to write a CV?"

Paseka shook his head.

That afternoon, he went to the old Morena's house so that the New Morena could help him write a CV. He made Paseka laugh a lot, telling him stories about his childhood in Maseru. His clothes were clean, and whenever he moved, like when he went to the kitchen to make him and Paseka motoho and bread, a smell of summer filled the whole room: bees knocking dizzily against each other over violets, lips made wet and pink by water arching through the mouth of a hosepipe. Paseka had never met anyone like him. When the rope of their conversation wound itself thin, he leaned over and pressed his lips against Paseka's.

Looking back, Paseka had played and replayed that moment over and over in his head, trying to remember the emotions he had felt. Some days, he was convinced that being in that room with the New Morena was the happiest he had ever been in his life. He hadn't even thought of the gruesome events of only a few days before. Other days, the memory of the New Morena was a distant disc of sun seen through hazy clouds.

He knew that since leaving the village, a different, much more profound, change had overcome him, more drastic than the physical transformations some of the village's children had gone through that year. One day in the city, he had finally come across Liako, but he didn't have the courage to speak to her. He had been at a coffee shop called Knobkerrie, and a peal of laughter threw him out of the novel he was reading. He put it down to see the woman he had known in Ha Ratau, all those years ago. Liako was as she was then, a fully grown woman, but something about her seemed to have made her a different person. She wore the same type of dress she was wearing on the first day of her transformation, and combed her hair neatly as she had then; but now, Paseka saw her smiling for the first time. She was happy, something Paseka hadn't ever experienced either in his life in the city, or back at the village on the heels of his transformation.

"Where have you been?" Paseka remembered Thabang asking him one day as he opened the door and snuck into the kitchen, the talcum smell of the New Morena's lovemaking still clinging to him. The house was quiet, with shadows resting in its corners, the smell of paraffin hanging in the air from the just-extinguished kerosene lamps. Thabang's eyes were like two orbs of light. Although Paseka was much taller than him, he refused to be intimidated.

"Why's that any business of yours?" Paseka said. "I'm a man, I work to feed this family."

Although his applications to find work in Maseru hadn't been successful, the New Morena had promised Paseka that they would keep trying. The New Morena knew Maseru better than Paseka ever could, so each day, he would take Paseka's CV and ID document and talk to people he knew in Maseru. Paseka had called himself a wrestler, so the New Morena had looked for jobs as a security guard for nightclubs and offices, or else, as a boxing teacher for young children. None of these were successful. To make sure that he could still feed his family, the New Morena had employed Paseka as his gardener, and had emptied the shed near the house for Paseka to sleep in. This was just so people wouldn't ask questions. When the New Morena came back from Maseru, he would make Paseka a bowl of pap and sour milk and, with a smile on his face, would watch Paseka eat. They would lie on the couch until the evening, or in the darkness take a walk towards the mountains and whisper jokes and anecdotes under the starlight.

The simple truth was this, the New Morena was the best person Paseka had ever known. What use was there in going to Maseru if it meant he would spend time apart from him? Even the plans to find Liako faded in Paseka's mind. He envisioned a life with the New Morena just as they were; when he came home, Paseka would be there to greet him, dirt from the garden still clinging to his clothes, stomach growling for New Morena's cooking. They would make love as the village slept, darkness surrounding everything, although with the New Morena deep inside him, it felt as bright as daylight.

Now Thabang told Paseka that their mother was sick, probably dying.

"I have to work to feed this family," Paseka told him, although this felt like something he was saying to himself.

"I have to work, I have to work, I have to work, I have to work," he told himself every day. And with each day he spent at the New Morena's house working for him, the more his family faded. Paseka was okay with this. What was his mother's eminent death compared to how large he and the New Morena had become? They were bigger than the village, bigger than Rey Mysterio, or the crowd roaring his name from where the spot-lights couldn't reach. This was the biggest Paseka had ever felt in his life. He had given himself over to a river far bigger, far more violent than any he had thrown himself in as a boy. Years later, every romantic partner Paseka went out with in the city, every boy or girl he ever made love with, he was chasing the rush of this river. None of them ever came close to matching its vivacity, or making him feel more alive.

That afternoon, the New Morena returned to his house, but no pap was cooked. No sour milk, either. It took Paseka a while to recognise him: his face was a blur, mottled with purple and red, his eyelids swollen, a tennis-ball-sized mound growing from the edge of his mouth.

"What happened?" Paseka said.

The New Morena couldn't speak until Paseka helped him into the house. He sat down and Paseka filled him a glass of water. But Paseka knew the answer before the New Morena could even say it: someone had intruded on the world they had worked so hard to build together. The ghosts of the village had finally heard them. Paseka was, even then, all too familiar with the roar of the river he heard in his ears, the language spoken in a primal realm: to have someone's skin against his. Anger and violence, the way he would lock himself into someone else's body during wrestling, was the greatest intimacy he had known. He knew how bodies functioned, how they could be moulded anew to feel a new and even enchanting pain. He left the house without closing the door and started running into the night.

Perhaps they were still drunk off the kill when Paseka had found them: Cosmos and a group of other boys, who had recently transformed, tottering in the field in the darkness, shouting obscenities at the moon, singing songs the old Basotho warrior used to sing;

Ke nna Cucutle
Masole a feta a bina!
Sefela sa ntoa se nfetile!
Se nfetile, se nyatsa kholiso ea ka!
Se kokota monyako oa Bonkuku!
Ke nna sesole se le lefifi!

"Cosmos!" Paseka shouted, stopping them all in their tracks. They turned back to look at him.

"You want to fight me?" Cosmos said, his words slurring, "U batla hong loants'a? How can you when you've become a woman? I should have known *what* he was when he said women didn't have to wear dresses anymore. He wanted to wear them himself! And now you wear them too."

The other boys laughed at the joke.

There are four main rules to scoring points in any wrestling match.

The first is the takedown, when you drive your opponent to the mat and pin them down so they don't escape.

The second is the escape itself, when your opponent manages to wriggle free from the trap.

The third is the reversal, when your opponent not only escapes the trap, but manages to trap you in the same manner.

The last is the near fall, when you almost pin down your opponent on the mat, but their shoulder hovers about the ground by a few centimetres. That night Paseka had followed all the rules, and even added new ones of his own. He had always wondered what it felt like to kill someone. But of course, as the breath left Cosmos's body, Paseka learnt that once you start something, it isn't as difficult as you had thought. After that, Paseka had flung his body into the darkness, the other boys chasing after him, although he was too fast for them.

He would remember that sensation: like he had truly mastered his body the day the water carried him away.

At Knobkerrie, for what felt like hours, even though it was only a few seconds, two sides of him couldn't agree whether to go after Liako or not. He only had a few seconds to act. Liako was with another man, and the way his hands rested on her waist told Paseka that they were lovers. They waved the waitress goodbye, and when they opened the door, the roar of the river outside filled the coffee shop. The rivers had been spreading all over the city like a virus. The government would regularly employ people to fill them up with soil and rocks, but just as quickly, new ones would form where the old rivers were dug out, until the whole exercise seemed not only pointless, but a running and noisy reminder that the earth could not be tamed, that humans lived in it only as visitors.

Paseka chased after Liako too late. He saw, in the distance, her lover taking her hand and helping her cross a muddy area where a smaller stream of water had branched off. Paseka was familiar with this one; it had formed just a year after he moved to the city. If you followed it by foot or car, it would lead you straight to his village, a place he had not been to in years. He didn't know whether it was to call Liako's attention that he jumped in, or whether it had been a roar building up in him so that he might feel anything other than his perpetual sadness. Neither Liako or her lover looked back. The people in the city didn't look at him either. The water was cold, and strong, and he tried to force his body to master it, to mould it just like he moulded his own body when he wrestled. But no sooner than he tried to grasp the tide, it changed shape, and carried him away.

self-awareness,
illusion, delusion and
deception

SOMETIMES YOU MAKE ME SMILE

Zanta Nkumane

*T*HE BODY HANGS over the toilet bowl as if in prayer. Its arms flop to the floor like vines overdue for a pruning. The overflowing water buoys the man's head and gushes over and across the office bathroom floor towards the door, as if running away from the dead body. A red tie streams around the neck, then down the man's back, the deathly loop that was his end. A dim, flashing light punctures the air.

Detective Mila waits by the door for the forensic team to finish up before approaching his lifeless friend. He pulls his shirt closer and wishes he was wearing the coat he left in the backseat of his car. He peels Mzwakhe from the bowl and lays him on the floor, to reveal eyes staring in shock, and a bruised head. Mila wonders if he knew his murderer, or it's the sight of death that provoked such staggering stupefaction. In all the dead bodies he'd seen in his ten-year career, all their faces looked different. Some had a look of surrender, as if welcoming their end. Others had a defiant look, as if fighting to stay. Others had no look, as if they cared neither to live or die.

He starts jotting down details of the scene. No sign of a struggle. No blood or body scrapes. No human trace anywhere, as if a ghost hauled Mzwakhe to his death. He brushes his hand over his friend's face, and the dead eyes wilt close like poppies at night.

A grey inkiness melts over the warm city and a chorus of generators roars in the distance as Mila drives back to the station on Commissioner Street. The building is always freezing, like the Arctic defecated inside it. Since many political activists were tortured and some killed in its depths by the apartheid police, Mila believes that the cold never left because ghosts float about in its hallways. Even in the swell of summer, there is always a coat in his car, like now.

He watches the city's huddled form take shape as he gets closer to the station. The twinkle of the Northern suburbs with their groomed gardens, hotel sundecks and middle-class homes shrinks into streets mottled with litter, abandoned buildings, and a barrage of people.

Mzwakhe is the third victim. The other two, Sandile and Jason, also met peculiar deaths, unlike anything Mila had seen since joining the force.

Sandile was found next to his pool, covered in flour like a dusted human loaf. The same flour had been stuffed into his mouth until he suffocated. His eyes were also wide with shock. Jason burnt to death in his bed. His electric blanket was tampered with and set off a fire. The killer had tied him to the bed. There had been no look to see with Jason.

Most of the traffic lights are off, and the ones that are on, he skips. Instead of turning into the station, he drives past it to Doornfontein.

As he takes off his clothes at the entrance, a sigh escapes Mila's body, as if he is shedding chains. He squeezes his way through the crammed bodies to the bar, the licks of skin against his already a better alternative to being alone in his flat or buried under mounds of paperwork at the station. He gulps five tequila shots like they don't make his throat burn, and watches the pile-on of naked bodies. An assortment of dicks and balls dangling, waists swaying to the music, all plump for plucking.

He used to be a regular when he started his job, fresh out of the police academy. He would just enjoy watching the other men smash against each other, while touching himself. Then one night, after half-a-bottle of tequila, he bent over to let a married man shove an Ecstasy pill up his bum. He could feel the cold ring between his buttocks, as the man fingered the pill inside him, then proceed to enter him. Sometimes he'd visit during his lunch breaks and return to his desk sex-sore, but relieved.

A hand sneakily rubs his buttocks, and he swats it away. He wobbles on the stairs as he descends into the basement, the smell of latex and balls growing more pungent as he goes deeper. He avoids meeting anyone's eyes in case he sees those wet eyes he witnessed earlier today. He wants to be sex-sore but relieved again. He has the rest of his life for more of the eyes. Moans sweep towards him as he feverishly knocks on each cubicle door. The last stall cracks open when he smacks the door, and he lurches in, tripping over the bowl of condoms and lube left on the floor. He steadies himself over the toilet, arms spread against both walls as if on Golgotha. Someone bolts the door behind him, and he knows to bend his body for the man.

I can't bear to hear their growls join the cacophony of jarring dance remixes, rhythmic thrusts and God hollering. Besides, the true satisfaction of the day is stiff inside a mortuary. A late-night rain wallops outside and I feel more here than not, like I can run my fingers over the ridges on the walls or step on a sticky floor. And really feel it. These moments of almost-solidity, I prefer to spend with Mandla or my mama.

MANDLA IS LIKE my Forrest Gump. Not like the movie, but like the Frank Ocean song. But the song is based on the movie, so maybe he is my Forrest Gump in the movie way, too. I hate rugby, but he asked me to come watch him play today. I also hate it because I must cheer him from the stands next to his girlfriend, who doesn't know that when she's kissing him, she's tasting a bit of me too. It's my weird consolation. I sit at the end of the row and prepare to pretend to be interested.

Last night, in his dorm room, he tried to explain again what a try was. "You run into the end zone and touch the ball down. That gets the team five points. Bro, I can't believe you don't know anything about rugby when your older brother was captain of the school team."

"I am not your bro. I told you that word makes me feel like I'm not close to you. Like we down beers every weekend and don't tell each other how we really feel."

"You're right. I don't kiss my bros."

"At least you're willing to be seen with them."

"Not this again."

"I know, but you don't even look at me. I just want to know it's different with us."

"If I looked at you, then people would see. I don't look at *her* how I look at you."

"Let me get back to my room before the other seniors return from the common room."

The boys look like rabid ants, running and tackling one another for the last crumb of sugar. There are moments when they are a pile, scrambling for the ball, then separating to chase each other. When they are piles, my eyes search for his orange boots, then I sit back when he emerges from the rubble.

I look at his girlfriend, down the row from me. I like Buhle. She told me I was cool once. Well, what I was wearing, not me. I was wearing my mother's St Michael's maroon cardigan in the bus back from mid-term break, and she said it as she and Mandla shuffled to the back of the bus, her voice gruff but comforting. It's still the nicest thing a senior has said to me.

Her long dreadlocks are pulled back in a high ponytail, each loc glistening like spiderweb silk in the morning sun. Her midnight skin has the same glow. Her plump lips form chants around his name – *Go Mandla, go Mandla* – as blue pom-poms fly above her like two frayed, flamboyant orbs. Everything about her is bright, like a sequined jumpsuit. I kind of understand. They look beautiful together.

But Mandla says I'm a better kisser, no competition. My mouth and skin never fail to fill him with heat, he says. Yet when the match ends, I watch him run to her and lift her up as if she is the weight of a droplet he won't let fall to the ground. Everyone crowds around him, a pat here and a high-five up somewhere. But a look my way: nowhere, like always.

On the way back to my room, Mzwakhe and his friends are sitting on a bench near the path to my dorm. Sandile is across from Mzwakhe and Jason across from Mila, each holding a fan of cards. Mzwakhe's father dates teenage girls, but everyone pretends they don't see because he owns buses and kombis. Sandile's father is the pastor of a big church, but his mom sometimes comes to church with bruises on her face. Sometimes, so does he. Jason is repeating Grade 12, but his father still bought him a car last year because he made captain of the soccer team. Mila, like me, is here on scholarship. Mila is his surname and his name is Mdu. Like me, he doesn't have a father. But his died. Mine left. Maybe that's why he uses his surname more – it keeps his father close. Boys like calling each other by their surnames, like sports commentators, like being a boy means that your surname means more than your name.

This is just another intrusion of teenage boys who will grow up to be a deceit of men. I pull my hoodie over my head as if it's an invisibility cloak. We aren't allowed to walk on the grass; if a prefect catches you, then it's two days on kitchen duty, washing pots wider than a car tyre. Mzwakhe calls me "Fruitcake" the moment he notices me. The intrusion laugh on cue, like the trained shits they are. Not bad; that's probably the nicest insult he has hurled at me.

"Fruitcake, I am talking to you," he shouts.

Just keep walking, just keep walking, I remind myself. That's what my mama said I must do. He quickly yanks me to the ground and stands over me. *Don't say anything, don't say anything. That's what Mandla said I must do.*

"Didn't you hear me call you, fruitcake?" His foot is heavy on my chest. "We need to clean out your fruitcake ears to make sure you hear me next time."

He signals to the others and chucks me over his shoulder, like I'm a large bag of ice he needs to smash into fragments. He marches down towards the quiet school bathrooms, his entourage behind us like a wedding procession. I want to scream, but fear it will make me look pathetic. Like I really am this thing he calls me. He kicks open one of the cubicles and instructs Sandile and Jason to hold me down, while Mila stands by the door. In the transfer, I try to shake myself free, but their hands tighten around my arms. Screaming for help is pointless; everyone is back at the hostel, waiting for afternoon tea and dry vetkoeks. We all watch Mzwakhe pee, his limp dick flopping like a fish out of water.

"Bring it here."

Inside the cubicle, they kick the back of my knees and bend me to the floor. They hold my hands behind my back and Mzwakhe shoves my head into the toilet. I hear myself whimper a *please don't* that only sinks into the sewer. The odour of his fresh piss punches me, wrenching my body as if it will vomit – but nothing comes up. It's the shit smells and potpourri toilet cleaner that make me feel I will never be clean again.

"Now your ears will be clean enough to hear me next time." He flushes.

THE BARBER SHOP smells sharp like purple spirit, but also earthy like coconut oil and Sulfur8. The clippers fill the room with a loud buzzing, and the banter foams around like lather. Mila waits by the door, declining offers of a seat in one of the barber's chairs when a space opens. Since he is balding, he cuts his hair weekly. But not here. Cheating on your barber is a transgression, even if all the barber does is shave everything off, nothing intricate like an undercut fade or line designs.

Mandla's head hangs over the sink, towel wrapped over his shoulders like closed wings. His barber dries his hair and directs him back to the chair in front of the mirror. Mandla notices Mila, and nods slowly like he wasn't expecting him. A man in a leopard-print suit, red loafers and garish sunglasses accuses his barber of being bewitched because of how well he treats his girlfriend. Mila wants to laugh, but this isn't his barbershop turf. The girlfriend must have put something in your food, the leopard man asserts. A wave of nods flows around the room. Why does loving one woman have to be witchcraft? the barber retorts. It's the only explanation, no man can be this whipped without a little help, another man in blue overalls adds. Everyone laughs except Mandla. His barber rubs shea butter between his hands and then slathers him with such might, his roots must taste it.

"What do you want, Mdu?" He pushes the recorder away from his face.

"It's Detective Mila. This is not a personal call, Mr Dlamini. I just want to know where you went after leaving Mzwakhe's office a few hours before he was found dead."

"Gym, then home. You can ask my wife."

"What time was that?"

"I don't remember … four? Maybe five? I am very busy these days, I can barely remember what I had for breakfast."

"I am sure you know Mr Thobela was drowned in his toilet. Do you know anyone who would want to harm him?"

"No. We weren't close like that."

THEY ARE WALKING towards Park Station. Mandla travels from Sandton into Braamfontein via the Gautrain to cut his hair, much to Buhle's annoyance. She even found him a barber who makes house calls, but he refused. Mandla finds the hurried spirit of the inner city hopeful, like the people still believe their luck can change. Here, the city feels like possibility. Its unpredictability comforts him and reminds him of all the dreams he once had. Sanitised Sandton stinks of routine and middle-classness; most times the performance makes his belly churn. There, the city feels like a ceiling. Buhle says she is a true North girl and never goes past Rosebank. She says it's for safety reasons, but everyone knows it's pretentious crap. Mandla is secretly glad there are places he can keep for himself, where her glittered spirit can't reach. What he also comes for is a plate from Mam' Ruby's, just off De Korte. He buys the beef stew and pap, then slathers it with home-made chilli relish. Ruby always warns him that he's putting on too much, asking for ulcers. He likes the heaviness of pap, the way it weighs down on the belly like three meals in one. Buhle refuses to cook pap in the house.

He insists on buying lunch for Mila, who shakes his head at the offer. "You remember Mvula from our school?" Mandla blurts out.

"Uh, yes? Two grades below us, neh? Heard he drowned few years ago."

"They never found his body, we can't be sure. He was a good swimmer, remember? It was the only sport he liked."

"I didn't pay that much attention to juniors."

After Mila leaves, Mandla settles on a bench just outside the station to eat, and thinks of Mvula for the first time in years. He first noticed him on the bus. There were always new faces after the mid-term break or at the beginning of the new term. He was one of them. He was gangly, and moved with the stealth of a cat. He was long. Long legs. Long arms. Long fingers. Mandla is not light-skinned, but next to Mvula, you'd mistake him as lighter than his medium complexion. That's what darkness did – it made the dullest of things appear brighter.

After school, when most of the boys played an informal game of football, Mvula turned out to be a great striker, especially since he was left-footed.

Then on the days he didn't feel like playing, he would disappear into the forest surrounding the school. What he loved most was swimming. Even in winter, as if the cold salved whatever burning angst seethed inside him. In May, when jerseys and blazers started being a common sight, he still walked around in short white sleeves like it was blistering January. Teachers started thinking his mother couldn't afford the winter uniform. But it was just him. Mandla had never seen anyone be more themselves than Mvula.

"THE SIZE OF your muscles makes me want to start gyming too. Nami, I want you to lay your head on something hard sometimes." Mvula pokes his shy arm muscles and pinches his soft chest in front of the mirror.

Mandla is getting dressed, before the supper bell rings. Seniors don't share their room like juniors. At his previous school, Mvula was in a dorm room with fourteen other boys and only three showers between them. But here at St Francis, he shared a room and bathroom with only one person, Zaire. Mvula's room could fit three times inside Mandla's. Just one of the privileges of being head boy. The personality-less walls had seen them writhe, tug, and drink from each other with such naïve ferociousness, they once broke the single bed.

"I like your body as it is. If you get bigger, how will I pick you up then?"

"It's the best way to test if you can live up to the meaning of your name. Mandla is also such an adult name. I can't imagine a baby named Mandla; what strength does a small thing have?"

"Baby me was probably still big enough to pick you up. You must also remember to be as light as your name suggests."

"Not all rain is light."

"You have an answer for everything, don't you?"

"And you make me smile. Sometimes."

Mandla dowses himself in deodorant, its fog swallowing all the mustiness in its wake. Mvula must walk out first, and Mandla follows a few moments later – or he walks on over to his other senior friends. If anyone saw Mvula leaving, the lie they'd agreed upon was that the head boy was punishing him for something. Joy lives next door to shame, and sometimes Mvula didn't understand the difference. Strong feels like another name for numb when you love someone who loves the world more.

Mandla wonders what would have happened if he had stayed in touch with Mvula after matriculating. If only he had answered all those Facebook messages. Maybe they'd be sitting here together, watching people run for the train and sharing a plate. Maybe Mandla had needed him to stay in the dark because Mvula saw the truth in him during daylight much too clearly. He stands up and heads down the escalators, quickly stuffing the leftovers in his bag before tapping into the station.

I WATCH HIM run across the platform like it's a rugby field, and wonder if he still smells like Herbal Protex and Axe Warm Amber deodorant. Possessing him had its uses, but it's our nearness that mattered more.

I DON'T KNOW where I am. I am not in hell. Neither am I in heaven. Those places don't seem to exist. It's just the after-death. It feels like I am everywhere all at once, but also nowhere. When I was a body, the restriction of being packaged into a sack of skin prevented this freedom. I move like breath. Like me, this place fades in and out of solidity.

Sometimes my mother's house will appear shimmering in the distance like a mirage. When I approach it and pry the door open, it dissolves into my dorm room. The room is bare except for the two single beds against the walls and the wardrobe. The wardrobe swings open and the windows rattle, like the room is terrified. The floor isn't a floor, but a field of grass like a football pitch. The toilet in the bathroom sounds like it's being flushed over and over. To stop its groaning, I try to lift the lever, but there isn't one.

Other times, it's Mandla's room. But the walls and the floors are mirrors, and everything is blindingly bright. I stand in the middle of the room and instead of seeing multitudes of myself, I have no reflection. I want to smash all of them, destroy the room until it dissolves into something else. But there is nothing to throw. No rock or branch.

Then there are the rare moments when it stays my mother's house. The house looks like I remember it, the lounge cluttered with furniture and the childhood things my mother refused to let go. From the kitchen, her soft humming accompanies the aroma of hard-boiled chicken and steamed bread. It's the meal she always made me when I came home from school. But every time I shuffle into the kitchen, I find no one there. Just three plates set on the table. Yet the humming gets louder, as if she is using a megaphone. Then it's gone, and I wait for it to appear again.

When I first arrived in this place, the heat was unbearable, the sun multiplied into a thousand suns. The heat, and its unkindness, pummelled me for a long time. My search for a way back to life would be interrupted only by my howls of frustration. After what felt like an eternity, I gave up the search. That's when the heat started subsiding into a welcome coldness, fondling this thing that I had become, but couldn't see. I could only feel my presence, but how far it stretched, I couldn't say.

But I can still see what is happening down there. Or up there. It's a strange comfort. The more people remember you, the closer you remain to life. Their thoughts of you power your existence this side. My mother named me after the rain, and every time it rains, she believes it's me. Or she lies down on my bed and plays some of my old CDs when the grief is too big. Her grief keeps me from disappearing. Maybe it's true: people live on in their loved ones' hearts. Maybe that's where I am, inside my mother's heart.

One Sunday, after church, she fell asleep on the couch because a storm disrupted the electricity supply. When the power returned, the surge sparked a fire in the kitchen. I panicked and screamed as big as I could. All she did was roll over, the sound of rain lulling her deeper into her nap. The flames hopped from the counter and climbed around, reached the kitchen curtain and snaked all the way up, onto the walls. *Mama, wake up. Mama, wake up.* I kept shouting, but my voice just fizzled into silence. As I stood above her, the feeling of tears all over me, it happened. Somehow, I fell into her body. I woke us up, and we were able to put out the fire.

I watched myself fade from Mandla's memory as the years went by, until my name didn't fit around his tongue anymore. I watched him marry Buhle, then have children with her. I watched him fuck many men in hotels, writhing like he used to with me. He kissed them so long and hard, he tore words out of their mouths. Even though he told me I was the only boy he ever loved or would ever love. But fucking doesn't mean love. It's just fucking. Maybe he was telling the truth.

Sometimes, if I could gather enough strength to solidify, I'd topple a vase or knock on the door in his office. I watched him become friends with Mzwakhe, Sandile and Jason, like he forgot the terror they inflicted on me. A terror he could have stopped.

Mandla's life continued. And I remained neither here nor there. I was not up or down; unmoored, rather. At times, it didn't feel like I was dead. It just felt like I had taken a step outside of myself.

Bundles and bundles of rain poured down this last summer, until the rivers couldn't swallow anymore. As the water flowed, my mother's thoughts made me solid for days. All I wanted was to touch him.

Last month, as he was driving to his office on Rivonia Road, I settled on the passenger's seat. I listened in on his work calls. He was firm and decisive without being too arrogant. People underestimated him because his eyes had a confused look. That's why he was a successful investment banker, with the typical trimmings of such a life.

I reached out to caress his cheek. He had grown a thick beard that he nurtured with cedarwood oil and combed obsessively. His stoutness bulged under his blue suit as he changed gears. He didn't play rugby anymore but sometimes he gymed. The gym was also where he found some of the men he fucked, eyeing each other too long in the steam room or the showers – the common signal. Most of them were married to women, like Mandla himself. Fucking other married men made the guilt less flogging.

As I reached over, I fell inside him like cane sugar into hot water. I was seeing the world through him. I moved his limbs, and our thoughts were one. I searched for myself inside his mind. Traces of me were nowhere, like he'd buried me in parts of his mind he couldn't find his way back to. I watched him vanish into a boardroom, his brown coat flying behind him as if angel wings were sutured into its edges. The trip from home now a haze in his head. I had to make him remember me.

THE COLD IN the interrogation room makes Mandla pull his suit jacket closer. He buttons it and waits for Detective Mila to return. The room is concrete, and the chair is hard. Mila walks in, a file in his hand. Mandla still didn't understand why he had to come to the station when a phone call would have sufficed. Mila flips open the file, and lays out a picture first of Sandile, then Jason, and finally Mzwakhe.

"Do these remind you of anything?"

"No, man. I've already passed your lie detector twice."

"We know you killed Mzwakhe. We found the bust you used to smack him before you drowned him."

"That's impossible. I swear I didn't do it."

Mandla wraps his arms around himself, rubbing himself desperately. He looks down at the three crime-scene images. He has never been to these places. He reaches for Mzwakhe's one, brings it close to his face, his nose nearly touching it. Mila watches him, Mandla's face behind the picture, hoping that he will finally confess. But when he puts the picture down, he just stares into Mila's eyes.

"Mandla?"

"He is okay. Don't worry about him. I'm Mvula. Remember me?"

"Mr Dlamini, I need you to be serious."

"But I am serious. I must go soon, but I wanted to make sure you tell Mandla that for the rest of his life, inside his jail cell, he will think of me every day. Because the rain never forgets."

Mila stands and rushes to the door, but it's locked.

"Don't worry, I won't hurt you. You are lucky I needed you, otherwise there'd be a fourth picture on this table."

"You're still dead, and what we did to you is still lodged in your memories. So what was the point?"

"The point? Suffering. You live without your friends; Mandla goes to jail. We're all connected by this now."

Mandla's body briefly stops moving, like a video buffering. He blinks and looks confused to see Mila standing up.

The room immediately feels warmer.

MANDLA AND I strike Mzwakhe from behind with the heavyweight glass trophy from his table. We make sure it's not too damaging a blow because Mandla is big. We drag his body towards the toilet, amidst concussed mumblings. We tighten the red tie to choke him, but not so much as to break his airways. We whip out our dick and take a piss, but there isn't an intrusion to witness us this time. All the coffee and beer we filled up on earlier flow through into the water. We grab his head and make him look at us. In the eyes. We shove his head into the golden glazed bowl, ensuring his head smacks the bottom of the bowl. We stand over him and pull the tie tighter, our left leg pressing his back down. When his choking sounds begin to subside, and his body is nearly deflated and desperate for air, for life:

We flush.

PASTURE

Aba Asibon

"Pour the chopped onion into the hot oil."

"Is it normal for it to splatter so much?"

"This is all your grandmother's fault."

"Did you really expect her to put her favourite grandson to work in the kitchen?"

"When we have a son someday, I will teach him to feed himself."

"Knowing you, he will be spoiled rotten."

"Have the onions browned?"

"I think so..."

"Okay, now add in your cayenne powder. Mm, about half a teaspoon should do. Uncle Jatau has just arrived."

"Did he bring his army-general of a wife?"

"Yes, and she is already in the courtyard rounding up all the aunties to tell them about her recent trip to Dubai."

"I suppose your Mma is rolling her eyes."

"More like huffing and puffing. Now, add in your tomato paste and stir."

"Wow, it's actually beginning to smell like stew!"

"Who knew a simple thing like making stew could get you so excited?"

"It's the closest I can get to home right now."

"A tiny bit of dawadawa would have made all the difference."

"Unfortunately, the African store ran out."

"Tsk-tsk, what a shame."

"What do I do next?"

"Add in your fresh tomatoes and stir."

"What's all that ruckus in the background?"

"Khadija and Sayed's children opening up their Eid presents. You know Mma likes to go all out for her grandchildren."

"I'm sorry I could not get you a present this year."

"It's okay, Amadu. Speaking to you over the phone is enough."

"I think my stew might be burning."

"You've got to keep stirring. Lower the heat and leave the pot uncovered."

"I can't mess this up. I promised Faraz a proper feast after his shift."

"Your cousin works too much. Even on Eid?"

"Here in America, they don't seem to take Eid as seriously as we do."

"Tsk-tsk, what a shame."

"I miss the early morning prayers and Grandmother's special Eid rice. Do I add salt now?"

"Yes, yes. Just a pinch."

"What are you wearing for Eid this year?"

"My maroon abaya – you know, the one with the gold embroidery."

"Aah, of course, I remember it well; the one that brings out the browns of your eyes."

"Have you been wearing the agbadas I made for you?"

"Not really, masoyi. They're not very ... practical."

"Practical?"

"Well, it's almost winter; the cold would bite right through the cotton."

"You could wear them to the masjid, then."

"I still haven't found one close by."

"Any luck at all with the job hunt?"

"Not yet. Faraz is still working on it."

"Didn't he promise you would be able to start work immediately?"

"You know Faraz, I'm sure he is busily pulling some strings. Something will come through."

"If you say so. Now, taste your stew. It should be almost ready."

"Ugh! This stew tastes like the Atlantic."

"Tsk-tsk. What will you have to eat then?"

"I'll go down the block and grab us some pizza."

"Pizza for Eid. Only in America. I wish I were there to cook for you."

"Soon, masoyi. Soon."

"I should go now."

"Already?"

"Mma is calling for me. She needs help with setting the table for lunch."

"Then you must go."

"I love you."

"I love you more."

On Tuesdays, Faraz's shift at the department store does not begin until ten a.m., which gives the two men time to eat breakfast together. On the other days of the week, he is out of the apartment at the first sign of light, to work the early stockroom shift. Amadu pops four slices of bread into the toaster and slathers them with margarine. The one-bedroom apartment has no dining table, so the men make do with a squat coffee table and the leather couch which doubles up as Amadu's bed at night.

The creaky headboard in the adjoining bedroom keeps him up on those nights when Faraz brings home one of his many female acquaintances. His cousin appears to have eclectic taste in women – Colombian, Senegalese, Vietnamese, Ukrainian and, most recently, an aspiring Finnish actress. He flips through them like television channels and they tiptoe out of his room before daybreak, clutching their shoes against their chests. Amadu pretends to sleep through it all, spying through semi-closed eyelids, speaking nothing of these comings and goings.

Now Amadu watches as his cousin shoves bread into his face, smudging his thick beard with margarine. Faraz slurps on his tea while going through yesterday's mail, tossing the bulk of the envelopes into the recycling bin.

"Bills, bills, bills," he whines. "America, the land of bills."

"I wish I had a job so I could help," Amadu sighs.

"Relax, Bro," Faraz places a hand on his shoulder and squeezes lightly. "The recession has complicated things, but we should be able to find you a good job soon."

Even though it has already been four months since his arrival, Amadu trusts Faraz to work something out. After all, his cousin is one of the most resourceful people he knows, the first in their family ever to make it outside the country. He had applied for and won the Green Card Lottery at nineteen, abandoning his studies at the university to relocate to America. Over the years, Faraz had managed to remit enough money to build his mother a mini-mart in the city and renovate Grandmother's house in the village.

Amadu and Faraz have always been close. Growing up, they spent school holidays at Grandmother's with all their other cousins. The days were for hunting birds with homemade catapults, the evenings for taking communal bucket showers in Grandmother's courtyard. And even after Faraz left for America, they still spoke regularly over the phone. It had been Faraz's idea for Amadu to come to America after he heard him complain about the government's reluctance to budge on increasing nurses' allowances, despite the rising cost of living back home. His younger sister Neina had long-overdue university fees to be settled, and his plans to marry Saran had stalled.

"Nurses are in high demand here, Bro," Faraz had said over the phone. "With your experience, you'll find work in no time."

The plan had seemed quite straightforward: Amadu would enter America on a tourist visa and immediately find a job that would sponsor a work permit before his visa expired. He had sold his trusted Toyota to cover the cost of a plane ticket and pocket money to keep him afloat during the transition. Faraz had been at JFK to welcome him, sporting ripped jeans and a graphic hoodie, a cigarette dangling from his lips.

"Man, can you believe it's been twelve years?" Faraz playfully slapped his cousin on the back. "You haven't changed one bit."

"You look like a proper American now," Amadu responded, returning the back slap.

The last twelve years had seemingly been kind to Faraz. He had bulked up in all the right places and now walked with a self-assured swagger. To Amadu's disappointment, they took the train, not a car, from the airport up to Faraz's apartment in the Bronx. The two men lugged Amadu's heavy suitcases up and down grimy subway platforms and into packed train carriages. Faraz showed him around the apartment on the fourth floor of the faded brownstone. He ushered him into the single bedroom which had space for a double bed and not much else. In the sparsely furnished living room, Faraz pointed to a white cordless phone and demonstrated how to use a calling card to make international calls. It had never occurred to Amadu that people in America would be packed into boxes the size of a chicken coop. They picked up McDonald's for dinner, and when Amadu asked if the burgers were halal, his cousin mumbled something inaudible under his breath. At bedtime, Faraz draped a fleece blanket over the couch and lent Amadu a pillow from his own bed.

AFTER FARAZ LEAVES for work, Amadu keeps himself busy by cleaning the apartment. He scrubs the bathroom tiles with bleach, working the brush into each crevice to remove the dark build-up. He pulls up the blinds and slides open the windows, giving the illusion of space. In between his chores, he checks his watch, calculating the time difference, determining what Saran would be up to at any given moment. In the morning, she'd be at the primary school, teaching English and mathematics to nine-year-olds; afternoons in the family shop at Orion Square, selling wax prints by the yard. He pictures her through it all, her slight frame gliding through each movement, her plum lips pulled into an enduring smile

With summer gradually passing on the baton to autumn, Amadu makes it a point to get out of the apartment once a day to savour the last of the warmth. Some days, he lingers close to Faraz's apartment building, watching the neighbourhood kids play Double Dutch on the sidewalk. Other days, like this one, he strolls down to the subway station to get as far away from the apartment as possible. When he first arrived, he had been intimidated by the convoluted New York subway system, thrown off by the numbers and letters marking the train lines. But after intensely studying the city map Faraz had given him, he has finally mastered which trains go uptown or downtown, and which ones go express or local. On the train, he is taunted by impertinent couples who kiss and nuzzle each other with little regard for their fellow passengers. He finds their tenderness with each other insulting. The last time he had been that close to a woman, Saran's head was tucked into his chest in the middle of the departure hall. She had held on to him, her sobs drowned out by the din of bustling travellers and overhead announcements. In their twenty years of friendship and three years of courtship, they had never been apart for more than a few days at a time. He had kissed her on the forehead, promising to call every day until the day they would be reunited.

"I'll come back for you as soon as I have my papers," he had assured her, but that had done little to quell her tears.

Sometimes, he smells her in his dreams – a marriage of jasmine and honey – only to wake up to the mustiness of Faraz's apartment. The train lets him off at the corner of 126th and Lenox, two blocks away from the Afrikiko African Market. The shop is easy to miss, a modest grey edifice nearly swallowed by the imposing high-rises flanking it on each side. Faraz first brought him here a few days after his arrival to help ease a fierce bout of homesickness. The aroma of freshly baked tapalapa bread and fried chin chin had done the trick.

"Welcome, my brother," he is greeted by the Nigerian shop owner from behind the till.

There are others in the shop, balancing baskets on their arms, speaking in tongues he cannot make out but which resonate with him all the same. A few smile and nod at him, as if to acknowledge an unspoken kinship. He likes to take his time perusing these aisles, examining price tags and clicking his tongue at how much things cost here in comparison with prices back home. He snags a bottle of palm oil and a chunk of stockfish, both marked down as part of this week's in-store specials.

"Will that be all, my brother?" the shop owner asks, ringing up his items.

"I'll have two five-dollar calling-cards please."

"How's the family back home?" she asks.

"Good, thanks," he responds, careful not to divulge too much.

Faraz has told him stories of other Africans in America who have snitched on friends and had them deported because of simple disagreements.

"There's something about this country that makes people turn against their own kind."

Back at the apartment, he chops fingers of okra into cubes and sets them on the tabletop stove to boil. He can hear faint bachata wafting in through the kitchen window and sticks his head through it to investigate the source. A group of older neighbours have set up camping chairs and a boom-box on the sidewalk below, swaying their hips to the catchy rhythms. The sight makes him smile. He pours in the rest of the ingredients and stands by as the fermented aroma of stockfish fills the apartment, transporting him back to Grandmother's outdoor kitchen in Bonu. When Faraz gets home that evening, they sit cross-legged around the coffee table, eating their dinner off paper plates.

"It's so nice to come home to a hot meal," Faraz says, licking palm oil off his fingers. "This is almost as good as Grandmother's."

"Well, Saran's been teaching me well."

"You're still serious about that girl, huh?"

Amadu raises his eyebrows: "Why wouldn't I be?"

"You've got to be open-minded around here, Bro," Faraz lets out a loud belch. "Having a woman back home complicates things."

"How so?"

Faraz opens his mouth to say something but ends up waving his hand in dismissal. "Never mind."

Amadu keeps his thoughts to himself as well, swallowing the urge to ask his cousin why he has never thought to settle down in all these years, and why he has chosen to live the life of a bachelor, subsisting on fast food and cigarettes. Instead, they both help themselves to more food, filling their stomachs with the taste of home until they can take no more.

WINTER ARRIVES IN a fury and snuffs a portion of light from the daytime. Amadu goes out only when necessary, borrowing one of Faraz's thick hooded jackets when they're running low on supplies. Outside, Christmas decorations are up and shops inundate customers with Christmas carols on repeat. The short days leave Amadu feeling heavy and reluctant to get out of bed some mornings.

"It's normal, Bro," Faraz consoles him when he complains about feeling slightly off. "It's called the winter blues. You'll soon get used to it."

Daylight saving puzzles him, this concept of tampering with clocks when the seasons change. To his annoyance, it adds yet another hour between him and Saran in the winter. They speak every day, lingering on the line, relishing even the occasional pauses between them. She brings him up to speed on happenings back home – her sister's new baby, the newly constructed mall in Mavu, the frequent nurses' strikes.

"You did well to leave when you did," she tells him.

He describes all the places he will take her when she gets to America. "I'll take you to the Bronx Zoo to feed sea lions and to Ellis Island to see the Statue of Liberty."

She is an effective distraction from the impending expiration of his visa. Going back home with nothing to show for it is not an option, but for someone who has not so much as committed a traffic offence in all his life, the alternative petrifies him. He withholds his anxieties from Saran, allowing himself to drown instead in her ceaseless optimism. He spends most of his free time cooking, filling the fridge with more food than he and Faraz can keep up with. He bangs his emotions on the chopping board, pours them into stainless steel pots and watches as they dissolve and bubble. One Wednesday evening, Faraz returns home while Amadu is preparing dinner.

"I wasn't expecting you back so early," Amadu checks his watch.

"Come and sit, Bro. I have news."

Amadu covers the pot of vegetable soup and seats himself next to his cousin.

"What's your news?"

"I've found you a job," Faraz is smiling, flashing his gums.

"Where? How?" Amadu asks, trying to breathe in between words.

"It's a gig at one of those posh nursing homes in Baychester."

"A nursing gig?"

"No, a friend of a friend is looking for someone to quickly fill a custodial vacancy."

"Custodial? As in janitorial?"

"Yes, something along those lines. It's not too much money, but it should sustain you until we can find you a proper nursing job."

Amadu searches Faraz's face, waiting for him to break character and declare it all a prank.

"Cheer up, Bro," he continues. "I know it's not what you were hoping for, but it's a good way to get a foot in the door."

"Won't they care that I don't have the right papers to work?"

"Nah, the manager is happy to pay under the table. It's a win-win for everyone."

"When does he need me to start?"

"Tomorrow," Faraz declares, fetching the remote for the television. "I told you I've got your back, didn't I?"

Amadu nods, absentminded.

"HELLO?" HER VOICE is a tinkle, music to his ears.

"It's me, masoyi."

"Amadu, why have I not heard from you in three days?"

"Forgive me. I've just started a new job and the hours are crazy."

"A new job? You should have said so earlier. Alhamdulillah."

"Alhamdulillah."

"Tell me more about this job then."

"It's at a nursing home."

"Hold on, Mma is asking what the good news is ... Mma, Amadu has just landed a nursing job in New York."

He cannot bring himself to correct this misunderstanding.

"We are all so proud of you, Amadu. Tell me, what's nursing in America like?"

"It's ... it's good. My colleagues are very friendly and the facility is well-equipped."

"Alhamdulillah. And are they paying you well?"

"It's not too bad for a start."

"You will soon make even more, inshallah."

"Yes, yes indeed."

"Do you know what this means, Amadu?"

"Tell me."

"It means that very soon you will have your papers and I can join you."

"Yes, but these processes take time, so we will have to be patient."

"Of course, but there is hope on the horizon now."

"I'm afraid my shifts are long and I might not always be able to call before you go to sleep."

"I understand."

"I will try my best to call whenever I have a chance."

"Yes, yes."

"I should go and get ready now. My shift starts in two hours."

"Of course, do whatever you have to do."

IN THE SLUICE room of the Oakwood Care Home, Amadu defies the manager's instructions and triples the required concentration of hospital-grade disinfectant. As he glides his mop across the vinyl floors, he hopes the caustic smell will mask the staleness that constantly hovers in the building. He gives special attention to any stains – the reds, the yellows, the browns and the in-betweens that are commonplace here.

At the nurses' station, he greets the on-duty staff, with whom he is on a first-name basis. There's Amy with the tight ponytail, Melody whose scrubs are at least two sizes too small, and Lynette with the thick Jamaican accent. He tries as much as possible to stay out of the way while they fill in medical charts and sort multicoloured pills into paper cups.

"302's soiled himself for the third time this morning," Melody complains, throwing her hands up in the air.

"Don't mess with 205 today," Amy whispers. "She's in a foul mood."

The nurses don't seem to notice him stealing glances at the residents' charts, trying to decipher the hurried scribbles and medical shorthand. Even though he disagrees with some of the courses of treatment prescribed for certain conditions, he keeps these opinions to himself and gets on with his work. He waits until the residents are moved to the rec room for breakfast to clean their rooms. He empties bedpans and trash cans, separating non-hazardous waste from the hazardous; he changes the linen and adds to the growing pile to be sent down for laundering. He can tell a lot about the occupant of a room by what is on their bedside table. Cards and flowers usually signal distant loved ones, a stack of books and magazines signals lucidness. He is careful not to put anything out of place, having experienced first-hand the tantrums some of the residents throw when they are unable to locate a personal effect.

The rec room is the most challenging of all his assigned work areas. In there, he navigates around the residents as he tackles juice spills and post-lunch vomit. Some of the residents acknowledge him with a nod or a smile, but most stare blankly through him. He knows each resident by name, although with the high turnover at Oakwood, he must make an extra effort to stay abreast with the roster. Some of the residents have grown on him, like the smiley Miss Alice everyone calls Scarlet Alice because she never leaves her room without a dash of red lipstick, chatty Mr Olvera who always reaches out for a fist bump, and funny Mr Jones who likes to break into the twist at the slightest sound of music. During Amadu's fifteen-minute orientation on his first day at Oakwood, the manager had been very clear that fraternising with the residents was frowned upon. A silly rule, in Amadu's opinion, given that the large sign at the entrance reads "Oakwood, A Warm-Hearted Community". He cannot imagine Grandmother in this place, away from her grandchildren and great-grandchildren, her sharp wit dulling slowly among the senile and the decrepit. The neighbours back at home would click their tongues, wag their fingers and call it a real shame that an old woman cannot be cared for by her own.

Lunchbreaks at Oakwood are strictly thirty minutes long. Amadu heats up the leftovers he has brought from home and sits with the other staff in the breakroom, watching them munch on their pricey salads and sandwiches from the food truck across the street. They point curiously at his lunch box: "Is that food from Africa, Ah-mah-doo?"

He nods, muting his desire to remind them that Africa is far too broad a generalisation. Now out-of-status, he would hate to cause trouble or make enemies around here. Sometimes, his lunch breaks are cut short by a request to clean up a catheter spill or soiled sheets. As the floating custodian, his hours at Oakwood are erratic, often dependent on whether or not the manager has found someone to relieve him. He takes the train home after his shifts, thankful for an empty seat when he can find one, occasionally dozing off and almost missing his stop. He has learnt to navigate the city with his head down, avoiding neighbourhoods with notoriety and a heavy police presence. He has allowed the city to swallow him, just another speck in a sea of scurrying bodies. On days when his shifts run late, Saran waits up for his calls, stifling her yawns. They converse efficiently, cramming their thoughts and feelings into what little time they have before Saran succumbs to sleep. She tells him her parents are beginning to question his intentions towards her; if he still has plans of paying her dowry. Their doubtfulness spurs him on to put in more hours at Oakwood, to continue to fill the old Milo tin underneath his couch-bed with green bills folded into neat squares.

THE DAY SCARLET Alice in 312 dies, it stings more than it should. Amadu shows up for his shift to find the night nurses telling the morning nurses she has died peacefully in her sleep. He is sent to strip down the room in preparation for its next occupant. His throat tightens as he gathers her personal effects into a plastic bag her family will collect later. As a trained nurse, he should be less affected by death. At St Michael's he could always entertain some level of hope for his patients, that with the right combination of care they would likely walk out of those doors better than they came in. At Oakwood, things are different – there is only one way out for its residents.

He thinks of Scarlet Alice on the ride home, choosing to stand in the half-empty train car, pondering over what might have scared her more: death or loneliness? As he makes his way up the musty stairwell and into the empty apartment, he thinks of her family – two daughters, from what he could tell from the photos at her bedside – and if they harbour any regrets at all. He picks up the cordless phone and dials Saran's number, yearning for her balmy voice.

"Hello?" The voice on the other end is gruff.

Amadu glances at his watch and curses at himself – it is past midnight on that end.

"Hello, Mma."

"Who's this?"

"It's me Mma, Amadu."

"Do you have any idea what time it is over here, young man? Is anything the matter?"

"Apologies, Mma. I lost track of time. I'll call back tomorrow."

A click. A long dead tone.

THERE'S CHATTER AMONG the nurses when Amadu arrives for his shift this morning. There's a new resident in Scarlet Alice's old room, the father of a popular New York real estate mogul. The old man has refused to go down to the rec room for meals with the other residents, insisting his food be brought to his room.

"Ah-mah-doo, I wouldn't go in there just yet if I were you," Amy warns him, waving a thermometer in the direction of room 312.

He heeds her advice and bypasses the room. Someone has scribbled the name "Holdebrook" on the dry-erase board outside the closed door. He is in the middle of stripping the bed in 310 when he hears yelling and the sound of metal clanging coming from 312. Rushing in, he finds Lynette at the bedside, syringes and plastic collection tubes scattered at her feet. Holdebrook, a bony man with an encroaching moustache, is sitting up in bed swinging his veiny arms at her.

"Everything alright in here?" Amadu asks Lynette, who appears to be frozen in place.

She composes herself and inches closer to the resident. "I was just trying to get a sample for Mr Holdebrook's bloodwork, but we're having some trouble finding a good vein, aren't we?"

She reaches out to take Holdebrook's arm, but he quickly pulls back and hollers, "Someone get me a nurse who knows what she's doing!"

Without thinking, Amadu approaches the bed and takes the syringe from Lynette.

"What do you think you're doing?" she hisses into his ear, her eyes wide.

"Trust me," he whispers back. "I'm a trained nurse."

Amadu wraps a tourniquet around Holdebrook's left arm, distracting him with talk of the Giants' recent win over the Patriots. The old man stays calm, allowing his arm to be manipulated in search of a good vein. When Amadu finds one, he cleans the area with an alcohol swab, sticks the needle in and draws half a syringe-full of blood which he hands to Lynette.

Back in 310, the adrenaline continues to pump as he replaces the soiled bedding. Even after a year and a half without practice, it had all come so naturally to him. He had found Holdebrook's vein with little effort – tap, tap and there it was, pulsing, begging to be poked. The possible repercussions of his actions pale in comparison to the lightness he feels. Lynette comes to find him as he wraps up in 310, hands folded across her chest.

"What you did in there was stupid, you know?" Her eyes spit fire. "If that man says one word, we're all finished."

He drops the bag of dirty linen and looks straight at her. "Sorry, I was only trying to help."

"Why have you never mentioned you're a trained nurse?"

"I didn't think it would make a difference."

She uncrosses her arms and allows them to fall limply to her sides.

"Thank you, though. You saved my behind in there. I panicked."

"It's okay, it happens to the best of us."

"Can I make it up to you? Let me buy you lunch, just as a thank you."

Her offer seems extravagant when he thinks about the mundaneness of what he did.

"I can't let you do that," he says. He would hate for her to think he did it to gain something in return.

"Please, it's the least I can do."

Worried about coming across as rude, he accepts her offer. They walk across the street to the food cart at lunchtime, where a woman in a white toque is turning slices of bread into elaborate sandwiches.

"What would you like?" Lynette asks, pointing to the menu scribbled across the front of the truck.

He shrugs. "I'll have whatever you're having."

When their order is ready, they seat themselves on a bench with a direct view of the verdant Oakwood grounds, where they can look out at the blue jays flirting between the milkweed bushes, nipping playfully at each other. They eat quietly, hunched over their cheese and tomato sandwiches, parading their table manners.

"Are you enjoying your lunch?" Lynette asks, wiping a smudge of mayonnaise from the corner of her lips.

He nods.

"Different from the food back home, I'm sure."

"Yes, very different."

"How long have you been away from home?"

"About a year and a half now."

"Do you miss it?"

He nods. "It is the people I miss most. My girlfriend, my sister, my grandmother."

"You left your girlfriend behind?" She raises an eyebrow.

"Yes, but she'll be joining me soon."

"You're lucky to have someone who is willing to wait for you."

"And you? You're Jamaican, right?"

She chuckles. "I guess there's no hiding with this accent of mine, huh?"

"How long have you been in America?"

"Nine years next month. I moved here to join my parents who left Jamaica when I was quite young."

"So, you're now American then?"

"I don't really believe in labels, Ah-mah-doo."

"What's Jamaica like?"

"People think it's all beaches and weed and reggae," she says, rolling her eyes. "It is a beautiful country, don't get me wrong, but we've got our issues."

"My country's beautiful too – we have mountains and beaches and freshwater lakes, but our government is failing us."

"Well, that's something we have in common," she says with a sardonic grin. "That's why we are both here."

They eat quickly, mindful of time.

"Where do you live?" Lynette asks.

"Inwood, with my cousin."

"Oh! I live in Fordham. Not too far from you."

"Yes, I know Fordham."

"Have you ever had Jamaican food?"

Amadu shakes his head.

"Well, we will have to rectify that. Why don't you come by my place one of these days so I can make you some? We'd better get going," she says, giving him no time to react to her invitation.

They gather themselves, dumping their paper plates and cups into a nearby trashcan. As they walk through Oakwood's automatic glass doors, Lynette pinches her nose at the strong smell of disinfectant: "I really hate the smell of this place."

"Hello?"

"Oh, it's you, Amadu."

"Yes, it's me. Were you expecting someone else?"

"We've just had news from the village about Grandfather."

"What sort of news? Nothing too serious, I hope?"

"He's ill. Mma and I are catching the night bus to the village."

"And how long will you be gone for?"

"It's hard to tell when we don't fully understand the extent of his condition..."

"This means I won't be able to reach you while you're away in the village, then?"

He can hear what sound like faint sobs on the other end of the line.

"Forgive me, masoyi, I didn't mean to be insensitive. I should be there supporting you."

"I have to go now. Mma needs help packing."

"You'll let me know when you're back?"

He stays on the phone long after she hangs up, oblivious to the loud beeping tone on the other end, grasping at the remnants of their conversation.

THE SIZE OF Lynette's place glorifies Faraz's one-bedroom apartment. A studio, she calls it, on the nicer side of town where shops do not bother to put grills on their glass display windows.

"Welcome to my humble abode." She ushers him in and points to a collapsible table. "Please, sit."

She looks more youthful without her drab scrubs. Her long braids, free from the bun she keeps them in at work, swing as she moves. On the table, she has laid out three Pyrex dishes, two glass plates and a vase of fresh flowers.

"Can I get you something to drink? Beer? Wine?"

Amadu shakes his head. "I don't drink."

"Of course," she cups her forehead. "Some juice then?"

While she fetches the juice from the kitchenette, Amadu's eyes wander. It is a well-economised space, thoughtfully demarcated with folding screens into a kitchen, living room and bedroom. Accents of blue are sprinkled all over – in the floral wallpaper, the fraying floor rug, the tartan upholstery. A printed copy of "The Madonna and Child" hangs on one of the walls.

"Are you Catholic?" he asks.

"Ah, someone's very observant," she says, placing a glass of orange juice in front of him.

"I'm Muslim."

"That, I have gathered." She takes a sip of wine from her glass. "But at the end of the day, are we not all God's children?"

She begins to heap his plate with coconut rice and curried goat and fried plantains.

He holds a hand up. "That's enough, please."

"No need to be shy around here. This is authentic Jamaican fare. I promise you'll like it."

"I didn't realise Jamaican food was so similar to our food," he says after the first forkful.

"Well, it's not surprising given that we share the same distant ancestors. Do you cook?"

"Only recently. My girlfriend's been teaching me over the phone."

"It must be tough, being so far away from her."

His chest feels heavy. "We grew up together in the same neighbourhood, went to the same primary and secondary schools. We've never been apart for this long."

Over the course of the meal, he learns Lynette is thirty-two, only a year younger than he is, even though he would have pegged her in her late twenties. She was once married, for a short time, to a fellow Jamaican she met soon after her arrival in America. She blames the marriage on the peculiar melancholy that comes with being in a foreign land, that overwhelming urge to fill a void. Had she taken the time to know him before jumping into a lifelong commitment, she would have known better.

"Do you miss him at all?" Amadu asks.

"It's the companionship I miss. This bustling city, ironically, can get quite lonely."

"I agree."

"Enough about me. Tell me about your life as a nurse back home."

"I was a surgical nurse, one of two male nurses in the entire municipal hospital, so I was quite the spectacle," he grins, a faraway look in his eyes.

"Why did you leave?"

"I was struggling to make ends meet on my salary."

"But how does a qualified nurse end up working as a custodian at Oakwood?"

Amadu fiddles with his glass of juice. The truth wriggles dangerously up his throat as he debates whether or not it would be wise to confide in her. She has opened up her home to him, given him no reason to question her sincerity.

"My cousin says nurses are in high demand here and that he can easily find me a job. Oakwood is just something temporary while I wait."

She plants her elbows on the table. "I'm assuming you know that you will need to be certified here first before you can practice?"

Amadu lays down his fork and looks up at her. "Faraz says my diploma will be accepted here."

"And what does Faraz do?" Lynette asks, her face crumpling into a frown.

"He's a stockroom manager at Bradley's downtown."

"Take it from me, then. I've been in this field long enough."

"What are the requirements?" His face feels hot.

"First, you will need to complete a Foreign-educated Nurse Course, which includes quite a bit of clinical practice under supervision."

"That doesn't seem too difficult."

She holds up a finger. "There's more. After that, you will have to pass the licensure exam and have your credentials evaluated."

"How long does all of this take?"

"It really depends on how quickly you finish the course and how long it takes you to pass the licensure exam. And let's not forget that it will cost you quite a bit of money."

His body goes numb. He remembers the incident with the mangoes all those years ago. Of all of the grandchildren, Amadu was the most skilled at tree climbing, which had earned him the nickname Bushbaby. He could climb anything, from a sausage tree to a marula tree, nimbly springing from bough to bough. Faraz had come to him one afternoon while he was dozing off on Grandmother's porch, announcing that Mrs Salim down the street had given them permission to pluck some mangoes off her pregnant tree.

"Are you sure?" Amadu had asked, aware of how protective Mrs Salim was over that mango tree. He had seen her pelt thieving children with stones many times before.

"I swear on my mother." Faraz kissed his finger and drew a line in the sand.

"We are not supposed to swear," Amadu admonished.

"The more reason why you should believe me."

He had believed Faraz. He would have believed anyone who had the guts to swear on their mother's life. Climbing up the old mango tree had been easy, the weathered bark providing more than enough friction with which to hoist himself. On top, the branches sagged with plump yellow fruit. He plucked and threw them down to Faraz, who was waiting on the other side of the fence to collect them in his t-shirt. As Amadu made his way back down the tree, he heard a screech and looked down to see Mrs Salim at the foot of the tree, brandishing her walking stick. Faraz managed to escape unseen, but Amadu had been led back to Grandmother's compound by the ear. It was the first time Grandmother had laid hands on him, spanking him with a neem switch until he could no longer feel his bottom.

He still remembers the look of disappointment on Grandmother's face as she swiped the switch back and forth, rebuking him for his foolishness. His immediate inclination had been to point fingers at Faraz, who was crouching behind the small audience that had formed in Grandmother's compound. But Amadu understood, even then, that at the end of the day, he was solely responsible for his own actions. So he had held his tongue, taking each stroke with a stifled wince.

Sitting in Lynette's studio, he pines for Saran. He would give anything to lay his head on her chest, to find comfort in the sweetness of her skin and the assuredness of her voice. Soon, there might be no bridge long enough for this widening chasm between them.

"Are you okay, Ah-mah-doo?" Lynette leans in across the table, placing a warm hand on his arm.

He rises from the table and makes his way to the window facing the eastern side of the city. Outside, the city is slowing down to catch its breath, but all who know it well know that it will never sleep. He should really be heading back to the apartment to get some rest before his six a.m. shift. Faraz will be back from work by now, watching the sports channel with his legs up on the coffee table, expecting dinner. *Faraz*: the name bites like fresh kola in his mouth.

He turns to face Lynette. "Can I stay here a little longer?" The words just tumble out, refusing to be restrained.

"Of course," she responds, clearing the table to make room. "I'll brew us some coffee."

He turns his attention back to the window. The sprawling New York City skyline he grew up seeing in movies and magazines now lies before him, shimmering seductively, flashing its gilded reputation in his face, wooing him shamelessly into its bosom.

SLEIGHT OF HAND

Josephine Sokan

$\mathcal{Y}$OU HAD SENSED black was appropriate, and you always did have a hunch for these things. All thefts had an ending; you either won or got caught. As the entire family watched you put yourself back together, readjust your wig, and slide out of a bed reserved for lovers, a bed that was not yours, you were certain that you and he had run your course. You had arrived at your inevitable destination, and the shame contained within the four walls of this room would be the resting place of what you had once shared. You were neither his mistress, nor a beloved sister. You had not even really been friends, for you cared nothing for any details of his life. He was boring, unattractive – and most likely a thief.

"Ada, what is the meaning of this?" you heard Ibrahim ask. You remained silent. Picking your bag up from the floor, you thanked them for a lovely evening and made your way down the stairs towards their front door. You would head to Sainsbury's for a bottle of Tassleton's Pinot Grigio – but not to drown your sorrows. Tonight, you were celebrating. You had won.

IT WAS ON your way upstairs that you noticed the opened door, leading to a bedroom. You had peered inside but for a moment when your eyes caught a silky dressing-gown with the words "Happy Anniversary Love" embroidered on the back. In an instant, curiosity and desire were aroused like summoned spirits. You checked the care label to confirm whether it was real silk. To your surprise, it was even mulberry silk! Then you spotted some lipstick: a Rouge Elixir Fatale 230. Why, that had to cost at least a hundred pounds! To your knowledge, Ibrahim hadn't mentioned receiving any discounts as part of his job. Or had he? You'd remember a thing like that. You were certain you'd have taken advantage of such a fact, had you known. Placed next to the lipstick was a large bottle of Clive Christian No 1. At this, you had gasped. It couldn't be. How could an ordinary cashier afford all this? And to spend such an amount on a woman like Amina? A woman who drew her eyebrows on with a kohl pencil and did nothing about the fine line of hairs standing to attention above her lip?

That was when your mind really began racing. You reached out, only to sample the fragrance and to see if the rouge 230 suited you when your eyes fell upon the soft Egyptian cotton sheets on the bed. You'd always believed this dangerous shade of crimson would suit a refined woman like you. You glanced in the mirror, enticed by your own appearance: you were right. The lipstick now smothering your lips flirted brazenly with you, the perfume beckoned you to bed, asking you to stay. You succumbed, falling into the soft sheets with a gracelessness reserved only for moments of privacy. You even loosened your wig a little. This was where your one-day love would find you. Armed with gifts of silk and diamonds, he would remind you of your incomparable beauty, your elegance and grace, before you crumbled in his strong arms. So lost were you in yearning for a man that did not yet exist, you did not hear the creak of Amina's footsteps on the stairs as she made her way up to find her missing guest. You did not hear the bedroom door swing open. You did not hear curious little feet rushing upstairs after her. When you snapped out of your fantasy, it was to a glaring Amina, her hands shaking with rage. Behind her stood two small children, puzzled, eyes squinting, unsure of what to make of the scene before them.

A wave of shame rushed over you, warm and all-consuming. You had no words to explain. This was not like being caught in the department stores. Those incidents were easy enough to explain away, and at the very least, you could always just pay. But here, in this moment, as repulsed faces waited for a response, and eyes accused you in this unfamiliar, vulnerable state, you were speechless. In haste, you removed the robe that did not belong to you and scrambled out of Amina's bed. You were buttoning up your shirt when Amina spat: "Wonders shall never end! Are you wearing my lipstick? Did you use my perfume? Ibraaaahiiiim!" The children gave way as a speechless Ibrahim emerged in the doorway. Your gaze held his for a moment as his bewildered eyes searched yours, desperate for an answer, yet also silently saying something else; a muted confession, perhaps.

AMINA OPENED THE door, and she was everything Ibrahim had described. She moved with precise glides, studied carefully before speaking, and seemed only ever to half-smile. As he had said, she was a simple woman: braids instead of lengthy waves, a long hem and high neck instead of displayed shapely curves and dips. Nothing like you. When she first laid eyes on you, she observed you slowly, almost drinking you in with her cloudy eyes. Moments later, with a careful nod which you could not interpret, she complimented your shoes before a quip about you hopefully now being "on the straight and narrow". You remained silent, disappointed that Ibrahim had obviously shared your story with his wife. What else had he told her about you? The night wore on. You ate and smiled through gritted teeth, praising the salty tomato stew, tough beef and clumpy rice. You laughed as the children repeated their knock-knock jokes; you even asked questions about the hideous portrait which Amina had hung on the wall. By ten thirty, you figured you had endured quite enough, and decided to call it a night. But first, you would head to the ladies.

THAT WEEKEND, AS you chose your attire for the big event, you moped beneath dark clouds. To meet Amina was to introduce reality into the cocoon you had built with Ibrahim. Surely he knew the truth: that you had neither care nor curiosity for his family? Or was he that naïve? That blind? That unassuming? You chose to dress the part of a woman in mourning as you sensed the approach of the end. You decided on your black shirt-dress, simple patent court shoes, and Theresa – your mid-length, brunette, loose-wave wig. Theresa represented dignity, grace, elegance; the sort of hair worn by a lady who was desired by someone, somewhere. Slicking on another coat of 002 Renegade, you glanced once more into your pocket mirror. With the nerves of someone approaching the "other" woman, the one to whom the throne belonged, you knocked on the weather-beaten door of Flat 4G.

SO YOUR LITTLE sailboat drifted down this new stream of male attention and affection. Until the tide turned and creeping winds began to rock your boat. After a few months, to your surprise, Ibrahim announced that it was high time your friendship came up for air. He said that he had told Amina so much about you, she was just dying to meet you. In that vivid scene, on the 170 bus as you almost choked on the last of your cinnamon waffle, you could have sworn blind you heard a balloon pop, a foghorn blast, a whistle blowing time. Could your party be ending? Why this exposing of your special thing to the fluorescent lights of the real world? Surely it's a little too soon, no? you had asked. He laughed, saying that it was proper that his family got to know a friend who was so dear to him. The word "friend" sent bullets through your frame. Had you just been *friends*? you wondered, but did not ask. The treats, the questions about your relationships, the compliments: had it all been just friendly? You realised that Ibrahim was waiting for your response. He was inviting you for dinner at his family home, and it was polite to accept. It was a chance to meet the whole crew – *they will love you*, he said. Amina and the twins would be overjoyed to have a new friend in this bustling city. *Friend, friend.* Again, that blasted word. You both agreed on the last Saturday in July, but for the moment, you decided that you would enjoy the thrill of exclusivity for as long as you could, even if it was a lie.

THIS THING BETWEEN you, this relationship of convenience grew on your bus rides home. You often wondered what exactly Ibrahim was getting out of it, though. He would ask about your day at work, the things you had been up to, whether any eligible bachelors had approached you that day, and if you had eaten. You would gush and blabber, stopping short of saying anything that actually made you vulnerable. The real stuff was saved for *him*: your ideal André, or Maurice, or Pierre. Once you were satisfied, only then would you let Ibrahim share his day – his thoughts, his concerns about how Amina and the kids were settling into life in England. It had been seven months; yet the kids still cried when speaking of home, and Amina had not yet managed to find work. You would nod, occasionally pose a question or two, and give an impression of interest. However, the trivialities of his standstill life drained your reserves of energy. His wife seemed like a snob, and his children, to you, sounded brattish. You would eventually hurry him along, finding a way to steer the ship back towards your own shores. Quite often, Ibrahim would purchase a cinnamon waffle from work and would watch your eyes sparkle with pleasure at the light-cream dotted wrapping and the warm, buttery smell. He would then laugh with all his teeth, as he would catch a glimpse of six-year-old Ada behind your wide eyes and easy smile.

In such moments, without meaning to or perhaps even realising, you gave a little bit of yourself away. You revealed aspects of your truth: a little girl who just wanted to be wanted. To be loved just because, without conditions, terms or prerequisites. Ibrahim seemed to require nothing from you. He had never made advances, and you were not entirely sure what you would do if he ever did. For now, he seemed happy to compliment your outfits, validate your feelings, your changing hairstyles, buy you waffles and listen to your voice. He was the temporary cure to the loneliness swelling within you, a Band-Aid, if you will. For now, it was enough.

IT WAS ON a wet October evening that you encountered Ibrahim for the first time. You had finished work and were feeling low. Retail therapy was usually the answer. You headed to a new place that you had visited a few times before, and had already successfully stolen from once. Jacob's Department Store, with its imposing silhouette, ornate, stained-glass Venetian windows and dramatic entrance, stood proudly in London's exclusive Marylebone. Normally you would peruse the aisles: cosmetics first, then shoes before heading to the food court for a snack and an overpriced artisanal coffee. Despite your healthy salary, here, you were always a window shopper. Perhaps it was for this reason that you decided to steal that night.

By now you were adept at "lifting". It should have been simple; a left-hand, right-hand switch, but that day, you were caught by the security guard on duty. Cue quiet sobbing, shaking hands and rehearsed babbling. The cashier was a smallish, balding man with a round, kind face and permanently smiling eyes. With a knowing glance exchanged between the two of you, he explained that he had made an error at the till, as he was still getting the hang of his new role. He was reprimanded sternly by the store manager, which he accepted humbly, as if he were a young child, not a man in his early fifties. You left the store confused, but relieved. And feeling another thing. Something heavy, sticky and maybe bitter. It left you with a rush of heat in your chest you could not explain.

It would not be for another week, on your journey home, that your paths would cross again. He, the cashier from the store, spotted you on the 170 bus headed towards Clapham Common, and made a dash for the empty seat next to you. He introduced himself as Ibrahim, and spoke with you, almost even scolding. But what was this? No, not judgement; it was more like concern. No – maybe interest? Or perhaps, compassion? Probably the latter. With urgent eyes, he queried your actions that evening in the store. He asked about your family and friends. Were they here or back home? Did you do what you did often? What compelled you? Why would an educated young woman of promise do such? Were you of faith? Why not live a better life then? In his enthusiasm, he relayed a patchy string of words, a nod to Christianity, the moral being the benefits of a life of righteousness. You fought back giggles that were determined to escape. You were sure he noticed. Nonetheless, you listened earnestly, despite having heard all this before. It was the attention, concern and tenderness; it was brand-new and delicious. Ibrahim, in all his bald, middle-aged, pot-bellied glory, was another thing to be stolen; a trinket to soothe the wound of loneliness.

NATURALLY, YOUR HABIT and skill had developed over time. You started with small items like office supplies and books, but soon progressed to jewellery, lingerie and perfume. Items your one-day love would purchase to surprise you just because, or to celebrate your anniversary, to congratulate you on your promotion or celebrate yet another trip around the sun. You were a good thief: nimble, quick-thinking, subtle and charming. You had been at it for about five months and were rarely ever caught. Whenever you were, you would feign ignorance, apologise profusely, then offer your black Ohler Co-operative card, and the matter would be settled. Besides, your work at Spellman & Tate equipped you with enough lingo and knowledge to avoid prosecution. They would had to have seen you, caught you on camera, or found you unwilling or unable to pay. In this regard, you were always careful and thus, to date, had escaped any consequences. On such nights, those occasional instances when you were rumbled, you were led to drink. On those nights, you had lost.

THE FIRST THEFT as an adult was a case of a forgotten item among other legitimate ones. You hadn't even realised until your journey home. Initially, there was panic, a sudden draining of blood from your head and then a most peculiar feeling, something you couldn't name. It left you buzzing like you had been reborn. You carefully checked the product labelling. It read "Long-lasting Matte Lipstick Shade 002 Renegade" – an oil-based chocolate-crimson colour. It was sultry, dark and alluring. You wore it every day, even in the spring when typically ladies wore pastel shades for a fresher appearance. You even wore it to St Bartholomew's on Sundays. There was something wonderful about wearing Renegade as you sashayed in black, noisy heels through the aisles for the twelve-thirty Mass. You would shimmy through the pews as the old biddies whispered and tutted in hushed tones about ladies like you, young women of nowadays with neither reverence nor home training.

THAT FIRST TIME had indeed been purely accidental. A St Ced's alumni, daughter of Chief Justice and Pastor Julius Chike, you, Adaeze Chike, were not the sort to be labelled "thief". When leaving for Britain, both parents had advised you to "remember whose child you were". You were destined for a higher purpose, a great calling. Bearing this wisdom in mind would keep you from a reckless life overseas, they said. You had heeded their advice, not wanting to shame the people who had toiled, who had on bended knee but with an iron fist encouraged you to eat, to read, to speak less, but be confident, study hard and excel, just like they had.

YOUR SALVATION HAD been the short days and long nights of your time at university. The lights and pace of London were the soundtrack to a new golden age. The city let you bloom. You found friends with names like yours; long, proudly African and awkward on the British tongue. You found salons that were adept with your natural coily-kinky hair. You met members of the opposite sex who didn't seem apprehensive at the idea of a date with you. They were not intimidated by hips, lips and thighs; instead, your thickness, your presence, your essence in all its melanised glory was even desired. You felt wanted and seen.

However, London proved to be a cruel lover; it was never a true community, but rather a cosmos with its own bitter orbit. University ended and friends began to leave to settle down elsewhere or go travelling. So, like all fortunate graduates, you found a job, a few boyfriends here and there, but nothing that led to the dreams you had dreamed when you first heard you were leaving for London. The loneliness led you first to shop, then to drink and date excessively, regardless of the calibre of the specimen. There was Derek with the fungal infection, who preceded Mishaal the bus driver looking for a woman who had papers, and Ayo whose music was about to blow – he could feel in his bones that this year was his year, man – and Derek again, because for a moment there, pickings were evidently slim. Slowly, dates turned into professional qualifications and further study, then dance classes, and even volunteering at the local shelter.

COMING TO BRITAIN at age sixteen, you had dreams of life in Notting Hill with friends like Julia Roberts and Hugh Grant. You would wear a wavy brunette weave and drink wine from oversized glasses with young idealist pals. You'd eventually marry a man with lots of hair and even more money, with an accent that no one could place. However, your reality in North Yorkshire was nothing like this. The two years of A-levels at St Ced's were among the darkest times in your life. Your only brief solace had been visits to Aunty Edith and Uncle Ambrose, who never missed the opportunity to remind you to "knuckle down" as you were being offered the opportunity of a lifetime. "Do you know what this costs?" they chided. *What your parents must have sacrificed? Just to give you the world? It is good for a child to work and study hard, then make enough money to return the debt to their parents,* they had said. You eventually decided that the covert bullying, boredom and bleak corridors of school were more palatable than weekends in Leeds with the childless couple. At least back at school, you were free to leave lights on, to talk with friends online, and sleep in at the weekend.

YOU WERE SIX when you first stole. You had always toyed with the idea, but could firmly recollect that thieves and liars went to hell – and would also likely earn a heavy spanking from their mama and papa. Nonetheless, an afternoon came when you rose to Lydia Dengu's teasing. Some people's family only pretend to have money, she had said. My mama and papa said your daddy is just pretending. So you took some money from your Mama's purse to buy candy at Mr Ojo's shop. Like the big, fancy girl you were, you were gracious enough to buy a round for you and your friends. Even that stupid Lydia, to whom you gave the dregs at the bottom of the bag. You were praised by all, and the candy was delicious. You had enjoyed the sticky, forbidden fruit, eating in hurried and then slow rhythms. Little did you know that you had met your soulmate, the only thing in this life that would ever stick by your side.

This thirst for belonging, for inclusion and the avoidance of "otherness" would both not only shape you, but feed your compulsion in later life. It was a demon you would never purge.

THE DARKNESS WINS SOMETIMES

Doreen Anyango

*M*Y DEAREST BABY-CAKES,

How are you? I feel like I haven't asked you that question in a long while. And even when we've spoken of recent, it has felt somewhat insufficient. And so, I'm ignoring your phone calls. And texts. And WhatsApps. I'm sorry about that. I'm not mad at you or anything. It's nothing you've done. I know how you overthink things, and I don't want you going crazy wondering now oba, what did I do to Phoebe? I'm just unable to right now.

And so, I'm writing you a letter. How quaint. How high school. Remember how we used to be so excited to get mail? Remember how we treasured our perfumed letters on those bu pastel-coloured note pads with the flowery borders and song dedications at the end? How our fourteen-, fifteen- and sixteen-year-old selves giddily opened the envelopes and lapped up the confessions of love and promises of eternity? Remember that one sentence one you received from Kasper that said simply *My heart goes boom*! in his spidery handwriting, with a ka doodle of a heart exploding? The drama! Such simple times. Such easily accessible joy.

I have been unsuccessfully chasing joy for such a long time that I'm completely depleted. To the point that my boss noticed something was off about me. Yeah, a self-absorbed arsehole who speaks of himself in the third person looked at me one morning and was like, what's wrong with you? He wasn't kind about it or anything, but still. It was all I could do not to break down into frenzied weeping in the office. I managed to compose myself long enough to go to HR and ask for leave for personal reasons. Me, whom they have to remind and practically force to take leave every year. Me, who has worked through every single heartbreak. Olaba I haven't looked at a spreadsheet in the three days I've been in hibernation. That alone should tell you how bloody tired I am.

I should be setting off for Dr Emma's office soon. My appointment is in the next two hours, but instead here I am still in my nightdress at midday, still sitting in my bed, writing to you. It is the only thing I'm able to do at the moment. Do you remember how excited I was about therapy at first?

How I was gushing about all the discoveries I was making about myself, and how I was being equipped to deal better with life, and how enlightened and empowered I felt? That feels like such a long time ago, even though it was only three months ago.

I'm now at the stage in my therapy journey where I'm just overwhelmed by how incompetent I've been at life in my twenty-eight years. I'm just not in the mood to spend fuel and 250k (in this economy!) to be told yet another way I'm fucked-up. Dr Emma says the discomfort is good. That this is how I will grow. That I need to let myself feel what I feel. That it is the nature of beginnings to be difficult. That all I have to start with is where I am, with what I have, and work until everything I loathe about myself is finally made beautiful. That I need to keep on treating myself in self-loving ways even when I don't feel I deserve it. Well, today self-love looks like staying home and writing a letter to my best friend.

Full disclosure, we talked about you last week. I can't tell you what was said about you obviously, these things being confidential and all. But you have been on my mind a lot lately, despite what my silence might be saying. I've been thinking about you and us, and fifteen years of growing together and fighting and crying and loving. I've been thinking about the things you say and do that make me love you and/or want to murder you:

I love you.

You don't say this often. Like only on birthdays and special occasions. You're more the *I love you too* kind of friend, and I've never told you how over the years I've felt like I was the better friend. That my love was superior because it was louder, more forceful. But I'm learning that love doesn't always have to be loud. And that loudness doesn't always translate into quality.

You were raised by a grandmother who was always the first to show up on Visiting Days at school. The first time I laid eyes on you, you were with your grandmother. It was the first day of high school, and she'd come to drop you off in your uncle's old truck even though she had a broken foot. You were walking ahead of her with that (sometimes incredibly annoying) leisurely stroll of yours, a brown envelope held to your chest, and she was lagging behind you, dragging her heavily bandaged foot, pursing her lips and pushing the one crutch she was using for support forcefully into the ground with each step. You, tall and dark and graceful, gliding; she short, light-skinned, fierce.

I remember watching the two of you and thinking *that mukadde looks small and weak, but I bet if anybody messes with her grandkid, there will be hell to pay*. It was the way she was watching over you. Like you were a precious thing that might break even though she was the one fragile and bandaged. And then my mum, from whom I get the never-able-to-mind-my-business gene, offered your grandmother a seat on the tree stump next to our van, and took over getting you registered at the office, and introduced us and volunteered me to you: This is my daughter Phoebe, talk to her if you need anything.

I took you as my responsibility from that moment on. And I've convinced myself that I have always carried you, when the whole time you've been there, watching over me, ready to fight anyone who would hurt me. Loving me quietly and steadily.

You were raised by a grandmother that had only you. It was always just the two of you in a cocoon of warmth. I'm the fourth of four girls, and was raised by a single mother who was hell-bent on trying to save the world. I've always had to fight to make myself worthy of love.

Phoebe, you're crazy.

I remember the first time you said this to me. It was a boring weekday night in our boring all-girls' boarding school dormitory. I came over to your bunk bed and stood on tip-toe so my face could be closer to your face, and I said you absolutely had to sign up for the first ever Miss St Joseph's High School beauty contest happening in a few months, and which had gotten the entire school in a frenzy of excitement. And you were like no, there's no way I can win, and I was like, absolutely there's every way for you to win. And you were like: Phoebe, you're crazy. I was like, no I'm not, and you are signing up and we are winning this thing. And you were like, we?

And I was like, yeah. And you were like, okay, but reluctantly. And I was like, we are winning this thing. And we worked hard and practiced every night after that, and you ended up as second runner-up in a case of broad daylight robbery. In an election so rigged that Museveni would have been in a corner with a thumbs-up nodding his approval. You were clearly the most beautiful, most graceful, most popular contestant. We were robbed of our victory. And it still pains me fifteen years later. Meanwhile, did you know that the chic who was chairperson of the judges committee is now a cabinet minister in Rwanda? I saw her gu face on Twitter recently and I was like, this chic is going to steal money and Kagame will throw her in prison. A thief is always a thief, and karma is a bitch, and I'm still waiting for the universe to avenge us.

Chill, we will reach when we reach.

I remember you saying this to me on that trip to Mbarara for one of your cousins' kuhingira. We were in first year at campus, I think. You'd said it would take a maximum of four hours to get to Mbarara, and we were over five hours in and I was losing my shit because you were like, we still have some way to go. How much longer? I don't know, like an hour maybe. *Chill, we will reach when we reach.* And then you turned from me to talk to the lady across the aisle who was convinced you were a sister to one of her old school mates.

I was already angry because you'd said we'd leave Kampala at eight a.m. only to show up at the bus park two hours later. And now I was angrier because you were relaxed and happily chatting with this stranger in your language when nothing was going according to plan. And I was on the brink of exploding with fury each time the conductor hit the side of the bus and it stopped to pick up a passenger. But we reached when we reached. And there was good food and music and that alcoholic porridge I fell in love with, and lots of warm hugs from your relatives.

To be fair, I probably will never be a hundred per cent cool with how you just wing it through life. But I'm learning to chill a little. I will always need a clear plan of where we are going and how and when we will get there and some commitment on your part to follow it – then I'll be more relaxed for the rest of the journey. I'm working on it.

Nah sis, he's not the one.

To be fair, you've never said this out loud. Or at least not in those exact words. But you don't know how to lie, KK. Whatever your feelings are about someone, they show on your face. And so I know you don't approve of John. You were going through your own stuff when I first introduced him to you, and even in your own pain, I could see you genuinely trying to be happy for me, but there it was, the ka ever so slight sneer (an imperceptible twitch of the lips to the untrained eye) whenever I mentioned his name, and the cool detachment in how you spoke to him. Then the constant questions about his kids and his ex, and how was I dealing with all of that? Anyway, you were right. Again. He wasn't the one.

So last Saturday afternoon, nga I'm all still high on endorphins from spin class that morning and I'm preparing to get ready to leave the house for Dr Emma's. Nga munange, doesn't he call me? Mbu, the kids' nanny has left suddenly and he has a meeting to attend and can I go and be with the kids? And I'm like, I'm going for therapy, you know that. And he's like, but this is an emergency, you can always talk to that so-called doctor another time. And I was like my mental health is an emergency. And he was like, you're just wasting money on white-people nonsense. The audacity! Anyway I told him I was going for therapy and I would see him and the kids later, and he would have to find someone else to mind his offspring in the meantime. Nga he hangs up. Nga also me I go for my session with Dr Emma (where we talked about you). Afterwards, I passed by CJ's for ice cream and brownies, as is my tradition after some emotional heavy lifting, and then I went over to his place.

The kids were dirty and playing outside even though it was getting dark, and the house was a whole mess, and he was in the sitting room with his two cousins watching Arsenal vs Man United. And there were all these bottles of alcohol on the table even though we'd had the conversation so many times over the past three months, about him supporting me in my sobriety journey by not having alcohol in the house. And I was just like, I can't do this. For the first time in my dating life, I'm the one who walked away. So maybe that's a small victory, I don't know.

There's this South African movie on Netflix called *Seriously Single* that I've been obsessed with. It's about these two best friends and their struggles with the men they're dating. And babe, you should find it and watch it because it is so us. There's this one scene where one of the girls is trying to get back with this guy her friend is not feeling at all, and they have a double date and the friend is giving this guy the stink-eye and throwing bu little verbal jabs here and there, but she's there. Like this is bullshit, he's so not the one and I don't like him for my friend, but I will show up. That is so you.

Imagine if I made a movie about my relationship dramas with men. It would be epic and way too long and people would be like this is an exaggeration, there's no way all of that happened to one person. But it happened. And you were there. From actual bar fights with women of ill-repute over some upcoming rapper, to eloping with a narcissist at twenty-two, to stalking that radio presenter after he made it clear that what we'd had was a one-night-stand, to getting pregnant for a married man so he would choose me over his wife.

There's this tweet I saw this week where this lady said she takes a solid thirty minutes out of every working day just to sit back and do nothing except fear men. And I shall be incorporating that into my daily routine henceforth, probably early in the morning, from 6 to 6.30, between meditation and breakfast.

Eh eh, naye Phoebe, the whole bottle is finished?!

In all this, the one thing I'm truly proud of is succeeding at staying sober. I've not touched alcohol for three months. I want to so desperately right now, but there's not a single drop in the house, and if I don't leave, I can add another second, minute, hour to my three months.

I don't know.

You say this a lot. And I can't tell you how far up the wall this always drives me. So far up, I topple over on the other side. KK, I'm at Javas, what do you want to eat? *I don't know. Anything. Whatever you get me is fine.* Baby-cakes, where should we go for your birthday lunch? *I don't know, any-where. What did you have in mind?* What are your plans for the weekend, KK? *I don't know. I have a few deliveries to make, and then we'll see.*

It's infuriating how you lead everything with not knowing. Full disclosure, I judged you hard when you found out about J's bipolar diagnosis, and led with *I don't know.* I judged you for not being strong for him. I judged you for being scared. I'm ashamed to admit that I even judged you a little for how completely undone by grief you were when he killed himself.

But now that I think about it, there is no guide on how to react when your boyfriend is diagnosed with a serious medical condition. There is no guide on how to grieve any loss. I'm learning first-hand that grief is a many tentacled monster that can just pop out of nowhere and crash you to the ground. Or grab you around the neck so hard that you can't breathe. Or wrap itself around you so completely that you cannot move at all.

Even when I was beyond certain that motherhood wasn't for me. Even when I made the choice to terminate my pregnancy. What is a tiny clump of cells in comparison to a fully formed person you held and smelled and loved and laughed with?

Forgive me my unkindness. I didn't know.

The darkness is winning.

This is a new entry that only came into your vocabulary after J's death. And a firm favourite. I've watched you remake yourself after the devastation of loss. I've watched you quit a job you hated and start a business with only a sack of potatoes, a phone and grit. I've watched you morph from a broken fragile thing to a boss babe, unafraid to go back to school at twenty-seven and start over to build the career you want.

But even as you win, you have never hidden from the fact that you stumble sometimes. My first favourite thing about you that first day of high school was how arrestingly gorgeous you were. And then over the fifteen years of knowing you, my favourite thing about you has moved between how chill you are, and how loyal. And how honest. And how present. And how kind. And how generous. My current favourite thing about you is how vulnerable you are. How I will ask how you're doing, and sometimes you'll say *Pheebs, the darkness is winning*. I wish I could answer the phone when you call and say I see you trying to be there for me, and I appreciate it more than you'll ever know. But babe, you're trying to love me like I love you when all I need is for you to love me like you love me. I don't need you to call me on the phone eight times a day or forward me motivational quotes on WhatsApp. You know what would be really nice? No talking. In lieu of therapy this afternoon, I wish you would come over here and lie in this bed with me like you did on another Saturday afternoon many years ago, when I saw my boyfriend of three years' wedding pictures on Instagram. Remember how you held me so tight, like the force of your arms would be what held me together? And how we lay there in silence for hours. Forehead to forehead. Heartbeat to heartbeat.

You may smile at me or make faces if you want, but nothing else. Not a word.

Eh, you chic, I'm really feeling this ka song.

This as you sway in your seat and bob your head, the one glass of wine already getting into your system. And then you'll stand up and keep dancing on the spot at the table, and then you'll slowly make your way to the dance floor, and then just like that, you'll be lost in the music and shaking all the parts of you that can be shaken, and people in the club will all be staring at you because of how alive and free you are.

We should go dancing sometime soon, babe. It has been way too long.

With all my love,
Your Phoebe

PS: Song Dedication
"Danger" – Lilian Mbabazi

N'GANGA

Emily Pensulo

*M*AYBE HE HAD swallowed Nono's fur. He did not know. All he knew was that he had had a cough for the past six months which was not going away. A deep cough, which produced thick dark-yellow phlegm. His grandmother told him fur was dangerous. Especially a cat's fur. Once it was swallowed, one would get a cough that would last for a lifetime. And although he had always hated cats, he let Nono stay when she came out of nowhere and sat on his verandah and wouldn't go away. It was out of necessity. Recently, he had begun receiving unwelcome guests. Thick rats who chewed clothes and paper. And he had had enough when they ate the corner of a bunch of hundred-kwacha notes he had saved for rent after being retrenched from work – because business at Glory Lodge where he had worked as an accountant wasn't doing so well during the lockdown. Overnight there were no guests or tourists at the lodge, so they had to lay him off. He thought of being angry because he had given ten years of service, but he knew the books; there was no other way.

As he coughed and spat the phlegm onto the dirt in his backyard, he told himself that Nono had been dead for two years, so it was unlikely that he had swallowed her fur. He coughed some more, his body jerking and his chest heating with every motion. At last he stopped, stood up straight, faced the sky, and beat at his chest. He took in a deep breath and had begun to retreat back into his flat when water droplets hit his face.

"Sorry," said the woman, holding an empty bucket.

Her name was Chimwewe and she lived in the flat next to his. He considered this as pure misfortune. Her stereo burst out kalindula music at awkward hours, and she had a multitude of friends who were always coming over. They danced and laughed the night away, disturbing his sleep. He often wondered about her; she was an unlikely person to listen to traditional Zambian music. She was a slay queen, although now redundant because her ex-boyfriend, who had paid for rent in Salama Park and bought her hair and clothes, now had a younger woman. And when their relationship ended, he took back everything he had paid for. So she moved to M'tendere to the one-bedroomed flats erected in a linear fashion. The rent here was cheaper, but even then she played hide-and-seek with the landlord every month.

He began to say something, but erupted in a coughing fit.

Chimwemwe moved closer and ran her soft hand over his back, easing his discomfort.

He gained composure and exclaimed, "Yaba."

"Sorry ey," Chimwemwe said. "Have you gone to the clinic?"

He nodded. "They gave me paracetamol and cough syrup and said it would stop in a week, but still nothing."

"Nanga TB?"

He shook his head. "The test came back negative."

"Eh," Chimwemwe said. "Sorry to hear that, Ba Henry."

He hated it when she called him Ba Henry, not just Henry. He wasn't much older, but the prefix widened their age gap and extinguished any opportunity for romance with her or her friends – he wouldn't have minded something short-term with benefits. He nodded again. Holding in a cough, he walked back into his flat and closed the door behind him. But before he could lie down, he heard a knock on his back door. He wanted to ignore it, but it would not stop. He found Chimwemwe waiting for him. He had not noticed earlier how low-cut her top was, and how the red lace appealed to his appetite.

She smiled and moved closer. "Nanga," she began, "have you tried Ba N'ganga?"

Henry coughed, "Ba N'ganga?" he asked, his body growing cold just at the mention of the word. He shook his head. "I can never go to Ba N'ganga."

Chimwemwe laughed. "But Ba Henry, do you not want to get well?"

"I want to," he said, "but I can't go to a witchdoctor."

"Ba Henry, Ba N'ganga's medicine sometimes works even better than modern medicine."

Henry managed a smile and shook his head. Back in the village where he had lived with his grandmother, he had once been to a witchdoctor's shrine, even though it had been by accident. It was shortly after his mother had wed another man and left to start a few life. That day, Henry had been in the bush hunting birds with his best friend, Chisomo. As he kept his eyes on a bird, the stone in his catapult pricking his thumb and forefinger, he did not realise how far he had gone into the bush until he stepped on a thorn. He looked down at his bleeding foot and stooped to wipe the blood. It was when he straightened that he saw a lone shrine with coral shells and withered heads of hyenas and lions all around it. Above the door of the shrine was a black doll with red wool hair. He stared at the shrine open-mouthed, and the hair on the back of his neck stood. He had already begun his retreat, still staring at the shrine, when a hand grabbed his shoulder. He had not heard branches crack under the weight of feet nor the swishing of grass. But here was someone behind him. He turned and his eyes widened further. Before him stood the boniest man he had ever seen. He wore a black kaftan. He had hair on the sides of his head that fell to his chest, and the brown of his eyes had turned milky. Henry wanted to scream, but something held his voice until the man removed his hand from his shoulder. It was then that Henry screamed, and ran and ran and ran.

He knew he had met Kalebwe, the N'ganga he had always thought was a myth. Something grownups used to scare children who wandered into the bush on their own. They always said, "Kalebwe will get you." He was the witchdoctor who lived alone in the bush. He had once caused heavy floods when British contractors had tried to pull down his shrine and build a railway. The contractors had been warned to keep away from Kalebwe, but they wouldn't listen. So after the floods, Kalebwe sent lions and mysterious diseases to kill the railway workers. Soon no one wanted to work on the railway, not even the British themselves, and the project was abandoned.

When Henry reached home, breathless from running, he told his grandmother what had happened, and she immediately called the village pastor. He came as fast as his bicycle, which was the village's main means of transportation, would allow. This bicycle took people to the hospital, and ferried household goods and produce sold at the market, providing service at no cost at all.

The pastor sat on a stool offered by Henry's grandmother, and asked him to narrate what had happened from the beginning to the end. He did the best he could. Then the pastor took some anointing oil, dipped a finger in it, and marked the sign of the cross on Henry's forehead. Then he laid hands on Henry's head and went on to pray in tongues. When he finished, he announced that it was done: Henry's grandmother did not have to worry about curses, hexes or seals on her grandson's life as a result of wandering into Kalebwe's territory. She thanked him and tried to offer something in gratitude, but he raised a hand and shook his head.

"I am here to serve," he said, "and I must do the work of Him who sent me."

Henry's grandmother tried to insist, but the pastor still said no, and as she walked him out of the kraal, they chatted. Henry heard the pastor say, "People go to witchdoctors for favours, but they are deceived because there are no good evil spirits."

The words had stuck with Henry and now played in his mind as Chimwemwe suggested he see a witchdoctor for his cough.

"Okay Ba Henry," Chimwemwe said, "in case you change your mind, let me know." She turned to go, and then stopped. "See here," she dangled car keys in front of him, "I went to Doctor Vumbi just last weekend. Yesterday John apologised and bought me a brand-new car."

Henry studied the keys and thought of how good it would be to own a car, and how good it would be if his cough went away. But he shook his head, remembering the words the pastor had said all those years ago: that there are no good evil spirits. Even though now witchdoctors had removed the "witch" and went by the name "doctor", they were still witchdoctors who conspired with evil spirits to cast spells that bound people's souls. And if this was their trade, how then could they bring about any good?

Henry went back into his room and lay down for the rest of the afternoon. He woke up in the evening for tea and boiled sweet potatoes, then went back to bed. This time he could not sleep. He coughed and coughed until he coughed out blood and his throat could not take any more coughing without piercing him with sharp little pins. He sat up for the rest of the night, afraid to sleep, afraid to let out a cough while his body lay in unconsciousness. He watched the darkness turn into day and at first sight of light, he knocked at Chimwemwe's door. She opened the door with her eyes half closed, eyeliner and mascara smudged around them.

"Ba Henry," she said.

"Doctor Vumbi," he began, "can we go see him today?"

Her eyes opened fully and she smiled. "I knew you would be back," she said. "Give me five minutes. It's best to go early before more clients go to see him."

Henry went back into his flat and changed his shirt. He had held back his cough since last night, and hoped he could hold it in until he received treatment from Doctor Vumbi. He went back to Chimwemwe's, stood outside and waited for her. Thirty minutes later, she emerged with foundation on her face and bright pink lipstick on her lips. A sleek weave covered her head, and she carried a brown doll with purple eyes and yellow wool hair. Around its waist were beads and coral shells. It smiled, but there was nothing friendly about the smile. She put the doll in her bag – "for good luck everywhere I go" – and led Henry to her silver Toyota Vitz. Before he got in, he asked, the words escaping his mouth: "Has Doctor Vumbi ever cast evil spells?"

Chimwemwe laughed. "Evil spells?" she asked. "Why? What you should understand is that there are spirits who watch over us, our ancestors. If they are good and we petition them, it's they who help us."

"But Ba N'ganga..."

Chimwemwe raised a hand. "If Doctor Vumbi was so bad, would I have a car today?"

Henry got into the Toyota Vitz. And as they drove from Mtendere to Rhodes Park, he thought of all the things he could ask Doctor Vumbi to do for him besides healing his cough. He could ask for expediency in finding a new job; a Mercedes Benz, preferably brand new; and a woman to marry. In an instant, the world of possibility came into view, and Henry imagined sitting in his office, driving his Benz with a beautiful woman beside him. So lost was he in his thoughts that he didn't notice the morning traffic, which stretched for miles and moved at a snail's pace, or how they had left behind the medium-sized houses in M'tendere and now drove through streets with high wall fences, which concealed big yards and spacious homes. After what seemed like forever, they stopped at the gate of one such yard.

"We are here," Chimwemwe said, then rolled down the window and pressed the intercom with the tip of a stick-on nail.

Henry sat up and took in the freshly painted black gate, the gold lion-head statues on both sides, and the green lawn bordered by brown lawns in neighbouring yards. He stared at Chimwewe, wide-eyed.

She laughed. "Yes, this is Doctor Vumbi's house," she said.

Seconds later a voice spoke, asking who was at the gate.

Chimwemwe responded and said she had come with a friend to see Doctor Vumbi.

The gate opened revealing a sprawling grey house that sat in the middle of a green lawn. Palm trees lined the paved driveway as they drove to the visitor's car park. Then they walked to the house, where a man in crease-pressed trousers and a black shirt with Assistant labelled on the right breast opened the door for them. He led them up a cascading stairway until they reached a room with a white carpet and furniture upholstered in gold fabric. On a sofa adjacent to the door sat a man cross-legged in a navy-blue suit with a sky-blue pocket square. His hair was cropped in a brush cut and he held a phone in his hand, moving a finger up and down the screen. When Chiwemwe and Henry walked in, he put the phone down, smiled and came towards them. He offered a handshake first to Chimwemwe, and then to Henry. The musky smell of perfume filled the room.

"Hello," he said, in a British accent.

Chimwemwe smiled coyly. "Hello," she replied, but Henry kept silent. His eyes were fixed on the face in front of him – clear and browned-skinned with warm brown eyes.

"Hello," Doctor Vumbi said again.

Henry muttered a response.

Doctor Vumbi clasped his hands. "We should begin," he said, and stared at Henry. "You've had a cough for six months."

Henry swallowed. His mouth dry, he looked at Chimwemwe: "But h... how did he know?"

Doctor Vumbi laughed. "The spirits know everything," he said.

Henry should have been scared to be in this place where spirits knew why he had come even before he said anything – but he wasn't. He was at ease even though images of Kalebwe had tried to intrude on his mind, and he himself had tried to conjure fear so that he could turn back and leave. He still remembered the words of the pastor, but this place did not lurk of evil but of calm and luxury; and the man in front of him looked like a man he could trust.

"Let's get into it, then," Doctor Vumbi said. "Please wait here."

Doctor Vumbi disappeared behind a door and returned with a black rug and a reed basket containing coral shells and wooden figurine heads of hyenas and lions. On top of the figurines was a brown doll with purple eyes and yellow wool hair. He spread the mat and placed the contents of the basket on it. He knelt and instructed Henry and Chimwemwe to do the same. He moved the items around using a wooden stick with a black feather attached. He hummed and hummed, and then said, "For the things you require, the spirits need an offering."

Chimwemwe reached into her bag and retrieved a fifty-kwacha note. She handed it to Henry, who placed it in the basket.

Doctor Vumbi closed his eyes and hummed again. He opened them and smiled. "Henry," he said, "the spirits have accepted your offering." He poked at the hyena and lionhead figurines again and said, "They say to say it is done."

Henry looked at Doctor Vumbi.

"Yes Henry, all you came for has been granted – even the Benz, the job and the wife."

The hair on Henry's neck stood. And then relaxed. Warmth spread from his belly through all of him, and he bowed low on the mat, saying "Thank you, thank you, thank you." Doctor Vumbi urged him up, but Henry would not move. Today was the last day of his troubles. Soon, he would be in a job, maybe even the next day, and he would have a Mercedes and meet someone to fill his lonely days, and for this he was grateful to Dr Vumbi. Eventually Henry sat up and Doctor Vumbi reached for the doll and gave it to him.

"Take this," he said, "for good luck."

Henry took the doll. Even though it was only as big as his palm, it weighed more than a brick. Then he and Chimwemwe walked to the parking lot where ten more cars had parked since their arrival, all clients waiting to see Doctor Vumbi.

Henry and Chimwemwe drove away. The tiredness and pain in Henry's chest had ceased. He tried coughing just to make sure it was all gone. But no deep cough or phlegm came out of his mouth. He sat back and tried again after a few minutes, and still his chest was calm.

He turned to Chimwewe: "Thank you."

And then they laughed and played kalindula music all the way home. And when they got there, Henry took the doll to his room, carrying it as if it were an egg, careful to keep anything from harming what would bring him good luck. He opened his closet and retrieved the suitcase in which he had carried his belongings from the village to the Copperbelt and to Lusaka. The zip still worked, even though time had eaten bits and pieces of the material.

His grandmother had given it to him. Actually, it was the pastor – when he heard that Henry had been accepted at the Copperbelt University to study accounting on a government bursary, he had brought a gift he thought the young man would need. He hadn't used the suitcase in years and had nothing to keep in it. So he gave it to Henry's grandmother so that she in turn could give it to Henry because gifts to the child had to first pass through the hands of the guardian to eschew any impression that they had failed to provide.

The suitcase was officially handed over at a small get-together that the pastor had advised Henry's grandmother to host in thanksgiving because a son from the village, and from her house in particular, was going to university. He would come back a success and make so much money he would feed the entire village. On the day he left, people whispered things they wanted him to send back to them. A friend of an uncle wanted newspapers even though he did not know how to read, an aunt wanted lotion and chitenge, and cousins wanted clothes. And his grandmother, even though she did not say it explicitly, wanted a monthly allowance. Only the pastor did not want anything other than a promise that he would do well in school.

As Henry placed the suitcase on the bed, a cloud of dust followed from his closet. It had been years since he last touched the suitcase. He had simply placed it on the upper shelf and never bothered with it. In it were things he would not need again: secondary school notebooks, test and question papers, which he had carried because he thought they had some value. What exactly, he did not know. But there was something satisfying in having things which told stories of past victories: A I test scores and notebooks in which teachers had written "excellent". He covered his mouth and nose to keep from sneezing at the dust, unzipped the suitcase and placed the doll inside. Before placing it back on the shelf, he looked through an accountancy book and smiled at how many times "excellent" was written in it.

Henry then sat on his bed and made a mental list of all the places he wanted to find work now that he could. He listed them in order of priority, with PricewaterhouseCoopers being the first and the government being the last. He wondered if he should write application letters or wait for them to call him; but how could they could call him if he hadn't written any application letters? But then again, Doctor Vumbi could do anything. Henry decided not to take any chances and took sheets of plain paper from a drawer of a bedside table. He wrote some application letters, and decided to drop them off first thing next morning. Today he would relax and enjoy good health, and plan what to do next once he got the job.

But as he sat there thinking, a loud bang cut through the air as if something heavy had fallen from the sky. Then there were people screaming and the sound of rushing feet. Henry got up and hurried towards the commotion. People had circled around, and in a few minutes, the crowd had already thickened. Henry followed a stout woman who pushed her way through. She gasped when she got to the front, and placed both hands over her mouth. Henry moved faster and pushed her out of the way, and then he saw it too. On top of Chimwemwe's car, there was a rock – or at least what appeared to be a rock. It was as black as a starless night, and it moved backward and forward, curving in the roof, shattering the windows, deflating the tires, crushing the Vitz to the ground. Eyewitnesses said it had fallen from the sky. And when it had crushed the Vitz flat, it began to reduce in size. People gasped, took photos and videos, and called for others who had not yet come. When Chimwemwe arrived at the scene, the crowd parted for her.

"That's her, that's her," they said, "the owner of the vehicle."

When she saw her Vitz, she yelled. Her legs weakened under her and she began descending to the ground, but two women held her on each side as she cried inconsolably. At first, the crowd was sympathetic, but when the rock disappeared completely, they threatened to stone her. Chimwemwe was a witch, they said, and should be put to death so the community could be safe again. But the two women led her away from the crowd and back to her flat.

Henry stared at the Vitz that would never be driven again, and followed Chimwemwe to her flat. She had calmed down a little, although her body was still shaking. The two women sat beside her as small drops of tears left her eyes. Chimwewe narrated, in a shaky voice, how she had had an argument with John, and in anger, had thrown the doll against the wall and stomped on it over and over. She thought she had seen blood ooze, but she wasn't sure. It could have been red cotton inside the doll. When she finished her account, one of the women asked: "Where is the doll now?"

Chimwemwe pointed to a handbag on the floor.

The woman went to the backyard and came back with a stick, placed it between the two handles of the bag, and carried it outside.

The other woman followed and suggested calling a pastor, but her friend said the pastor would come later to pray for Chimwemwe because she had put her hand to evil. She said a prayer and pleaded for the blood of Jesus to overcome this evil. Then she took some matches and set the bag alight. It exploded in a ball of yellow, red and black flames. Then it disappeared, like it had never existed.

Henry stared wide-mouthed. His knees were numb and urine ran down his thighs to his feet and soaked his shoes. He pointed to the place the bag had sat before it disappeared: "There was a bag there," he said.

The women nodded.

Henry found his feet again and turned to leave. He thought about the doll he had in his suitcase. Right then, he heard the pastor's voice in his ears, as clear as it was all those years ago, and it said to him: "There are no good evil spirits."

SECTION 47

Sola Njoku

*W*ONU WAS TURNING into her mother. Like a passenger in a car racing towards a crash, she could see it happening but was powerless to stop it – much as she wished she could, much as her world depended upon it.

Some of her earliest childhood memories were of her mother setting arithmetic questions and waiting, her leg vibrating with the effort of holding in her impatience, as the terrified six-year-old Wonu attempted, repeatedly and unsuccessfully, to solve the tasks presented to her.

"Are you sleeping over there?" Wonu's mother would finally explode, jolting the child who had been dithering at the dining-table-turned-classroom, hoping to delay the inevitable force of her mother's rage.

She would jump to her feet and approach cautiously, proffering the exercise book opened to the ink-smudged page she had been working on. Wonu's mother would snatch it from her hand and address her glower to the page.

If the glare remained in place, Wonu could tell, with relief, that she had managed, not by any method she could recollect but by pure chance, to solve the maths problems. She would be rewarded with even more problems to solve, to prove to her unrelenting taskmaster that she had grasped the lesson. Although bent to the task well into the evening, the lesson would be so fleetingly stuck in her mind that by the next day Wonu would again be struck dumb by the same homework, to the constant frustration of her temperamental teacher.

If her mother's glower switched to a small mirthless smile, followed by a rueful shake of her head and the beginnings of a harsh laughter, Wonu knew that the book would soon be flying in her direction, accompanied by the lash of her dad's belt, borrowed for the day's lesson. And then her mother's words would follow, so hurtful that they seared her ears on their journey to lodge themselves in memory. Decades later she could recall them with the clarity of a school bell. It was during these years of childhood that Wonu mastered the art of stringing hurt like endless coral beads.

Her mother would go on inform her that she was a useless,

good-for-nothing Olodo, a collector of noughts, and foretell that, in years, Wonu would, mark her words, be perambulating the roadside hawking peppers and tomatoes, slapping about in flipflops with holes worn into their soles. She would conjure ever more humiliating and dire destinies for Wonu for having so woefully failed at such easy mathematics. Only the sound of three short horn blasts beyond the double gates of their two-bedroom bungalow, indicating the return of Wonu's dad, would silence the tirade. Wonu would never know if this was because her mother was distracted by her dad's arrival or because her beration was a thing she hid from him, their own hurtful secret; but she spent many gloomy evenings anticipating the sound of his Peugeot 504 horn.

Wonu observed herself now in the incandescence of her own anger. She was crouched on the floor beside her son who sat on a low toddler stool. She forced his hand to the paper for the umpteenth time to shape the number five. She had been teaching him to write numbers up to twenty for some days, in readiness for entry into nursery school. The boy had been excited to hold the pencil and the number grid sheet, to muster something more meaningful than wriggly lines and droopy-faced smileys with feeble stick figures. He had started off a keen learner, reciting the numbers that he already knew by heart as he slowly and deliberately embedded them on the paper. But he always got stuck on the five. Half the time they looked in the opposite direction, the rest of the time he failed to manage the sideways dome of the numeral. Soon his delight gave way to boredom and then despair over the repetitive task.

"Again! Hat," and grasping his pudgy little hand in hers, Wonu drew the horizontal top of the number. "Neck," she said, making a right angle by connecting a perpendicular line to the former, "now, the belly," she said, drawing an exaggerated roundness for the number's base. Then she released his hand, drew back, gave him the pencil and watched him fail yet again to achieve any form that was a recognisable five.

Mayowa was tired, she knew that. She had read many online parenting articles that advised that the attention span of a two-year-old was a maximum of six minutes. They had been going at this for twenty minutes, and he had managed everything else but the five and the fifteen. But he needed to learn this, and she could not leave it until tomorrow because she would have even more important knowledge to impart then. Between her long shifts as an A&E health assistant and the long commutes to the hospital, no time was left on the days she worked. All teaching and learning had to be crammed into her infrequent days off, trailing in importance behind household chores that piled for days into a mountain of things, prolonged mealtimes directing spoonfuls into an unwilling mouth, and endless play-dates and playground visits.

"Again," she said to the now morose boy, her voice hoarse from the effort to restrain herself from shouting at him.

"I'm tired, Mummy," ventured Mayowa tearfully. "I don't want to write anymore."

"You have to," she snapped. "We're not leaving here until you write me a decent five. I don't know what's so difficult about it. Remember, head, neck, big belly. Simple."

And Mayowa again bowed his head and put his pencil back to paper.

WONU STUFFED THE loose pages of paper, the now blunted pencils and the blackened eraser into the knick-knack drawer in the kitchen and reflected tiredly on her performance. She was proof, if anything, of the wisdom of adopting a different tack from her mother. She made the obligatory weekly phone call to the bungalow house her parents still lived in, phone calls that consisted of small talk about the weather and remonstrations over the lateness of her maintenance payments to them. It was entirely a chore.

Now a parent herself, her earlier resentment of her mother had evolved, if not to forgiveness, to an understanding. She now had an inkling how the burden of parenting defied logic or detachment. Everything was catastrophic, critical, and personal. She had sent Mayowa, exhausted, to his room for a time-out, could hear him crying, and knew how silly it was to punish a toddler for his inability to manage a particular sequence of scrawls.

But she was tetchy and exhausted from the effort of the failed tutorial, and could not bring herself to dispense comfort. Instead, she started on dinner, cutting up the peppers, onions, garlic and tomatoes that she would combine into a stew, sighing as the noise of the blender drowned out her son's distress.

BEFORE MAYOWA WAS born, Wonu had watched a Victoria Derbyshire exposé on BBC2 titled "How British Education Fails Black Boys". The presenter had, through voiced-over clips and interviews with experts, highlighted that Black boys on average came into education twenty points above their Caucasian counterparts and came out of it trailing twenty-one points behind them. Wonu could not recall what the points were based on, nor was she able to retrieve the information despite repeated Google searches. But this horrific statistic lodged itself in her mind even then, when the idea of having a child, possibly male, and attempting to raise it in Britain, was largely hypothetical. Yet here she was, doing those exact things with a fierce determination to thwart a system intent on undermining her son's potential. She would not relent, and neither could she permit him to.

From the day Mayowa was born, the British child of Nigerian parents, Wonu felt that he might well be their ward, but that the structures of Britain had made it clear that he was first the Queen's subject. From the midwives' insistence on taking the new baby to intensive care to be tube-fed mere minutes after birth because he was exhausted and had no interest in approaching the nipple, to the intrusiveness of another who – without waiting for a response to her cursory "May I?" – pinched Wonu's milkless nipple so hard it squirted colostrum into her triumphant face. Then there was the prohibition that meant she could not bathe the baby for the two weeks that they spent in hospital, a taboo that kept her own mother awake at night in the belief that he would develop lifelong body odour. There were also the room temperature restrictions issued by the health visitor, which left the new mother shivering in a house cold as a dog's nose, and the GP's disapproval of Mayowa's circumcision, a Nigerian custom that Wonu did not particularly care for, but nonetheless went along with to abate the panic of the baby's grandmothers.

Wonu remembered once in a children's centre feeding Mayowa fresh orange juice diluted with water to soothe his constipation. A middle-aged nurse had swooped over to challenge her on the natural remedy she had picked up from her own mother. The steely-eyed matron had insisted that she was as good as poisoning the child with her "concoction." Wonu had felt at the time that she might as well leave Mayowa at the relentless mothering mercy of the ubiquitous harridans who constantly looked over her shoulder to offer scathing critiques of her childrearing.

The day Mayowa began primary school, Wonu walked him to school, feeling the weight of dejection dragging at her feet. Her child sizzled with excitement beside her in his bright blue sweater, grey trousers and shiny black Clarks shoes. Wonu dreaded the cutting of the psychological umbilical cord that bound him to her and made her the only source through which Mayowa derived his knowledge and esteem. She knew that she was submitting her son to an authority that would as likely hinder as help him. Her eyes roamed over the redbrick school building as Mayowa was ushered in by a sing-songy teaching assistant. As she slowly made her way out of the school gates, she wished she could see what was going on inside. What ideas were being implanted into his young consciousness by this sea of white faces? Daily, when she picked him up from school, she hoped to encounter a black or brown face and discover that they were teaching staff, but Mayowa progressed through school steered by an unending line of Mrs Smiths and Browns and Pearces in swishy calf-length skirts and flowery blouses, with crisp voices and smiles that were always fixed in place.

Wonu watched with alarm as the school system began to undo her son. His teachers' words became gospel to Mayowa even when they spouted ignorant ideas: "Timbuktu is a fictional location that has intrigued mankind for centuries... Racism has ended... Britain ended slavery."

He insisted, one day, on colouring his Jesus peach-skinned for his RE homework, despite Google's obliging display of swarthy Middle-Eastern approximations in answer to her question: "What would Jesus have looked like?"

He was also made to think that learning had to be fun, had to be aided by colourful props, performance or media. If learning was presented as graft, as a task that required perseverance, he came unstuck. He pronounced his own name wrong, displacing the vowels to arrive at *Moyawa* or *Moya*, acquiescing to the distortion of teachers and friends. He compared notes with his classmates and wanted liberties and excesses like fidget toys, video games, fast food, sleepovers, Halloween... She made up her mind to do all she could to ensure that he didn't grow, like they did here, into a lippy delinquent, entitled, intent on vandalism and self-destruction; they had nothing to fear, hence nothing to respect, she thought. Her own upbringing made her see inflexibility, asceticism and curtailment as necessary components of parental love.

Wonu countered these changes by insisting on him speaking Yoruba when addressing her, even in the presence of his friends, and by purchasing a copy of *Black Heroes: 51 Inspiring People from Ancient Africa to Modern Day USA* on Amazon. The book went on at length about the NAACP and failed to hold even her own attention, with its overtly American perspective on a global racial experience, dropping off their nightly reading after they had covered Hatshepsut, Tutankhamun, Obama, Mandela and Shaka Zulu. She booked Kumon classes and bought 11+ booklets two years advanced for him to practice on. The fact that the mathematics and non-verbal reasoning answers often eluded her, so she had to resort to surreptitiously consulting the answer booklet before issuing emphatic corrections, did not deter Wonu from her pursuit of Mayowa's academic excellence.

WONU ARRIVED HOME from work one day just as Mayowa was settling down to a YouTube video of the three times table being rendered by Mr DeMaio to the tune of Uptown Funk. The video had garnered an impressive seven million views. She clicked off the TV and ordered him to his Kumon booklet. Mayowa's loud groans, growing more elemental by the second, called her from her bedroom ten minutes later.

Wonu knew that her frustration did not really lie with him, but with the diabetic amputee who hissed "wog" and pinched her arm whenever she wheeled her instrument trolley over to record her hourly blood pressure and sats, but she did not waver in her resolve to get Mayowa productively engaged.

Mayowa was slumped in the dining chair, yet to lift his pencil to a single multiplication. He issued another groan that sparked a primal reaction in his mother. The boy's voice was cut off mid-grunt by the yank of his mother's fingers and thumbs on both of his ears. The anger coursing through Wonu delivered adrenaline-induced strength to her forearms. She was jolted to the present only when her gaze met his tear-streaked face at eye level and she felt him treading air. She dropped him to his feet as suddenly as she'd hoisted him, and he ran off to his room, having regained his voice, screaming and clutching his smarting ears.

AT SCHOOL, MAYOWA was a sensible, competent child not used to being singled out for attention. Because of this, he had been excited when his teacher perked up at the words he spoke during the newly introduced *Personal Social Health and Economic* (PSHE) education class. She asked him to stay behind while his friends ran off to lunch.

When the class had emptied, Mrs Shillcock approached his desk and sat in the chair vacated by his friend Oliwier. Her bottom hung off the edges of the child-sized seat and he remembered Goldilocks breaking the little bear's chair. She looked at him so intently that he was struck by the gold flecks in the grey of her irises before she began to gently remind him of what he had said to gain her attention.

"Mayowa, you said that your mummy has a cane. Tell me about it."

"Yes, she has a cane she keeps by the door. When I don't listen, she goes to get it."

"And when she gets it, what does she do with it?"

"She chases me up the stairs," Mayowa explained, remembering his excited terror whenever his mum raced up the stairs behind him, finally giving up as he rounded the corner and launched himself laughing into his dad's arms. "Luckily, I am a fast runner."

"...and then..." the teacher prodded.

"...then I take my clothes off and my dad gives me a bath."

"But what does your mum do with the cane?"

He tried hard to remember. "I don't know," he conceded, embarrassed at not knowing the answer. "Maybe she puts it back?"

"Does she ever touch you with it?"

"Sometimes she gets my bottom, but I try to run faster." Mayowa sensed that his answer had not quite satisfied his teacher.

"Does it hurt?" she asked kindly

It didn't, not really. It felt more like a tap or a pat on his bottom, but the teacher's sympathy made him think it must have. "Yes," he said quietly, tears filling his eyes.

He saw Mrs Shillcock discreetly wipe the corner of her eye. "Does your mum do anything else that hurts you?"

Mayowa thought for long moments. He did not have a good memory – he was constantly forgetting to put his toys in the right places and getting told off by his parents – but he finally remembered something his mum did some yesterdays ago that really hurt. He had been "not focusing" on doing his homework. He had sat petulantly for long minutes not picking up his pencil despite his mum's repeated demands. The Kumon multiplications were repetitive and mind-numbingly boring and he hated having to do them, so he had refused until she had shouted at him, grabbed him by the ears, and sent him to his room for a time-out. He had wailed for a long time until she had come to soothe him, explaining that she was disappointed that he was not putting in his best because the tasks were not difficult, and he was a very intelligent boy. She had wiped the tears he shed at his failure to please her. She had given him a hug and told him to go finish his task so he could watch some more Mr DeMaio before bedtime.

Now, as he sat with his teacher, the memory filled him with new anguish. "My mum lifted me up by my ears. And it was very painful." The teacher nodded wordlessly, patted his shoulder and mentally lodged details of their conversation.

THE NEXT DAY, Mayowa was playing "The Floor is Lava" with Caspar when the headteacher Mrs Nippon called him over. He followed her imposing figure into her office, mesmerised by the swaying flowers on her large skirt as she walked ahead of him. In her office sat two women, who smiled at him and asked how he was.

"Good," he replied shyly.

Although rambunctious and playful with friends, he was uncertain around adults. His young mind tried to work out why he'd had to speak to his teacher yesterday and was now speaking to his headteacher and these two smiling women, who were asking him the same questions.

"Does your mummy hit you?" Yes, when he's running up the stairs for his bath.

"Does it hurt?" Not so much. He had forgotten that yesterday, he had said it did, but he remembered his ear being pulled had hurt, so he mentioned how his mum had lifted him off his feet.

"And what made her do that?"

"Because I wasn't focusing on learning my Yoruba," he replied, muddling up the memory of the task. "But I know many words, I can say 'Good morning' – Ekaaro." He was rewarded with smiles.

The headmistress and her companions huddled over the computer afterwards, typing in variations of the strange language he'd mentioned, until they came upon Yoruba, described as a West African language. They did this after looking him over for signs of injury, speaking to him reassuringly, restraining themselves from touching him unnecessarily. They had patiently waited as his little thumbs and fingers had struggled to get the buttons undone on his polo t-shirt. They had encouraged him to sit on the carpeted floor and take off his shoes before attempting to remove his trousers. When the boy was self-consciously naked before them except for his underwear, they had turned him by his shoulders, this way and that, their expert eyes searching for marks that would indicate discipline that went beyond "reasonable chastisement".

After Mayowa was clothed and dismissed, he had hurried off, relieved to escape their prying eyes and questions, unaware of their complex deliberations on his behalf.

WONU HAD PLANNED a big surprise for Mayowa's birthday. He wanted a movie night with all the works: *Sonic 2*, salted popcorn, strawberry jelly, chocolate ice cream, and the biggest treat of all, a sleepover in her bed. He had made these requests repeatedly during the countdown of days leading to his birthday. He also wanted a slime kit and plushies for his birthday present. She planned to surprise him by inviting his friends Caspar, Josh and Maya. Wonu had gone to pains to reiterate the surprise aspect of the party while issuing sporadic invitation and party reminders on the WhatsApp group into which she had hastily corralled the invited mums.

Mayowa was turning seven, an age that Wonu dreaded, the age by which Aristotle had famously declared that a child had become the man he would grow up to be; his emotional, psychological and cognitive behaviours set in stone, with no allowance for parental do-overs.

Mayowa's birthdays always filled Wonu with a plethora of emotions, ranging from joy to despair, but none more than this birthday. Though unreligious, she had issued insistent proclamations over him at dawn; she had walked him to school, lying convincingly for the umpteenth time about how much she would enjoy having him with her in bed tonight; and had stood to the side eavesdropping on his birthday announcement to his class teacher, ready to intervene should the latter fail to respond with appropriate excitement in the morning crush.

Back home in her kitchen, aided by Googlecast's display of pictures of past anniversaries of the day, she devoted her mind to reminiscence as she poured flavoured gelatine into tiny plastic containers. She contemplated images that jumped from their mawkish faces moments after Mayowa's birth, still joined by the umbilical cord, to the one-year-old cherub with a cake-smeared face, to the more recent rangy golf-club-wielding version from his last crazy-golf birthday party.

She remembered the bright Sunday morning when he was born after a night of fitful epidural-aided sleep that had culminated in an hour of straining. He had emerged, bloodied, bright-eyed, unblinkingly but quietly appraising her, making her worry that he wasn't issuing that most anticipated wail that indicated the presence and commencement of life. She had looked to the midwife: "Why isn't he crying?"

The other had shrugged: "He's looking right at you, even better."

Wonu had gazed into the long-lashed eyes focused on her, tinged yellow from the sunlight streaming in from the open ward window, and felt suffused with love and dread. Long forgotten notes of a Shakespeare play rose to taunt her: "You have murdered sleep ... you shall sleep no more." And how true those words remained. Today, on the cusp of his eighth year, she felt the presence of the anxiety that she had birthed as solidly as the child. The one that had kept her company every night since, after she had put to bed all the changing iterations of her child.

Mayowa's birth had been Wonu's rebirth – her life suddenly profound for acquiring an appendage, her pains more acute for being his, her blunders more unforgivable for their impact upon him, her actions more desperate for being so significant in the long-term. Her constant question: was she intentional enough, doing enough, being enough to guarantee the happiness and success of this life she had called to the earth from her own arrogance and ignorance? The unwavering answer: "No."

As she shut the fridge door on the jelly pots, the doorbell pinged. She continued her tasks when she heard Tunde get up from his home office station to attend to it. The female voices that she heard mingling with his stopped her as she was poised to crack another egg into a mixing bowl to begin making cake batter. She returned the egg to its crate and made her way to the voices.

Two white women of roughly the same size-fourteen build, one in an impractical red polka-dot summer dress on a none-too-summery day, the other in a light blue shirt tucked into smart, navy trousers. The latter, in a business-like manner as indicated by her choice of dress, introduced them both. "I am Police Inspector Sarah Macpherson and with me is Julie Drayton from Child Services. Are you Mayowa's mum?"

And to Wonu's nod of assent, her voice having fled in momentary alarm, the PI replied, with a brief smile that didn't engage her eyes, "It is you we have come to see."

WONU WAS A magnet for racist experiences, large and small, personal or communal. She collected them like precious pearls that she strung, one painful experience after another, until they formed a giant noose upon which she hung the world.

When the nursery teacher told Mayowa he could be a bin collector rather than a doctor, she strung the hard lump that had knotted in her chest; when, after sending out hundreds of applications detailing her double degree qualification for jobs where A-levels were "ideal" and Tunde, always methodical, had taken pains to uncover the mystery of her lack of success, swapping her consonant-laden Nigerian name for a lilting English one, after which the interview invitations had come, she strung a golf-sized ball of bewilderment on her lengthening tally; when her NCT friend gossiped that she didn't "fit in" with the group and one of the others laughingly told her about it, her string of injustices acquired a hard new kernel. George Floyd dropped a boulder on her; the two murdered Black British sisters, photos of whose naked corpses were taken and distributed on WhatsApp by members of the police, nearly broke her. The smiles devoid of warmth that briefly appeared on white faces when their gazes collided with hers, leaving her certain that they had been directing evil thoughts her way; being followed around a shop or accelerated past at a zebra crossing; the time a gang of lanky, acned hooligans surrounded her, asking if she could score them any weed. She picked up little slights every day, shining them into a gleaming animosity that radiated from her person.

Her injuries were not restricted to human interaction alone – the self-checkout machine at Tesco insisted loudly, "Please place scanned item in bagging area" long after she had done so, and subsequently flashed red to summon a cashier to check her purchases; the security doors at Morrisons beeped as she exited the shop even though she had no groceries stowed away on her person; the automated call service of Barclays bank failed to recognise her intensifying, enunciated voiced sign-in requests. She day-dreamed that her string of hurts would stretch and stretch to infinity, loop around the earth, and hurl the globe with all its vain cruelty into oblivion.

Wonu gazed weakly at her unexpected guests and steeled herself for the biggest one yet, the colossal asteroid that would wipe her out as clean as the dinosaurs Mayowa so loved in their extinction.

"Is Mayowa alright?" Wonu asked once she was able to dislodge her tongue from the roof of her mouth.

"He is, we have just spoken with him at school. May we come in?"

"Yes, please," Wonu consented, showing them to the dining room and indicating the chairs.

Once seated, the PI began. "Mayowa has made some concerning disclo-sures about being assaulted by you, and we are here to launch an investiga-tion. In the meantime, we have placed him under a Section 47 order."

Wonu stood rooted to the spot, the receding terror rushing back as salty acid into the back of her throat. She knew her way around these terms from her work at the hospital's paediatric unit. Section 17 was an intervention to help parent and child. Section 47 was the big guns – child protection.

After a brief pause for a response that didn't come, the Inspector contin-ued. "He told us that you have a cane that you hit him with, so we are going to have to confiscate and take it into evidence."

Rage and incredulity replaced terror. "He said I hit him with a cane? Which cane? You mean these spindly things?" She stormed to the bin by the kitchen door and retrieved two twigs cut from the grapevine in the back garden.

To the visitors, she appeared crazed, just as they had expected. Differ-ent from the poised woman who had welcomed them at the door. "Yes, occasionally I tap him with them, but what harm can these tiny things do? I can try them out on you if you want..." She ran out of steam, and stood waving the sticks in the air as if to dispel her belligerent offer.

"He says you hit him with them and also lift him up by his ears when he does not learn *Yaraba*. I am guessing that you have been teaching him your native language? He is very proud of that ... he taught us some words," the inspector offered, aiming for a less combative note.

Wonu was silenced for the minutes it took her to compose herself, feeling Tunde's hand on her shoulder, interpreting it as an appeal to co-operate.

"These," she said finally, waving the canes about again, "are never correction. I never use them when I am angry. Usually when his dad calls him up for bath time and he does not go, I grab a cane and chase him up the stairs. He's laughing and screaming as he runs up the stairs. He begs me to do it sometimes. What does it matter if it occasionally lands on his butt? It is never punishment!"

The policewoman and her silent companion did not respond, but disbelief coloured their silence. This was a lot less sensational than their own interpretation of the situation – a type of jungle household where violent clashes ensued amongst near-primitive creatures. A child who needed to be rescued from this bedlam.

"This," Wonu continued desperately, yanking at her own ear, "is correction. In my country, it is what we do!" Her words were a deluge now, pouring out of her. "Why? Because it is not painful. Can I do it to you?"

Julie finally piped up, offering her arm warily. "Maybe try it on my arm."

Wonu blustered, thinking on her feet. "No, that will be painful because it is flesh. The ear is cartilage, and that is why it doesn't hurt as much. That is why pulling a child's ear is how we correct them."

The caustic reply, "But you don't just pull, you hang them by their ears! Believe me, if we had found a mark on him, you would be in handcuffs right now, so count yourself very lucky."

They let this threat sink in before they proceeded to ask questions about her and Tunde's backgrounds to determine their penchant for grievous bodily harm: whether Wonu's anger would abate, how well the pair spoke English. They ran their eyes over the house, noting things that Wonu would never guess at – how many toys they could see around the house, the child seat attached to a dining chair, the child's many artworks stuck clumsily onto the fridge with magnets. There was nothing alarming to see, but their prejudice made a stronger argument than their own eyes did.

"Can we get him from school? It's almost pick-up time." This from Tunde who did not know what a Section 47 was, and, being on the outside of the interrogation, maintained an awareness of time.

Wonu made to silence him, unwilling yet to confront the implication of their visit. It came anyway, sundering her heart. "We have decided that until we conclude our investigation and gather more evidence, Mayowa will be placed in safe care. We hope that you will co-operate with the investigation and comply with the arrangements we have made. If you have any questions, please do not hesitate to contact me," the PI finished, holding out a contact card.

Wonu charged bitterly at their retreating backs, "Do you know it's his birthday today?"

"Yes, he was very excited about having a sleepover with you. We will do our best to explain things ... make sure to let foster care know about his birthday," Julie answered, deliberately missing the significance of Wonu's words.

TUNDE UNRAVELLED WITH the efficiency of habit. Tears streamed down his face as he recalled the WhatsApp invite, poured congealed eggs down the drain, tossed set jelly in the bin, and banished Sonic the Hedgehog from sight. Then he withdrew to their room and howled loud and long, striking Wonu by how much like their son he sounded.

The twigs sat forlornly on the table for days, Wonu too scared to remove them for fear that her interlocutors intended to return for them, afraid that she would be accused of tampering with evidence, convinced that moving them, moving anything around, would solidify her nightmarish reality, trap her in this alternate existence where she had lost her child as certainly as if he had been strangled by his cord and never taken a breath. She had handed him over to the state as irrevocably as if she had gift-wrapped him in a swaddling blanket and delivered him to a church doorstep.

One dawn, she woke up from a nightmare in which she had lost grip of Mayowa's arm to a pale, faceless spectre that carried him off into the distance. She rose from Mayowa's bed, put the kettle on to boil, and emptied its contents into a basin. She found the plastic canister of ground red pepper placed on a high shelf out of a child's reach. She emptied its contents into the water. With a soft hiss, a plume of spicy steam rose into Wonu's face to induce a forceful bout of sneezing. Undeterred, she carried her stewing mixture to the table, and tenderly picked up the abandoned twigs, caressing them. They were tauter, dryer now, for their exposure to the cold air. She immersed the full length of them gently into the water, waiting patient moments for them to absorb the heat, then in one swift motion grabbed them by the tails and flung them against her bare back. They had been right, she noted with bitter irony: the tiny twigs could deliver excruciating pain, which suited her perfectly. Again! Dip... Lift... Strike! Again! And again! And again ... her screams rising to a crescendo that woke the world from its slumber.

ELSEWHERE

Kabubu Mutua

*B*EGIN ... WITH the boy. The house with the white filigree. The country with the heat. There he stood, smoking on his balcony, his olive skin warm in the evening light. And I asked Dalia what she thought of him, rebellious or simply brave, for smoking in a country that outlawed such an act.

Rebellious? These people do what they want because they can afford to do what they want.

And I laughed, and I said she was bitter because she'd not been born a man in a country that supplied the world with all its oil. I was watering the small bushes of frangipani near the pool, and she was detangling her hair on the balcony. She said the desert air cleaned her lungs, and every afternoon unwound the iron cord from the laundry room to the balcony so she could iron with a view. How ridiculous, iron with a view. Even in her servitude she sought luxury.

We met in a recruitment office in Nairobi, run by a big agent who refused to speak to anyone around noon when his secretary massaged his feet. We'd taken all the blood tests. We'd sworn against our mothers that we were loyal servants. We'd said: we cook, we clean, we cut grass, we wash. And that's all he wanted, that big agent with eyes like marbles – loyal submissive hearts, hearts that could take pain, hearts that said yes, have me all you want on the condition that you pay me.

Dalia had seven children, and she began to cry when we were accepted to fly. She said: What to do, my man, with all these children looking into my eyes for their lives? And I said, was this not what she'd always longed for, to work elsewhere, where she would never lack? She was South Sudanese, and the day Salva Kiir was announced president she gifted me a tartan bedsheet which I still keep. And the way her cheekbones popped from her face reminded me of my sister, who – God bless her – was asking me to send money for her failing tailor shop every other week in short telephone calls. She who feared for my life and kept asking, Are you okay? on every call. The rain came last week and all the kente is soaked, she once said. Or, I need to hire two more tailors, I have a whole bridal party from the neighbouring town.

Oh God forgive me, but when I looked at that Dalia all I remembered was the girl, and it filled me with an overwhelming sadness that I had left home, and here I was and there she was, and how we were separated. Make no mistake, Dalia was not without her faults. I knew that Dalia could not keep a man, that she'd kept several husbands who had hit her and bought her love back with cheap Lady Gay and Lux soaps and pomades. I knew this because she'd told me. Each of the children is living with their father, and they are eating well and going to school.

How I pitied her.

So back to the boy. I thought him sweet like a baby. All innocent and unaware of all the shit that life could grant you. I suppose I pictured him as a person I would have loved to befriend. You know, there are people like that. People that you see and know you'll be safe with, you'll never need to run, you'll look into the pools of their eyes and say, I'm here, take me as I am. So, all I could do was to churn out a story to poor Dalia so I could keep him in my mind. You see, there is nothing to do in this country except shape small flower bushes and water them and repeat, and the next thing you know, Dalia is sticking her nose in the direction of the sanded horizon and the sun is setting.

Do you know the boy is not married? I said to Dalia.

And why do you care? You snoop and these nasty Arabs find you, and the next thing they are tearing your ears out.

But he is so composed. Wouldn't you want a man like that?

Dalia said of course the man was handsome, but he was Arab, and so there was a boundary, a wall that couldn't be penetrated.

But wouldn't you want him inside of you? I wanted to know.

And what have you been taking? Is it the Sahib's hookah that you slip out to smoke at midnight? Oh, it seems that you will die in this country.

But Dalia, can you imagine how things would be without a little imagination? No news, no radio. Scraps of old newspaper in the bin if we are lucky.

Just then, Sahib's long car honked at the grilled gate. Oh, there she was, the queen herself, sticking her nose out as if we smelled of shit. She took his hand and they walked into the house. The entire time Dalia pinched my back. Dalia hated that woman well-well for smacking her face because she had burned her chiffon dress. Dalia with the trembling hands had run the iron on full heat and the entire house was smelling of burnt fabric, and the queen herself was rushing to the balcony with her gown trailing behind her, and she slapped the poor woman.

What was a chiffon dress, Dalia had cried to me the following day, when she can buy this world and the next if she wishes?

And so Dalia accumulated little hatreds for the queen, cursing under her breath whenever she called her name, even pinching an extra spoonful of salt into their dinner stew one night so that the queen and the Sahib fought for the first time since our arrival. You see, the queen always cooked Sahib's dinner – you should see how that crazy woman looked as she scoured through pages and pages of cookbooks looking for exotic things to please her man. There were Mediterranean cookbooks and Chinese cookbooks and West African cookbooks and Zanzibari cookbooks, all opened in various stages of reading. Sometimes she burned the food because she was in the bathroom preparing her face for Sahib's return from work, or she was filing her nails or she was gossiping on the phone. And oh, how she loved to gossip. Talking about cheating husbands and wives as if her life was pure and without trouble. But how did we know her language, you want to know? Because all gossipers look the same, laugh the same, in that light way as if they are afraid of being caught.

The boy from the house with the white filigree came out to walk his dog one Saturday morning and the sun was glowing. I was trained on a patch of Sahib's garden when I smelled him. He was scrolling through his phone. He looked up for a quick second and our eyes met. My stomach melted. My hands trembled. He walked on. I suppose he was stretching his legs, something that has troubled my mind for a long time. Why does he stretch his legs when the entire time he spends doing nothing?

That evening I said to Dalia: The boy seems to be rude. He passed me as if I was a tree.

Dalia, who was oiling her jet-black air with shea butter from home, said I was delusional. And did I want him to stop and ask how my day was going?

Of course, no, I said. But imagine the way they see us. As if we are mere machines and not people. You there, scratch my back. Wash this room. Do this, do that.

Walk well. Have you heard that Ndila, the girl who cleans at the house with the red dog, died? They said it was a heart attack. She fell in the pool. They found her in the morning.

I had seen the girl, a thin thing with frog eyes.

And the agency has refused to pick up calls from the family, and the family says they don't have money to take her body back.

I listened and felt a coldness flow into my ears. There were always deaths, and we comforted ourselves by deciding we were the safe ones, it would not touch us. As if we bore a mark that said to death: Hey, I'm taken by something else. You can't have me.

The year we left Kenya, a local newspaper ran the headline, "African workers in the Gulf dancing with death". And I imagined, each year, swirling in a bright ballroom with diamond chandeliers and a quartet playing on a platform, me in the centre, death before me asking: Will you give me the pleasure of dancing with you?

On the third day, I called my sister and she said: Oh, how I missed to hear your voice, and have you heard they are harvesting organs now and selling them to Thailand?

What organs? I wanted to know.

And she said: your organs, those of you that leave.

I said it was a lie. I had not heard of such a thing. You see, newspapers will do anything to keep their silly headlines fresh.

But there's this girl from the village across the hill who returned with a missing kidney ... Christ, are you listening to me?

I hummed yes.

Yes, that girl from the village across the hill returned with money and she was plump and healthy and her people celebrated her return because she'd returned alive and well. They gave her the best husband. But the night after their wedding, oh God. Are you there? The husband touched her back and felt a scar, a thick scar at that. And they took her to hospital and ran a scan and the girl from the village across the hill was missing a kidney.

Oh God. True story?

True story. She paused; and I wanted the old times to roll back, when we were children, when we were happy.

Take care Bi, she said.

Back to the boy from the house with the white filigree. I said to Dalia that he seemed thinner than he'd appeared last week and did she think that the cigarettes were affecting him? Dalia laughed and said she'd noticed the change too; the boy from the house with the white filigree could be sick. And true to our suspicions, the boy was coughing and leaning on the railings until a short woman appeared to take his hand. We read their lips. Come down Junior, Dalia guessed. Away with the cigarettes, I guessed. And days later we heard an ambulance speed through the estate in the dead of night. And Sahib said to the queen that the boy from the house with the white filigree was dead. Funeral within a day. And how did we know? We saw the procession snake past our flowers, the body clothed in white, rolled like a giant sausage. The short woman headed the procession veiled in black, her eyes protected by sunglasses. I thought her beautiful even in her mourning. The following day, we heard Sahib describe the house as cursed because two maids with origins in our country had died there, drowned in the swimming pool.

I have my suspicions, said Dalia.

Tell me, I said. I bit into a clump of dates. Sahib's record player played softly before it died, its needle crackling into silence.

The boy is a killer. He pushes them into the pool. Perhaps he takes pleasure. Afterwards he might touch himself. But it is all in the stare. The charm, the way he moves, like a snake.

But he's dead now, I said.

I suppose the deaths will stop.

Oh, death will always come for you, I said.

At this point, my dear Dalia left saying that her back hurt; she needed to apply some creams to feel better.

Now, you might not believe me, but I saw the boy from the house with the white filigree exactly seven days after the funeral – God bless his soul. I couldn't sleep because the winds were howling from the desert mountains and the heat ... oh, did I tell you that my room and Dalia's are unair-conditioned? I woke up and walked to the balcony and there he was, across the street, smoking with his slender fingers.

Oh, my mouth went dry. My legs trembled on account of this sight. I clutched the railing so I could stand, for that was a ghost, you can't tell me otherwise. He was there, and you cannot tell me otherwise. Dressed in his long white robe, staring straight at me. But the thing is that his eyes seemed to speak to me, to ask me of things I completely knew about myself and yet did not wish to come to terms with. Sexual things.

I said, let me go to Dalia and let her see what I'm seeing. Poor Dalia was speaking in her dreams, scolding her eldest daughter for burning her beans.

You little brat, the beans again, the woman was saying.

I knocked thrice on her door before I realised that it was open. I had to pinch her fat neck so she would wake up. That one slept like a cow, even in all her troubles.

Oh, Dalia! How I have seen things. Come see for yourself.

I led her through the carpeted hallways, to the balcony and the entire time she was saying, Oh my beans. Why have you burnt the beans?

But, dear friend, the ghost of the boy from the house with the white fil-igree was gone. The house was cast in a yellow light. And a sharp wind tore into our faces. Dalia said, why I was disturbing her sleep, and I said I was only here to show her a miracle, and she looked at me with anger and said I should keep my madness to myself.

Perhaps I was mad. But the second time? The third time? Is that madness, too? There he would be, smoking and staring into the stars, the starry wide sky, as if it was his fate to wake from death and watch stars.

A plant locked in darkness will grow towards the light, and so I imagined him, waking from his imposed state, looking for the things that gave him pleasure in life. Cigarettes. And yet I imagined that my memory was playing with me, giving me glimpses of things I had sought and lost, things I now mourned with a kind of silence, things I had kept to myself. In this country, stories abound of djinns locked in bottles, stories I had read in Kiswahili Kitukuzwe as a little boy. Now I was a believer.

After Dalia's disbelief, I kept to myself, often waking up in the middle of the night to watch the ghost of the boy from the house with the white filigree. But a distance existed between us. I wanted to ask if he'd met my beloved Cucu in the afterlife. To wave and ask how he was – dead, how did I think?

My fear of ghosts had died. Perhaps I was emboldened by the familiarity and the closeness of him, by the fact that he was someone I had known in this life. Besides, what can they do to you, these weightless victims of death? I remembered when as a young man I had contemplated suicide, and this ghost – a friend of my father's who'd come to drink chai and talk politics in our childhood home – appeared to me in a dream, or rather came to me and poked me, and said it had observed me from the other realm, that I would never find peace in the world of the dead if I killed myself.

I often wondered why the ghost of the boy from the house with the white filigree came and not the ghosts of all those women who'd died in that house. After all, ghosts linger in the places from which they've transitioned. The soul remembers, seeking completion for what could've been. I would wave at him, but my overtures for friendship were avoided. He would remain in that trance, and the next minute he would be gone, that small balcony left empty, reflecting a blue iridescent light from the pool beneath. And should I say that those moments of absence drove pieces of sorrow into me?

I called my beloved sister and asked about the progress of the returned-girl-with-the-missing-kidney. She sighed and spoke of an approaching flu, and went on to narrate how things were going in the village of the returned-girl-with-the-missing-kidney. Arrangements were underway to conduct seances whereupon her kidney would be located. It was a special case and the *Voice of Kenya* was particularly interested in the girl's side of the story. Naïve girl, my sister was saying, blowing her nose. And she went on to say how the girl said she'd never argued with her employers, that she'd never received any harm. They might have drugged her one night and slit her back open. And now she is defending them, saying, *The food I ate was meant for a queen, the bed I slept in* ... Oh, and my sister stopped to cry at this point.

So, regarding the matter of the ghost of the boy, I asked my sister what she would do if ever she encountered one. She laughed and said I had too much time, and why had I suddenly acquired the need to know about ghosts?

I am reading books now, I lied.

Reading books, you say? It is the Bible you should turn to. Oh, and I have heard good things about sage.

Sage?

Yes, remember that smelling plant that used to grow in our backyard? I hear it gets rid of them.

I wanted to tell her it was not getting rid of a ghost that I wished. Rather, I wanted an audience with one, but I lacked the proper questions to ask it if ever it came to me.

Days later, I discovered that I touched myself more after the times I saw the ghost.

Soon I observed a change in my dear Dalia. Once she'd taken only a little interest in her appearance, only concentrating on her hair. But now she wore a floral scent. Her nails she painted red. I asked her: Dalia, what is all this? And she laughed, her whisky-coated laugh, and said, Bi, this long nose of yours, where will it take you? Oh, how astonished I became. How afraid. Because something in her had changed. What, I couldn't place. I said: Dalia, you are hiding things from me. We were preparing the backyard for a special tea ceremony in which Sahib would honour his queen for staying as a wife. I strung a light on a balcony railing. I said: You know there is nothing long that has no end. She said she'd only been thinking, that life was too short and so why not to wear good smells, why not to live in the present moment and not wait for a happy place that might not even exist? I said, alright.

Back to my ghost story. I woke up at that hour to which my mind had trained itself, and walked to my balcony. Now I called it my balcony because, for a moment, I slipped into my world where I imagined things with the ghost of the boy from the house with the white filigree. Things I cannot even speak of. I would stay there watching him until the night passed, before the rest of the house woke up. But this particular night something happened. I bumped into Dalia; I shall not even lie to you. She was not sleepwalking, for her eyes were wide open and alive like a cat's. And she smelled of Sahib's hookah, that mint and coconut scent. I said to myself: If it is not the devil himself, then who is it? And Dalia asked why I was awake at such an hour and I said since when did she care about my sleeping patterns? I did not wish to reveal that my ghost-sighting routine had become like a ritual at this point.

I could not sleep, so I went to clean my lungs, she said.

I thought I saw a light flicker in the end of the hall. I shall always remember this night because it was the night when the ghost did not fade into the night, but rather remained so that Dalia saw it. She screamed and soon the queen and Sahib were running into our faces.

And Dalia was saying she'd seen a ghost, in full view. The queen, searching for a small trouble with Dalia since the day she had first arrived, thought her to be mad, and asked Sahib what she'd done to God to deserve this – a maid, a salaried maid, who saw ghosts. Sahib kept asking her to quiet down, for she was now pacing about the corridor, touching her forehead and crying that her blood pressure was rising. And hadn't Dalia brought enough trouble to her life? Dalia was trembling and crying. The entire time she leaned on me and kept saying: Tell them I'm not mad. Will you?

Sahib invited a mullah, a man with a long beard to conduct a cleansing of the house from ceiling to floor. He burned incense and called upon his gods, and the whole time I watched from a half-opened door. I found his designation mysterious, he who could commune with the dead. A part of me resented him, what with the way he pretended to move through the house pointing at objects where ghosts might take refuge: the ornamental porcelain plates on the walls, the macrame, the table lamps, even the table cloths, he said. I watched as the man pressed money from the couple and I pitied them – forgive me, but a little mercy is good. Word was sent from the agency that they'd found a replacement for Dalia, but things were said between the queen herself and Sahib, and after a deep consultation, they decided not to let her go. Dalia told me this one afternoon, the first time in a long time she'd brought the iron out.

Sahib is such a good man! she said.

I thought I heard a softness in her voice. You know the way you speak when you adore someone, say someone you go to bed with? That way.

Now I called my sister and said what was left of the returned-girl-with-the-missing-kidney and she paused to sip from a cup – that donkey took the loudest sips you'll ever hear.

The girl-with-the-missing-kidney has finally admitted there were some nights she never dreamed. She simply slept and darkness overcame her as if she was dead. She confirmed this with her grandmother, who said she has been a loud dreamer since she was a baby. And she was on the radio! Can you imagine that fame can find you in such unexpected ways? The poor girl cannot even know which direction the sun rises and that upon which it sets. They say that's how they sliced her; those devils put pills in her food or water and waited for sleep to snatch the thing. Then they performed the act.

Oh lord. The things I shall hear. Have you been eating well? I wanted to know. And she laughed, and said of what use was my concern when I was kilometres and kilometres away.

WHAT TO SAY, when the ghost stopped coming? I came out one night and the balcony of the house with the white filigree was empty. I came the next day and the next and the next. But my eyes really suffered from all the straining into the darkness. Who could tell if the owners of that house had called upon a mullah of their own to perform a cleansing as I had seen Sahib do? I said: I will tell Dalia tomorrow, the very day she died.

The day Dalia died, I thought she was playing games with me. She'd never swum in her entire life, she'd told me once, her voice filled with longing, and I said it was so easy, never fight with the water, as if I was a master myself. I found her floating upside down, her dress filled like a balloon. Her hair was spread in the blueness, black and full and beautiful.

I said: Dalia, what are you doing? And she did not answer. I said: Dalia, the ghost never came yesterday, and the day before and the one before it. I think I'm losing my mind. But she remained that way, looking into the bottom of the pool.

When the agents came to pick up Dalia's things, Sahib said: Stupid girl, she sneaked to swim at night. I thought of all the ways dear Dalia had changed in recent days, the hair, the floral scent, the painted nails even, that lone trip when she saw the ghost and cried. Perhaps there had been many trips, trips taken to the wrong rooms, trips that had killed her. After the police came and went, after the employment agents came to pick up Dalia's things, I waited for the night, to see if her ghost would appear.

THE GIRL WITH THREE FACES

Khumbo Mhone

*T*HERE ONCE WAS and never will be a girl with three faces. Growing up as the only child of a well-to-do farmer, the girl spent most of her days tending to animals and keeping her father's affairs in order while he was away. Of all the animals on the farm, three were her greatest friends: the bull who was strong and dependable, the hen who was adventurous and picky, and the cat who was curious and aloof. The girl spent every day in the company of these friends, and she felt no desire to leave her father's farm.

One day when her father returned from a long trip to the big city, he brought with him a woman and her two children. The woman had long black hair different in texture from the girl's, and her eyelids were painted green.

"This is your new mother, and these your new sisters," her father said.

The girl was confused; she didn't understand how it could be so easy to replace one mother with another, her own being buried under the rose bushes in the field behind the farm. Her stepmother hugged her while the two daughters watched. When her father wasn't looking, the woman pinched her before whispering, "Behave and we won't have a problem."

Her new stepmother was quick to take over the affairs of the farm, stating that the girl was too young to understand the magnitude of the tasks involved. Instead, she was to focus on securing herself a good match so as not to be a burden on her father. So the girl spent every day practicing the skills her stepmother said would make her a well-respected member of society. She woke up every morning and swept and mopped the house, she cooked breakfast for her stepmother and stepsisters, combed their hair and washed their clothes. Although these were supposedly life skills, the girl's stepsisters were not required to learn them.

One afternoon the girl went to visit her mother and cried so profusely on her grave that the pink rose petals bloomed three months early. When she visited the next day, she found a beautiful teardrop mirror covered in pink rose petals under the bushes. That night, while the rest of the house slept, the girl looked into the mirror for the first time, and saw a face looking back at her. A shadowy face with a big smile and stars for eyes.

"What is it that you wish for?" the mirror asked.

"I wish ... to have a great love, one that will take me far away from here."

The next day the girl woke up waiting for her great love. She answered every knock at the door and opened every letter, but day after day he didn't come. Frustrated, the girl confronted her starry-eyed companion. "Mirror of Magic, why has my love not come?"

"A wish made is not a wish granted. What do you wish for?"

"I wish ... to go on great adventures, to see lands beyond my wildest dreams."

The next day, the girl was asked by one of her stepsisters to escort her into town. There was to be a big party at the chief's house, and all the eligible young ladies were invited. The girl spent the entire day walking around glass-fronted shops displaying multiple gowns in beautiful wax cloth designs. She sat dutifully in every store as her stepsister tried on dress after dress in a bright orange colour that did nothing for her complexion. When she got home, carrying the ten bags of cloth and accessories that her stepsister had left in her care, her stepmother looked at her and smiled. "Looks like you finally got to go on an adventure."

The girl was distraught, and her anguish was made worse by having to watch as her stepsisters got ready for the big party and left, their heels clicking down the driveway.

Then she sought out her mirror. "Mirror of Magic, I wish to no longer be a servant. I want to be waited on hand and foot. To have every request treated with the highest regard."

The girl awoke to the screams of her stepmother the next day. It wasn't an unfamiliar sound, but the girl wasn't used to hearing from her stepmother this early. She heard approaching footsteps, then her bedroom door burst open and her stepmother called her by name: "Sindikusiya! What is this nonsense?"

She threw the *Village Herald* newspaper down on the bed, and there, on the front cover, was the chief's son, a muscular young man who was renowned for his carpentry and prowess in hunting, and beside him in a flowing pink gown, hair pinned back in pearls was ... her. Sindi looked at her stepmother in confusion. "I don't understand."

"Don't play dumb with me. You clearly left this house last night and stole away to the party. All this time I believed you to be a dutiful girl. How dare you steal the chief's son away from your sisters?"

"But it's impossible, I was here all night."

"And who will vouch for you, silly girl, the farm animals?"

Sindi realised there truly was no one to testify in her defence, her step-mother having dismissed all the farm hands who had previously lived on their land.

That was how Sindi found herself locked in the highest room in the house as punishment for her alleged crimes. Despite these precautions, however, a strange occurrence continued to present itself. Every morning without fail, there was a new story in the paper about the girl with Sindi's face, and her dalliance with the chief's son. Her stepmother tried every-thing, putting bars on the windows, snakes outside her door, planting thorn bushes under her window; but with every morning, there came a new picture of Sindi and the chief's son.

One afternoon Sindi was watching the cat balance precariously on one paw as it crept stealthily from the frame of her bed to the windowsill, losing balance at the very last moment and toppling to the ground. It lay so still that Sindi was afraid it had lost its last fight with gravity. Just as she was about to pick it up, the cat shook itself, jumped back onto the windowsill, squeezed through the metal bars and disappeared.

"Perhaps I too have more than one life," Sindi thought.

As her stepsisters kept vigil outside her door, Sindi asked the mirror if she could see herself. It showed Sindi's face smiling coyly back at her, her hair bone-straight and black, her eyes lined with kohl, and her lips red as blood. When the face of Sindi stepped back from the mirror, Sindi saw a bedroom the size of their farmhouse behind her, draped in finery. She laughed loudly and easily at the sound of the voice of a man just out of sight.

The sound of her older stepsister's voice forced Sindi to break eye contact with her other self, and her reflection was once again her own.

"It's simple, I've left the apple soaking in cassava all day. When we give it to her tomorrow, she'll barely even taste it."

Cassava water was widely known as a solution to various everyday problems. A few pieces of raw cassava soaked in distilled water overnight could be used as a permanent solution to the issue of a philandering or abusive husband, or even a person who seemed to be outliving their hefty life insurance package.

That night Sindi barely slept. She was the first to see the red rays of the sun peek over the hills that sheltered the farm. In her smallest bag, she packed three dresses and her mirror.

"Mirror of Magic, I know a wish made is not a wish granted, but my life is in danger – please help me escape this prison."

Just then the cat jumped through the bars of her window, landing lightly at her feet. It licked its paw exactly three times and walked around her twice, its tail lightly brushing the backs of her legs.

Her entire body tingled as she shrank, her bedpost looming above her until she was no bigger than the cat standing before her. The ground beneath her shook as her stepsisters thundered up the stairs, the clang of dishes on a metal tray hurting her ears. The cat hissed and dipped down so that Sindi could climb on his back. The wind was knocked out of her as the cat leapt from the floor to the windowsill. She surveyed the space beyond the window as though she were a sailor coming face to face with the open sea, with no land to call home.

The screams of her sisters could be heard as the cat jumped down ledge by ledge until they reached the ground. As soon as Sindi dismounted, she returned to her original height. She ran full tilt beyond the gates of the farm. With no cart and no money, she had to walk all the way into town, but her boots were strong, and she had never been a stranger to hard work.

On the edge of town, she met three of the chief's guards. They frowned when they saw her and bowed. "My lady, you should not be out in this sun. Let us escort you somewhere cooler."

Before Sindi could protest, they took places on either side of her and walked her to where a palanquin stood waiting. The inside was indeed cooler, and soon Sindi fell asleep on the plush cushions. When she awoke, Sindi found herself in the main compound of the chief's home. The guards called two young women dressed in matching blue and white wax print to escort her inside.

"It's very strange for you to want to leave the compound alone, my lady. Perhaps you are more nervous than we first thought."

"I'm not really..."

A door opened and Sindi was ushered inside a huge bedroom. Everywhere she looked, she saw windows, sunlight streaming in and lighting up every corner. The bed was carved from a single piece of dark brown wood that gleamed. A large mirror with a table covered with bottles and powders stood on her left, and to her right was a bay of sunflowers growing out of giant clay jars.

"Is that you, my love?"

Across the room, another door swung open to reveal a young woman wrapped in a towel. Her hair was black and bone-straight, and her lips were red as blood. Both women stood and looked at each other for a long while.

"You," they both said at last. "You're the one who's stolen my face."

Sindi frowned until she could feel the creases in her forehead, a trait she had supposedly learned from her mother, and one despised by her stepmother.

"I think you're mistaken. It is you who has stolen my face. I am a simple farmer who is being accused of consorting with the chief's son."

"A farmer? No, that can't be right at all. You're a thief!"

"Excuse me?"

The other Sindi walked over to her dresser and returned with a *Herald* newspaper from another town. This one showed a picture of another girl who looked just like Sindi. Her hair was matted and wild. In one hand she held a small grey sack, and in the other, six golden eggs.

"My husband-to-be has been beside himself, wondering how I could possibly be a thief when I have everything I need right here."

Sindi was barely listening. She took the mirror out of her bag and confronted the face with the starry eyes.

"Mirror of Magic, show me myself."

Both Sindi's watched as a third Sindi filled up the reflection in the mirror. This Sindi was loud and brash. She moved with a steady confidence as she gave out rations of food to a mother and her child. Next to her home, a simple two-roomed bungalow, a large mango tree stretched into the clouds, its leaves somewhere in the heavens.

"You see, there are two of you masquerading in my place. You will ruin my life with your falsehoods. I know that because I am so beautiful, it's hard not to want to steal my life, but this is treason."

Sindi looked at the girl with her face. This person with the blood-red lips was nothing like her at all, and she wondered what strange punishment was being handed to her.

"What's your name?" Sindi said.

"Sindi."

"Where are you from?"

"I am from here."

"Before here, before the chief's son, where did you come from?"

There was silence as the other Sindi frowned, the creases in her forehead non-existent.

"Where is your family?" Sindi pressed.

The other Sindi seemed to lose her balance for a second, and Sindi had to steady her.

"How ... how can I not remember?"

"What is your earliest memory?"

"...The party."

There was a silence between the two of them, punctuated by the meow of a cat outside the window. Sindi stood up.

"We need to go and find the other girl with our face. Maybe she has the answers."

"But tomorrow is my wedding day."

"We'll be back before then," Sindi said, crossing her fingers.

Together the two Sindi's stood side by side as the cat licked its paw three times and circled around them twice. The sun was halfway across the sky when they left, but by the time they got to the next town, the world was bathed in moonlight.

The other Sindi had spent the whole time loudly declaring how uncomfortable she was, how the royal palanquin would have been a better form of transportation, how she should have left a note.

"At least you have a ride. I walked all the way to you."

At last the cat stopped and stretched, throwing both Sindi's off its back as it skulked off into the night.

The bungalow was dark except for a single candle burning in the front window. When they knocked, an elderly woman answered the door. The knitting needles she clutched in one hand showed the beginnings of a sweater. She rubbed her eyes and they widened as she looked from one Sindi to the other.

"I knew that girl would anger the spirits one day," she said, her needles clattering to the ground as she bowed low. "Oh great spirits, do not take me along with the actions of that foolish girl. I am but a bystander."

"Is she here?" Sindi asked.

"No, she is in the spirit realm again. I told her after she stole money from the spirits that it would not end well, but so much time passed and we lived so well. And then she stole that chicken that lays gold eggs, and I knew it was just a matter of time before our judgement came."

The other Sindi stepped forward. "Are you her mother?"

"Me? Oh no, I am just the person who takes care of this house."

The other Sindi bowed her head as Sindi thanked the old woman and led them to the base of the giant mango tree.

"How do we even get up there?" asked the other Sindi.

Sindi removed her magic mirror from her bag.

"Mirror of Magic, I know a wish asked for isn't a wish granted, but let us get to the top of this tree so that we may meet the girl who has taken my face."

"Our face!"

A chicken appeared at the base of the tree. Sindi recognised it as the chicken from her farm, with its distinctive red tail feather in a sea of white. It pecked at the ground five times, then began to grow: first until it was as tall as Sindi's waist, then until both Sindi's had to look up into its glasslike eyes. Getting onto the chicken was a little more difficult than the cat, and after much squawking, both Sindi's finally settled on its back. The dust blew in their faces as the chicken flapped its wings furiously and slowly started to rise up into the air, past the gnarled tree trunk of the mango tree, through the slowly budding leaves, and into the clouds.

In the distance, a three-story thatched manse stood against the blackness of the stars, a path of crystallised rain leading to it. The chicken was about to touch down on the path when an almighty crash thundered through the skies. All twelve windows of the manse lit up, and the clouds were flooded with light as though from the sun. Sindi dug her heels into the chicken's side, urging it to fly on. As they got closer, a small figure emerged at one of the windows.

With unruly hair and clothing usually reserved for a male farm hand, the third Sindi scrambled out of the window. Under her arm was a cow-skin hide drum that was playing itself. From behind her, came another crash.

"Ah Eh Ih, who dares disturb a spirit like me?"

A foot twice the size of any building seen by man or woman stepped out of the manse. As the third Sindi ran, she saw two people flying towards her on a chicken. "The gogo was right," she muttered, "stealing from the spirits will make you mad."

Nevertheless, she waved her arms, calling for help. The chicken landed in front of her as the drum beat faster, calling out to its master.

"Get out of here now!"

"Ah Eh Ih, who dares disturb a spirit like me?"

Black hair thick as tree trunks coiled out of a skull that dwarfed the moon. Three brown eyes and one green looked around over the expanse of the sky as the spirit, dressed in nothing but a long wax cloth tied around its waist, began to pursue them.

The three Sindis aboard the chicken raced towards the top-most branches of the mango tree.

"What happens if that spirit follows us into the human world?" the second Sindi asked.

"I don't think we should find out," the third Sindi said.

"Ask the mirror for help!"

"Mirror of Magic, I know a wish asked for isn't a wish granted, but the village below us will be crushed under the weight of this spirit's revenge. Please help us."

The deafening steps of the spirit behind them shook the leaves of the great mango tree as the chicken swooped down, avoiding wayward tree branches as it hurtled towards the ground. The trunk of the tree began to vibrate, large green mangoes, big as boulders, narrowly missing their heads.

"Is that ... a bull?" the second Sindi asked.

On the ground below them, with horns as large as a small house, was the bull from the farm. It pawed the ground five times and ran full tilt towards the tree, ramming its horns into the base again and again. The leaves above them shook as the spirit grabbed the top branches, while below the base of the trunk cracked under the charge of the bull's horns.

The three Sindis scrambled off the chicken's back and ran clear of the now falling great mango tree. Above them, in a hole left in the clouds, four eyes glared down at them before disappearing back into the night.

The third Sindi looked at them now, her eyes squinting from one face to the other in the dark.

"I've heard that when the spirits come to take you away for judgement, they appear as your greatest fear," she said.

"You're afraid of yourself?" asked the second Sindi.

"Isn't everyone?"

Sindi stepped forward. "I don't know why this is happening to me. I am the one and only Sindi, yet here you two are running around with my face, living lives that I have only dreamed of, whilst I am cursed with wishes that don't come true."

"The bull saved us – that wish came true."

"The things I actually want are never granted! I wished to no longer be a slave to my stepmother and sisters."

"Are you a slave now?" the third Sindi said.

"I ... I wished to go on great adventures."

"You left your home and travelled to two separate towns on a cat, entered the spirit world on a chicken, actually saw a spirit face-to-face, and lived. What greater adventure is there?" the second Sindi said.

"There's still one wish."

When Sindi pulled out the mirror from her bag, she found it slightly cracked, a network of spiderlike threads etched in every direction.

"Mirror of Magic, I know a wish asked for isn't a wish granted, but I wished for a great love, one that would take me away from my suffering."

The face with stars for eyes did not appear: instead Sindi saw only herself in the shattered ruins, a single face. Behind her, the two other Sindi's had disappeared; and before her lay the world.

WITH OPEN PALMS

N.A. Dawn

*I*T IS NOT at all clear how, or why, things come about the way they do. Furthermore, there is the equally elusive matter of what to do about it. Starting with the pain. That is always the most obvious part; and so, we tend to think, the most important. Chiefly, for the Prefect, the agony of a stomach digesting itself. The abdomen implodes, a self-immolating pit. He staggers forward, half-blind, too exhausted even to brace against the barbed nettles, diminished with every step. Limbs, armoured or otherwise, ache and fray, splintering like wind-battered branches. Liquid life-force spills upon the green earth, glittering in the daylight like a comet's trail. Multiple fractures shoot fire throughout his body. His vision blurs, his legs give. The strain eclipses him. He collapses, reuniting with the soil. Here he lies at last, dwindling to the song of the nearby river, where time trickles peacefully past.

BIRDS NATTERING. TREES purring in the warmth of summer.

Breath fills and leaves him, fading him in and out.

A memory tingles on his skin: practiced hands cleaning his wounds, dressing them. A glowing haze where a face should be.

When he awakens, he remembers only hunger, hears only the chirruping waters.

THE BODY IS unravelling; these wounds will not close, the scars will not heal. They will grow and multiply, becoming the domain of vermin. This is already mundane, like the unfurling of blossoms and the howling of wolves. No spectacle survives the Cycle. The mind dims, a jungle of lost things; thoughts like dust hovering in the afternoon, then evening, then night.

If he could fill a gourd with all the words he had ever said, how many would remain once he poured out all those spoken in ignorance or cruelty? Ayu would know.

Invisible spirits whisper.

THE RULE OF bureaucrats knows no apotheosis. No marvels of the mind, no mysteries of the cosmos. Mastery is lost on them: they are too preoccupied with pleasing their masters, or becoming them. Adventures belong to pilgrims; spirit is the province of poets. Soldiers know courage; sages, nothing, allegedly. The Prefect was destined for the simpler path: authority. Mostly beneath it, until near the end. Clerical vassals seek first to serve, so that in time they may be served.

And serve he did. Lord Kajhangpaan of Iridas knew abundance in many things, neither patience nor mercy among them. Ayu said he stank of dead flowers. The courts, wreathed in foreign fineries, glowed with his machinations, nameless busybodies fussing at his whims, sweating before his judgments. Flocks of functionaries settled on their perches, roosting on nests built by others. Betters instructed; lessers obeyed: all the fair-faced gentlefolk pretending to be gods.

The Prefect saw his station correctly. Diligence is first and foremost worship, its currencies effort and attention, specifically, applying them to matters alien to the passions. The call of drink, the pang of lust, the will to leisure. A noble pedant wears his mantle for all to see; he has paid for it in serenity and earthly joys.

In solitude, so easily confused with merely the absence of noise. In connection, confused with its paltry transactional substitute, conversation. In patience, conquered always by hatred. The sound of that strike still rings in his head. Even now, his knuckles sting from the blow. She shrank that day, retreated. But she will outlive him, any moment now. For her to reclaim that lost ground, any sacrifice will do.

At least the scrolls were timeous, even if their contents spared no one the war. In that way, as in most other respects, scrolls are preferable to people. Tell them what to say, and they say it to the letter. The moment something breathes and eats, it must work, and that means risk. If it can speculate and communicate, the risks increase with every mouth. It is so much easier to take from another than to create for oneself.

"Baaggha?" she had said to him, staring mortified upon them through the carriage window. Droves of them, ragged and moaning with palms bared.

"Look away, Ayu," he commanded. "They're beggars."

"Why are they so angry?" she asked. "And dirty?"

Her lips trembled at the sight of a fellow child, his cheeks hollowed and ribs stark.

Of course, there could be no answer.

Her horror was plain, unguarded. "They're so ill, Baaggha..."

Dust loosened by their march choked the streets in golden clouds; their rasping pleas swallowed the carriage. Inside, the passengers exchanged glares, drawing their clothes about them.

"Quiet now," the Prefect said. "I said, come *away* from there, Ayuvashni!"

But he recognised that look in her eyes. Mosindra's defiance had blazed just as terrible.

He yanked his daughter from the window with the same strength he had reserved for her mother.

Senseless beings in a sensual world, always reaching and never touching. Consumed by illusions, driven by want. Too much this, too little that; too sweet or sour, too hot or cold. All that was not too soon was too late. Perhaps hereafter will return him as a creature of contentment: a mushroom sprouting in the crenelations of an elder tree, or a caterpillar devouring until it sleeps itself into bright-winged heaven. Even the labours of anthood would be a vacation after his mortal career: free from decision or debate, and the tedium of other people. An ant is an ant is an ant; why was he so obsessed with being different?

Why was he so obsessed, in general? Perhaps he did not laugh enough. Destiny surely gave him ample opportunity. Plates are too empty until stomachs are too full, and all the good food ended the same way as the bad. She would have laughed at that. The clever and beautiful grew old and silly; somehow she seemed all these things at once. Those who strove for self-control without self-knowledge saw lessons only as mistakes, avoiding the one thing they truly needed. He certainly did. Once elected, virtuous candidates were tainted by office, nullified by colleagues, or ousted by rivals. Replaced, he supposed, with people like him.

All that time earning money. He never had enough of either, for all that was priceless.

It's a pity, but predictable. Did that make him a cynic? Agitators might say so, they who always seemed to gain more than he from their imaginations, that unruly realm. Then again, fatalism is easier to swallow when you're not so hungry.

THE DIRT WILL be his last bed. This he knows with the certainty with which rising suns all eventually set. For the most part, he is as gradual. As he drains, blood becomes sublime: this gift, so easily lost; an inner river, richest of all streams, carrying through its corridors the speechless wisdoms of life, whose passage unlocks every gate of chi and chakra. The flow must continue, so he must cease. No one body holds it forever; now it is his turn to give. It pools at his face, fills his mouth, clogs his nostrils. He sputters across the scarlet moat.

Finally, generosity: soaking the soil darker and darker. He finds himself listening, perhaps for the first time.

See? I did learn. Just a little late.

What a mess, even at the end.

Am I too late?

All his quests for perfect things go unfulfilled.

HIS CHEEK PRESSES close to the earth, that primordial place. Ayu's heart does not beat there, but he hears it all the same. No heart beats there; only others' hearts elsewhere. Buried beneath, floating above, and briefly upon the world's mortal carpets: the feral landscapes of the north, the frigid cliffs of the south, searing dunes he once glimpsed on shores on voyages which now appear so fruitless and wasteful.

"Where are you going now?" she hissed.

Nowhere that matters, he answers back in time.

"Why then?"

The lush wilds his forefathers tamed, his foremothers forged into bowls of hot *koku*, boards decked with grilled catch and dried harvest. Every one of them, dead.

The wave learns it is the ocean; the leaf learns it is the tree. What does he learn, here at the close? Awe, he sees, was never merely wonder, but terror too, And in rare moments of supreme, self-annihilating gratitude, also reverence. It takes dying to appreciate true power, and its absence. So it takes living to believe in better things.

I didn't know what you do, he sobs. *Who taught you the meaning of enough?* His last sight is the overstory, where melodies become prophecies.

So, he sighs with dimming eyes, *I was fragile after all.*

THE CIRCLE OF HISTORY

Salma Yusuf

NANA SAT ON the mat folding banana leaves for the mikate ya nazi she was about to smoke. She moved her hands in a circular motion, estimating the suitable sizes for each dough. A leaf could accommodate one or two doughs, depending on its size. The elderly woman knew the proportions just from feeling the textures of the leaves and knowing their seasons. Next, she assembled the charcoal for the smoking. Her right hand fanned the grill until smoke came out like a volcano about to erupt. She then started smoking the mikate. After testing Narman's patience for over forty-five minutes, she began narrating the story.

"Hapo zamani za kale, there was an old man who lived by the sea. He spent his days fishing and spent his nights talking to the moon and listening to the sounds of the waves. He appeared lost in thought, as if he was holding onto something from the sea, as if he was waiting for the sea to vomit out something valuable it had taken from him. So the locals at the sea of Buntwani named him *the old man and the sea* after an Italian pizzeria opposite the beach, which in turn was named after Ernest Hemingway's book."

"The old man's skin was discoloured by the scales of fish and the barbarism of the ruthless jinns that lived under the sea. He was wasting away like days off a calendar. His eyes became shrunken pods. His fingers were calloused by the pain he carried like a snail's shell on his back. His hair became spasms of shades of grey. Yet his face stored a deep secret of his spirit, his whole life."

"Sixty years back, he had fallen in love with the sea, the same sea that drowned his blood."

As she continued smoking the mikate, Nana said, "We will stop here for now."

Narman leaned forward, her petite hands pressed against her face. She carried enthusiasm on her shoulders. She was soaked in story. She always had been. Ancient stories, especially those about her Malindi community's heroes and heroines, fuelled her. Partly because the heroic stories in history class were always about white saviours she knew nothing of. But stories of her people, by her people, reminded her of the grit and tenacity she had been denied from experiencing herself.

She opened her mouth to demand, but she knew her grandmother. When Nana paused, it meant a pause. It meant she was being tested for patience. Waiting and waiting and waiting until Nana was ready to share the next piece of the puzzle. Narman waited.

WHEN KHALID MARRIED Humeirah, he was not prepared for the baggage she carried with her. She was brought up in Stonetown, Zanzibar, by parents who gave her everything she ever wanted. She did not know how to wash her body with pumped seawater. She did not know how to eat urojo with her hands in the streets of Forodhani. She did not know how people scrambled and shared sweat and tears at Darajani Bazaar. She was accustomed to tasting the sweetness of her father's mansion, where the large wooden doors displayed the amount of wealth they possessed. The butterflies that flew in their garden, sucking on the nectar of the roses, the friends she collected like seashells and dropped like sand when she grew bored with them.

She grew up with hunger that could not be satiated. Like a hyena, she devoured everything – until her parents did not know what to offer her anymore. She started embezzling the family wealth by gambling. She pawned and pawned and pawned. Her parents' concern grew, and the locals complained about her inconsiderate behaviour. Knowing that the dough they had kneaded with their own hands had fallen flat, they started being harsh with her. But it was way too late – maji yakimwagika hayazoleki. You cannot rescue spilt water. Disputes started escalating until the house built with intricate craftsmanship, with all the expensive furniture in the world, became a pit that sank into the brown tablet of the earth.

Two weeks after another major fight with her father about her reckless tendencies, Humeirah put on her black buibui and left her home with her passport and a bag containing all the money stored in the family safe. When a trade ship headed to Mombasa Island docked at Zanzibar Port, she boarded it. The hunger that she still had could no longer be satiated in Zanzibar, and it was time for her to start afresh in a new place. The twenty-three-year-old did not look back.

WHEN THE TUMAINI ship from Zanzibar arrived in Mombasa with containers of cloves and herbs, Khalid was on his day shift as a yard clerk at the Mombasa Port, performing his regular routine of recording containers coming in and out of the port. But that day, he was interrupted by a woman wearing a black buibui.

"Alsalam aleikum. Where is the exit of this port?"

"Waaleikum salaam. Follow those men wearing the orange reflectors. They are heading to the main entrance – or wait, I can take you."

In their thirty minutes together, Khalid had learned enough about Humeirah for them to exchange contacts. She was an attractive one whose eyes glowed like fireflies. Her hands were soft, evidence of someone not accustomed to household chores. She spoke so delicately that he wanted to take her into his own world. There was a gap that he wanted to fill, but he had never yet found someone suitable to occupy the space that had been vacant for fifteen years. Vacant ever since the sea took his affianced. Khalid's heart was so empty that he wondered if he could ever learn how to love again. Yet in those thirty minutes, something had happened. An invocation, an awakening of a spirit once dead.

That was where it all started.

NARMAN SCRAPED COCONUT with the mbuzi. Using the wooden mbuzi with its sharp tooth to extract bits of coconut for coconut milk is the first kitchen lesson a Swahili girl learns in her initiation into womanhood, soon growing familiar with the sound the scraper makes as it learns to know when to stop scraping.

Nana folded her green banana leaves, she folded and unfolded, folded and unfolded, folded and unfolded until she found the right size for her mikate ya nazi. Her eyes peered at Narman occasionally to see if she was getting her chore right. Then she muttered, "What closes the wound of the sea?" Narman replied almost instinctively, "Closure by the same sea."

"When the old man grew tired of waiting, Izrael took his soul. But the people of Buntwani honoured him by creating a landmark at the shoreline with his initials. The landmark has stood the test of time; even when the high tides come in, it still survives, it always has."

"But Nana, what was his story with the sea?"

"His son's wife had planned a family retreat to Sardegna Island to celebrate the engagement of their grandson. They hired a boat in Buntwani and sailed away with the old man's wife, his son and the wife, his three grandchildren save one, and the fiancée of one of his grandsons."

"Why did the old man not go?"

"He had gone fishing on the other side of Buntwani."

"Why was one grandchild left behind?"

"That is not important for now, Narman. Allow me to proceed with the story.

"They had planned to snorkel along the coral gardens in the lagoons and the fringing reefs and mudflats. They had planned to eat barracuda fish and rice at Sardegna Island and take strolls along the serene mirror-reflection water and play with the starfish and turtles and crabs that sometimes came out from the sea to meet the other side of the circumnavigating world. They had planned, but the sea had other plans."

"What happened to them?"

"Everything happened. Please help me fan the grill. The yeast in the dough has risen. It is time for the assembling."

Narman helped Nana fan the grill. Her mouth was watery, as if she was thirsty and hungry all at once. But with her Nana, she had learned to press the buttons only when necessary, where necessary.

KHALID ASSISTED HUMEIRAH in finding a safe place to rent. Since she was new in Mombasa, he took time to show her around. She was mesmerised by the similarities and the differences between Zanzibar and Mombasa, like gardens of pomegranates and olives. Whenever the pair of them met, he was drawn to her charisma and liveliness. She was adventurous, with a tint of danger and enigma roaming her eyes, like a fierce owl. Yet he fell deeply in love, his soft heart drowned slowly and slowly even though he was afraid of drowning, fearful of the deep waters. He had been tested before, but it seemed as if the seas enjoyed teasing him; and now he was ready to take a step – no, a jump – into the waters with no lifesaver whatsoever.

What started as a coincidence, as a game of fate, turned into something serious. The two continued meeting frequently, and one day, Khalid dropped the question. The question he had often pondered, tossing in bed, his pillow wet in tears. The question brought back memories of his lost love Lailatu and the genuine love they shared. But he had made up his mind to move on. Time was skyrocketing past, and he was not getting any younger. He had to set himself free from his first love, set her away from his heart to allow it to heal and love again.

So one day, when they met up in a restaurant in Sargoi, he asked her. "Humeirah, will you marry me, ala-sunnatillah-warasul?"

She glanced at him. His broad shoulders. His half-smile. His rough hands. His caramel skin. His hair shining with an eco-styler gel. He was too good to be true, too good for a deceitful woman. But he was also perfect for her plan. She had set her bait hanging off the boat, waiting for her big fish. She brought her attention back to his question.

"Yes, I will. Yes, I will."

He wiped tears off his face with his handkerchief. He smiled as if he had regained closure simply through Humeirah's consent to his proposition. He had never known if he would find love again. But here he was; love had sailed from the other side of the world to find him. What if Humeirah was a gift sent by Lailatu? What if she was what he had lost?

THE WHITE AND grey pigeons were always on time. They paced around Nana's verandah, waiting for her to feed them sesame seeds. When she delayed feeding them, they started fights amongst themselves. They would fight until they left feathers on the floor, until Nana opened the door to feed them. They were so used to her scent, her wrinkled hands, and her skill in handling them that they never wanted anyone else to do her work.

Narman added vinegar and pepper to the one-litre bucket of mango pickle. She stirred the mixture with a spoon and left the sun to handle the drying.

"Nana, what happened to the old man's family?" she asked. She had been waiting patiently for the continuation of the story for three weeks. She had even gone to Buntwani to see the landmark for the old man on the shoreline, fighting with all its muscle for survival. She asked the locals what they knew of the old man and the sea. Most of them said that they feared talking about it. It was unsafe to wage war with a waterbody with more strength. The waters in Buntwani had ears.

"It was Maghreb and by sunset, all the boats, however far they had sailed, had come back to the shore for refuelling and rest. The old man had already got back from his fishing. He sat on the shore and touched the sand, felt its texture, pressed it hard and released it back to where it belonged. He had a gut feeling that something was wrong. The other boats were back and anchored at their respective stations. He started to worry. He asked around. The other fishermen and sailors knew of the cadaver of a blue boat on which was written mla nae hufi nae: you will not die with the one you eat with. The boat was timeworn, but it still had the power to take away and give life. Two of the sailors confirmed that they had seen it sail away around Dhuhr when the tides had not come into the shore. One of the fishermen had tried to call the number of the boat owner, but there was no response. The old man called all his missing relatives; there was no response either. The swimmers of Buntwani swam into the deep seas to see if they could find anything, rescue anything, or find floating bodies. But."

"But what, Nana? We have to finish this story today. It's the longest you have taken to finish a story," Narman said.

"I have to tell this story with the right pace; the pace that it deserves, Narman."

KHALID WAS EARNING enough at the Mombasa Ports to care for a wife. He was in a place in his life where he really needed a partner to close the open gap that had been empty for so long. Humeirah had informed him that her parents would not be able to accept their union because of their difference in social status. In fact, she said, it was for that same reason she had left her family to begin life in another place.

Khalid called Nana to inform her about his engagement with Humeirah and his plan to go to Malindi to celebrate his big day with the community and his younger sister, Narman.

"Are you sure she is the one? I am not against you getting married. I am in fact extremely happy for you, but have you done a background check? Or do you want me to do it for you?" Nana said on the call.

"I am sure she is the one. I am also keen to marry someone outside our community. Maybe because of my past, or maybe because otherwise it would make me feel as if I am doing an injustice to Lailatu."

"Lailatu went to her Lord fifteen years ago. You have faithfully stayed single for all these years, crying your heart out. Khalid, if you have done your research, then tawakul. Alilililili." She ended her words with a ululation.

Khalid and Humeirah packed and left for Malindi two days later. They were received with rose garlands and poetry. Nana, with the help of Narman and the neighbours, had decorated the cement verandah with fairy lights. The aqeed ceremony was conducted in the mosque on the same day. Humeirah was dressed in a green dress and adorned with gold jewellery. After the mosque prayers, Khalid returned for the masah, where he opened Humeirah's veil and kissed her forehead. Her face shone enough to make the moon jealous.

Their wedding celebrations continued for six days, with the community eating and drinking and dancing; because Khalid's marriage was a sign that anyone could find love again, even after losing the petals and buds of love.

After the wedding, the newlyweds returned to Mombasa to kickstart their new life. Khalid was hopeful that this was the beginning of their ever-after.

Khalid returned to work after a fortnight, and Humeirah stayed at home to handle the household chores. Since the wedding, he had noticed that she appeared anxious, and would always hide her phone from him. He had seen her eyes several times carrying mountains of tension. Something fishy was going on, but he dumped his blind eye on a pillow, assuming that what he was thinking was just an illusion – the illusion of catastrophes constantly following him like a shadow.

Calls started coming in like the rains, and he started getting concerned. What was she keeping from him?

He asked her on one night after an exasperating day at work.

"Who keeps calling you all the time?"

She was wearing a pink silky flowery nightdress. She turned to look at herself in the mirror while she detangled her brown curly hair. She turned a deaf ear to what her husband asked, until he held her shoulders tightly enough to cause her pain. She turned red. Tears came out of her eyes, trickling down her cheeks and onto her nightdress, forming an expanding map. But Khalid had no sympathy in the beam of his attention. He had a strong gut feeling that something was amiss, and he was not ready to fall into the trap of her tears.

"I am asking you again, who keeps calling you all the time?"

"It's no one. Don't you trust me?"

"Why do you always appear tense, then? You were not like this before we got married. If there is nothing or no one to worry about, then your gestures should indicate so. I love you, Humeirah; do not ever think of hurting me."

"You like to create mountains out of molehills. Trust me, I love you. I know your past, so I will never hurt you."

Khalid was easy to appease, and Humeirah knew how to appeal to his soft side. He kissed her on the cheeks and they went to bed buried in their thoughts. Khalid was thinking of his past and Humeirah was thinking of her present. They turned their heads away from each other, too ashamed to face their fears, until the moon lulled them to sleep.

THE CLOUDS HAD unruffled themselves to create heaps and heaps of cotton wool. The sun was sluggishly awake as Narman hung the clothes on the clothesline and placed the assorted pegs on the ends of each item. Nana was burning oud for the Juma'a prayers. She was wearing a red and black dishdasha with an embroidered black lesso that hung on her right arm like armour. She sat on a crooked wooden kibao, letting the air soothe her with the overpowering scent of freshly burnt dukhan.

She asked Narman, "What do you do when your whole life crumbles in front of you into broken glass?"

Narman squeezed one of the wet maxi dresses before she hung it on the clothesline. She replied, a peg between her lips, "You start afresh."

"The fishermen and sailors went far and wide for three days. The old man also followed them, hoping that the sea would throw something out of its mouth. But there was nothing the sea could offer except sea moss and plastic that had swum across the tides. After three days, the trumpet was blown by the chief who announced that a guy had been found on the shores of Madhubah in Mombasa. He was immediately resuscitated and rushed to the Coast General hospital, where he was going to be under observation until further notice."

"Did the chief know that the survivor was linked to the old man?"

"Yes, he knew. But he could not deliver the hurricane in one go. The old man had not only lost his wife; he had lost his son and the wife of his son and his grandson and the fiancée of one of his other grandsons – the one who was washed ashore."

"I do not know what I would have done if I had been the old man, or the survivor who saw his family fall from his hands like pearls. But what about the other grandchild who was left behind? What is the story?"

"The granddaughter that was left behind had chicken pox and was left at a caretaker's home, not knowing that the caretaker was going to have to become her mother, her grandmother, her everything. She shared her bread and butter with her, loved her with the intensity of the five restless souls who were lost at the sea, a grandfather who died of a slow cancer, eaten away by sorrow and despair, and a brother so depressed he never ever wanted to fall in love again. Until recently,"

Nana wiped the tears that were trickling down her face. She then faced Narman, who sat on the floor, her hands touching her head while she tried to find the right words to say.

"So this is my story? Why did you hide it for so long?"

Nana replied between sobs: "Because you were not ready to receive and I was not ready to give. I am not your maternal grandmother, as you have always thought, but I have loved you more than ten grandmothers would. When I heard the news from your grandfather, I made up my mind that I would give you the world. You always thought that your parents went overseas to search for greener pastures, but Sulum and Karima are not your parents. Karima is my daughter and Sulum is her husband. You were too young to carry the grief with you. Where would you have offloaded it? You might not want to forgive me and that is okay, but I did it for your own good. You are now eighteen years old, ripe for marriage, and I wanted to relieve myself of this story that I have carried for fifteen years."

Nana spread her arms and let Narman into her arms, which flapped open like wings. They hugged until asr when the muadhin announced the call for prayer. Narman offered a prayer to Allah to grant her family Jannah, and went to bed earlier than usual to escape from her own thoughts.

KHALID DID NOT like the suffocating smell of tension at the police station. Yet he had to be there. Humeirah had escaped with all her belongings and his savings three days back. A week before, Nana had called him while he was drinking his zaatar tea and said, "My grandson, brace yourself for the thunderstorm that is about to hit you. I was searching through channels while I waited for my Zee World series to continue when a certain headline at Zanzibar Plus caught my attention. It showed a picture of a girl from an upper-class family who had escaped Zanzibar via a Tumaini ship headed to Mombasa. The girl had stolen over two hundred and thirty-three million Tanzanian shillings from her parents and gambling mates, and she was under search. The passport picture shared looked so much like Humeirah. Please come to Malindi as soon as you can."

Khalid was shaking like a leaf in a gale. He stopped drinking his zaatar tea and decided to think of a plan before involving the police. But the days went by so fast that before he could actualise anything, the woman with whom he shared a bed, the woman supposed to be his newly found love to replace his Lailatu lost to the deep seas, had deceived him and had left him poorer than when she met him.

The formalities at the police station took all day, but there was no sight of Humeirah. Her phone was off; no ships were going to Zanzibar that month, and why would she go back to where danger was looming? Khalid left the police with all the necessary information that might help them track her. He then borrowed money from a friend to go to Malindi to be with Nana and Narman. If darkness had existed before, it had now revisited him with an audacity that was beyond him.

Days became weeks and weeks became months, and there was no news from the police or his friends and family. Humeirah had disappeared into thin air. She had come fast and left even faster.

Khalid started going to the sea of Buntwani. He spent his days there and then his nights. Nana and Narman sat with him sometimes to listen to the sounds of the beasts, the wracking sound of a sea that laughed at him. His eyes became shrunken pods. His fingers wilted like dead flowers. His willpower was squashed like citrus. He did not know whether he was looking for a past that embraced him, or his present eating him and his demons away. But he stayed to continue the legacy left behind, beneath the landmark of his grandfather, the old man and the sea.

CHANGES IN OWNERSHIP

Moso Sematlane

*T*HE OLD COUPLE came in arguing. The man, at the last minute, had decided that he didn't want to sell the chest of drawers. Katleho watched them, hidden in the shadow of a nook in the shop, waiting for the moment he could swoop in and diffuse the situation by introducing the clear logic that if the man sold the chest, he could use the money to buy a new, better one. He would ramble on about how, in second-hand shops, you never really lose anything; the magic is in knowing that you forfeit a precious item and open up space in your life to get something much better in return. He would smile and hope that something in its charm suggested he, too, was created from magic. Like the shop. His boss Annie had organised the displays in a haphazard way to make customers bump into items, creating the illusion that the items had found *them*, instead of the other way around.

Katleho had been working at the shop for two years, yet he still lacked the social skills expected of clerks; the ability to convince customers that their purchase was perfectly suited to them in an easy, meandering chit-chat meant to make them feel they were talking to a friend. Something in him hesitated to take that leap outside of himself. He saw the old couple arguing as a test the day had given him, yet he couldn't shake the feeling that he had already failed.

"Please, put some sense into him!" the woman said to Katleho as he approached them. Her eyes were blue and watery, and yet open in a way that most white peoples' in Ladybrand were not. He looked at her husband, but *his* attention was fixed on the chest, as if its legs might come alive and walk away. Outside, Tumelo waited to hear if he should load the chest back into their car.

"I've had that chest of drawers for twenty years!" the old man said. "Ten from our years in London, and ten from our life here. A man should be allowed to change his mind. Is it so wrong for me to change my mind?"

"Nothing wrong with that," Katleho said. "I've always wanted to visit London. It's amazing how much life can be carried inside a single piece of furniture."

"Oh, he's just a *hoarder*!" the woman said. "We bought a house in Cape

Town to be closer to our daughter. She just had her first child, and at our age the trips there and back are too exhausting for us. Plus, this is a dead town, I'm sorry to say."

Katleho kept quiet. He couldn't exactly disagree with her. Katleho had learned that as much as you can choose to live in a place, it has to choose you back. On his Sunday jogs he liked to stand at the border long enough to watch the sun turn the morning mist into nothingness, revealing Maseru in the distance. Like a curtain parting onto an empty stage. If it was quiet enough, he would swear that he could hear cars hooting and imagined all the people he had known throughout his life inside them, and the errands they were running. Ladybrand seemed unable to dislodge the weight Lesotho had cast in his chest, a weight he sought to remove by moving there in the first place.

He admired the breezy way the old couple talked about moving between London and Ladybrand, and now Cape Town, as if places weren't living organisms with preferences of their own, experienced differently when you're black or white, rich or poor.

"Think of selling this as a fresh start then," Katleho told them. "Move to Cape Town with new furniture. No need to drag things that should be forgotten from this dead place, as you say."

The man looked at the chest in silence. Then Katleho and the old woman watched him hobble to the door. "Do what you want with it," he muttered, before stepping into the sunshine.

"That's all the business there is then," the woman said. "We need to get out before he changes his mind again."

Katleho joined Tumelo and they hoisted the chest up to their waists and carried it to the storeroom. As they exchanged money, the woman complained about Ladybrand; how very *quiet* it was, how it felt like it was caught in a silo, suspended in a pod while the world hurtled towards the fourth industrial revolution happening around it.

"It got worse after the pandemic," she said. She asked Katleho where he came from *originally*, and her eyes brightened when he said Lesotho.

Katleho was forced, as he so often was these days, to re-evaluate the place he called home under someone else's gaze, with the necessary distance to see all its contours. He told her that, like Ladybrand, Lesotho is dead, although if you look carefully enough, there is beauty to be found. In the mountains, in the September evenings when the sunsets coat everything in honey.

He didn't tell her that he'd left Lesotho because the boy he loved didn't love him anymore. His move to Ladybrand was his way of making himself anew, without being tied to Lesotho. For so long, he and Tekane had felt like they were refashioning the country for themselves. In their eyes, Lesotho was recast as a place of coffee-shop dates in summer, the freedom of holding Tekane's hands when they visited Maletsunyane Falls and watching the water steam up from the ground as if a great God lived under there.

It had been a hackneyed end-of-love story, the calls between them growing infrequent, the hand-holding colder, until finally Tekane came to his flat and told him that he had found someone else.

"So what were you doing with me? Passing the time?"

"I wasn't. My feelings are mysterious to me, but I know that what I felt for you was real."

"You used me."

"I didn't. I just ... changed. I don't know how better to describe it."

Tekane had married his new partner by the time winter ended, and Ladybrand had allowed Katleho to be numb. On Saturdays, there was nothing to do except watch sports and reality television in his house, or go to his eleven o'clock crocheting class. Sundays were the worst. On Sundays, the loneliness of the whole world crashed on top of him: the church bells; the empty streets; the families lunching together. He felt like he should have been doing something significant on Sundays, when time slowed and could be bent into so many shapes and sizes that the memories he'd tried to leave in Lesotho would come back as fresh as if they had just happened yesterday.

He told the old couple to enjoy Cape Town and surprised himself at the warmth in his voice. He was getting better at being a clerk. He'd test himself again tomorrow, with someone new. As he watched them drive away, a longing rose up in him. Perhaps one day, he could go to Cape Town, too. Any place but here.

Katleho faced the quietness of the town once more, and with nothing else to do, he took out his phone in anticipation of the long night that awaited him when he got home. He looked over the texts that he and Lunga had sent each other over the past week, shrugging off Lunga's curt responses to his own desperate ones. Lunga's discomfort was apparent, but Katleho took the fact that he was responding at all as a sign to push through anyway.

— *I stay alone ... You can come to me anytime ... We don't have to have sex ... We can talk over drinks and you can decide if it's something you want.*

— *You are pressuring me.*

— *I really like you, Lunga.*

Lunga had been the store hand before Tumelo until he had found a new job in Johannesburg as a security guard. It was a great surprise to run into him after his Sunday jog. Lunga had told Katleho that Johannesburg didn't work out, that someone else had gotten the job before him, so Katleho had asked Annie for help on his behalf. She had called up a friend who ran the flower shop to hire him.

Katleho had invited him for drinks at a bar next to the industrial area, and they had gotten drunk and had kissed after midnight. Katleho couldn't remember who had initiated the kiss, but he remembered Lunga clutching his wrists as if he wanted to pull away. And yet his lips remained in a steady dance against Katleho's. When they withdrew, Lunga cupped Katleho's face in his rough palms and said, "You are beautiful."

He had left Katleho standing alone in the street, his chin stinging from stubble, the taste of the Maluti beer Lunga had been drinking all night hot in his mouth.

On the Sundays that followed, Katleho would go past the florist to try to reinitiate their tryst, but as soon as Lunga saw him, he would lift a hand up in greeting and disappear into the shop. One night, he had been thinking of Tekane, the memories of his time in Lesotho keener than they were on most days – almost piercing his heart – when he texted Lunga and asked him if he would like to have sex. He wanted to plant the idea between them, in all its pulsing, primal shape, so he could undercut Lunga's evasion. Courting was futile with men like Lunga; only the draw of another wordless body next to theirs could pull them from the shadows.

— *Do you want to come over ... we don't have to do anything ... just talk. I really want you to come over tonight.*

When Annie came to lock up the shop, Katleho told her about the Cape Town couple, and she admired the chest and declared it would look spectacular in the light that came through the store window. As was their routine, Katleho got into Annie's car and she dropped him off at his house on the way to her more affluent neighbourhood. He poured himself a glass of Chardonnay and showered. When he got back to the living room, there was a text from Lunga.

— *I come once and never again.*

— *Okay. You don't have to ever see me again after tonight.*

Lunga didn't reply, and as the hours wore on, Katleho lost faith that they would ever speak again. Maybe it had been a mistake to come on so strong.

Towards midnight there was knock on the door and he opened it to let Lunga in. Although this was the first time Lunga had been to Katleho's house, he made straight for the couch and sat there without greeting Katleho. He put one leg over another, supporting his head with his palm as the TV cast patterns of light on him.

"Do you want a drink?" Katleho said. Lunga shook his head. Katleho went to the kitchen to pour himself another glass of Chardonnay, and returned to the living room to sit on the chair adjacent to Lunga's. He pretended to watch the television, casting glances at Lunga. Lunga didn't seem to be pretending at all, and appeared genuinely absorbed in the film that was playing; something in black and white, from a screen adaptation of a novel Katleho remembered doing for his high-school English class.

"Why do you call me here?" Lunga said, without looking away from the screen. The sound from the film filled the endless space between them.

"Do you not want to be here?"

"No choice," Lunga said. "I come here so that we don't speak ever again."

"But you came," Katleho said, anger colouring his voice. With the glare from the television profiling him, Katleho was reminded again why Lunga wasn't so much someone to fill the need for another body next to his, but was also a way for Katleho to harm himself. Seen by the light from the screen, Lunga's features were unflattering enough that Katleho was repulsed by him, and this appealed to Katleho's sense of his own soul being ugly. But just as quickly, Lunga's posture assumed the kind of frame that had often attracted Katleho in the past; big and tall, the promise of violence and passion woven into every tendon. Lunga was pouting, and this increased his irritation. Lunga wasn't a victim here, his sulking was merely a crafty way to evade the fact that they were bound to each other by an act they had both partaken in.

"You came," Katleho said. "Didn't you?" He stood up to go sit beside Lunga.

"Why do you do this?" Lunga said. "You are beautiful. But you are here with me. You should go to Lesotho. Ladybrand is not good for you."

Katleho's laugh sounded hollow against Lunga's unsmiling face. "Why do you say that?"

"How old are you?" Lunga said. "I think in Lesotho young people like you are partying, not wanting to have sex with old men like me."

"I'm thirty-nine," Katleho said.

Lunga let out a booming laugh that bounced on all corners of the room and although he didn't mean to, Katleho smiled.

"You're lying," Lunga said, "You're not thirty-nine. I'm thirty-nine."

Katleho didn't have an answer. In the silence, Lunga shifted his body so that he was facing Katleho. It was too dark to figure out his expression exactly, though the steel-forged presence of his stare was more intense than any sort of attention Katleho had received from a man recently.

"You're thirty-nine?" Lunga said. He looked away from Katleho and faced the TV again. "Why did you leave Lesotho?"

"There was nothing for me there."

"So there is something for you here?" He didn't wait for Katleho to answer. He stood up, walked past the TV and stood by the window. He parted the curtain slightly and looked out. Under the weak light from the street lamps, his body again aroused something in Katleho that was both urgent and alive. He stood up to go stand beside him. He put a hand on Lunga's broad shoulders.

"I just want you tonight," Katleho said.

"I'm not a good man for you," Lunga said after a while. "My life ... it's too hard. It's way too hard."

Katleho kissed him. Unlike their first kiss at the bar, Lunga didn't kiss him back. His lips parted and he exhaled into Katleho's mouth with powerful breaths. Katleho was persistent. He stepped back to the couch and found that Lunga followed, his hands now resting on Katleho's waist. Katleho took Lunga's clothes off and then his own, dropping them on the floor. Katleho lay Lunga down on the couch and took all his dick in his mouth. Lunga didn't make a sound, which cut Katleho's pleasuring of him short. When Katleho reached up to Lunga again, he saw that he was looking up at the ceiling. He was about to kiss him again when he saw a cluster of tears sparkling at the edge of Lunga's eye.

"Do you want me to continue?" Katleho said.

Lunga didn't answer. All of Katleho's nerve endings felt exposed to the sheer beauty of him. He wanted to wrap himself around Lunga, Lunga in him, him in Lunga, Katleho didn't care, as long as by the end of the night he shared something vital to his being with Katleho.

Lunga's lovemaking was slow and quiet. Only when Katleho entered him did Lunga make any noise, moaning quietly. Lunga was one of the few men that Katleho had been inside. Entering him was the only response he could think of to Lunga's perpetual inertia. The feeling that, even with all their breathing and sweating, something between them was dead, and he was trying to resurrect it.

THE WEEKS FOLLOWING the Cape Town couple's visit were slow, and Katleho could tell that Annie was getting worried. She instructed Katleho to rearrange the shop, and they spent the early mornings moving around paintings, furniture and books to give the store a fresher configuration. It was during one of their morning sessions that Katleho noticed a truck with a Lesotho number plate outside. The truck's driver was talking to Tumelo, but by the time Katleho could pause his item logging to see if it was anyone he knew, they had moved towards the storeroom. When Annie left, the truck's driver followed Tumelo inside.

"Hello," he said.

Katleho's first instinct was to hide. Then the sinking in his stomach was replaced by sheer joy, a joy that was reflected in Tekane's face as he reached to hug Katleho.

"I didn't know you had a truck," Katleho heard himself saying.

"It's not mine," Tekane said. "It's my father's. He loaned it to me so I could get all these things here."

Katleho looked out at the chairs, the old computer, books and carpets that Tumelo was unloading from the truck. "They belonged to him?" Katleho said.

"No," Tekane said. "To me ... to us. Me and Seliba. I'm moving to Joburg soon. These won't fit my life there."

"You want to go through the rollercoaster of buying furniture again?" Katleho said.

"I've already bought some of it," Tekane said, smiling. "But you're right, it's a rollercoaster. I wish I had an assistant to do it all for me. To *ride* along with me."

They walked outside to help Tumelo unload Tekane's things from the truck. The sun was hot against Katleho's face, the concrete glaringly white, and they soon took to the shade, unused to the heavy labour.

"It's really good to see you," Tekane said, as they watched Tumelo unload the final batch of Tekane's things on his own.

"It's good to see you too," Katleho said. For the first time that day, the weight of the past seemed to stretch a distance between them, filled with all the unsaid words. Tekane smelled of sandalwood perfume, the same scent he had used when he and Katleho were together. Once the rift between them was acknowledged, albeit silently, Katleho found it hard to look at Tekane. He became conscious of his own sweating, and he walked towards the entrance of shop where it was cooler. Tekane's voice stopped him.

"Do you want to go to dinner with me? I don't have to be back in Lesotho until nine. My father isn't expecting his truck until then."

Katleho stood with his back to Tekane, consulting his chest. After finding an unexpected calm there, he turned around and agreed.

Evening came, and Katleho berated himself for dressing up for their date. He wanted not to care enough to present himself as anything other than what he was. However, by the time he got to the steakhouse, Katleho was glad that he had taken the decision to look good. If there was any vengeance to be found in their reunion, it was in letting Tekane see that he was still as attractive as he was when they were together, perhaps even more so.

Tekane's truck was already in the restaurant parking lot when Katleho arrived. There was something touching about picturing Tekane squeezed into it with all the stuff he shared with his husband, packed at the back, ready to move on to their next chapter.

Katleho sat down next to Tekane as they had many times before, in a different lifetime, in a different country.

Tekane handed Katleho a small yarn animal with uneven proportions. "For you," he said. "I made it at the crocheting class while I was waiting for you. It's supposed to be a fish."

Katleho inspected it in the dim light. "I think this is the most beautiful gift you've ever given me. You made it with your hands and didn't buy it like all the others. I appreciate that."

Tekane laughed. "It's really good to see you, Katleho. Really. And you look good. Beautiful as always."

"You look good, too."

Katleho ordered a burger and Tekane a steak. While they waited for their food, the fish watched them from the edge of the table. Katleho picked it up and played with it in his hands, smiling at it to avoid any awkwardness. But it was hard not to look into Tekane's eyes, although they rested firmly on Katleho; he felt at ease, unburdened from the rituals that are only performed when one has expectations of how the night will end.

"When do you move to Joburg?" Katleho said.

"Next week."

"Must be exciting."

"It is," Tekane said. "I know how much you talked of leaving Lesotho when we were together. I never got the urge, to be honest with you. I never understood it. Things were always fine the way they were around me. But after the divorce, it started feeling like I had no place there."

"Divorce?" Katleho said.

Tekane gave him a conspiratorial smile. "I didn't tell you?"

"No."

"I'm moving to Joburg alone," Tekane said. "Seliba is staying behind."

"I'm sorry," Katleho said, without missing a beat. He stashed the news of Tekane's divorce in a secret compartment in his mind to figure out how to feel about it later. He didn't know Seliba, or even what he looked like. Although he'd known photos of Seliba and Tekane's life together must exist somewhere online, but, after deleting his own photos and memories of Tekane, Katleho had resolved not to torture himself with the social media roulette of bringing back old, stinging feelings.

"Are you going to say *I told you so*?" Tekane smiled as if he and Katleho were in on a joke together.

"Why would I celebrate you being hurt?" Katleho said. "I'm over all those feelings anyway. It did hurt when I found out you got married, but I had to move on. Life moves on."

"Life moves on," Tekane repeated, idly taking the fish from the table where Katleho had paused his own tinkering with it. "I always felt so guilty ... like I hurt you and didn't say sorry."

"You said sorry," Katleho said quickly.

"No, no," he said. "It wasn't the same. Wasn't like *now*. I suppose I really felt I was in love and didn't want anything to convince me otherwise. I'm so dumb. All my life, I always saw myself as this guy who could have everything he wanted. Any boy, any girl, any job. I fucked up in a big way by thinking like that, 'cause now I'm literally a few months away from being forty and I'm realising I didn't know what I was doing at all. There's so much stuff about myself I need to figure out, and it feels like time is running out."

"Forty is still young," Katleho said. Only a few weeks earlier, he'd had the same conversation with Lunga. He had tried, afterwards, to erase Lunga's expression from his mind at finding out that they were the same age, an expression Katleho could only describe as a *face aged by sadness*. It was as if, at that moment, on top of his thirty-nine years, Lunga had aged another nine and was now like every older person that Katleho knew, marching towards his grave.

"You flatter me too much," Tekane purred.

Their food arrived and they ate in silence. Tekane bobbed his head along to the music as he ate, Katleho assumed in an effort to lessen the renewed unease. Finally, he looked up to Katleho.

"I had to come here and see you. I confess, selling my stuff in Ladybrand was just an excuse to see you. I looked everywhere for you, but couldn't find you. Your mother told me you lived here now. You should have seen how hard it was at the border getting all this stuff across, but it just felt like there was a chapter I had to close."

"I've been living here for a very long time," Katleho said.

"Do you enjoy it?"

Katleho shrugged.

"You don't enjoy it?"

"Ladybrand is Ladybrand," Katleho said. "It's peaceful here."

"What do you do for fun?"

"Crocheting classes, like you," Katleho said. "There isn't much to do here. You just work, then go home to sit with your thoughts. But I like it that way. A boring life is a peaceful life."

Tekane laughed. "That's going in my memoir, *Forty Quotes For Forty-Year-Olds*. A beautiful man like you shouldn't be bored."

"I'm not bored," Katleho said.

"Ah," he said. "You seeing anyone?"

"Yes," Katleho said. He described Lunga to Tekane. He told him that Lunga was a beautiful man, though often quiet. That, on Sundays, they would watch sports, even though Katleho didn't like sports much. He told him that Lunga treated him with nothing but kindness, which made the lonely, boredom-filled days in Ladybrand easier to bear. Katleho didn't know why he lied to Tekane, except that he started and he couldn't stop. He hadn't seen nor spoken to Lunga since they'd had sex a few weeks back.

Each day the memory of Lunga stretched farther and farther away, and yet a far more horrible truth approached. Slowly, an image of Lunga as a broken man had crystallised in his mind, tangible enough to touch. This was the true legacy of their night together. No matter how many times Tekane called him beautiful, those tears in Lunga's eyes had made Katleho feel ugly.

He could cry all day if he allowed himself to think about Lunga too much. If only people could be restored, like the furniture Annie took to Johannesburg and returned to the shop with new varnishes. Katleho could no longer bring himself to share in her joy at the beauty of restoration, and faked his wonder. Although the furniture was objectively beautiful, it was the fact that it had been previously owned that made him think of it as undesirable. Palimpsests with hands and hands upon them. Perhaps he would not make a good sales clerk after all.

"I'm happy that you're happy," Tekane said. "Really." Katleho could see that Tekane meant what he said.

It was an easy night, despite the intrusive memories of Lunga, one that recalled the happy nights they'd had together in Lesotho, whether in a restaurant – where all they did was talk, laugh, talk, and laugh again – or in the privacy of their own bedroom.

"You should really go back to Lesotho," Tekane said. "I think you'll be happier."

"I don't look happy to you?"

"You do," Tekane said. Katleho wondered if he imagined the glimmer of mischief in Tekane's eyes. "But your mother misses you a lot. I could tell from speaking to her. As for myself, I don't think I'll be setting foot in Lesotho for a very long time. Me and Seliba are good, it's not like we're angry at each other. But this is why I asked you what you do in Ladybrand because it's the same thing in Lesotho. What do you *do* in Lesotho?"

Katleho laughed.

"No, really," Tekane said. "You go around in circles, meeting the same people. Going to the same events. And what's really fucked up is how people *think*."

"And you want me to go back to this?"

"I will say this," Tekane said. "I knew I needed to be in Lesotho when I needed to be there. It's strange, but I think even my divorce ... it happened for a reason. Your story with Lesotho might be unfinished."

"I don't know," Katleho said. "I don't know."

They stayed in the restaurant long past the time when Tekane was supposed to go home. On their way out to the truck, Katleho resolved to call his mother. It had been almost a month since they had spoken. Since leaving Lesotho, their conversations had avoided the topics that they should have been talking about all along: why Katleho left the country; Katleho's sexuality, which he had disclosed to her shortly before leaving. She would ask Katleho if he was still working at the second-hand shop. She would, in a steady flow of speech that Katleho found hard to interrupt, much less desired to, tell him small details of the things his brothers had bought her: grocery items, appliances like irons or kettles. Perhaps tonight Katleho would bring up the subject of visiting Lesotho.

Tekane said he wasn't worried about making it past nine, that his father would be "placated by the money he got from the thrift". Katleho, so loud that he heard his own voice echoing back from two streets down, said that he wished him well on his way back. He meant it too. He watched Tekane get into the truck and start the drive back to Maseru. With him gone, the only thing to do would be to get into bed and wait for a sleep that would never come. Or look outside the window at the empty streets, like Lunga had on their night together, because in this town, even looking at noth-ingness was more interesting than being present with your thoughts. He stood in the same spot that Tekane had left him in, watching the unchang-ing darkness that had swallowed the truck, that swallowed everything but the street lights.

appendix

Salma Abdulatif Yusuf is a recipient of the Global Voices Scholarship Award currently pursuing a Masters in Creative Writing (Poetry) at the University of East Anglia, Norwich. She is a winner of the East African Writing Contest, The Coastal Essay Contest and her work has appeared in the *Coast Woman Magazine*. She has been involved with various literary engagements including Honey Badgers in Uganda, Bookmart in Tanzania, Hekaya Arts Initiative and the Heroe Book Fair in Kenya. She was longlisted for the Griots Well Programme for BAME Writers. Her work has been published in *Lolwe*, *Ink, Sweat and Tears*, *Arts Against Extremism*, and *Doek!*, among others.

Aba Amissah Asibon is a Ghanaian writer, and an SSDA Inkubator Fellow 2022. Her poetry and short fiction have been published in *Guernica*, *adda*, *The Kalahari Review*, The University of Chester's *Flash* Magazine, *African Roar* and *The Johannesburg Review of Books*. She has been shortlisted for the Commonwealth Short Story Prize and the Miles Morland African Writing Scholarship. Aba was also long-listed for the 2016 Short Story Day Africa Prize and featured in the prize's anthology, *Migrations*. She is a recent nominee of The Rolex Mentor and Protégé Arts Initiative. Aba's work focuses primarily on contemporary African narratives through prose, and she aims to use her writing as a platform to challenge perceptions and push boundaries. She has had her work discussed and highlighted on online magazines such as *LitNet* and *Africa in Dialogue*.

Doreen Anyango is a Ugandan fiction writer, scriptwriter and biotechnologist, who was born and raised in Kampala. Her short fiction has appeared online in several journals. She has published short stories in print anthologies with FEMRITE, Writivism, Short Story Day Africa and *Riptide*. She was long-listed for the Writivism prize for fiction in 2016 and the SSDA prize in 2020. Her novel manuscript titled 'A Darkness with Her Name On It' was shortlisted for the Island Prize for debut African novelists.

N. A. Dawn writes essays, poetry and literary speculative fiction, chiefly concerned with ecological politics and the prickly problem of human flourishing. He holds a BA in English Literature and Environmental Science from the University of Cape Town, South Africa, and has been featured in *New Contrast*

Literary Magazine and Short Story Day Africa. He is known for philosophical digressions, drumming on everything, producing improbably vivid sound effects with his mouth, and for someone who spends so much time at a desk, his roundhouse kicks are actually quite nimble. Follow Nick @nadawnauthor.

Khumbo Mhone is an actor turned marketer and entrepreneur living and working in Malawi. She received her undergraduate degree in Theatre and English from the University of Denver in Colorado before moving to New York where she worked as a professional actor for a year. Khumbo moved back to Malawi in 2015 and is currently the Business Development and Marketing Manager at Unicaf University. A contributor to *Enthuse Magazine* (an online publication based in Zimbabwe), she spends her free time writing her fiction blog, helping the community through Rotaract International, and working on her new novel about rain priestesses in pre-colonial Malawi. Follow her @kcmhone.

Kabubu Mutua is an SSDA Inkubator Fellow 2022. He grew up in Machakos, Kenya. He was longlisted for the 2021 Afritondo Short Story Prize and shortlisted for the 2022 Peters Fraser and Dunlop Queer Fiction Prize. His work appears in *The Hope, The Prayer, The Anthem* anthology by Afritondo,

A Long House, and the Commonwealth Writers *adda* magazine. Follow him @kabubumutua.

Sola Njoku is a freelance writer and editor, children's author and mum of two living in Berkshire, England. Sola is currently researching Yoruba culture and anglophone African literature with a view to progressing onto a doctorate programme. She has been engaged in literary and arts journalism for over a decade, and had worked with BBC Africa, The Caine Prize and *Granta*. Her writing has been featured in *Wasafiri*, *Next Newspapers*, *The Guardian*, *The Punch* and many other Nigerian publications. She has recently published Moyò àti Kayin Books, a series of bilingual children's books in three Nigerian languages in a bid to promote early multilingualism and create an avenue for children to develop simultaneously a love of languages and literature. Follow her @yorubamama and @readerinafricanliterature.

Zanta Nkumane is a writer, journalist and ex-scientist from Eswatini. His work has appeared on *Okay Africa*, *This Is Africa*, *Mail & Guardian*, *Racebaitr*, *Kalahari Review*, *City Press*, *Arts 24*, *New Frame*, *Amaka Studio*, *Doek!*, *Lolwe*, *Olongo Africa*, *The Republic* and *The New York Times*. He has contributed essays to queer anthologies *We're F**king Here* (2021) and *Touch: Sex, Sexuality* *and Sexuality* (2021). Zanta is the non-fiction editor at *Doek!* Follow Zanta @Zanta_Nk.

Emily Pensulo is a Zambian writer masquerading as a banker during her weekdays. She holds an undergraduate degree in Business Administration and a Master's degree in Economic Policy Management. She's written a biography of a local conservationist which is yet to be published and her writing has appeared in local magazines such as the *Bulletin and Record* and the *Zacci Journal*. She has also been published by the Kenyan magazine, *Down River Road*. In 2018, Emily was longlisted for the Kalemba Prize for her short story, "Dowry". And in 2020, she worked as a scriptwriter for a film project called "Lifeblood", directed by a BAFTA nom-inated director.

Josephine Sokan is a Nigerian-born writer who moved to the UK as a child. She fell in love with literature in those tender years and now writes poetry, short stories, audio and stage scripts and articles on faith and motherhood. She is currently working on her first novel. Josephine relishes filling blank pages with stories that ask important ques-tions. She enjoys exploring the delicate and difficult. Her work often deals with themes such as female identity, moth-erhood, the perceptions and attitudes towards mental health, "otherness"

and faith from an Afro-European and very personal lens. She is a wife to her best friend and a mum to two cheeky little boys. She is a lover of romance but despises love stories. She is also a Nollywood connoisseur and enjoys experimental cuisine (eat at your own peril).

Helen Moffett is an author, editor, poet, academic, activist, and SSDA enthusiast. Her publications include university text-books, a treasury of landscape writings (*Lovely Beyond Any Singing*), a cricket book (with the late Bob Woolmer and Tim Noakes), an animal charity anthol-ogy (*Stray*, with Diane Awerbuck), and the *Girl Walks In* erotica series (with Sarah Lotz and Paige Nick). She has also published two poetry collections – *Strange Fruit* and *Prunings*, with the latter the joint winner of the 2017 SALA prize for poetry. She edited three previous Short Story Day Africa anthol-ogies: *Migrations*, *ID* and *Hotel Africa*. She has written a memoir of Rape Crisis, and two green handbooks: *101 Water-wise Ways* and *Wise About Waste: 150+ ways to help the planet*. Her children's book, *Toast*, was the hundredth title published by literacy NPO Book Dash, and her debut novel *Charlotte* (a *Pride & Prejudice* sequel), was published by Bonnier in 2020. She lives in Cape Town with four cats and a very feisty kombu-cha scoby, and can be found on Twitter @heckitty.

Rachel Zadok is an editor, writer and designer. She is the author of two novels: *Gem Squash Tokoloshe* (Pan Macmillan, 2005), shortlisted for The Whitbread First Novel Award and The John Llewellyn Rhys Prize, and long-listed for the IMPAC Award; and *Sister-sister* (Kwela Books, 2013), shortlisted for the University of Johannesburg Prize and The Herman Charles Bosman Prize, and longlisted for the Sunday Times Fiction Award. She is the managing editor of Short Story Day Africa, a project to promote and develop African writers, and as such has published seven anthologies of African short fiction (including this one), and three collections of stories written by young African Writers. She attended the Caine Prize Workshop in 2012, was a Sylt Foundation Writer in Residence and the Rhine-South Africa Fellow in 2015, and participated in the Sylt Foundation's "Transformation And Identity – Trauma And Reconciliation" workshop in Myanmar in 2018. She lives in Cape Town.

*T*HE BRITISH COUNCIL is the UK's international organisation for cultural relations and educational opportunities. We build connections, understanding and trust between people in the UK and other countries through arts and culture, education and the English language. Last year we reached over 80 million people directly and 791 million people overall, including online, broadcasts and publications. Founded in 1934, we are a UK charity governed by Royal Charter and a UK public body. We receive a fifteen per cent core funding grant from the UK government. www.britishcouncil.org

ACKNOWLEDGEMENTS

*T*HE SSDA INKUBATOR that birthed *Captive* was supported by the British Council Cultural Exchange programme, which supports cultural organisations, festivals, artists and creatives between the countries of sub-Saharan Africa (SSA) and the United Kingdom (UK) to create art, build networks, collaborate and develop markets and share artists' work with audiences.

Captive would not have been possible without the exuberant help of my co-editor Helen Moffett (affectionately known to all at SSDA as Mama H) who believes in SSDA and its cause more than I do at times, and without whom I may have thrown in the towel on this project, and all that came before, many, many times.

These stories would not reach readers across the globe without the co-operation and patience of our publishers which, like SSDA, are small, independent, and women-led organisations. I am eternally grateful to Jessica Powers, SarahBelle Selig and Ashawnta Jackson of Catalyst Press, and to Karina Szczurek of Karavan Press; SSDA is lucky to have publishers who share our passion for African stories.

SSDA would not have received the British Council grant without the partnership of Emma Shercliff of Laxfield Literary Associates. Fortune smiled upon the Inkubator fellows when she generously agreed to do this with us. She not only gave her time during the Inkubator, but has left a door ajar for these writers that extends beyond the project.

These stories were shaped in part by the Inkubator workshop facilitators Karen Jennings, Tochukwu Okafor, T. J. Benson, Doreen Baingana and Olumide Popoola. I am particularly grateful to Karen, Toch, and TJ for their ongoing support of SSDA over the years; their small gestures of belief make me believe that SSDA makes a difference.

Printed in the USA
CPSIA information can be obtained
at www.ICGtesting.com
JSHW080044110424
60986JS00001B/1